PRIDE and JOY

PRIDE and JOY

a novel

Louisa Onomé

ATRIA BOOKS

New York | London | Toronto | Sydney | New Delhi

An Imprint of Simon & Schuster, Inc.
1230 Avenue of the Americas
New York, NY 10020

First Atria Books hardcover edition March 2024

ATRIA BOOKS and colophon are trademarks of Simon & Schuster, Inc. For information about special discounts for bulk purchases, please contact Simon & Schuster Special Sales at 1-866-506-1949 or business@simonandschuster.com.

The Simon & Schuster Speakers Bureau can bring authors to your live event. For more information or to book an event, contact the Simon & Schuster Speakers Bureau at 1-866-248-3049 or visit our website at www.simonspeakers.com.

Interior design by Joy O'Meara
Illustrations by Andrey Kotko/Dreamstime.com

Manufactured in the United States of America

1 3 5 7 9 10 8 6 4 2

Library of Congress Cataloging-in-Publication Data

Names: Onomé, Louisa, author.
Title: Pride and joy : a novel / Louisa Onomé.
Description: First Atria Books hardcover edition. | New York : Atria Books, 2024.
Identifiers: LCCN 2023024748 | ISBN 9781668012819 (hardcover) | ISBN 9781668012826 (paperback) | ISBN 9781668012833 (ebook)
Subjects: LCGFT: Novels.
Classification: LCC PR9199.4.O66 P75 2024 | DDC 813/.6—dc23/eng/20230920

ISBN 978-1-6680-1281-9
ISBN 978-1-6680-1283-3 (ebook)

To my family, living and otherwise.

Family Tree

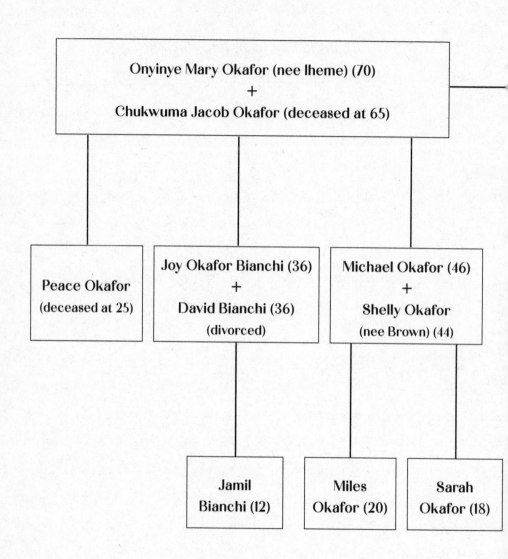

Onyinye Mary Okafor (nee Iheme) (70)
+
Chukwuma Jacob Okafor (deceased at 65)

Peace Okafor
(deceased at 25)

Joy Okafor Bianchi (36)
+
David Bianchi (36)
(divorced)

Michael Okafor (46)
+
Shelly Okafor
(nee Brown) (44)

Jamil
Bianchi (12)

Miles
Okafor (20)

Sarah
Okafor (18)

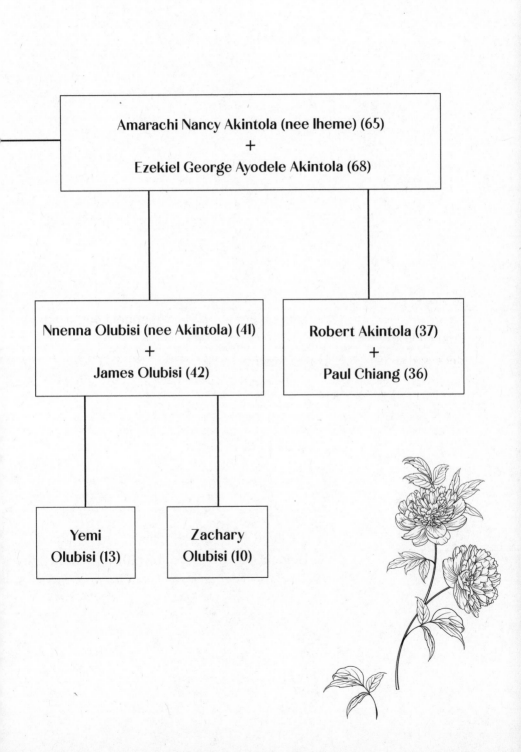

Amarachi Nancy Akintola (nee Iheme) (65)
+
Ezekiel George Ayodele Akintola (68)

Nnenna Olubisi (nee Akintola) (41)
+
James Olubisi (42)

Robert Akintola (37)
+
Paul Chiang (36)

Yemi
Olubisi (13)

Zachary
Olubisi (10)

PRIDE and JOY

— 1 —

Mama Mary Okafor is turning seventy today, Good Friday, and at first, no one was happy about this. Simply put, if there's anything anyone, including Mama's daughter, Joy, knows about Mama, it's that she would rather die than upstage God, and yet, here she is turning seventy on a holy day.

Joy couldn't believe it. Clearly, this was cause for celebration. Mama didn't think so. When Joy suggested they do something to mark the occasion, Mama huffed, saying, "People will already be going to church."

"No, Mom, I mean to celebrate your *birthday*."

Mama was stubborn, but after her friends, fellow Nigerian women who had grown accustomed to the sweetness of life abroad, boasted about an event they went to that served crusty and dry gizdodo, Mama changed her tune. "I want a *par-ry*," Mama had told her. "With *fresh* gizdodo. Not that one wey dey like stockfish."

Joy was elated. Initially, anyway. Then came the crushing realization that she had to plan a party to appease her family, including relatives she'd never meet but who would undoubtedly hear about it in her paternal village in Nigeria.

Seventy was a huge milestone and, once the menu was sorted, Mama began to see it as divine timing. Joy wasn't so sure. "I mean, it's just a coincidence," she had said, to which Mama had scoffed, set her eyes on Joy, and replied, "Gịnị *coincidence*? Chukwu adịghị ehi ụra, o." *God does not sleep.*

If God did ever want to sleep, Joy supposes He would pick the same six-bedroom mini-mansion backed onto a ravine outside of Toronto that Joy chose (after careful deliberation and an extensive pros-and-cons list) for Mama's party. Usually, the local Nigerian community does hall parties, loud and festive occasions in rented community centers or banquet halls. But Mama had said she wanted a different kind of party for this birthday.

"Is there a pool?"

"Hm?" Joy raises an eyebrow, but she's zoned out on the cars in front of her. From the moment she left her townhouse in North York to the second she got on the highway, she's been inundated with worry. *Please let this weekend go well, or . . . or . . .* she's not sure. What will it prove? She's not a good daughter, not a good kid? She can't budget and was right to fail advanced mathematics in high school?

That she can't persevere the way she always thought she could.

She taps her fingers against the steering wheel as the car inches forward. Traffic on the 400 is uglier than she expected. Who would've guessed that this many people would be trying to escape the city on Easter weekend?

"Mom. Pool?" Jamil prods again from beside her. This time, she tilts her head and blinks rapidly before she's finally able to snap out of it. Her son has one eye on his game device and the other on her. She's not sure how that's even possible, and she tries to think back to when she was twelve and could multitask without crippling anxiety. The memory doesn't come. *Yeah, because it doesn't* exist, *Joy.*

"No. And you don't even know how to swim," she says finally.

"Yeah, but Sarah said she'd teach me."

"Your cousin?"

"Mmhmm."

She didn't know Sarah could swim. The only thing she tends to remember of her brother Michael's daughter is that she had a very public emo phase when she was starting high school. And she looks a lot like Michael, which is to say she looks a lot like their dad.

When Joy thinks about it, it's a bit rude that children have the audacity to look like anyone but their mothers. She never used to have thoughts like this until the long separation, and finally, the very recent divorce. Now whenever she looks at Jamil, she sees more of David than she'd like. He's still a boy, on the cusp of adolescence, but she knows he will have the same chin as David. She can see it. They already have the same eyes, that rustic, hazel color Joy finds herself thinking of from time to time. Sometimes they pronounce words the same way, and Joy thinks it's because Jamil is spending too much time with his dad. But then she stops herself because, really, what is "too much time with your present and involved father"? Shouldn't she be happy? At least they agreed to shared custody. It could be so much worse.

Joy unintentionally jerks the car forward, startling Jamil from his game. "Sorry," she murmurs. "A-and forget it, you don't need to learn how to swim."

Jamil snorts, his curls bouncing as he throws his head back onto the headrest. "Why? Are *you* gonna carry me during the apocalypse? Everyone knows it'll be, like, every man for himself."

Joy purses her lips and just nods, thinking back on when she was secretly obsessed with aliens as a preteen. Jamil couldn't get away with casually referencing the end of days in front of Mama, but it reminds her that even though David has claimed his face and vocal intonations, Jamil Bianchi is truly her child and Joy has his heart. Not that it's a competition or anything. Also, not that she should be proud he's apparently prepping for the apocalypse.

It takes an extra half hour to see their way out of traffic before a breezy hour's drive gets them to the rental property. Jamil gapes in awe at the winding driveway leading to the grand house. It looks just like the pictures: glass where there could be brick and manicured gardens that reflect the high property value. Off to the side, Joy can see the pathway into the expansive yard where they will hold Mama's birthday celebration. She gets nervous just thinking about it. Everything has to happen on schedule. Everything has to be perfect.

Jamil unbuckles his seat belt and launches himself out of the car the moment Joy slows to park. "Hey, hey, wait a second!" she calls, but Jamil is too busy marveling at the motion-sensor walkway. It lights up even though it's bright outside.

"Come help me grab stuff," Joy says as she steps out of the car. The air feels cleaner this far from the city. She knows she's imagining it, though. "Jamil?" She looks around and spots her son taking pictures of the exterior. "Jamil, I don't have strength, I'm not calling you again."

"Coming, coming." He hurries over, stretching out his hands for whatever Joy is sure he can carry.

Joy rifles through her trunk for their suitcases, a bag of CDs with old Igbo music for the party, and her sunhat, but freezes when she hears her ringtone from the driver's seat. "Shit," she curses, which earns her a sharp inhale from Jamil. "Don't— Just, hold on one second," she says before scuttling around to the car door.

Joy didn't mention it to anyone, because she knows if she'd told her mom or even her cousin Nnenna that she was bringing her work phone, they'd tell her it was a bad idea. She knows this now. After a hectic week at her life coaching job, the last thing she needs is to be fielding calls outside of work hours. She told everyone she was taking this weekend off, but she knew that wouldn't stop Coral.

Coral was currently going through a painful breakup. Normally, this would be the perfect time for life coach Joy to impart her non-judgmental wisdom to help facilitate healing, perpetuate growth, and establish some semblance of client/coach boundaries. But Joy, who was adjusting very well with her divorce until she wasn't, could barely muster up enough strength to appear put together in front of her kid, let alone clients or strangers. She hadn't even formally changed back her last name yet. Her identity was being held somewhere in limbo and her boundaries had all but collapsed.

She kept trying to pass Coral off to other coaches, but it was no use. Coral seemed to vibe with Joy and Joy alone, even going as far as to say, "We just *get* each other, you know?" at their last session. *Classic transference*, Joy told herself, and then proceeded to talk for the next hour about why boundaries were important.

"Be the adult," Joy whispers to herself as she takes the call. She preaches the importance of boundaries all the time, but for some reason, she can't seem to make them stick in her personal life. "Be the adult ... be the adult—"

"Joy?"

"Coral, hey! How are you?"

"Joy." Coral's voice goes limp, dissolving into a whimper over the phone. Joy's heart drops. This will be a longer conversation than she was hoping for at 10:00 a.m. on a Friday. On *Good* Friday. Quickly, she signals to Jamil, telling him to go inside, before turning her back to focus on the phone call.

Coral takes a deep, shaky breath. "I'm so sorry to call like this, but I needed to talk to you. I'm—it's—this morning, I was watching the news, right ..."

"Right, right."

"And I saw them mention, um, the park." She chokes back a sob.

"Mmhmm, mmhmm."

Joy listens as she busies herself with getting what she can out of the car and locking the door. She wishes she had taken the time to marvel at the exterior, too, because now as she rushes to the front door, nudging it open with her foot, it's all a blur. She treats the entranceway like she's been there a hundred times before. Kick off your shoes here against the spotless shoe rack, set down your luggage beside the front table—keep your keys snug in one of the many silver cups designed for trinkets and loose change—glide past the grand stairway, glance at the hanging crystal chandelier, ignore the shutter doors leading to the den, the living room, the entertainment room, waltz into the kitchen, shield your eyes from the glass panels that decorate the back of the house, squint into the distance because—is that a greenhouse out there? Was that in the ad? Forget it, forget the ad. Instead, go straight to the lush sectional, sink your way in, and listen to Coral go on and on *for free.*

I can't do a free session, for fuck's sake. Joy sighs, tapping her forehead lightly. At some point, she will have to tell Coral that this is actually, technically, a little bit illegal since Joy is not a crisis center. At some point, she will have to interject and hang up. At some point, she'll have to locate her child and her mom and the caterer who should be hanging around somewhere and maybe the DJ will be showing up early to do a quick setup and there might not be enough chairs and tables in the backyard . . .

There's just so much to do before the party tonight. *So* much. And, as always, she feels like she's doing it all alone.

Please let this weekend go well, or . . . Or? She still doesn't know. She just wanted to do something nice for her mom. That's it. Contrary to what she bets her cousins are thinking, this isn't about Joy. She just wants her mom to have a nice weekend with her family. She deserves it. Isn't that good enough of a reason? For her busybody Nigerian family, maybe not. But for her, it could be.

Joy takes a deep breath and says, "C-Coral? Coral?" The line goes silent with Joy's interruption. Panic creeps into her words. "I didn't mean to cut you off. I'm so sorry, but I'm not available this weekend, remember? I told you on Wednesday. I don't have my computer with me so I don't have your file—"

"Oh, that's okay. I can just explain—"

"N-no, no, I, um, it wouldn't be fair." Joy clears her throat. "Why don't we, um, reschedule?"

"Reschedule?"

"Or, um . . ."

"Or?"

Joy hears footsteps coming down the hallway behind her, and she turns just in time to see her mother arrive. Joy has matured to the point that now Mama's presence is calming, like when the tide comes in and brushes the shore. As a kid, her mom's footsteps meant trouble—she forgot to close the fridge fully, or worse, she didn't get a good grade in school. But as an adult, Joy is conscious of the soothing, otherworldly quality Mama has. She's like an anchor and has been that way for years, especially after Papa passed away five years ago.

Mama says nothing; just smiles, her eyes crinkling, and waves at Joy on the phone as she circles into the kitchen. She moves through the house with such ease, as if she is the matriarch in a Nollywood movie whose son built this multimillion-dollar home with money from a relative who died under suspicious circumstances.

"Joy?"

Coral's voice brings Joy back to her unfortunate reality—that she sucks at enforcing the boundaries she loves to advise on.

"Coral? I'm *so* sorry, but I *will* get back to you. Bye," Joy says quickly. A flimsy, vague apology is the best thing her mind can come up with. She would much rather be here, present and semiorganized, than have to relive each pain point in Coral's breakup—and, by extension, in her own.

As soon as she puts down the phone, Joy is enveloped by the bustle of the house. She stops and stares around at faces and bodies, most of which she doesn't recognize. The people rushing back and forth with tablecloths and wires, chatting among themselves as they set up the outdoor space, must have been here from the crack of dawn. The party is tonight and these people are absolutely not running on Nigerian time.

Joy gets to her feet, ignoring the million-and-one things running through her mind, and gravitates to the large glass window overlooking the yard. She watches as staff place tables in an accessible pattern, while others decorate with what looks like a pulpit at the edge of the dance floor. Her heartstrings tug. Weeks of vetting professionals and calling fifteen different DJ Ebukas around Toronto has finally paid off.

Although it looks as if they might need one more table.

If it rains (will it rain today?), the canopy above the high table might not reach the pulpit.

And did she okay those specific centerpieces on *all* the tables?

"Shut, shut up," Joy hisses to herself, and allows one deep breath to flow through her. "No more worrying. Take a break."

"Ị sị gịnị?"

Mama approaches Joy, reaching out to steady herself. Joy roots herself in place, feeling the weight of Mama's grip.

"Mom," Joy says.

"Ke kwanu?"

"I'm fine."

"Eh-heh."

Joy bristles at the response. In her mom's voice, she can hear a tiny tinge of judgment, the kind that has yet to disappear, even at Joy's big age. She heard the same *eh-heh* when she was fifteen, decided she didn't want to go to church anymore, and made a PowerPoint presentation to state her case. She heard it when she was twenty and decided to pursue psychotherapy instead of something reputable like aerospace engineering.

She heard it at twenty-five, at Peace's funeral.

"You got here early, huh?" Joy asks, squinting into the distance. "Who drove you? I said I could come get you. I'm not too far from Etobicoke now."

Mama shakes her head; gives Joy's arm another squeeze. "It's fine. You know that, eh . . . my bosom friend, Amara"—she snickers at this, leaning in and wiggling her eyebrows to really sink in the fact that she hates this woman—"she drove me on the way to that her work. The hospital. She's a nurse."

"I know, Mom."

"And she almost *killed* somebody! With paracetamol. Which kin' nurse is that?"

Joy's lip twitches, biting back a smile. "Wo-ow. She's your friend, Mom. She drove you here."

Mama snickers. "Who asked you? Anyway, where is that my son? My beautiful baby son."

Mama always heaps a lot of praise on Jamil because he's the young-est of her grandchildren. She would always call him things like "my beautiful son" and a part of Joy wondered if it was because Jamil was hers, or because Jamil was David's. Mama really likes David, as people often do, because he's charming and statuesque and funny in that way that you can tell is genuine. He is very good-looking, with his dark, wavy hair and intense, hazel eyes, and he is also, unfortunately, quite amiable. It was one main reason why the separation and divorce were so hard. They aren't enemies by any means. They just aren't the people they used to be.

How can you explain the pain associated with growing apart? It wasn't just sharp like a knife in the side. It wasn't even dull, like a constant, steady throbbing. Being both and neither of those things brought on an exhaustion that Joy wasn't prepared for.

Her family didn't understand. Her mom refused to. "Why would you get *divorced*?" Mama had asked when Joy finally dredged up the courage to tell them two years ago. She had come to pick up Jamil from Mama's place after coming back from a fruitless therapy session, which Mama thought was pointless anyway. "Therapy will not fix a marriage. Did therapy give you the strength to birth your child?" is something she would always say. And she said it that day, as Joy was gathering up Jamil's things in a hurry. Joy didn't have the strength to tell her that it actually, truthfully, and honestly made no fucking sense.

"He's Catholic, *Roman* Catholic," Mama had continued, following Joy up and down the living room with a scowl on her face. She held the corner of her tied wrapper at her waist, clutching it as if it would unravel. "Catholics don't divorce. It's sinful."

"You think Catholics genuinely care about sin? Haven't you seen those documentaries?"

Mama frowned. "Which documentaries?"

"About the priests."

A look of shock so grave came to Mama's face that Joy was sure time had stopped. After a moment, Mama whispered, taunting and low, "And what about them, Joy?"

She knows, Joy thought. *She just wants you to say it so she can yell at you.* Joy couldn't believe she watched this entire conversation blow up in her face. She kept forgetting she wasn't the fun child. She could barely make a nonjoke about a Catholic priest without it turning into another intervention. "Uh, n-never mind."

Quickly, Joy had resumed grabbing books and clothes and, wait, where was Jamil? She stopped, held on to the staircase's railing, and called, "Jamil? Come on, we're leaving!"

"Okay, nwa m, ndo, let me just talk to him," Mama had said, holding her hands up like this was her last offering. "Let me talk to him and then we will see."

Joy let out a sharp breath and stared at her mom, incredulously. "Mom, no, why? You weren't even married to him."

She frowned. "He's my son-in-law—"

"Well, not for much longer."

"Ah!" Mama had hissed and snapped her fingers above her head. The shrillness of her voice rang out through the living room and Joy, heart thumping with anxiety, froze in place. She didn't look at her as Mama said, "You think I won't slap you? Is that why you're saying such foolish things?"

A sigh fluttered from Joy's lips, pulling frustration and sadness with it. Suddenly, her eyes stung with tears. She turned away, unwilling to cry in front of her mom.

Mama took a firm step forward in that relentless, purposeful way she had, and grabbed Jamil's bag from Joy's grasp, picking up where Joy had left off. "Family is very important," Mama told her quietly. Joy watched as she tucked the last book inside, zipped up the bag, and placed it at the foot of the stairs. "God has His hands in my life. He won't ever rest. Everything will be fine."

Joy thinks a lot about how Mama is so sure of this ever-present God, this watchful God who doesn't sleep. Standing in their rented house, she watches staff carry a new table into the yard and forces herself to come back to the present, to stop thinking about how Mama was so sure her God would fix a problem that wasn't orchestrated by Him in the first place. Instead, she lets her mind run back into overdrive. Where is the caterer? And where's the, uh, the DJ? And, and, and. *I'm too tired for this shit.*

"Where is David? Tell him to come."

Joy's heart thumps, first with the shock of Mama bringing him up—and then with annoyance that, no matter how many times Joy has explained what divorce is, Mama still doesn't get it.

Joy opens her mouth. "Ah . . ." and breathes out. Turning back to the window, she tries to remember . . . What are those things she keeps preaching about to her clients?

Oh, yes. Boundaries.

— 2 —

Joy stays quiet long enough that Mama's question dies in the air between them. *Thank God,* Joy thinks. They watch the staff move tables. They say nothing.

Mama breaks free of Joy's arm and wanders into the kitchen for her breakfast, which she brought specially wrapped from home. Caterers from Omotola's Kitchen have filled the fridge with drinks and meal prep for later this evening. "The woman said they would be back. She left some of the dough for the chin-chin here. All we have to do is fry it," Mama tells Joy, who follows her, stopping to lean against the gleaming countertop.

"What kind of caterer makes food for the party they're catering *at* the venue?" Joy asks, scrunching her nose.

"She's frying some here and some there," Mama says with a shrug. "You know chin-chin doesn't finish, so, anyway."

Joy pauses, unsure if this is something else she should add to her growing list of stressors.

"Biko, I need your help." Mama unwraps her packed lunch, boiled yam and stew, before signaling Joy over. "For the party later, I want to read a very important Bible verse. It's my birthday, but it is also a holy day. You understand?"

"Of course."

"So, anyway . . ." Mama has this habit of trailing off, leaving her sentences behind as she goes. She takes her plate to the microwave, punches the one-minute button, and spends two, three seconds watching it spin before coming back to join Joy at the island. "Help me look through the Bible to find a good verse."

Joy's eyes skip to the microwave, doing a very noticeable leap to avoid Mama. She hasn't read a Bible in ages, which, if not for the divorce, is probably the number one character flaw her mom would say she has. *She's a nice girl, but she doesn't read the Bible.* In fact, Joy is sure that Mama has uttered those words about her to her church group.

A lightbulb goes off in Joy's mind just as the microwave starts beeping. "Oh! Jamil can help you," she says. She always loves when Mama spends quality time with her son, even though as a kid herself she hated those moments when her parents would sit them down to tell village stories about relatives who had turned into goats. Jamil won't get those experiences from her, and she knows it. She is too in her head, too westernized. Jamil is fortunate, Joy thinks, to have this opportunity.

Mama frowns, but the brightness behind her eyes shows that she doesn't completely hate the idea. Joy can see that the wheels in her head are turning—"Get him into Jesus now before he turns out like his mom," probably.

She says, "Eh-heh, kpọọ ya ebe a," with a small smile as she retrieves her food from the microwave.

Joy breathes a sigh of relief, the very same kind she used to feel when she got out of going to church or singing worship as a kid. She used to offer up Peace in her place, but now she's substituted her son for her sister. It was a bit unfair, but as she wanders back to the main hall, she makes a silent promise that if Jamil ever said he was sick of going to church with David's family, she would support him and tell him to quit. She'd tell him that he would be happier as an adult the sooner he started to make his own decisions. That he should be careful not to hang on to her approval too long, the way she did with her family.

"Jamil?" Joy calls. Her voice all but echoes in the hallway. She takes in the details, this time approaching the grand staircase, her focus drifting to the lush carpet runner that leads upstairs. The chandelier glitters across the second floor and the landing leads to a circular opening, almost like a rotunda, where each of the bedroom doors are visible.

Jamil pokes his head out of the one closest to the landing. "Jamil," Joy calls again, but he quickly holds out his phone, shaking it as if to say he's busy. Joy's eyes connect with the screen. He's in the middle of a call. She whispers, "Who are you talking to?"

"Dad," he answers quietly, and then returns the phone to his ear.

Joy pauses.

She hears her mom's voice repeat in her head, *Call him here*, and she narrowly avoids another David-induced spiral. "Hang up the phone," she tells him. "Grandma wants your help picking a Bible verse for the party."

He makes a face like he doesn't understand what she's saying.

"You gotta read the Bible," Joy explains, "and pick something that sounds cool, like a really interesting anecdote or—or, you know, like, a verse."

Jamil squints while he thinks. "So just, like, something about Jesus?"

"Yes." Joy grins, clasping her hands together. She's thankful Catholic school is paying off. "Say goodbye to your dad. Tell him you'll call him later."

"Okay. Did you wanna say hi first?"

Jamil extends the phone before she can say no. It takes all her willpower to not jump back. If there's one thing she and her ex had been really particular about, it was making sure Jamil didn't feel as if there was an actual separation.

She and David are still friendly. She is known to meet his eyes during dropoffs; she still manages to smile around him. But that sort of ease brings its own discomfort. It brings up family members prodding and judging, wondering what the point of being separated even was.

It makes her wonder, too. *We got married when we were pretty young, so I don't know, people change, don't they? People are allowed to change.* No reason was good enough. It would've been easier if she hated him; if they had fought each other over Jamil until he, too, spiraled into his own emo phase.

Joy swallows. She is sweating. "I'll call him later. I gotta do something first."

Jamil nods and turns to say bye into the phone. It's only after Jamil descends the stairs and Joy can hear the emptiness of the rotunda does she allow herself a minute to breathe. She takes a step forward, her feet sinking into the luxury carpet, before she realizes she has no idea where she's going.

Each bedroom door is ornate and adorned with a gold trim. The main family will be staying here for the weekend. Her and Jamil have one room, her cousin Nnenna and her family have another, her cousin Robert has his own, then Mama will be on her own. And if her brother, Michael, ever decides to show up, then he and his family will have their own room, as well. Joy rolls her eyes at the thought. God forbid Mama's eldest child would plan her seventieth or, honestly, even show up on time. He should be the one worrying about Bible verses and if there are enough chairs and why the caterer is planning on frying chin-chin at the house! Seriously, what kind of caterer does that?

It wouldn't be this bad if Peace were still here. This is what she tells herself often. If her twin sister, the Peace to her Joy, were still around, then maybe things would be different for her.

She tiptoes down the hall and pokes her head into each room. Some rooms have two queen beds; some have just one king. Some rooms feature their own TVs while others have mock fireplaces and gold-tinted bedside tables to fit the aesthetic. This place is very fitting for both her mother's birthday and an Easter weekend getaway. The family will be impressed. They'll laud her for her attention to detail and her dedication to Mama—and, who knows, they may even stop asking where her husband is.

Ex-husband, *ex*-husband.

Joy makes her way into the room her mom has already settled into and glides her way toward the large bay window. From here, she can see the yard and the accompanying ravine. *It's all coming together so well*, she thinks to herself.

"See? No need to worry." She touches her cheeks lightly. "Take a break." Quickly, she turns, maneuvering her way around the excessive number of suitcases her mom brought with her, and finds her way to the bed.

The mirror sits directly across from her. Joy swears this is bad luck in some cultures, if not her own. There were so many superstitions associated with her Nigerianness that sometimes it was hard to keep track. Don't do this, don't say that, don't walk there, don't talk to witches.

Peace could've done well with that advice.

The doorbell rings.

Joy pushes all thoughts of her sister from her mind and rises to her feet. As she comes out of the room, she hears her mom downstairs, saying, "Who is that? The door is open, anyway . . ."

The closer Joy gets to the landing, the more voices she hears. Step by step, she descends the stairs, coming into full view of the foyer— and her cousin Nnenna and her family.

"This house na wa, o. Look at this place!"

Joy involuntarily cringes with her whole body. Her eyes dart to the front door. She knows she couldn't make it out in time even if she tried.

— 3 —

The first thing Nnenna Olubisi does when she enters the grand foyer is take off her shoes and set aside her luggage, making sure the embroidered double Cs of her Chanel bags are visible to her approaching extended family. Flying from Baltimore with two kids and not enough snacks was its own challenge, but no matter how exhausted Nnenna was, that didn't mean her Chanel carry-on didn't deserve to be seen. She didn't haggle with a third-party seller on Marketplace for nothing.

"Wow!" her son, Zach, whoops from beside her. He's ten and looks like the spitting image of her husband, James: clean-shaven, large ears, and a snaggletooth that always seems to be visible at every angle. She likes that he's spirited, but finds it hard to chase after him sometimes when she's wearing her Louboutins. And she's always wearing her Louboutins.

Zach is already rushing to get his backpack off so he can shoot off into the house. His sister, Yemi, is much more reserved, much more reminiscent of how Nnenna was as a child. "Take off your shoes and jacket first," Yemi scolds him in a tone that is too adult for a thirteen-year-old. She assists him before he goes bounding down the hall, straight into Mama's arms. Yemi glances back at her mom, locking eyes with her as if to say, *Can you* believe *this kid?* It makes Nnenna want to laugh. It also freaks her out a little.

James kicks off his shoes and steps past Nnenna, staring up toward the chandelier. "Are you sure we're the only ones here? In this big house? He-ey!" He breaks into a cackle at his nonjoke. "Mama. Mama, kedu k'į mere? Happy birthday." He approaches Mama for a hug after Zach has finally let go and wandered off.

Mama reaches out, warm and glowing, as her eyes flutter from him to Nnenna. Unlike her own mom, her auntie Mary always looks as if she's been waiting to hug you, no matter how short the time is since she's last seen you. And Nnenna knows that it's been ages since they've seen each other. They've . . . well, James has been too busy with his church duties, as head pastor for the New Apostles in Pentecostal Glory African Church. They pull in almost every West African family in the Baltimore area, so Mama should be happy that James is quite literally doing the Lord's work.

"Wow, wow . . . ah-ah," Nnenna says and grins, marveling at the interior. Bright, airy, but exotic and reminiscent of a beachside vacation home. She wishes she knew how much it cost, but she figures asking Joy about it right away would be crass. They stare at each other across the foyer, as if neither is sure who should approach first. An uncomfortable smile comes to Nnenna's lips as she inches forward. "Joy, my baby cousin," she croons, slowly outstretching her arms, although from far away it probably looks like they're being cranked open against their will.

Joy is no better. She doesn't fully lean into the hug until Nnenna is directly in front of her. "Nnenna, sis. You made it on time."

Nnenna pulls back. Was that a jab? She studies Joy's delicate features, a reflection of Mama in her younger years, and isn't sure what to think. Her smile falters as she clears her throat, tossing the length of her twenty-two-inch wig over her shoulder, and says, "Well, I sent you our itinerary, didn't I? We arrived at the Pearson airport at nine fifteen, just like I told you."

"Yeah, o-of course, yeah."

Joy is nodding but Nnenna isn't done. She turns to Mama, sharp like a hawk. "Mama, kedu. Please, I told everyone our airport arrival time was nine fifteen, no?"

Mama glances at Joy. "Ah . . . I don't know, o. You know I am not good with, eh, comp-u-ter." She emphasizes the word, spitting it out harshly like it's something disgusting.

"Yeah, you did," Joy cuts in, holding out her hands in surrender. "I just meant that, you know . . . 'You made it on time. Welcome.'"

Nnenna raises an eyebrow. "And why would I not make it on time?"

The air seems to crackle with Joy's inability to answer.

Nnenna is Mama's sister's daughter, and her personality rivals the intensity of Auntie Nancy. Joy can't stand the way Nnenna wears "pastor's wife" on her forehead like it's a badge of honor. As if she'd get into heaven just by proximity. People like Nnenna don't understand you have to actively *not* be the worst for all that praying and shit to hold water, but Joy would never say that around her. Nnenna would attack her with her heels and strangle her with her hair.

Nnenna's eyes travel toward the staircase. "Which room is ours?"

Perfect. Joy breathes a sigh of relief. "Yeah, lemme show you upstairs. You can take a tour of the house after."

"Well, it's not much of a 'tour' if I'm just walking around by myself, is it?" Nnenna hums as she pokes at the polished wood railing, admiring its precise curve. She doesn't see Joy's eyes blank behind her, her soul fighting to stay present in her body. "Show me the rooms."

Suddenly, James snaps his fingers in their direction. He waves his hand haphazardly around the entranceway, around the luggage taking up most of the space. "Nne, take these things upstairs. Keep the kids' stuff to one side, too."

There are more bags than Nnenna has hands. A normal person might say this would be an impossible feat to do alone, but Nnenna barely bats an eyelash as she reaches for the first of the suitcases. "Where are you going?" she asks him while she rolls the closest one toward the stairs.

James cocks his head as if he doesn't understand the question. "To see what else needs to be done. The staff needs direction, na."

Joy bites her tongue so she doesn't snort aloud. James is standing with his bald head shining in the morning light, and Joy swears he's sticking out his chest. Posturing, as if it even means anything. For sure she didn't miss this, how her cousin-in-law stepped so easily and effortlessly into his machismo whenever he sensed too much estrogen. She isn't sure what she hates more: James being James or Nnenna being Nnenna. Choosing the lesser of two evils was never really her strong suit.

And yet.

"Let me help you with those." Joy snatches a few of the lighter bags and maneuvers around Nnenna toward the staircase.

Nnenna smiles, then swoons, "I hope we have the best view. Ooh, preferably of the garden. Don't give the garden view to Rob, o. I know I'm your favorite, anyway."

Nnenna's comments don't let up as they lug the bags upstairs. She *oohs* and *aahs* at the simple beauty of the railing and the doors while she asks, "So where's David? Oh, this is a nice detail here, I like this a lot . . ."

Joy pretends she doesn't hear as they shuffle along the hallway. "This one's yours," she says, nudging a door open with her foot. Light cascades in through the large bay window, illuminating two queen beds, a restored oak dresser, and the path to a walk-in closet.

Nnenna gasps, throwing her bags to the side, and rushes to the window. "Come see, o! Wow . . ." The view isn't of the garden (Joy is thankful, because the last thing she wants to see right now is James reordering the tables or something), but Nnenna is still in awe of how much she can see of the fountain in the front yard from here. "It must be marble," she says, nodding to it.

Joy shrugs. "Maybe. I don't know."

Suddenly, Nnenna spins to face her. Joy sits uncomfortably under her cousin's gaze, shifting her weight back and forth on her feet, unsure where to land.

Nnenna asks, "How's Jamil?"

"He's good. He's here," Joy adds, gesturing to the doorway. "He's helping my mom with picking a Bible verse to read at the party later."

Nnenna's eyes light up; her posture changes. Suddenly, she seems warmer, more open. Joy knows if there's anything Nnenna does well, it's reading and reciting Scripture. No, not even James could best her at it. And yes, it is a competition. "Exciting, exciting! Are you going with something classic? Like a Matthew 26:26–29 situation? Or does she want something more aligned with a birthday? Like—oh, 3 John . . . I think 1:2 would be cute. The King James version starts with 'Beloved . . .'" She tilts her head toward Joy, waiting for the continuation.

Joy doesn't know the rest of the verse. If she focuses real hard, she's sure she can hear her work phone ringing somewhere.

After an uncomfortably long pause, Joy asks, "'Beloved' what? You don't know it?"

Nnenna's eyebrow twitches. "Don't be stupid. Of course I know it. Sounds like you don't, though."

"Of course I don't."

"Well, then it's good that Jamil is the one helping Mama." Nnenna kisses her teeth with an exaggerated roll of her eyes. "In fact, this weekend will be good for him."

"Yeah, because he hasn't seen his cousins in forever—"

"I meant, he'd be exposed to what an actual Good Friday celebration should be like."

"All right."

Nnenna narrows her eyes. "I bet the poor boy hasn't been to church in ages."

"Sure."

"You must be proud."

"I feel no ways about this."

"Yemi says he has a YouTube channel." Nnenna cringes, probably disgusted at the idea that her twelve-year-old nephew would be selling his soul online. Joy distinctly remembers hearing Nnenna say once, in all seriousness, that there's no reason for strangers to perceive her children on the internet.

Joy shakes her head right away. "No, no. Sometimes he'll film things like he has a YouTube channel, like a fake one. He doesn't have one in real life, he's way too young. And it's weird, right, a kid with their own channel."

"It's unnatural."

"Okay."

"How's David?"

Joy purses her lips, then lets out a nervous chuckle. She can't help it. It's one thing to be confronted about him by her mother, but by her cousin who she barely sees? Who she barely talks to? Joy is almost curious as to what she's heard from across the border. Almost.

"Mm, what's so funny?" Nnenna asks. Her gaze is like a hawk's. It's everywhere in this room. Joy can feel it bouncing off the beds, the paintings, the window, the walls.

Quickly, Joy waves away Nnenna's question. "He's . . . I don't know."

"He's not coming?"

"We're not together, Nnenna," she explains with a frustrated exhale. "You know that. *Everyone* knows that."

Nnenna crosses her arms and turns up her nose. She leans back into the windowsill as if to get a better look at Joy, scanning her from head to toe, finding the next thing she wants to scrutinize. "I don't understand you and these weird customs."

It takes all of Joy's strength not to roll her eyes—and she still fails. "Divorce is not a 'weird custom,' Nnenna. It's actually pretty common. Most first marriages end in divorce—"

Nnenna claps her hands together loudly. "Ah! Enough. Don't say those kinds of things."

"It's *true*—"

"Maybe for people like *you*," Nnenna says with a shifty glance to the floor. "But for African people—for Christians, it's not."

Christians divorce. Joy knew that because some of her clients happened to be Christians working through divorce. But apparently Nnenna had already decided that anyone who didn't attend church with the passion of a thousand burning suns wasn't worthy of breathing her air, so there was little Joy could say to get through to her. In the end, how much did it really matter? If Nnenna thinks Joy is a heathen for getting divorced or buying a phone for her child, then it's really not Joy's business.

Nnenna sighs. "Divorce is a cop-out. You're essentially just giving up."

Joy holds her breath. *It's just one weekend, and then Nnenna will be gone. . . .*

"You think other couples don't have problems? You think marriage is supposed to be *fun*?"

There will be a border between them. All Joy has to do is survive the weekend and let Border Patrol do the rest.

"I didn't want to say it, but I will, okay? Maybe if you married someone Nigerian, someone African, this wouldn't have happened to you."

Joy lets out a sharp exhale.

Nnenna glances away. Her grip on her own arm tightens, as if she could cross her arms harder, posture stronger, be more right.

She's fucked, Joy reminds herself over and over again. *This is what she does. This is just how she is. Don't let her get to you.*

The room is tense with Joy's silence. Truthfully, she's stayed here too long. She's stayed in a room with her semipsychotic cousin for longer than is necessary. It's like a law, it's physics: the longer you stay in Nnenna's periphery, the higher chance she'll say some fucked-up shit. The higher chance there is for her to dig her claws into you, nudging just enough until she finds the exact nerve that makes you yelp in pain. And then she keeps digging because "It didn't hurt *that* much, right? You're fine."

Joy clears her throat. "First of all, you don't know what you're talking about. Second of all, no one asked you," she says sternly.

Nnenna raises an eyebrow. "Joy, please, I'm on your side here."

"*This* is you being on my side?"

"I'm—"

"Okay, actually, let's just not," Joy cuts in. "We don't need to talk about divorce and, um, fun marriages. To be honest, we don't even need to talk, so . . ." She clears her throat and looks around the room, counting the suitcases as if she knows how many Nnenna's family packed. "I'm gonna go grab the other bags."

Joy doesn't wait for Nnenna to agree before she exits the room and makes a beeline straight for the foyer. Mama is waiting at the bottom of the stairs. She clutches Joy's work phone with a sour look on her face. "It was just ringing and ringing. Ah! It was giving me a headache."

"Sorry, Mom," Joy mutters as she takes the phone. Two missed calls, both from Coral. She suppresses a groan.

Mama looks to the top of the stairs before setting her eyes back on Joy. "Where is Nnenna? Why is your face doing like that?" She reaches out to pull at Joy's cheeks, but Joy takes a swift step back before she can do so. "Is Nnenna all right?"

"Nnenna is always all right," Joy answers. She surprises herself with how even-toned she sounds even though she'd rather smack Nnenna in the face.

Then Mama says, "You know she loves you," in a soft, pacifying way. Joy hates it. She stuffs her phone in her bra and busies herself with grabbing two more bags from the entrance. "She's your cousin. Nwanne gi. My sister's daughter," Mama goes on. Her voice is like an echo following Joy around. Like a bee that won't stop buzzing, telling her to be nice to her cousins, the same way she did when Joy was growing up. It was always "be nice to them," but never "don't let them talk to you anyhow." If Joy had had the opportunity to fight Nnenna once in hand-to-hand combat when they were kids, maybe things would be different now!

"It doesn't matter what she says," Mama goes on. "She loves you. So just forget about it."

Joy bites her tongue, swallowing down her frustration. The fact of the matter is that love doesn't absolve Nnenna from being accountable. And for once, Joy would love it if Nnenna showed some restraint. Just because her husband is a pastor, it doesn't mean she can run her mouth about things she doesn't understand. The two things aren't even related, as far as Joy is concerned!

Mama follows Joy upstairs. She holds out a hand before Joy disappears inside Nnenna's room. "Where is your brother?"

Joy scoffs. "I wish I knew."

"All right."

"Mom, you really should yell at him," she goes on. Joy is joking, but only a little. "Like, for once, just tell him he's stupid."

"He-ey. Bad mouth. You think I won't slap you?" Mama chuckles through her usual threat. "Your brother is not stupid. Ekwula ya ọzọ. Bush girl."

Joy laughs.

Mama reaches forward again, gripping both of Joy's forearms. Joy knows Mama's secret, that she doesn't need to hold on to anything for balance. She's strong, even at her age. But there must be something about keeping your children close even when they're all grown up. Joy is an adult, she is thirty-six, and she has a son. It must be different spending time with your adult child, being able to talk with them in ways you couldn't have before.

She says, "Your elder brother is still your brother. God says you must give grace, so . . . biko, don't be so hard of heart."

"Ugh, okay."

"When Michael gets here, tell him to go help James."

"Technically, James shouldn't *need* any help because it's not his job to *do* anything."

Mama gives a knowing look, a wink-nudge type of smile. "Well, anyway. My beautiful son picked a verse for me, so we will read it together later."

"Was it one of the classic ones?" Joy asks, using the same term Nnenna used earlier. "Something for Good Friday?"

Mama shakes her head. "Numbers. 6:24–26."

Joy nods. She has no idea what that one is.

Mama immediately chortles. "You are nodding like this." She emulates it, an exaggerated version of Joy's subtle compliance. "Ah-ah. You don't read the Bible, o, so I don't know why you are pretending. Bush girl."

Joy laughs. "I'll look it up."

"Yes, o. Go and read. As for me, let me go and rest small." Mama gives Joy's forearms one final squeeze before traipsing past her down the hall. "Come wake me in one hour. Wake me when my sister arrives."

"Okay," Joy says. At this rate, Auntie Nancy and Uncle Ezekiel—
hell, even Robert—all of whom are flying in from Maryland, will get
here before her useless brother. *Don't call him* useless, *Joy,* she tells herself. *Remember what Mom said: have grace.*

She shakes off her bitterness and carries the last few bags into
Nnenna's room.

Nnenna, who is sitting poised at the edge of the bed closest to the
window, turns and gasps. "Oh, it's you. I was just thinking, actually.
Isn't it weird how our kids are pretty much the same age, except you
got pregnant out of wedlock?"

Grace, Joy. Have grace.

— 4 —

The last time Jamil saw his cousins was at Christmas three years ago. He was nine and after Yemi said that they weren't allowed to watch cartoons past 6:00 p.m., he'd spent the remainder of the trip clinging to his dad and asking to play games on his phone. He didn't really like that about Yemi. She was such a buzzkill. Any time he wanted to do something fun—like, any time even Zach wanted to do something fun—she would say no right away. She was worse than his teachers, for real.

That's why, as they huddle on the large living room sectional, Jamil doesn't really expect much when he asks Yemi and Zach if they want to play Mario Kart. "No," Yemi says right away, as if the word is an extension of her being. She says it so easily. She must hear it a lot.

Jamil scoffs. "You don't even know what Mario Kart is, probably."

Yemi bristles, visibly irritated by the accusation, but Zach just laughs. His smile is missing three teeth. He says, "I know Mario Kart! Ryan at school has it."

Jamil shrugs. "Cool. I don't know if this place has the cables to connect this to the TV, though . . ." He taps the edge of his device, staring around at the room. Adults are rushing back and forth, carrying stuff here and there. It makes him excited for his grandma's birthday party later, but also a bit nervous. His mom looks tired already, so truthfully, he can't wait until this is all over so she can sleep in. And, by extension, so *he* can sleep in.

Yemi is scowling. She looks at the TV, then tosses her braids over her shoulder. It reminds Jamil a lot of his auntie Nnenna. "Zach," Yemi says, homing in on her brother. "If you play that game, I'm telling."

Zach gawks, staring at his sister. "That's not fair!"

"Today is Good Friday," she goes on, this time directing her gaze to Jamil. "Do you even know what this day is about? Not *you*." She smacks Zach's hand away when he shoots it up to answer, and then settles back on Jamil. "My mom says your mom says you guys don't go to church because you don't have to."

"What?" Jamil asks.

"My mom says your mom says you guys don't go to church," she repeats.

Zach gasps. "How come?"

Jamil shakes his head, though he isn't sure he has a good reason as to why they don't go. Well, his mom, maybe. He goes sometimes with his dad's family, with his nonna when he sees her every other Sunday, but they don't really bother him about it otherwise. His dad doesn't even go that often, but he never hears that side of the family make such a big deal about it like his mom's side. He really doesn't get it. Suddenly, Jamil asks, "Wait, will I die if I don't go? No, don't answer that," and he waves his hands frantically, hoping to wipe the question from their minds.

Yemi cocks an eyebrow and says, "Yes."

"For real?"

"One hundred percent," she goes on. "In the Bible, it says that you have to throw away other gods and only pay attention to *the* God, or you won't get everlasting life, so it probably means you'll die if you don't go to church."

Jamil scratches his head, thinking. "Okay, wait, wait, wait . . . So what if I go to church sometimes with my dad?"

"Doesn't matter."

"What about if I helped Grandma pick out a Bible verse for today?"

"It . . ." Yemi pauses a minute, then glowers at him. "W-what are you talking about?"

Jamil lets out a sigh. "So, before you guys got here, my mom said I had to help Grandma pick a verse from the Bible to read because it's her birthday and stuff. So we were reading and she asked which ones I liked, and I said I didn't like any because I didn't know any. Then she kept talking and showed me some verses in the book that she liked, and then we picked one. I think it was in Numbers. . . ."

Yemi listens carefully, but the more Jamil speaks, the more he notices her eyebrow twitch and . . . heat. She's starting to emanate heat. *That's probably not normal*, he thinks.

Yemi's breathing quickens, building and building until she forces out a cough. Disgruntled, she spits out, "A-and you don't know *which* verse?"

Jamil shakes his head, then shrugs.

Zach asks, "Can we play Mario Kart?"

Yemi snaps, "No one is playing Mario Kart while I'm here!"

Suddenly, Jamil's phone rings. He searches his pockets until he finally finds it.

Yemi watches on in intrigue. Her parents let her use her phone only during the weekdays and only after she's done homework. She wonders how many good deeds she'll have to do before her parents let her take her phone out of the house. But as she hears Jamil utter a quick "Ciao, Papà," she wonders if maybe she'd have a better chance if she had a white parent, too.

"Who was that?" Yemi pipes up the moment Jamil is off the phone.

"My dad."

"How come he's not here?" she asks, feigning innocence. She knows from eavesdropping on her mom's conversations with other aunties that Jamil's mom is what they refer to as a "heathen" because she got "divorced." Honestly, Yemi doesn't understand why being "divorced" is such a bad thing (the dictionary tells her it's just when married people break up, right?), but if her mom thinks it is, then it probably is. *Majorly.* The way they talk about Auntie Joy makes it seem like she doesn't know right from wrong or something; that this being "divorced" means she is "selfish."

And that's a sin.

What Yemi knows of sin is what she's seen outlined in the crisp pages of her Bible, the one she received at her baptism, and it sure feels like, sometimes, everything is illegal. If she didn't have the guidance of her parents, she'd feel stuck. Her mom is the definition of perfection and she admires the way her dad leads the church with power and passion. If all she has to do is listen to what her parents preach and reflect every Sunday (and Saturday, and Wednesday sometimes), then she'll be okay. She'll get into heaven.

She couldn't say as much for her brother. Zach is young, but easily led astray. As his older sister, Yemi supposes it's her job to help him out. She's fine with it, though. It would actually suck if her brother didn't get into heaven with her and her family. Oh my God, she doesn't even wanna think about it. It would actually be so embarrassing.

Jamil didn't appear to care about those things. It's so weird because when Yemi asked about his dad, she was sure he'd look rattled or guilty. Instead, he pauses a bit to think, as if trying to figure out his dad's exact schedule.

In the end, he shrugs. "I don't know. I forgot to ask."

"Okay, but how come he's not coming?" Yemi presses. *Say your parents are divorced,* she prods in her head. Suddenly, she thinks hearing the words will be a big deal; a real scandal.

"Him and my mom aren't married anymore," Jamil tells her. She watches his lips twist awkwardly around the words, as if he's been fed them a million times and is trying them on for size. "But, like, they don't hate each other," he rushes to say. "I have two houses now. For a week, I'm with my dad, and then for the next week, I'm with my mom. This is my mom's week."

"So is your dad coming to get you tomorrow?" Zach asks.

Jamil frowns. "I don't know."

"He should come to Grandma's party," Yemi challenges, a smug look on her face.

Jamil shrugs. "Okaaaay. Sure. I wanna play Mario Kart now." He leans back into the sofa. Zach wriggles excitedly before curling in beside him, eyes wide and mouth slack open at the lit-up screen.

Yemi falls into the sofa, too, keeping her eyes trained on her cousin—but not the game. She's not interested, obviously. Zach reaches over to ask Jamil for a turn, and she pinches him hard until he scowls at her. "If you play that, I'm telling," she hisses. He sticks out his tongue at her.

"Telling what?"

Yemi sits up straight the moment her mother comes around the corner, as if her mom's presence requires Yemi's perfection. "Mom."

Her mom stops in her tracks, looking around to find the source of the voice. "Kids," she says, approaching with a cautious smile on her lips. Her eyes fall on Jamil, who sits up a bit straighter, too. "Jamil, ah-ah. Is this the first time I'm seeing you?"

That means he's in trouble. Yemi bites her lip to keep from gloating. Rule number one—no, rule number zero for a Nigerian kid: always greet your elders the millisecond they arrive, or face the wrath of the family. And probably death. "Sorry, Auntie," he says. "Good afternoon."

Her mom's smile widens. "It's all right. I can see you all—"

"Mom, Zach was playing video games."

"—are doing fine. Yemi, wetin?" She turns to her daughter, frowning. Under her gaze, Yemi can feel herself deflating. "Anyway . . ." She watches her mom check her watch, then turn toward the staircase. "It's almost been an hour since Mama went to lie down. Go and wake her to come eat something. Your grandma will be here soon, too."

— 5 —

Yes, I can hold . . ." Joy murmurs into the phone as she circles the entranceway. So far, everything was falling into place for Mama's party, but if Joy could just confirm with the bakers that the cake was in transit, then she could rest. This is what she's been telling herself since she arrived. One more confirmation, one more check-in. Everything has to run smoothly. She owes it to her mom.

And the family, I need the family to see that I actually picked a bomb-ass cake, she thinks, spite filling up every crevice of her body where compassion can't reach.

Her niece Yemi passes her on the way to the staircase. Joy gives a warm smile, pulling the phone from her ear briefly. "Yemi, what's up?" she whispers to her.

Yemi bites her bottom lip, glancing away. She's scowling. "Hi, Auntie. My mom said I have to wake up Grandma."

Joy gives an exaggerated wince. "Good luck with that. She can sleep through anything."

Yemi shrugs, her shoulders rising and falling with preteen indignance, and turns to make her way upstairs. Joy watches her go, praying silently for the day the kids will get to an age where they want to actually have a conversation with her. She might have to wait a while. It had only been a few years since she herself felt more comfortable to chat with her own mother, besides the noncommittal "How are you" and "I'm fine."

Joy is still on hold as she saunters into the living room. Nnenna smiles when she sees her, but from far away, Joy gets strong vibes that it's actually a grimace.

"You're on the phone?" Nnenna coos.

"Mmhmm." Joy swivels the device around to make sure they didn't hang up on her. Nope, still connected. "Just confirming with the bakers."

Nnenna tilts her head, her eyes scanning Joy from her head to her toes. "I'm excited to see this cake. I . . ."

"I . . . ?" Joy furrows her brows, watching as Nnenna's focus shifts from her to something behind her head.

She follows Nnenna's gaze to Yemi, who has made her way back downstairs, stumbling past them. Nnenna calls, "Um, hello? Miss Yemi?" but Yemi's tunnel vision leads her right to her brother and Jamil, both curled up on the sofa. She rattles them, shaking Zach by the shoulders and commanding him to get up. Her jaw is set; she won't stop blinking. Joy glances at Nnenna, wondering if they're both seeing the same thing.

The three kids disappear upstairs, urged along by a restless Yemi.

Nnenna frowns. "I don't like that, o."

"Don't like what? Kids *playing*—oh!" Joy startles when her call connects. "Y-yes, hello?"

"Yes, Ms. Bianchi? Our driver will be on his way within five minutes, he says," came the assistant's reply.

A sigh of relief burst through Joy's lips. "Okay, perfect. Can you send me updates as he drives or, like, what's the procedure here?"

After a beat of silence, the assistant says, "We don't offer that service, ma'am."

"Oh! Yeah, no, of course you don't, I'm sorry." No one would offer a play-by-play delivery update service for a cake.

"Well?"

Nnenna's narrowed eyes and upturned nose are awaiting the moment Joy signs off and hangs up.

"Cake is good. It's on the way," Joy tells her.

Nnenna's face stretches with a smile. "*Perfect.* I can't wait to see what you chose." She raises her eyebrows in a way that makes Joy feel self-conscious. Maybe she should've run the cake choice by the family? Maybe she should've done samples and tasting with them?

Suddenly, a thundering of footsteps sound on the floor above them. Nnenna jumps a little, and the two of them listen as the noise tracks all the way to the staircase. Yemi, Zach, and Jamil materialize with Zach racing forward, a look of frustration on his face, as he nearly crashes into his mom.

Nnenna holds out her arms, catching him before they both tumble to the floor. She resets him, standing him upright like a doll, before unleashing her anger. "Ah-ah! What's all this? Why are you running in someone else's house?"

"M-Mom! Y-Yemi was—" Zach takes a deep breath. "Mom, Yemi was supposed to wake Grandma and she couldn't!"

Joy watches as Nnenna's eyebrows furrow, as if Zach is speaking to her in tongues. "What do you mean you couldn't wake her up?" Nnenna asks, her voice sharp as a knife.

Joy and Nnenna share a look, which freaks Joy out because since when has she ever been on the same page as her cousin?

"Did you . . . ?" Joy clears her throat while she stares around at the kids. She's used to kids having wild imaginations, but this isn't making any sense. "Like, did you . . . *try* to wake her up?" she asks plainly.

Yemi nods right away. "Yeah! And she wouldn't wake up."

"And her skin was weird," Zach puts in, eyes downcast. "Felt weird."

Joy takes a deep breath. She is acutely aware of how Jamil watches her and, for a moment, she tries to look composed. But the breath won't come out. It stays trapped in her chest, building. *No, Joy, don't do this, not now.* She tries again. Nothing.

"O-okay."

She looks over at the sound of Nnenna's voice. "Okay, okay. Let's just, uh, let's just go see. Hm?" At this, she nudges Joy, her eyes telling her what her mouth can't—*Just keep it together, okay? Keep it together*—and they make their way down the hall and back upstairs.

No one wants to step into the room first. Nnenna places a hand at Joy's shoulder and ushers her forward, the kids hanging at their backs, breathing unevenly, their hearts pounding nervously in their chests. Joy wishes she could be there with them, in the back. She wishes she didn't have to ... she wishes her older brother could be here right now.

You're overreacting, Joy tells herself as she tiptoes in. Mama's sleeping figure looks so calm. *The kids are just being kids. They say bizarre shit all the time. It's fine. Remember ...* She creeps closer. *Remember when you were ten and you said you had seen fairies in the bush or whatever, and then Peace made fun of you? You know damn well you never saw one fucking fairy. Why'd you say that shit, huh? Why?* She comes around the side of the bed. Her eyes fall upon her mother. She takes a deep breath, and crouches down.

"M-Mom." She clears her throat and tries again, reaching out to touch her arm. "Mom, wake up. It's time to eat."

Nothing.

Why'd you say all that? Fairies and stuff. Did you see them? Were you lying?

"Mom?" She reaches out for Mama's forearm. For her pulse.

You were. Or maybe you weren't. It doesn't matter anymore.

Zach starts to whine with discomfort. Nnenna is shaking. She clasps her hands together tightly. Jamil tries to step forward, but Nnenna holds him back.

Jamil asks, "What's wrong with Grandma?"

Joy takes a ...

She takes a deep ...

She chokes.

"O-okay, okay." Nnenna turns and snatches the kids, hands on wrists and her chest at their backs, as she walks them out. "Oya, go downstairs, all of you. G-go play. Just go."

Yemi frowns—then glowers at her brother when he starts to cry. "Why are you crying? Just shut up!" she snaps at him and he starts to cry even harder.

"Why are you telling your baby brother to shut up?" Nnenna snaps back, eyes narrowed at Yemi. "He's a small boy, na."

"He's *ten*!"

"Oya, enough, enough." Nnenna kisses her teeth and manages to wrestle them just outside of the door. Jamil stands on his tiptoes to try and see around Nnenna but she blocks him. "What?"

"Is my mom okay?" he asks, his voice small. "What happened?"

"Nothing. Nothing happened," Nnenna tells him sternly. "Go— Yemi, you take them and go help your dad outside."

Yemi frowns. "But, Mom—"

"*Mom*, wetin? Ah-ah!" she snaps. "I said, take your brother and your cousin and go away from this place. Non-sense." And she slams the door shut.

— 6 —

The tears creep up on Joy and soon her face is a riverbed. She wipes them away as fast as she can—she feels her breath hitch in her throat and she hiccups, hiccups, hiccups, until a gut-wrenching sob breaks free from her lips.

She's on the floor in minutes. Nnenna rushes back from the door to be at Joy's side, her eyes teary, panic rattling her voice. "Joy . . . ah-ah, Joy," she whispers. "Joy, what do we do, na? Oh my goodness. Oh my goodness . . ."

Joy can't speak. As her cousin's voice rings in her ears, her mind pulls images from memories she doesn't want to face. From a pattern that seems to be forming. Family members, dying.

Peace died, and Joy cried as hard as she ever had, up until her dad's passing.

Then her father died, and Joy cried as hard as she ever had, up until now.

Now her mom is . . .

Nnenna's hand shakes Joy's shoulder a little, bringing her back from wherever she was headed. "Joy, what should we do?" Nnenna asks again.

"I . . ." Joy croaks, then coughs. She feels delirious, as if she's not really here. *What if I'm not? What if this is just a bad dream?* She looks at the bed. From where she is on the floor, her mom's figure looks serene, as if she's in a deep sleep. But when Joy holds her breath, when she waits for the room to stop spinning, the realization that there's no sound sets in. There is no other breathing.

Except for Nnenna, who is wheezing by Joy's shoulder.

"I don't know, Nnenna," Joy mumbles, trying to brush her off.

"You don't *know*?" Nnenna gasps. "Ah! So if not you, then who? Should I go and call my husband?"

The thought of James coming in here to give directions—the sheer thought of James coming in here, period—is enough for some life to return to Joy's eyes. "No," she tells Nnenna. "I can do this just fine."

She can't, actually, and she knows this.

Joy has always been the one to set things in motion, to execute where others couldn't, but she was not in the room when Peace died. She wasn't even at home when her father passed away. Even though she was good at *doing,* she had never done *this* before. Be the first one to respond to a tragedy. Not have a game plan written in red ink somewhere. Not be able to go through something without knowing her mom would be there.

"Let's, um . . ." Joy crawls to her feet, uneasily. "Let's figure this out, o-okay?"

Nnenna nods, her head bobbing up and down like a rabbit. Joy figures Nnenna will agree with whatever she says, which only makes Joy feel worse. Joy, the reliable. Joy, who has buried more family members than anyone else at this point. Joy, who has never once dropped the ball.

She can't look at her mom.

Joy crosses the room on shaky legs to shut the blinds.

She can't look at her.

Nnenna begins pacing, muttering under her breath, crying, "Jesus . . ." and invoking some sort of holy law. Suddenly, she crosses the room—Joy gasps—and grabs the blankets on the bed with two tense fists.

Joy screams, "What are you *doing*!"

Nnenna stops, but her hands are shaking. "What does it look like? I'm covering the body!"

"What? Because she's *cold*?" Joy rushes over and hustles Nnenna away from the bed. "Please, can you not right now?"

"Well, what's your idea, then? We have to do something. And we can't just leave Auntie's body like this for anyone to see! Isn't that why you closed the blinds? So how is this any different?"

Joy narrows her eyes at her cousin. "It's different because I'm not *touching*—I'm not touching anything!"

"Ah-ah!" Nnenna forces out a shaky sigh. She brings her hand to her chest, trying to calm herself down. "I'm going to scream, Joy. Is that what you want? You want me to scream?"

"Nobody is asking you to start screaming, Nnenna. Just l-let me think, okay?" Joy takes a deep breath. She runs her hands down her face. She paces.

"Let's wait for Michael, then."

Joy walks away, trudging until she reaches the far wall, pretending like she didn't hear Nnenna's suggestion. *He should've been here already* . . . he *should've been* here, Joy thinks bitterly.

When Peace died, Michael made no real efforts to help coordinate plans for her funeral. Joy remembers that he hugged her, said he was sorry, and faded out of the picture. He's the first son, the only boy, and he didn't help drive their parents to talk to the funeral director. He didn't help design the program; he didn't help invite Peace's friends. And then he showed up late, using his children as an excuse.

Same with when their dad died. Their dad had always been so lenient with Michael, and even then, that wasn't a good enough reason for him to take point on the planning. He left their mom to call Dad's relatives back in Nigeria, to plan the menu, to coordinate who would sew funeral clothes for the family. And when he arrived, his white agbada glistening in the summer sun, people heralding him as the first son, the only boy, Joy swears she had never felt such anger in her life.

Because when he wasn't there, she had to be. That's why she can't wait for him.

"No way," Joy grunts. "No, if he chose not to show up by now, that's his problem. He's already proven that he doesn't care."

Nnenna grimaces. "Listen, you two are very annoying. Okay? Very annoying people. This isn't the time for sibling rivalry."

"*Rivalry*? That's—"

"So you're blaming him because he didn't know his mother would be—that this"—Nnenna gestures to the bed loosely, her arms flailing about her—"and so, okay, now that's more grounds to fight him, abi? He deserves to be here—"

"I didn't say—"

The doorknob rattles.

Joy jumps, nearly stumbling over her feet at the shock. In a split second, Nnenna rushes to the door and presses it shut. Joy hisses, "Why would you do that?"

Nnenna squeals, "I don't know I don't know I don't—"

"What's going on in there?" Michael's voice booms out loud and clear from the other side of the door. The doorknob rattles again as Joy tiptoes over. "Somebody better come and open this door," Michael says. "I just got here and the kids say something is wrong with Mama."

Nnenna groans and slides her way down the door, collapsing on the floor. "Ah, what's wrong with kids these days? They don't know how to lie again?"

Joy grabs Nnenna by the arms and pulls her away from the door just as Michael manages to get it open. He nudges it softly, poking his head in first, before stepping through.

And when he does, he's pissed.

A frown so fierce is pinned on his lips, and for a moment, Joy is reminded of their dad whenever he got angry or, to be honest, mildly inconvenienced. Auntie Nancy or Nnenna would call Michael "ejima nna," "Papa's twin," or "Papa's boy" as a joke. Michael really does look so much like him. It's like a carbon copy of her own father resurrected to come and judge her.

Joy avoids eye contact with her brother as he enters the room.

Her heartbeat quickens, watching him take in the scene. She wonders when he will notice.

"Why is it so dark in here? Why did you close the blinds?" he asks, gesticulating toward the window.

Joy blinks, her eyes following Michael's hand from the wall to the window. "W-what?" She doesn't understand the question. She doesn't get why he doesn't *see* it.

Michael's frustration seems to grow with each wave of his hand, with each new observation. Joy waits. She just waits. And as she does, her anger blossoms, small at first before ringing in her ears like a siren. *Is he dumb or what?* She narrows her eyes at him. *He showed up late and all he cares about is a window?*

She steps forward and looks at her brother. She's annoyed, like usual. It feels like sometimes she can't go a whole day without being annoyed by him. "Where the hell were you?" Her voice comes out harsher than she imagined it could, especially at a time like this. Even Nnenna, crawling slowly to her feet by the door, shivers a little at the harshness.

Michael kisses his teeth, "Joy, abeg . . ." and moves past her. He doesn't give her a second look. Instead, his eyes float around the room, taking in every detail, until they land on their mom's sleeping figure. Joy holds her breath. She watches Michael watch Mama. How she's lying on her side on the bed. How she's . . . she's sleeping.

He frowns. "What's going on here? Why is Mom—"

"Michael, we've b-been here since nine a.m.," Joy cuts in, the quiver bleeding into her voice. "Mom was hoping you'd come earlier. *I* was thinking you'd come earlier."

The room is quiet.

Joy shares a look with Nnenna, unease pushing tears to her eyes. "My God . . ." Joy murmurs, bringing her hands to her mouth. Her and Nnenna have never been on the same page. Judging by the way Michael grimaces, Joy bets he's also offended that she and Nnenna are sharing looks. Sharing secrets. *But it's not a secret, it's right there.* Joy takes a deep, shaky breath into her hands.

Michael turns back to Mama. He says, "Joy . . ."

She takes a steadying breath. Her shoulders tremble.

"Joy?"

Her lip quivers, but she says nothing.

Quickly, Michael turns. "Nnenna," he addresses her.

Nnenna begins to cry. Within seconds, she hides her face and folds, crumbling to the ground again. Loud and heavy sobs shake through her body. Michael takes a step forward to help her up, but he—he hesitates. Joy's heart thumps loudly. She watches his eyes, watches him piece it together.

Michael circles the bed slowly and carefully until he is facing their mother, but it's Joy he watches. Joy's eyes well with tears when he pauses by the bedside. Her bottom lip quakes with the same fear and sadness that has overtaken Nnenna.

Michael looks down at Mama's face.

Her lifeless face.

Her lifeless body.

"He-ey . . . Mama . . ." He drops to his knees, bringing his hands to his head in shock. Nnenna cries louder.

Joy turns, breathing slowly into her palms. What is it she always tells her clients? Steady breathing. Triangles, triangles. Think of sharp lines and hard edges before you can fall back into the softness of life.

You have to do this, she tells herself, *or no one else will. Breathe. Come on, breathe.*

Slow at first, then quickly, Joy takes a step toward Nnenna and helps her off the floor. "Okay, g-get up, get up, come on," she mumbles. So used to doing busywork, Joy can feel all the emotions in her brain fighting for dominance: get up and take control of this before everything turns to shambles, or—perish. Just perish.

As Nnenna stumbles to her feet, Joy turns her attention to Michael. He is touching Mama's hand, frowning as his fingers roll over her skin, her . . . skin. Joy guesses it is cold now. Clammy. Frigid. *How would you even know? Can we focus, please?*

She approaches Michael. "Don't—d-don't touch her," she says, her voice still shaky. As Michael straightens up, stepping away from the bed, Joy fidgets, clasping her hands together. "Y-you can't, you're not supposed to."

Michael kisses his teeth, frustration pushing through his lips, and falls back, pressing himself as close to the wall as he can. "Ewoh . . . damn." He shakes his head. "Who did this to her?"

Joy straightens.

Whatever sorrow hanging in the air a moment ago is quickly replaced with—

"Excuse me?" Nnenna croaks. She rubs her eyes, smudging tears across her cheeks. Nnenna, the professional mourner, has been replaced with Nnenna—just Nnenna. There is barely a hint of distress in her voice when she speaks, and when she turns to Michael, she looks like she's ready for war. "Who did what?"

"How did . . . how did this happen?" he asks, this time firmer.

Nnenna's mouth is slack as she turns to Joy. For a moment, neither of them speak. Then Nnenna turns her attention back to Michael, sheer villainy building with each inch she rotates. If Joy listens really hard, she bets she can hear a flute in the distance, the flute in village movies that signals someone evil is brewing potions. "What do you mean?" Nnenna says. "Wait, wait, are you implying we did something to Auntie?"

There had been so much disorientation that Joy almost forgot about this side of Nnenna, the sharp-tongued side that she weaponized at will. By the flustered look on Michael's face, it's evident he forgot, too.

Nnenna straightens out her dress and points a manicured finger at him. "Michael. So you came in here, saw two women crying, and assumed what? That we are just here, crying, doing what? Ritual?"

Michael waves away her accusations. "No. It's just . . . h-how could this have happened? She was healthy. Right? When was the last time she went to the doctor? The last time she had blood work done? Can we check her medication?" He turns to Joy, who is there to match his gaze. Except she's mad. Why wouldn't she be? He would know these things if he were around. Simple as that.

Joy narrows her eyes at him. "You're . . . joking, right?"

Michael scoffs. "Why would I be joking?"

"You—" Her voice breaks. She clears her throat and tries again. "If you had bothered to keep up with maybe *one* thing outside of your own life, you would know half of those answers already."

Michael scoffs again, shaking his head as he paces away from Joy's line of sight. "You always say that. Eh, Joy? Always." He lets out a deep sigh before telling her, "You're not the only one with hardship. You're not the only one who has children, Joy—"

"Oh, okay, here we go." Joy throws up her hands in mock defeat. "I don't understand anything because I don't have teenagers. I don't know what it's like to have a son at fucking Oxford, or a daughter who, I don't know, wears corduroy unironically. Okay, cool, got it. Next?"

Michael bristles, his nostrils flaring, but he stays quiet.

"And that's not a knock on Sarah's style, by the way," Joy cuts in, looking at both Michael and Nnenna. "She's adorable. She always styles the fuck out of those corduroys and I'm proud to have her as a niece."

Nnenna nods slowly, contemplating. "Hmm." She turns to Michael. "How are the kids? Are they good?"

"They are, thank you, *Nnenna*," Michael says pointedly, casting a glance at Joy in the process. "Miles couldn't be here because he's still in England. Sarah's downstairs with the kids."

"And where's Shelly? She didn't come?"

Michael bristles again—and Joy catches it, pointing at him immediately. He doesn't react to her accusatory finger. Instead, he buttons his lips, his jaw square, holding words he's not about to spill. *Something's off*, Joy thinks. Now that she thinks about it, Shelly would've shown up with him. She would've come upstairs by now, asking what the holdup was. She would've said something snide about Joy not being able to take time off from work.

Michael claps his hands together, startling Joy and Nnenna. "Okay, no more of this," he says. "We need to decide what to do."

Nnenna begins to nod. "Exactly, exactly. Right, Joy?"

Joy grunts, "Mmhmm," but she is glaring at Michael. Who does he think he is, anyway? Shows up late, has never partaken in any after-life planning ever, and decides *he* knows what to do?

"Mom can't . . . she can't just stay here," Michael says, letting his eyes fall upon their mother's figure. "The party is tonight. People think they're coming to celebrate her birthday. So . . . um."

Suddenly, Joy barks out a laugh. "No, no, wait. *Wait*. Don't even. If you dare say we should turn this into a funeral, so help me, God."

Michael groans. "Joy, please. I was going to say that we—"

"Pray."

All eyes focus on Nnenna right away. Nnenna already has her hands clasped together, her head tilted back as if she needs to concentrate and dig through her memory on every Bible verse she knows.

Honestly, she's astonished they haven't thought of this sooner. Prayer is the language of miracles. Although, as for what kind of miracle they're looking for, well, she's not sure. But it's always given her peace in the past, so why should now be any different?

She looks at her cousins, waiting for them to get on board with her idea, and is shocked—and disgusted, truthfully—to see discomfort and aggravation in their eyes. Joy shuffles back on her feet, folding her arms, holding herself tightly. Michael scratches his head, letting out a hefty sigh. Nnenna doesn't wait for them to turn her down before she pounces. "Excuse me, what's wrong with you people? Mama is a Christian."

Michael and Joy glance at each other before shifting away from one another.

"Are you people serious? Ah-ah. We need to call on the Father and pray for her soul. For our souls. For the souls of her grandkids who had to . . . had to see her like this." Nnenna gulps, uneasily. "It's very important."

Joy lets out a sharp exhale. "Sure."

"You don't believe me?"

"I didn't say that. I said 'sure.'"

"Joy—"

"Nnenna, if you didn't notice, I'm kinda going through it right now."

"Well, that's why—"

"Okay, ah-ah, please." Michael grumbles and rubs his hands down his face. "Nnenna, you can call God. *I* will call nine-one-one."

Bush man, she thinks as she makes herself comfortable at the foot of the bed. She dusts off her skirt before she gets down on her knees to begin praying. "O Heavenly Father . . ."

Joy listens as Nnenna recites any and every prayer she knows by heart. She desperately wants her cousin's words to be a balm, but they refuse to soothe. She is rattled and raw and unmoved and she feels ugly standing watch.

Michael brings out his phone, gravitating to the other side of the room while he calls 911. A few moments later, Michael returns and says the paramedics are on their way.

"Cool. Okay," she utters in response.

The words "That's it?" tumble out of his mouth quickly. He quickly backtracks with: "Sorry. I didn't mean that."

Joy grimaces. She knows he did. There may be a truce, but the war is always raging.

Downstairs, the doorbell rings.

"Who would be ringing the doorbell?" Joy utters. "We don't even *live* here, like, we don't even really live here. This isn't our house. And the door is open already. It's *open*."

And she bursts into tears.

— 7 —

Joy waits for another ring, but nothing comes.

Maybe they're gone, she thinks.

Then she kisses her teeth. *And where would they go, Joy? To where? There is nothing around this house but roads and more bush.*

Michael appears beside her. "Who was at the door?"

"Look at me, Michael," she whispers. "I don't *know.*"

The footsteps come fast.

Joy barely has the opportunity to step back before the door bursts open, announcing the arrival of her auntie Nancy and uncle Ezekiel.

Wait.

She panics.

The first words out of her mouth are "How'd you get up here?" and she knows it's the wrong thing to say for two reasons. One, being that, naturally, someone presumably let them in. Two, essentially asking "What are you doing in my house?" to a Nigerian elder is suicide. Joy knows right away that starting on the wrong foot with Auntie Nancy can lead to a lifetime of macroaggressions (Nigerian people don't do "micro" anything).

Auntie Nancy's face morphs. Where there was slight curiosity

etched in her high cheekbones and wide-set eyes, there is now an in-
kling of fury at Joy's accidental disrespect.

Nancy's eyes rake over Joy from head to toe. "What are you talking
about? Is that any way to greet your auntie and your uncle after they
have arrived from a long journey?" Her voice is sharper than Mama's.
Nancy doesn't have the same soft, cajoling spirit Mama does. She
stands half a head taller, five years younger, and ten times harsher than
Mama ever was. Beside her husband's tall, thick stature, she appears
feeble, but that's only to those who haven't seen her cut a yam or, to be
honest, oil up a child.

"N-no, s-sorry, that's not . . . I didn't mean to say that," Joy murmurs. "Good morning, Auntie. Good morning, Uncle."

A weary smile stretches across Uncle Ezekiel's aged face, and he is
about to reply, "Good—"

Before Nancy cuts in, "Which morning again? Is it not afternoon?"

"Ah-ah," Ezekiel tsks. "Nancy, wetin na? The girl is greeting you."
Then he gestures haphazardly toward Joy's face. "And she's been crying
anyway."

Quickly, Joy touches her hand to her sticky cheeks, wiping away at
the dried tears.

Nancy frowns. She takes a step forward. "Joy. *Joy.* Gịnị na-eme?"

Joy opens her mouth to speak but no words come out.

Michael speaks up, his voice as calm and measured as Joy has ever
heard it. "Auntie, Uncle, o-our mom is . . . she's . . ." His voice trails off.
He gestures to the bed, taking a step back so that their aunt and uncle
can see; probably so he can be absolved of ever having to say the words
himself.

The room falls silent.

Auntie Nancy is the first to come over. She walks in quick, short
steps, circling her way to face Mama lying on the bed.

And she looks at her sister.

Nancy watches Mary, the way she always used to when they were children. She has always idolized her elder sister. When they were girls

growing up in the village, Nancy would love whenever Mary did well in school, or successfully sold well in the market with their mama. She felt as though if Mary could do it, then so could she. Mary gave her a blueprint for her life and Nancy, dutiful and pious as she was, followed it almost to a T.

When Mary got married to Jacob, excused him his transgressions, and decided to start a new life with him, Nancy thought maybe she could love a man as much as Mary loved Jacob. She married Ezekiel and they had Nnenna while they lived in Abuja. Now they both had children.

"Anyị chọrọ ịga . . . Canada."

Nancy still remembers what it was like to hear Mary say those words. Night had fallen on Mary's compound, and Nancy couldn't see what her sister's expression looked like. She couldn't tell if Mary was excited or nervous. Her voice wouldn't betray her. And Nancy hadn't known if she should be excited or nervous on Mary's behalf.

After a beat of silence, Nancy had asked, "Maka gịnị?"

The sounds of the city had engulfed them momentarily. Nancy could hear cars in the distance. Honking. A sign of traffic, but also a way of life.

Mary's voice was small. *So unlike her,* Nancy thought. This was so unlike her sister. "Better life," Mary answered in English. "For a better life."

Nancy hadn't really understood what had been happening with Mary and Jacob. As far as she knew, their marriage was as sound as any. Jacob was a good man, all things considered. He tried his hardest; he was kind to his wife. This was as revolutionary, as free an experience as any woman could hope to have in Nigeria at the time. To go all the way to Canada would mean starting over, bearing your differences, and being othered. Being "Black," not Igbo. Being just "Nigerian," not Igbo. Nancy didn't understand why anyone would willingly choose that.

Nancy was unsure how serious Mary was until she, Jacob, and Michael left. She didn't know how bitter she'd feel seeing her elder sister, the one she looked up to all those years, just leave her. She also didn't think she and Ezekiel would, less than two years later, pack up and move overseas, too, to the United States, in search of that "better life" Mary had abandoned her for.

It seemed Nancy was always one step behind. Always one step.

But not today.

She finally looks into the eyes of her daughter, her niece, and her nephew. Her voice breaks. The tears start to fall. And she says, "God *f-forbid*. Oya, bring everybody downstairs *now*-now."

— 8 —

James Olubisi had finally hit his stride in the backyard. He met the head coordinator, a mousy sort of woman named Melinda, and asked to see the floor and seating plan for the event. She'd presented it with pride, of course, because she had twenty-five years of experience in the business and had formulated this schedule based on what she and Joy had talked about. Melinda produced the most accessible floor plan, even down to a high table for the family with a ramp to accommodate their grandma's poor knees.

"Hmm . . ." James takes the plan and flips it upside down—literally. He twirls the page until it starts to make sense. "Oh, eh-heh. So . . . she wants three tables here? And two here?" As he speaks, he walks the length of the backyard, pausing and pointing to the aforementioned areas. Melinda follows, nodding. "He-ey. No, o. I don't think this will work."

Melinda's face falls. "O-oh?"

"Yes." James folds the plan and hands it back to her. "We need more space here so that people can wander easily."

"I . . ." Melinda stares around. Her staff are already carrying out the original plan, and it wouldn't make sense to switch things up now.

Plus, Joy is the one signing her checks, not this guy, whoever he is. "S-sorry, sir, but the plan can't change. Mrs. Bianchi specified that we should arrange the tables like this because—"

"Missus who?" James tilts his head forward, leaning in with his ear as if he didn't hear the first time. "Please, she's my in-law. Joy. And she's divorced now, anyway, so she's not a missus anybody."

"O-oh, um—"

"I'm telling you, the plan will be better this way," James says. He stops a nearby worker and asks for a pen, snapping his fingers until he gets it. Melinda stays pin quiet while James, pen ready, draws lines all over the current floor plan. "Move this here. Throw this away. Don't put this here. Make this place bigger." He throws out commands left and right, ignoring the growing concern on Melinda's face.

He only stops when Nnenna appears at the sliding glass door, a grave expression on her delicate features.

James glances at her and continues with finding the perfect place for the decorative pulpit. Keeping it at the edge of the yard seems so archaic, honestly. In his opinion, they should be inviting God *into* the party, not keeping Him at the outskirts.

"J-James." Nnenna clears her throat, then speaks a bit louder. "James."

He waves her away. "I'm busy here."

"It's important," she says. "Come inside. Now."

He grimaces. Nnenna wouldn't have ever raised her voice at him or spoken to him in such a stern tone before. "What?" he snaps back. But then he sees how her eyes water, how her jaw is clenched tight, as if there's some word in there she doesn't want to come out. As if she may open her mouth one more time and there it will be, spilled on the ground in front of her.

Before James can speak, Michael appears at the doorway. "James, come inside," he says.

James might be imagining it, but the same look flashes across both Nnenna's and Michael's faces. He bristles with irritation. "What's going on?" he asks, his voice sharp, on edge. "Why are you people looking like that?"

"Enough, na. Just come." Michael's word is final and he disappears back into the house without looking to see if James will even follow.

James grumbles his way toward the door, muttering under his breath. When Nnenna reaches out to touch his shoulder, he brushes her off and marches straight into the house, into the living area where . . . where everyone is gathered. "What's going on?" he asks aloud, staring around at the long and confused faces of his family. Well, everyone's face is long and confused, except for Mama Nancy, whose eyebrows are knit together like they're hiding a secret in their folds. She sits beside Papa Ezekiel in the center of the sofa, staring around at each person as they gravitate toward her. And . . . wait.

James counts each family member. There's Joy, who has her arms crossed and her eyes downcast. She doesn't look at anyone. Not her brother, who has come to join her at the front of the room. Not Nnenna, who is hanging by the kitchen. Not her own son, who is huddled with James's children and Michael's daughter, Sarah, in the corner. Not even Mama Mary . . . wait.

That's strange. Why isn't she here?

Joy sighs out.

She shuts her eyes and touches her fingertips to her forehead. *Come on, steady breathing, focus on the present, focus on the present.* Out of the corner of her eye, she spots Jamil and his cousins. Oh goodness, she can't cry in front of her kid. She's sure she should wait until he's at least eighteen to invoke that sort of mental trauma.

She lets her eyes fall on her aunt, who stares back at her with an expression Joy can't quite read. Frustration and disappointment and anger and disbelief all in one. Joy feels each emotion tenfold.

Then Auntie Nancy speaks. "My children," she says, with a soft *c* that makes it sound more like "shi-dren." "I don't know what to tell you people, o. Something very wicked has obviously happened in this house."

Wait, what?

Joy's tears dry up with a quickness. Her confusion shocks her into a semiresponsive state. "W-what, sorry? Sorry, I just . . . what?"

The doorbell rings.

Nnenna wails. "Why is this doorbell ringing up and down, up and down—"

"Can someone get that?" Michael says aloud. Then he tuts, shaking his head as he moves toward the hall. "Never mind. I'll just—"

"Don't!" Nancy points an accusatory finger at him. "Don't go anywhere. Wait first."

He lets out an uncomfortable chuckle. "Ah . . . but, Auntie, it's probably the paramedics."

"The paramedics?" James echoes. His face screws up with discontent, his lips jutting forward as if he's smelled something bad.

No one moves.

Joy bristles as she watches James look around the room. Of course he's the only one who doesn't know yet. At first, she's unsure if she should feel bad about this, but given how condescending and commandeering James can be, she realizes she doesn't care.

"Oya!" James's voice booms out. "Somebody start talking *now-now*. What's going on?"

"Please!"

Everyone turns when Nnenna cries out. She fidgets in a way Joy has never seen before. Her cousin is usually more put together. A pastor's wife, Nnenna is a true woman of God. She probably can't lie or she'll feel the ground start to open up under her feet. "If . . . *ulp*"—Nnenna hiccups—"if we stand here any longer and draw this out, I will *scream*. Is that what you want?" She looks at Joy; looks at Michael. "I have to say it—someone *has* to say it! We've all seen, anyway."

Joy gulps. "Nnenna, no—"

"Mama Mary is dead."

It feels as if the air has been sucked out of the room. No voices. Minimal breathing. Somber faces. Nnenna hides her face and chokes out a sob, a long and dramatic sob, while the truth settles in around her.

The doorbell rings again.

"Jesus," Joy mumbles. "I'll get it—"

"No, I'll go." Michael steps out, maneuvering his way back down the hall before Joy can stop him.

What would Michael even say to the paramedics? He didn't find her. He wasn't even in the house when she . . . when she . . .

Joy's heartstrings tug. She can't—she can't stop shaking. Oh God. She looks at her hands. When did this start, the rattling in her wrists? Why didn't she notice it?

"Oh my God . . . fuck." Joy covers her face. She takes a deep breath into her hands.

She hears Sarah in the corner as she attempts to usher her young cousins away. "Come on, guys. L-let's go downstairs."

She hears James's voice. "Nnenna, wetin? How can you say such a thing on a holy day?"

She hears Nnenna's crying. "It just—she was fine, and the kids tried to w-wake her up . . ."

"Oya, okay, please, let's just calm down." James holds his hands up, but Auntie Nancy rushes around the sofa to where James is standing and smacks him on the shoulder repeatedly. She is smaller than he is, but her hand, which has probably given many slaps, is still strong. James jumps and shields himself. "Ah-ah! Mama, what's going on? Why are you beating me?"

"Instead of you to be looking after your wife, you are here making mouth," she says with grit. "You don't hear her? She says my sister is dead and you are here doing, 'Oya, oya, calm down' . . . Useless man!"

James frowns. "Mama . . ." He glances around the room nervously without meeting anyone's eyes.

Nancy spots the parade of uniformed medical workers from where she is in the living room, and scoffs. Joy feels her eyebrow twitch with irritation, though she can't explain why. She doesn't like it—she just doesn't like any of this. *It's being handled wrong. All of it is wrong,* she thinks. She remembers when Peace passed away and her mom and dad, they . . . they were unreachable, emotionally, but they never once pretended they weren't grieving. As Joy watches Auntie Nancy steel her gaze on the room, she can't help but feel the differences. *What would Mom do?* She is too in shock to remember.

Nancy says again, "My children. Listen to me very carefully. Because I have heard you. You have said to me on this Good Friday that my sister is dead." When she says it, a shiver runs down her spine so fast that her shoulders constrict and she kisses her teeth, loudly and with arrogance. "But I am telling you people . . . I know my sister. Na me wit' am share the same house as babies. My sister will not come and *die* on such a holy day. She will not!"

Joy suppresses a groan. She doesn't know what else to say. "Auntie. I don't think Mom made that decision herself."

Auntie Nancy claps her hands and then spreads them apart, like she's laying out the facts. "So. You see."

"N-no, I don't—"

"If my sister has died today, it is because of juju."

Joy groans. "Oh . . . no."

"Yes!"

Joy is speechless. She turns to Nnenna, to her uncle Ezekiel— hell, even James, as stuck-up as he is—*anyone* to come and save her from this. She can't believe this is happening. Her mother passed away on her birthday (to be fair, Joy didn't even know dying on your birthday was allowed) and Auntie really dares invoke witchcraft as the reason? She shudders, absolutely trembles, at the accusation. Auntie should know better than to say that. Especially after what happened with Peace.

She swallows down the discomfort, the need to run upstairs and cry or hide. Instead, Joy looks into her auntie's eyes and says, "We did not kill my mother," her voice wavering.

"Well, somebody did," Nancy goes on without missing a beat. "Somebody is using my sister for ritual. Where is Michael's wife?" she asks, looking around. After a moment, once she realizes none of the faces staring back at her are Shelly's, she scoffs like that's confirmation enough. "So, you see."

"No," Joy growls. "I really don't. Besides, what does it matter that she's not here?"

"Why does it matter? She's your brother's *wife*," Nancy says, her voice rising as if this is the climax in her long story. Here, finally, we arrive at the point. "Now she's not here and my sister is dead!"

"Auntie, I guarantee you Shelly wasn't using Mom for ritual," she says aloud, but in her mind, the smallest conspiracy theorist, fresh off several five-part village movies, murmurs, *You don't know that, though. Like, genuinely, how would you know?*

"Then how can a healthy woman of seventy just die on her birthday? On Good Friday? The day our Lord was killed? What is it if not juju?"

Joy throws up her hands in defeat. "An accident, maybe? Bad timing? I don't know."

"Accident ke? On Good Friday? The day our—"

"Okay, I got it."

"Let me tell you something," Auntie says, narrowing her eyes. "And you people won't understand because you were raised here . . ." In the corner, James opens his mouth, probably to protest and remind them that, actually, he was born and raised in Nigeria and only came here for university, but Ezekiel, most likely sensing that James is about to assert himself, quickly hisses—a sharp, pointed exhale—and James shrinks immediately. Nancy goes on: "If someone is doing juju, there are two things they use. Fire . . . and accident."

Joy suppresses a groan. "Auntie—"

"*Auntie* wetin?"

"I—"

"Joy." Michael reenters, holding a bevy of cards and pamphlets. Behind him, Joy sees—nothing. She's trying not to see. There are paramedics standing around. They're doing something. A body on a stretcher, maybe zipping it, maybe just covering it, maybe, maybe, maybe. She doesn't know. It all looks blurry when she tries to focus. And she's definitely trying. Absolutely.

"Joy?" Michael snaps his fingers in front of her face to get her attention. He holds up a few of the papers. "The paramedics talked me through some next steps. They haven't gone yet, but they're asking if Mom had a will. D-did she?"

Joy bites her lip. She doesn't have the energy. Her body feels heavy and her mind clouds like a muddy river. "I don't know," she utters and turns away.

Auntie Nancy scoffs. "So, you see."

Joy also doesn't have the energy to explain to her aunt how infuriating it is that she is using every banal, basic thing as proof of witchcraft.

"Maybe Mom is right . . ." Nnenna pipes up. Her voice is hoarse from her wailing. She has to clear her throat a few times before the words come out properly. "Think about it. It *is* really weird for Mama Mary to just die like this. She was reading the Bible, and then she went to lie down, and just like that, she died? No, it doesn't really make sense."

Joy swallows, shaking her head. "Nnenna, please don't do this."

Nnenna frowns. "Do what? So I can't ask a question again?"

"You're not—"

"You're not asking a question, Nnenna," Michael cuts in angrily. His temper flares up, surging in each word. "You're making an accusation. You better be careful, o."

"He-ey!" James rushes over, pointing a finger at Michael. "You better not be accusing my wife of witchcraft! I'm warning you, Michael."

"What?" Joy and Michael speak at the same time. Quickly, Joy steps in front, between them, before it turns into something it really shouldn't. James's chest is puffed out as normal, glaring daggers at Michael. Michael is growing more and more irritated by the second at the fact that this balding man would choose to challenge him. Nnenna's arms are crossed as she looks from wall to wall, avoiding the catastrophe she set in motion a moment ago. Uncle Ezekiel is trying to call Auntie Nancy back to the sofa.

And Joy can't believe this is happening. She can't believe she has to deal with her family making a mockery of her sorrow, of her grief—*their* grief, for fuck's sake—on top of all the other shit she had to organize. Of course they probably don't see it that way. They don't ask who booked the house, they don't mention whose idea it was to do the weekend staycation, they don't even wonder how many different DJ Ebukas exist in the Greater Toronto Area! All they know how to do is fight and take and argue and take, and take, and take, and take.

She's so tired of it.

"Okay!" She throws her hands up. "We're not fucking doing this. We're not gonna start arguing over my mom's d-dead body."

Auntie Nancy gasps.

"What we *need* to do is come up with a plan," she goes on, looking around. "We have people coming later for a party that can no longer happen f-for various reasons."

"For *one* reason," Nnenna mumbles.

Heat rises in Joy's chest but she pretends she didn't hear her. "Michael has all these pamphlets and cards, so we're going to call around for a . . . uh, a mortuary. A mortician. Or something."

"I'll figure it out," Michael pipes up. "We'll try and locate a will, too. Then we need to cancel all this—"

"We need to pray."

Auntie Nancy's voice cuts through Michael's rambling. Of course Auntie would suggest this. Nnenna suggested this earlier, and she is Auntie's daughter, after all.

Auntie Nancy stares back, almost challenging them to say otherwise. If only she knew how little energy Joy had. If only she knew how tired Joy was these days, how exhausted she is from rolling with the ups and downs of her own life. From having to be present all the damn time. And now, having to deal with this. Having to grieve her mother in a place where they don't seem to want her to rest.

The moment he hears the word "pray," James springs into action. "Oya, let's join hands. Good idea, Mama, good idea." He winks at her before moving to the center of the room. Quickly, he gestures for everyone to form a circle around him. "Let's call the kids."

"Just to pray?" Joy blurts out. She knows it's wrong the moment the words leave her mouth.

"'Just to pray'?" Auntie Nancy mimics her voice, then scoffs. "See you. If you had gone to church like your mama asked you, eh. If you had gone ... "

Joy doesn't want to know how that sentence might end.

The kids come upstairs, each searching for a spot beside their parents. None of them speak, not even Zach, who is clutching Jamil's handheld console as if it were his own.

Once everyone's hands are clasped, Auntie Nancy nods to James. "Oya. Begin."

James takes a deep breath. He stands tall, his chest out, so everyone can understand how seriously he's taking this. Then he opens his mouth, sucking in air, before he says, "O Heavenly Fath—"

The front door crashes open.

"Am I late? Shit, I think I'm late. I thought we were on African time ..."

The family stands still, hands growing uncomfortably sweaty, as the voice grows louder the closer it gets. Joy can hear it marvel at the chandelier and the staircase just as she did when she first entered. She can hear it admire the design, the brightness, the beauty of the house. She can hear it balk at the sight of paramedics in the hallway. "Uh, s-sorry, are y'all here for the party, too, or ... ?" the voice asks.

From around the corner, her cousin Robert Akintola appears. Rob is clutching a clear bag of take-away plates and a bottle of nonalcoholic wine, the kind Nnenna's family drinks by the gallon.

"I'm ... here." Rob chuckles nervously as he stares around. "Good, uh, good afternoon. Is it afternoon? Yeah, I guess, uh ... wow. Sorry, customs at the airport took forever." He holds up the bag. "I brought take-away plates. I figured, like, a Nigerian party might need more take-away plates, so, yeah, I got extra. Uh, I'm here without Paul. Yes, I'm making it awkward. No, I won't apologize, ha. Okay, sorry, wrong time. Wrong *time*, am I right? Like there are ... Did y'all see the paramedics in the front? Are they waiting on something because they're just, like, standing around or whatever. Maybe they're here to resuscitate this, uh ... sorry, I lost the joke—oh! Joy! Hey. Heard about the, uh, the divorce being final. Or 'final.'" He air-quotes. "That sucks. I liked David a lot. Sorry, I don't know if you're—if *we're* allowed to talk about him. Are we? Is that weird? Is he coming? Maybe I won't be the last to arrive. That would be cool. Oh, no, wait, speaking of the last to arrive . . . where's Grandma Mary? She's late to her own party? I mean, did someone forget *her* at the airport? Nah, just kidding, I know she wasn't flying in."

— 9 —

The only thing Robert's mother said to him was, "Robert, bịa. Come pray," before he was ushered into the circle and told to be quiet. He had heard those words many times before: come pray for this person, come pray for that person, come pray for your soul. Despite what his family would believe, especially after his marriage to Paul, Rob still maintained a good relationship with God. He prayed often. He volunteered sometimes at his church in Baltimore, one where he wasn't the only gay man who frequented. "But how many Africans go there?" his mom would ask, and he would roll his eyes because did it really matter? God is God, love is love, and all that other stuff. But to his mom, it mattered. To her, it wasn't the same.

This is why when his brother-in-law was praying for what felt like forever, he kept his eyes open, watching others slowly get tired of James's droning. The kids were always the first to go, but Rob was surprised to see Joy join them. She didn't close her eyes once. She had a listless look on her face, as if she was in a trance of some kind. Rob tried to get her attention, staring at her real hard, even wiggling his nose at an alarming rate all so his septum piercing would catch her eye, but nothing worked.

And then he heard the words, finally, from James's mouth: "We pray for the spirit of our Mama, Mary Okafor, er, Madam Onyinye Mary Okafor, who has left us today, O Lord . . ."

Rob's blood went cold. His hands went limp, nearly slipping back to his side. "Auntie Mary is dead?" he whispered aloud.

Joy looked over at the sound of his voice, but that listless look in her eyes didn't go away.

She had it when the prayer ended, when she tore her hands from those near her and left the room.

And she has it when she reemerges ten minutes later, joining him, his parents, and Michael at the bottom of the stairs.

Suddenly, his mom turns to his cousin Michael, reaches out for his forearm, and gives it a squeeze. "Ejima nna," she says, before addressing the rest of them. "Joy, call your husband. Robert. You people be well. I must go to the hospital." She exhales a bold sigh. And people say *he's* the dramatic one in the family. He's nowhere near as bad as either his mom or his sister. Honestly, Nnenna is like a reality show contestant without the reality show.

"To do what?" Rob chortles, then quickly sidesteps what would've been a smack on the arm from his mom. "Mom, I'm serious."

"Will you be quiet?" Nancy tsks at him. "Is it every day you'll be doing jester? Somebody should go there to be with my sister. God is asking me to come. I still have more prayers." As she says it, she stares at Joy. "Will you join me?"

Joy visibly bristles, taking the tiniest step back. "Oh, n-no, I . . . um." She clears her throat. Rob watches her gaze around the foyer, looking to latch on to anything that might get her out of riding shotgun with his mom. She blinks back a fresh set of tears, and Rob realizes this may not be about his mom at all. She looks scared. "S-someone has to look after the kids," she eventually says.

Nancy shrugs. "Nnenna and James are here. Michael will be here."

"A-and to cancel everything," Joy adds. "My name is signed on the house and with the caterer, so I-I should—someone should—"

"Ah-ah. I ask you one question and you're doing yanga. Just say you don't want to come," Nancy cuts in, waving her hand at Joy's excuses. Quickly, she reaches for Ezekiel's hand and ushers him toward the door. "We will be back. Eh, Robert . . ." Rob watches as his mom tries to find the words for whatever wayward question she's probably going to ask him. He has his money on "Where is that man you live with?" since his parents sometimes have a hard time referring to Paul as his husband. It's not like him being gay is a surprise, and as far as he's concerned, it hadn't been a surprise for a very long time. He recalls being a kid and being very emotionally invested in the underwear models in the men's section. He used to collect the boxes, for God's sake.

In the end, his mom says nothing. Just turns away and disappears out the door with his dad.

Well, you dodged another bullet, then, he tells himself, just to make himself feel better. In reality, he was hoping he'd have time to tell his parents something pretty important.

Usually, for any other thirty-seven-year-old man who owns a condo, has a stable job, and is in a healthy relationship, uttering the words "Mom, Dad, I'm moving" wouldn't be such an issue. But Rob is both Igbo and Yoruba, which he feels gives him a particular kind of stubborn, enterprising intensity. No, if he wants to move, leave his job and his city, he'd better have a good reason. He's afraid "I got a job with an NGO in Accra, so Paul and I have to pack up and leave by the end of the month" won't cut it. She would say, "Family needs to be together." He can hear it in her voice already. She said the same thing when he dared to ask about attending a West Coast college or spend one—*one!*—New Year's Eve with friends as a teenager.

As Nancy leaves, she gives Michael one final look. Rob can see the irritation building in his cousin's features: how his eyebrows slowly pull together, how his jaw tenses. He knows Michael hates being called ejima nna, but his mom doesn't care. She always calls him that, no matter what. But on today of all days, when their mother has died, she couldn't take two extra seconds and maybe consider his feelings a bit? That's stone cold, even for Amarachi Nancy Akintola.

Suddenly, Michael scoffs.

Rob and Joy look in his direction, but it's only Joy's sharp, "What?" he hears.

He grunts. "Nothing."

Rob doesn't think it's nothing. He watches Michael as he gazes past him toward the living room, squinting into the distance. "James said he'd talk to the staff, tell them what's going on. Not sure if it's okay to leave him with that."

"He lives to boss people around," Rob pipes up with a snort. "He's in his element. Don't feel bad for him."

That earns a smile from Joy, however feeble. "He should go tell them to fry the chin-chin in the fridge, then," she says, her voice cracking. She reaches out for a hug from him and they embrace firmly. "How've you been? Sorry that I'm so distracted today."

"Who's complaining? Please." Rob waves away her concern. "It's . . . it's weird. I wouldn't wish this on anyone. I'm really sorry, y'all." He offers a sympathetic smile to the two of them. "Your mom was always the nicer sister."

Michael snorts. "Don't let your mom hear that."

Joy attempts another smile. "Uh, how's Paul? How are things?"

Rob's smile widens, but it feels robotic. He feels like a liar. "He's good." That's not the lie. "He's at home. His parents are in this weekend, so." Not the lie, either. "We . . ." *We're moving to Ghana soon because I got a job over there. Because I applied and didn't tell anyone.* His cousins have just lost their mother in what is arguably a Good Friday disaster, so he really isn't sure if now is the time to bring up the ins and outs of an international move. Instead, he touches his chin while he carefully chooses his words. "Paul is . . . also sorry about your mom." Not a lie! Paul is a very compassionate person. He learned Thai just to speak to the old woman who lives next door to them.

"Thanks, bro," Joy says.

"Do you need us to help with anything?" Then Rob smirks, wiggling his eyebrows. "You said there's dough for chin-chin in the fridge? I got you. We can fry it and eat it. I'd do anything for my family, you know, so family-oriented."

Michael chuckles. "Abeg, is that all you know? To be eating?"

"I take pride in my talents."

"Just leave those for now. I have a feeling we'll all need something stronger than chin-chin after all this."

"Amen."

Joy's phone rings—her work phone. The sound is becoming all too familiar today, and she mentally kicks herself for not putting it on silent or "do not disturb." *But then what would be the point? Who keeps a work phone on silent? Why have it at all?* At times like this, she feels she sounds a lot like Coral, someone who can't keep her boundaries straight. She's usually so good at helping people in situations like hers, but today, she just . . . she can't seem to get it together.

She wishes David were here. She does. She won't say it. She'd literally rather have an honest conversation with her brother than admit that she misses her ex-husband to her "divorce isn't real"-ass family.

"You should take it," Michael speaks up, gesturing to the phone. It's hard not to hear the judgment in his voice. He eyes the device with amusement, like it's a toy that doesn't belong here. "I'll spend some time getting things in order. Call the mortuary, probably."

"Okay, but you probably need help," Joy replies. When he raises an eyebrow at her, she answers, "Well, how do you know calling the mortuary first is a good idea—"

"Joy, I know what I'm doing."

Does he? As if he knew what to do when Peace died—oh, no, he was out of town, or with friends, or being useless somewhere. As if he knew what to do when their dad died—oh, no, once again, he was fucking out of town, or with his fucking friends, or being a useless fuck. God, she wants to scream. How dare he show up now and pretend he has any sense? She can't stop looking at him and thinking, *It's just you and me now,* and then immediately wanting to cry because it isn't fair. Her feet feel itchy. She wishes she were somewhere else instead.

Deep breath.

No, she's fine. She probably just needs to eat something heavy, like pounded yam or that specific style of cake only Nigerian aunties know how to make.

"I'm only offering my assistance," Joy says carefully.

He scoffs, then juts his lips toward the phone in her hands. "Why? Aren't you busy? The way your phone is ringing, I would think you're at work. On the day our mom died, too."

Her heart drops.

She's going to kill him. She absolutely is going to murder him. It'll be a double burial—

"Is it David?" Rob interrupts, nodding to the phone.

Before Joy can open her mouth, she sees the tiniest eye roll, hears the lowest tongue click, from Michael. Her insides ignite. Suddenly, she is a teenager again, filled with envy and spite for her older brother who always gets away unscathed. She deserved to have a screamo phase!

She bites her tongue and shifts toward Rob as she channels her inner fifteen-year-old, and says, "Actually, it's Shelly," as she lifts her phone. Michael narrows his eyes at the mention of his wife. She says, "Be right back . . ." and scuttles off before Michael adds to her impending headache.

Neither of them see Joy reject the call and quickly dial out David's number. *Wait, maybe Jamil should call and ask?* She wonders about the etiquette behind asking her preteen to call her ex-husband and invite him to her newly late mother's birthday party, which is most likely no longer happening.

It doesn't matter. She just needs to talk to him. Her palms sweat the more nervous she becomes. She ducks into the den, a large expanse off the main hallway with a very ambitious nautical theme. No, this is too close to the family. What if someone overhears? Quickly, she turns and takes off running for the backyard, heading straight for the greenhouse.

Joy knows nothing about plants. It was her mom who was the gardener of the family. She would plant tomatoes and basil every year, and whenever the harvest came in, she'd proudly say, "You know, my papa was a farmer," as if that explained her green thumb and Joy's inability to grow anything. "But then he's *my* grandfather, so where's my gardening talent?" Joy would always say. Her mom would just laugh. No answer; no justification. Just that soft, warm, omniscient laugh.

Maybe coming in here wasn't such a good idea.

She turns, nearly runs into a small row of geraniums, and stumbles back just as the call connects. "Yikes, wow."

"Joy?" David's voice sings clearly in her ears.

She pauses a moment. Rests. "Y-yes. Hello."

"Hi . . ."

"Hi. Um." She clears her throat. "Hey, uh, Jamil said he wants you to come to the house." What is she, twelve? "Never mind, I don't know why I said that. I'm going through it."

"Yeah, you sound pretty shaky. What's going on?"

She swallows, hesitates for a moment, locks eyes with a petunia. "I don't know if Jamil called you recently, like in the past one, two hours, recently."

"Maybe? Did something happen to him?"

"No, he's okay. He's fine."

After a second, he asks, "Did something happen to *you*—"

Did something happen . . . ?

She shuts her eyes for a moment, feeling around for words that won't seem to come. Won't seem to form.

She exhales. "C-can you just come over?" she asks. "I'll text you the address." As she speaks, she pulls her phone away from her ear to copy-paste the address into their text chain. "What time can you get here? It's just over an hour away from your place, maybe longer, depending on traffic."

"Oh, like *now*? Uh . . ." He sighs, thinking. "Yeah, okay. If it's important, then, yeah."

Joy is so soothed by those words, but she has to admit it's both comforting and infuriating. *He should've just told me no, that he's busy, that he's dating someone new and she hates me.* Her mom's voice echoes in her head, all her motherly wisdom filtering through the crevices in Joy's mind: *Family is very important.*

David will always be your family.

God doesn't sleep.

Also: *Only people who aren't Christians divorce.*

— 10 —

Nnenna watches as Michael crosses the hall with his phone in one hand and a card in the other. He gives her a short nod before he says "Hello?" into the receiver. Nnenna has grown up with Michael here and there, and they're pretty close in age, but she has never seen him act so maturely. *Finally.* She would've thought having two teenagers—no, a teenager and an actual adult child—would make him more ... just *more* like he ought to be. A man, she thinks. Someone like James.

Everyone is so preoccupied—the kids in the basement, Joy running to the greenhouse, Michael floating around the offices—that no one even looks her way as she shuffles off to cry in the bathroom. How embarrassing for her. Nnenna Olubisi, losing her composure like that, in front of her children, her husband. Her mother.

She sighs, then reaches into her bag for a compact and does her retouches. "Dear God in heaven, please grant me the strength to be more of what you ask. . . . Please guide my words, my actions. . . ." Quickly, she swaps the compact for her lipstick, a dull red that she was planning on replacing with a bolder red in the evening. Now she's not sure if there will be a point, since Auntie Mary is ... "U-um, and please,

please look after my cousins." Her voice drops an octave. God forbid someone else hears her. After she finishes with her lipstick, smacks her lips, and readjusts her wig, she adds, "They've been through a lot and they deserve grace, so . . . please, Jesus, be a shield. As always, we exalt Your holy name—"

Suddenly, a rush of loud, clunky footsteps can be heard outside the door. A voice that sounds like her mom's. Her dad's. She pauses, straining her ears to make sure she hears what she thinks she's hearing. No way would her parents be back already. How far away is the hospital? Why did they even go if they were gonna come back so quickly? Immediately, she wraps up her prayer, "KeepourfriendscloseandourenemiesfarawayOLordinYouwetrustAmen," before dusting off her hands and prying the door open.

She turns the corner to a frantic scene. The caterers are carrying a table through the front doors, just as her parents are making their way in, pointing and arguing with James, who is waving his arms around, saying, "Don't scratch the walls, o!" as if it's his credit card on the deposit.

"These people should bring these chairs back, na," her mom says, frowning at the workers moving furniture past her. When she looks to Ezekiel for agreement, he simply throws his hands up and shrugs.

Nnenna approaches them, casting a glance over her shoulder at another set of staff walking toward her with fold-up chairs. "Mom? You're back? What's—"

"Nnenna, you're in the way," James grumbles, waving her out of the path of the workers. "Can't you see these people are working?"

She purses her lips. Her eyes stay focused on the latest group to walk past her while Ezekiel croaks out, "Bush man," letting his eyes wash over James. "Do Joy and Michael know you are sending these people away?"

"Ah, Papa," James says. "They're grieving—we're *all* grieving. We have to help any way we can. That's why we're here."

Nnenna doesn't technically think he's wrong, but still. If there's anything she knows about Joy, it's that she'd want to be annoyingly involved in every decision. Joy doesn't know how to ask for help and, to be honest, it's very unfeminine of her. She knows it's not her place, but sometimes Nnenna wonders . . . you know, she'll never say it out loud or anything, but exactly *how* much of Joy's marriage problems are because she doesn't know how to just relax and not take over things? Nnenna has met David multiple times, and she absolutely doesn't understand why her ye-ye cousin would let a man like that go. He is kind and responsible and seems to actually not mind the fact that Joy is neurotic.

"I have to tell the guests not to come," James goes on, tapping his chin while he thinks.

Nnenna frowns. "Where will you get the guest list?"

"Joy must give it to me."

"Okay, let me ask," she offers. "And then I can call—"

"No." He shakes his head. "*I* will call."

"Does . . . it make too much of a difference?" she asks cautiously. "You're busy doing this, so I don't mind calling."

James bristles, tilting his head as if to take in what she's saying. "Nnenna, please," he says, and waves her offer away. "Just get me the list."

"No one is getting any list." Nancy smacks her hands together to get their attention. "Go and call eve-ry-bo-dy to come here *now*-now. I have something very important to say."

Nnenna sighs. "Mom, I don't think—"

"Nnenna, nwa m, ngwa ngwa," Nancy cuts in, shaking her head. "This very day, I had a premonition, and everybody must hear it."

Nnenna is quiet.

She glances at James, whose ego has deflated enough for him to let Auntie Nancy's voice settle into his ears. "Ah . . ." He swallows, uneasily. "Mama. A premonition?"

All Nancy does is smile.

James and Nnenna head in different directions to find their family members. As Nnenna approaches the adjacent hallway, the one leading to the side of the house Nnenna hasn't had time to explore yet, she spots Joy exiting what looks like a games room, face blotchy as she clutches her phone and some loose papers. Nnenna stops instinctively, unsure if she should make herself known before Joy bumps into her. Joy doesn't seem to care. She glances at Nnenna once before maneuvering her way past. "W-wait," Nnenna calls.

Joy stops and turns. She silently raises an eyebrow.

Suddenly, Nnenna is aware she doesn't know what she wants to say. *Come to the hall. My mom had a premonition* seems trite when her cousin is clearly distraught over the passing of her mother. She and Joy have never been these people. Cozy and comfy and considerate of one another. It would be weird to start now. Off-brand, even.

"My mom said she had a premonition," Nnenna spits out. The words bounce between them. Nnenna sees how they ricochet off Joy's head; how they refuse to sink in, most likely because, yes, they are ridiculous. Midday premonitions feel kinda dramatic. If this was a nighttime premonition, a dream from their ancestors or a spirit coming to warn them of inevitable harm, then Nnenna would expect a different reaction. "She wants us all to come to the hallway or something," she says. "It seems important."

"What kind of premonition?"

"Joy, please. Does it look like I know?" Nnenna sighs and tosses her hair over her shoulder. Her eyes fall on the papers in Joy's hand and she nods to them. "Are you, um, going with a Christian funeral home?"

Joy is quiet. She stares back at Nnenna, unmoving, unwavering. Not even the slightest twitch of her eye or lilt of her lips.

Nnenna knows she's touched a nerve. But her nerves take over and soon she can't stop rambling. "B-because, obviously, Auntie Mary was Christian. A-and we have to contact all her friends, everyone she might want there. She was baptized Anglican, right? So we have to take that into account first."

"Nnenna—"

"It's very important, Joy," Nnenna says, her words firm and harsh. Panicked. "D-don't you want to make sure your mom's soul is taken care of?"

Joy sighs. She shuts her eyes, looks down while she exhales. "Nnenna, I really can't do this right now. Isn't it bad enough that your mom is having premonitions before we've eaten?"

Nnenna says, "I just wanna make sure you're not rushing through the process." What she means is, *I've never lost a parent before. I don't know this grief.*

She says, "What's Mama's local parish? They can also assist with next steps," when she means to say, *Tell me what I can do to help. We're family, you and I.*

She says, "It's just important you take your time, that's all. Don't look at me like I don't know what I'm saying," when she should've said, *I'm sorry. I'm really sorry this is happening.*

Joy breathes out. She says, her voice quiet but firm, "Leave me alone, Nnenna. For the love of God. Just leave me alone," and moves to walk past her.

"Is that any way to talk to your sister?"

Joy and Nnenna both startle at the sound of Nancy's voice. They look around before they notice she's waving at them frantically from the opposite side of the hall. "And I asked you people to come here, not to be gallivanting up and down, up and down—"

Nnenna growls. "Mom, we are *not* gallivanting—"

"Mechie ọnụ! Non-sense!"

By the time Joy and Nnenna get to the hallway, joining the rest of their family members, Auntie Nancy has rushed up the staircase and positioned herself on the balcony, like a royal about to address her subjects. And with the way she leans forward, her arms spread and grasping the banister, a confident smirk on her face, well, they wouldn't be too far off. They think: *This is not the face of a woman whose sister has just died.*

"God has put a special message in my brain," Nancy says with a sage nod. "And He said I must share it with you."

Rob makes a gagging noise, but covers it up with a cough. Nnenna glares at him.

"As my husband, Ezekiel, and I left this compound earlier today, we ran into trials and tribulations. . . ." She speaks, gesturing first to Ezekiel and then to the door. Everything about the way she's telling the story, the dramatic way she points, the overpronunciation of "tribulations," is building up to a climax Nnenna isn't sure she's prepared for.

"First, the car wouldn't start. I said, 'He-ey, Jesu! All I want is to see my sister. To see my late sister.' Anyway. It's all right. The car started and we were on our way. My heart was very heavy. We were driving, driving, driving. And then!" She snaps her fingers above her head. "One brown cow appeared to us."

Michael's eyes widen. "*Excuse* me?" He glances around, hoping that he's not the only one who thinks . . . Well, to be fair, he doesn't even know what he's thinking. His eyes start to sting, as if he might cry from his aunt's audacity, but no tears come. He spots Sarah trying not to laugh. He sees Yemi, stars in her eyes, seemingly enthralled by the idea that God spoke to her grandma through an animal.

"Yes." After a moment, Nancy places a hand on her chest. "You people won't understand, but when I was a girl in the village, I went with my uncle to collect meat from the farm, and those cows resembled this one. There was always *one* brown cow. . . ."

Michael looks at Joy. Her bottom lip trembles ferociously and he knows at once that she's trying not to burst into tears.

"And then I told my husband, 'Ah-ah, stop the car,' and we went to the side of the road, like this," Nancy explains, using her hands to show how a car parks on the road's shoulder. "At that moment, in my mind, eh? As we were approaching the cow, *gbak-gbak-gbak*, like this. The cow is looking at me. If you see een face, eh? That is when God spoke to me. Real God! No be all these juju people. In fact, no be juju at all." She clears her throat, and moves to raise her arms, palms open. "God said that my sister, nne Onyinye Mary Okafor, will be resurrected in the name of Jesus in three days. This one na real prophecy. As our Lord will rise, so, too, will our dear sister and mother. Yes. If anybody dare try and put her in the ground before her time, I will personally come—me, Amarachi Nancy—will personally come and deal with you."

The hall is silent.

Michael's mouth hangs open. That reassured look on his aunt's face, the confident way she is holding the rail . . . yes, he's sure Nancy

Akintola has lost it. From the corner of his eye, he sees James, beaming and watching on in awe, fully engulfed in the story of the prophetic cow or whatever.

Nancy drops her hands and clicks her tongue against her teeth. "You people must say 'amen,' o."

There is one person more taken with Auntie Nancy's story than James is, and that's his daughter, Yemi.

Yemi is buzzing. In fact, she's vibrating with something that feels like fear, but also feels enthralling. A real live resurrection! She looks to her mom, who looks—well, terrified. Shouldn't her mom be excited, too? Yemi sure is. She looks around now, trying to find another face to match her enthusiasm, but everyone has expressions like they just got slapped.

Well, no matter. Yemi throws both her hands in the air, grinning, and says, "Amen!" as a feeling of utter euphoria washes over her. She's sure this is what God's love feels like.

— 11 —

For a moment, you could hear a pin drop.

Then, slowly but surely, the hall erupts in questions—"Uh, sorry, *how* do you know this is real?"—and accusations—"Mom, that's a bit much, even for you . . ."—but Auntie Nancy fields them all as if she's being secretly instructed on how to do so. Divinely instructed, obviously. She nods sagely at each question, answering like a politician. "Faith is knowing. That's all I can tell you. Ọ dị m n'ime, n'obi m. Next question," she says, which makes Rob chortle.

Yemi shoots her hand up. "Should we do anything to get ready? Is there, um, a hymn we should sing?" She glances at her mom while she asks. Joy can see she's hoping to lock eyes with Nnenna, hoping to see her mom look back in adoration of her question. But Nnenna has a grave look on her face, wide-eyed and stiff-lipped.

Nancy answers, "We must tell everybody of what I saw."

Joy gasps, "No way!" at the same time Michael kisses his teeth, "Auntie, no, please." Neither of them acknowledge the other is speaking, but to anyone watching, it's obvious they are sharing the same grief. This is their mother Auntie is talking about. Joy can't believe she could be this careless, and—and—and opportunistic! She doesn't even have the words to argue. This entire day, from start to finish, has been a shitfest and she'll be happy when she wakes up tomorrow and doesn't have to deal with any of it. She really should be planning her escape, not imagining a brown cow delivering a sermon.

"You people are screaming 'auntie, auntie,' but I didn't even finish talking, o," Nancy goes on with a frown. She pouts as if the gravity of the story is enough to weigh her down. "This is a very serious premonition. You know that, eh . . . my friend. My husband knows who I am talking about." Eyes shift to Ezekiel, who doesn't move an inch. "My friend whose friend has a daughter here in Canada. She works for a very important TV program. Everybody watches AJAfrika TV."

Joy bristles. AJAfrika was one of those fringe programs that aired sporadically, hosted and produced by Alice Karim, a Nigerian woman who married this Moroccan billionaire and decided she wanted to live out her dream of having a TV show. She mainly reports on cultural events, like Igbo Day (which Joy didn't realize was real) and the christenings of random chiefs' babies. Of course something like this, something like a resurrection would be easy ratings for Alice.

"She will be here soon to ask us about what I am telling you, about my message from God," Nancy goes on loosely. "Maybe in a few hours. She has to drive from, eh . . . I don't know. Kitchener. Where is that? I don't know." Slowly, she holds up her phone to reveal a WhatsApp chat box. "I have already told my people back home, and my people at my church," she explains. Joy feels her heart drop, sinking further and further into her stomach the more Auntie speaks. "Jesus said to spread the good news that He is risen, so we must do the same for my sister. Tomorrow, we will also arrange for a spiritual man to come to the house to pray and commune with my sister's spirit."

James gawks. "Mama, but what about a pastor?"

Nancy swats away his question as if it's a fly. "Eh, chefuo ya for now."

"No, no, wait," Joy interrupts. "Okay, so why—why not a pastor? What kind of 'spiritual man' are you calling here?"

"Ah-ah! Onye nsogbu! He is a spiritualist, na," Nancy explains, as if it's common sense. "He is one of us. He is gifted. He knows how to talk to spirits."

"How do we know he'll be telling the truth?"

"Joy—"

"I just don't see the point of calling a 'spiritual man' to the house," Joy bites back. She's angry, she's frustrated, but it'll do nothing to show it in front of her family. So they're okay inviting this spiritualist here when the family makes such a big deal of her not going to church on a regular basis? How is that okay, but somehow she's a heathen for being a divorced nonbeliever who studied psychotherapy and was vegan once?

"He is coming because he will be able to speak to your mama," Uncle Ezekiel tells them. The hall falls into silence at the sound of his voice. He doesn't speak often—he isn't at all like his wife who will take any chance to give a proclamation on high—but when he does, the family knows to listen. Even though Joy is vibrating with anger, she finds herself slowing down. Taking it in. *He will be able to speak to your mama,* meaning, *He can speak our language.*

Nancy claps her hands together, startling them from the fleeting sense of calm they had a moment ago. "Oya, everybody, be prayerful. To-morrow night, there is work. We must prepare for the vigil."

Nnenna whispers, "Vigil?" and looks around. Most of the family have begun to disperse, heading upstairs or to different parts of the house. In their walks, she can see hesitation, confusion. Anger.

Michael and his daughter, Sarah, hang back, whispering to each other. Nnenna hears Michael warn Sarah not to tell her mom, and Sarah snorts. "Yo, it's really not up to me to tell her that this side of the family is crazy. When we're being interviewed on the news, or they're taking Grandma Nancy to jail, then she'll see it."

Nnenna crosses her arms. "Abeg, who's crazy?" She approaches them, a stern look on her face. Sure, her mother's delivery and tac-tics were a bit over the top, and sure, calling a second-rate vanity reporter to the house was uncalled for, but who's to say she didn't have a real premonition? Their people, Nigerian people, have always been a deeply spiritual group, and their family was no exception. People back home have dreams that predict events all the time. Hell, they even famously had an uncle in the village who met his brother in the spirit realm before he died, so this isn't new for them. Nnenna kisses her teeth, giving Sarah a quick once-over. Immediately, she blames Shelly's influence. "Listen, just because *you* don't personally believe that God can send people visions, that doesn't mean she's crazy. It happens all the time!"

"I know she's your mom and you feel you have to say that," Michael shoots back, "but even you have to admit, this cow nonsense is—it's taking advantage."

Nnenna gasps, then glances over her shoulder to make sure no one heard. Rob catches her eye, but she turns, trying to compose herself quickly. "She's not taking advantage! My mom has just lost her sister—"

"Yeah, and I j-just lost my mother," Michael says, his voice cracking. Sarah places her hand on his back. Nnenna can see his lip quivering; how he gulps and purses his lips to keep from crying.

From beside Nnenna, Rob steps in, resting his hand on Michael's shoulder. "Hey, listen," he begins. "I'm . . . sorry. I'm not gonna pretend to understand what my mom might be smoking"—Nnenna gasps—"but I think her heart is in the right place. And who knows? Maybe . . . maybe she's telling the truth and Auntie Mary really will, you know, get back up. Rise. We just have to wait and see."

Nnenna is ready to pounce on Rob's words until she hears them. In fact, she thinks there's a hint of truth in her brother's statement: there's nothing they can do but see what happens. She begins to nod slowly, much to Rob's surprise. "Exactly. We just have to wait."

— 12 —

Jamil had gotten so used to the plush, open basement space that he lay on a sofa, his feet up and a pillow over his face, as if this was his own house. Or, one of his houses. He didn't think about it often, but sometimes he felt a different level of comfort at each of his parents' places. Being in-between two homes is weird. And now he feels even more displaced because his mom is upstairs somewhere freaking out that Grandma is dead, and he is one of the last people to have seen her alive.

He is one of the only people who has seen her dead, too.

At church, they talk about things like souls and everlasting life, and he thinks that he now knows what it looks like to not have one. A soul. The way his grandma lay there, so lifeless, so impossibly still, it was almost as if her brain had lost the mechanism that made her go. Like it just stopped, just broke. She was inanimate, like a rock. A chair. His handheld that Zach won't give back.

"It's not like the movies at all," he whispers to himself, low enough so his cousins peppered around the basement won't hear. Slowly, he presses the pillow on his face until it's smushed against his nose, covering his mouth. Letting little air escape.

He really wishes his dad were here.

Suddenly, the pillow is jostled from his face. Sarah towers above him and she doesn't look happy as she tosses the pillow aside. "Don't do that. You'll suffocate," she grunts, and then makes room for herself at the edge of the sofa.

Jamil sits up, letting his curly hair fall into his eyes. Sarah was way nicer before, but he thinks she's allowed to be mean if she wants since Grandma Mary just died. And, since her mom isn't here.

Sarah crosses her legs, slouches into the sofa, and resumes her end-less doom scrolling. When Jamil asks where her mom is, she cuts him with a sharp look. She doesn't even know why she's being so strict. Jamil is all right—he's not borderline manic like Yemi—and, besides, it's really not his fault that her dad is treating her like a glori-fied babysitter. Plus, she feels she might understand Jamil on a differ-ent level, since her mom, like his dad, isn't Nigerian, either. Granted, Sarah's mom is Jamaican, but she'd be lying if she said she didn't feel a stark cultural difference every time she was around her Nigerian family.

Sarah sighs out her frustration and tries to sit up a bit straighter. "She's not here."

"How come?"

"Well, where's *your* dad?" she says with a snort.

Jamil rolls his eyes. "My parents are divorced, so they don't have to go everywhere together anymore."

He's right, of course, but there's no way Sarah can admit that the same thing might be happening with her parents. She's not dumb. It's not her place to spill the secrets of her family, partially because she doesn't really understand it herself. It wasn't an overnight thing by any means. It wasn't as if one day she woke up and her parents be-came more distant, or that they had a large blow-out argument and have been walking on eggshells ever since. No, it was more subtle. Less laughter. Less togetherness. The vibes were off.

If she's being honest, she feels this is just par for the course for many relationships—especially hetero ones.

When Jamil isn't looking, she swipes back into her text conversation with Mel. Her girlfriend. It isn't like Jamil will care or anything, since Uncle Rob has a whole-ass husband, but she doesn't need him accidentally telling Auntie Joy and then Auntie Joy accidentally telling Sarah's dad—although, to be honest, the chances of that are slim considering her dad and Auntie Joy don't seem to like each other very much. She shrugs as she types faster. Not her problem.

Yemi joins them, sitting on an ottoman with an intricate pattern, and Zach crawls over to lie on the carpet by Sarah's feet. Yemi is sporting a sour face. Sarah can understand why, given the circumstances, but for as long as she can remember, Yemi has always been like this. Always so serious, like a mini deaconess. And Zach is quiet, as quiet as Sarah has ever seen him. He plays through Jamil's collection of games with absolute concentration. His eyes are glazed over, if only to blink lazily every now and then, and his lips are pulled into a tight frown.

Sarah nudges him with her foot. "You all right?"

He wiggles away from her. Doesn't even make a sound. Sarah winces. This kid might need therapy. Hell, they all will, most likely.

"O-okay." Sarah clears her throat and pockets her phone. Time to be the adult in the room. Eighteen is legal in Canada, right? "Listen up, guys. I think we should all talk about our feelings," she tells them.

Yemi grimaces as if Sarah suggested something offensive. "But why?"

"Because you're all going through it," she jokes, but then softens once she sees how Yemi bristles, how Jamil pulls his knees into his chest, how Zach taps buttons harder, faster, without ever acknowledging her presence. She puts her serious face on and tries again. "Because you guys all are dealing with something big."

"You mean Grandma Mary," Yemi says, "and how we found her when she was dead."

Sarah gulps. "Yes. That's exactly it."

"Zach touched her."

Sarah follows Yemi's pointed finger to her brother on the floor. Zach is so focused on the end of the level that he barely registers the sound of her voice or his name being called.

"O-oh?" Sarah is way out of her depth here. It's one thing for them to have to witness a dead grandmother, but to *touch* a dead body? The thought makes her skin crawl. All she can say is, "Fuck, man, that's scary."

Yemi frowns.

"Yeah, it was," Jamil pipes up, his voice timid. He and Sarah lock eyes before he averts his gaze and stares down at his knees. "Do you think . . . she's okay?"

"Grandma?" Yemi cuts in. "She's not. She's dead."

He glances at her. "That's not what I mean."

Maybe Sarah had been a bit too ambitious with this "let's talk about our feelings" plan. Kids are much more candid, much less forgiving, than adults. They can't lie the way adults usually do. She needs a new plan of action. As she thinks, she taps her chin. "Um . . . well. Who knows what happens when people die?" she asks, looking around. "You too." She nudges Zach with her foot, but he just grunts and rolls away.

Jamil frowns. "They stop breathing and then they—then you bury them. And they never come back."

"R-right," Sarah goes on. "Their body immediately starts to decompose. So maybe when you touched Grandma . . ." She looks down at Zach. For a moment, the slightest second, he looks back at her. It's barely a form of acknowledgment, but she'll take what she can get. "Maybe when you touched her, she was already . . . decomposing. And that's why her skin might have felt different."

Zach holds his breath.

"It must have been really scary," she tells him.

He doesn't say anything. Just sniffles, appearing to hold back a noise in his throat, and nods slowly.

"You sound like my mom," Jamil says with a small smile. "She's always saying, like . . . things about people's feelings. Talking about what people are feeling and stuff."

Sarah nods, smiling. "Well, she's a therapist, right?"

"I think so."

"I think maybe I wanna be that one day. I'm not sure yet," Sarah says with a sigh.

Yemi crosses her legs and arms. *A perfect little madam*, Sarah thinks. Yemi says, "That's not all that happens when you die."

Sarah shrugs. "Yeah. I mean, your . . . muscles stop tensing so I've heard you also shit yourself."

"No, I meant, like . . ." Yemi inhales sharply before she says, "If you were a good person and you were saved, then you go to heaven. If you were a bad person or a heathen, then you go to hell and you can never gain everlasting life."

Sarah tries so hard not to roll her eyes, but she can't help it. Suppressing a groan is hard enough. It's one thing to have to sit through both sides of her family, her aunts and uncles, reciting this stuff in their sleep, but for her young cousins to parrot it back to her with such ease—well, it really pisses her off, she can't lie. Immediately, she jumps on Yemi's words. "Do you really believe that?"

Yemi raises her eyebrow, confused at the question. "Uh, yes? It's true."

"Is it?"

"*Yes*, it is."

"Okay, but how is that supposed to be comforting?" Sarah grimaces. "Who gets to say you're a good person?"

"You have to be saved and accept Jesus as your savior, obviously," she tells her.

"Is that the only criteria?"

"What?"

"Is that the only thing that makes a person good?" Sarah asks. "What if someone is saved, but they're also a murderer on the side? Or a pedophile?"

Yemi's mouth drops open.

She is silent for long enough that Sarah knows she maybe took it too far. What did she think she'd try to accomplish having an existential debate about religion with a thirteen-year-old, anyway? It's so pretentious of her, ugh. "Never mind, forget I asked that," she says, waving it away. "That was stupid of me."

"Y-yeah, it was," Yemi snaps back. "Do you even go to church?"

"Doesn't matter," Sarah says.

"Is it comforting?"

Both Sarah and Yemi turn at the sound of Jamil's voice. He didn't think such a throwaway question would get their attention, but he's really curious. He wants to know if he wouldn't feel so uncomfortable and weird in his body if maybe he had just believed a bit more in God. If his parents had forced him to go to church, would he be okay with what's happening now? Could he have made sense of it all somehow?

Would his parents still be together?

"It . . ." Yemi quickly loses steam when the question fully sinks into her brain. She pouts, trying to form the words. "My parents use the word . . . 'reassuring.' Like, it's 'reassuring' to know that when people die, God will take them to heaven, and they can meet other people God has saved, too."

"But how is that reassuring?" Jamil mumbles, eyes downcast. "No one actually *wants* to die. Right?"

The doorbell rings upstairs. The cousins look at each other, frozen, waiting for moving footsteps above their head. "Is it your mom?" Jamil asks Sarah at the same moment she asks, "Is that your dad?"

"Why not both?" Zach utters from the floor, his voice groggy from underuse.

Jamil hesitates for a second before he climbs off the sofa and makes the trip to the staircase. The carpet is lush under his feet, but he still can't believe how big this house is and how long it takes to finally reach the steps. Sarah is behind him by the time he gets to the ground floor.

And then he hears him.

". . . weird that no one else showed up early."

His dad.

"Well, you know . . . Nigerian people, African time, all that fun stuff."

And his mom.

He hangs by the wall for a second longer, enjoying hearing the two of them talk to each other. As he takes one deep breath and sighs out, he realizes that he didn't know how badly he needed some kind of normalcy today.

Sarah comes up behind him. "Come on," she says, and she gives his shoulder a squeeze as they approach the door.

Jamil approaches quietly. He takes in the way his mom looks much less tense, and feels a sense of comfort from knowing that if she can be okay, then maybe he can, too.

His dad greets Sarah first, reaching out for a hug from her. "Sarah, hey, how've you been?"

She grins. "I'm good. Just, um, surviving." When she steps back, she almost knocks into Jamil, who has his gaze fixed firmly on the ground.

David frowns, tilting his head so he can get a better look at his son. "Ay, cucciolo, what happened?"

Jamil takes a deep breath and shakes out a sigh. He can't speak. Actually, he really hates that his dad is using his childhood nickname, but he knows if he opens his mouth to say anything, he'll cry. And he absolutely doesn't want to cry in front of his dad, his mom, and Sarah.

Within a split second, he rushes forward and throws himself into his dad's arms, biting his lip, his tongue, anything to force the tears away. They fall anyway.

His head throbs. He can hear his dad's voice echoing outside of him, "Che è successo? Stai piangendo, perché?"

Jamil clings tighter. Every time he tries to speak, his voice gets stuck further and further down his throat.

Then he hears his mom: "We should go upstairs."

And Sarah. "Or, I could just go . . . ?"

Finally, his dad. "No, why would you?"

Jamil can't take this any longer. Just like Auntie Nnenna told everyone in the living room, he swallows his fear, the feeling that saying it will bring back the memory of seeing his grandma's body lying still on the bed, and he says, "Because . . . p-piango perché m-mia nonna è m-morta!"

Joy freezes. She's not sure why. It's not like *she* can understand Italian. And for what it's worth, David isn't fluent, either. She chooses to believe that's why his brows pull together, why he stares curiously back at Jamil without saying a word.

And then he asks, "Chi?"

Jamil shivers. "Nonna."

Joy gulps as David turns to her. She puts on her best stoic "I'm an adult" face: chin tilted upward, stiff upper lip, fighting the endless desire to blink more than is necessary. And she thinks, *I can't believe Jamil can speak Italian.* She's crying inside, but her mind won't stop looping around her son speaking whole sentences. She could've sworn she and David promised he would eventually learn both languages, both Igbo and Italian, at the same pace. Not that Joy even knows much Igbo to teach him. Truthfully, she can't even really speak it. That was supposed to be her mom's job. Well, her mom said she would help, anyway. "I don't want him to end up like you," her mom had said in a joking way. Joy remembers how Mama's face lit up when Joy asked her. Nothing made Mama happier. She would sing to Jamil when he was a baby in Igbo—when Joy was watching, anyway. If Joy turned her back for a second, Mama would start through a chorus of hardcore Nigerian gospel tunes.

She promised she would . . .

It's Joy's fault. It is. She was really bad at staying on top of it, not knowing how or when a baby was supposed to acquire a second language. But she didn't really expect Jamil to be practically rapping in Italian the moment her mom passes away! It makes her feel a special kind of loneliness.

Jamil has stopped trembling, if only a little. He pushes away from his dad and quickly wipes his face.

His dad asks him again, "È morta, tua nonna? Jamil, non va bene mentire. Lo sai, no?"

Jamil frowns, his frustration growing. "Non mento, Papà, è vero! L'ho vista . . . lying down . . . morta."

Joy crosses her arms, watching this exchange, understanding only what she can see on their faces. Jamil's restless words draw out a kind of fear in David's eyes that she hasn't seen before. His brows furrow as he listens, weighing the gravity of what Jamil is telling him. It terrifies her, too.

Then David turns to her, a curious look on his face as he tries to piece together their son's words. "Is . . ." He stops, takes a casual look down the hall. And a smile breaks out on his lips. A light chuckle, too. "I don't—I don't actually . . . uh. Okay." He clears his throat and asks, "Joy, is your mom dead?"

Joy inhales deeply. She feels the sting of tears behind her eyes again.

And she turns to Jamil, her voice small as she speaks, "Since when a-are *you* . . . fluent in Italian?"

David groans, "Oh my God" before he says, "Okay. Can we talk upstairs?" He doesn't wait for her answer before he heads up, leaving Joy to give Jamil a quick hug, whisper, "G-go play with your cousins, okay?" and jog up after him.

David pokes his head in each room until he finds one with Joy's things lying outside of their suitcase. She follows, shutting the door behind her and immediately launching into her explanation. "Okay, okay, listen—"

"Joy, what the fuuuuuck?" he groans, running his hands through his hair. "Are you serious? Noooo, are you *serious*?"

"—in my defense—listen to me for one second, okay—"

"Why didn't you say anything on the phone—"

"In my defense, I am currently having a-an unconventional response to a traumatic event—"

"Joy, my God, look at me, okay? Look at me—"

"David."

"I'm not one of your patients, okay? Don't talk to me about unconventional trauma responses and shit."

"I-I *saw* her . . . David. Lying there." Her lip trembles and soon she is shaking with the memory of seeing her mother's lifeless body. Not how her mom would laugh or dance while she was cooking, or sing sweet summer songs to Jamil when he was a baby—but the crass ugliness of how Joy tried to wake her. How she cried. How she prayed, even. The helplessness overtakes her, and she feels her knees weaken. David catches her before she hits the floor. She sobs selfishly onto his shoulder, and her words spill out of her mouth without pretense. "I didn't know what to do, I just kept crying, and Nnenna wouldn't stop praying, and I can't stand how she thinks that will fix everything when it hasn't ever, like, my sister is dead, my dad is dead, my mom died on her birthday, and I don't know what to *do*, like, clients won't stop calling me, a cow told my aunt that my mom is being resurrected, and everyone thinks I know what I'm doing but I don't and I just—I just wanna go home, I just wanna go home . . ."

She clings tighter, cries harder.

"I miss my mom."

The realization does not come easy for her. When she misses her mom, usually she would call her, visit her, sing a song her mom liked. Oh, and Mama loved all those old highlife songs. She knew all the words, so Joy learned them, too. But now, missing her mom has become abstract. It comes with the stark, unsettling knowledge that there is nothing to be done anymore; that missing her mom can't will her into existence. It won't change things. It won't give her more time. She just has to carry this grief forever, and when she forgets, it will come back to remind her that she is nothing.

That's the thing about grief, she thinks. Some days, she feels like she is done and ready to move on, but then it comes back, cold, calculating, and conniving as ever, just to say, "No, I think the fuck not," over and over and over and over again.

She feels David's arms wrap tighter around her the more she cries. He says, "I know. I'm really sorry, Joy. This isn't fair."

It really isn't.

Mom always said, Chukwu adịghị ehi ụra, but Joy is sure He is slumbering now.

— 13 —

The good thing about a house this big is there are so many rooms that normally no one in the Okafor family would have a use for. This is why no one thinks to check the games room, let alone the second-floor office, the attic loft, the library, or the second living room. Sarah is taking it all in. She loops into each room, snapping pictures to text to Mel, with captions like, *Look at all the books!* or *How do they keep this many plants alive?* Mel reacts with an emoji to each.

"He-ey, Sarah, be careful." Sarah nearly collides with her auntie Nnenna as she rounds a corner. Quickly and feverishly, Sarah hides her phone.

She notices her aunt glance at it, but thankfully, she doesn't think to ask who Sarah is texting in such a hurry. Instead, she clings tighter to a crumpled list in her hands. From the looks of the crossed-out names, Sarah guesses it's the guest list for Grandma Mary's party. Or, what *was* the guest list, anyway. *Auntie is weird, but she's not, like, actually telling people Grandma is dead and might come back from the dead, is she?* Sarah guesses Auntie Nnenna is probably lying, telling people that there's a flight delay or a problem with the house, at least until the resurrection is confirmed. In all honesty, Sarah would do the same. They all learned the art of deception from the same source, after all: their family.

"Sorry, Auntie," she mutters, and ducks away. She walks fast, past the main living room and down the opposing hall. At the end, she finds an open lattice door that leads into another space. Along the walls, she sees trophies, dart boards, and shelves that house board games and gaming consoles. "Jesus," she gasps, staring around at the largest games room she's ever seen.

Her uncle Rob comes into view, holding a pool cue as he circles the pool table by the window. "Welcome!" he says and, after seeing the shock on her face, he cackles. "What? Did you think rich people play games in the same room where they eat? Like *peasants*?"

Sarah snorts as she enters. She takes in the large TV on the opposite side of the room. "No cables," she says, pointing to the clean display. "Is anything even hooked up to it?"

"I think it's voice activated," Rob tells her. "Not sure. Maybe Joy knows?"

"Ah, hmm. Y-yeah, never mind." The thought of asking her aunt anything right now terrifies her.

Rob shrugs. "Or, your dad might know? He's been on and off the phone for the past hour, I think. I could hear him in random parts of the hallway, but it's like his strong aversion to fun prevented him from seeing this room."

Sarah laughs but it fades as quickly as it bursts out. The gravity of the situation washes over her, as she thinks of her dad calling around to funeral homes or mortuaries or wherever, trying to figure out what to do with grandma's ... dead body. And then what's Grandma Nancy thinking, having some weird reporter come to the house? She shivers. "This all really sucks," she mumbles. "Honestly. I just can't believe it. It's Grandma's birthday, too."

"Yeah." Rob reaches out for Sarah's hand and she gives it freely. "This is so shit. But at least we've got each other for now."

"What do you mean 'for now'?" Sarah asks midsqueeze with Rob's hand.

Immediately, Rob's face falls and he moves to the other side of the pool table. "Let's play a round. Do you know how?" He ignores the way Sarah watches him curiously, how she looks distrusting of the pool cue he hands her. "Oh, come on," he grunts with a roll of his eyes. "Let's play one round. *I* will explain, and then, uh, *you* can tell me how things are going with Mel." And he gives her a knowing look.

Sarah really does burst out laughing this time, a loud sound that tapers into a nervous chuckle the longer she goes. "O-okay, fine," she says.

Neither Rob nor Sarah know how to play pool.

After missing the ball and having to use his hand to roll it into the nearest pocket, Rob sets down his cue and declares: "Let's not do this because it is fucking embarrassing."

Sarah giggles and drops her stick, too. "Yes, agreed."

The two of them settle on the sofa in the corner that looks more comfortable than it feels. "Shoulda known." Rob kisses his teeth. "It's just for decoration."

"You sound like my mom."

"How's Mel?"

"After, after." Sarah blushes as she waves away his question. "What's with your ominous 'for now'? Are you . . . sick?" The word lands on her mouth heavily. Honestly, she wasn't expecting it to. She and her uncle Rob are always joking and they're rarely ever serious. *It's just the day,* Sarah thinks, biting back bitterness in her mouth. *Today is just a heavy, shitty, horrible day.*

Rob places a hand on his chest and shakes his head. "Oh, no, no, I'm not."

"G-good."

"I'm . . . ugh." He takes a deep breath before he says, "I got a job offer for this NGO."

Sarah gasps. "Oh my God, congrats!"

"You won't be all 'oh my God congrats'-ing me if you knew where it was," Rob mumbles. "It's in Accra. In . . . Ghana."

"Oh my God, congrats!" Sarah repeats with a cheeky grin. "That's actually awesome, though. Haven't you told anyone? I know this isn't the right time for it, b-but, I mean . . . maybe after, we can celebrate?"

"Celebrate ke? No way," he scoffs. "Listen, the second my mom finds out Paul and I are moving to Ghana in a few weeks, she'll kill me. And there will be no prophetic cow to bring me back."

Sarah raises an eyebrow. "Why would she kill you? What's the big deal? You're, like, a real adult. You can live wherever you want."

Rob grimaces. "You sound like Paul."

"Isn't that a good thing?"

Rob doesn't reply. Sarah shifts uneasily, feeling more of a gap in their ages and experiences than ever. She wishes she could understand where he was coming from. At the end of the day, they're in the same family. If anyone should understand, wouldn't it be her?

So she tries, offering a hesitant, "Is it because of your mom, maybe?"

Rob lets out a breath and purses his lips, a sour look coming over his face. "Well. Family is the most important, you know." Sarah feels herself shrink, remembering all too well the unofficial-official motto of the Okafor and Akintola families.

Honestly, when she thinks about it, she can't remember if her uncle Rob has ever lived far away from his parents. He didn't go to a faraway school, or take a faraway job. Maybe he felt an obligation to stay close. He can't hide the bitterness in his voice, but Sarah thinks maybe family *is* important to him, too, in a way, and he just doesn't know how to say it. She understands, though. *It's cultural,* she thinks. *It's just . . . how we operate.*

Sarah offers a comforting smile, a near-grimace of solidarity, and says, "I get it. Your mom is scary. Better to save the news for another day."

Rob looks at her, barely meeting her eyes. "Yeah." He sits up straighter, but then slouches back when he realizes this sofa wasn't made for comfort.

"A-anyway, um." Sarah clears her throat and holds up her phone, a sly smile playing at her lips. "I have updates about the trip idea."

Rob's eyes light up. Sarah had already told him and her uncle Paul about Mel, for obvious reasons, and she's so happy she told them when she did. It would kill her to have a secret this big and not be able to share with people she's close to. Rob and Paul are both in their midthirties, like her auntie Joy, but they're infinitely cooler than she is. Sarah feels she can talk to them about anything, so the moment she decided she wanted to spend a weekend in New York City with Mel for their six-month anniversary, she ran it by Rob first. "She said she's down," Sarah says, squealing. "I'm amped. I don't know how I'm gonna convince my dad to let me cross the border, though."

"Say you're coming to visit me," Rob says with a shrug. "That we're, uh, going . . . for a weekend in the city and we want you to come."

"Well, that's suspicious." Sarah snorts. "My mom already might think . . . A-actually, never mind."

Rob's brows furrow instantly. Sarah thinks he looks a lot like Grandma Nancy this way. "Might think what?" he asks, then gasps, "Wait, do they know?"

Sarah gives an exaggerated shudder. "N-no." She feels uneasy right away. Her mom . . . Well, her mom isn't the most welcoming of people. She says homophobic things sometimes without thinking. Or, well, if Sarah is being honest, she says it while thinking, too. And she always seems to save the worst comments for when Sarah is within earshot. Sarah really doesn't understand why. After all, she doesn't think anything about the way she presents in front of her family gives her away. She sweats in fear at the thought that there's some part of her identity she overlooked that is manifesting itself some other way. Is it her hair? Her choice in socks? Does she maybe go *too* hard for Megan Thee Stallion?

When Rob's concern doesn't let up, Sarah makes a point to shrug and chuckle, as if the act could make her worries fall from her shoulders, too. "It's nothing. They've been fighting a lot, so maybe she's just being the worst on purpose. Don't say anything, though."

"Ooh, trouble in paradise." Rob grimaces.

Sarah glances away, a nervous chuckle rolling off her lips. "P-please. It was barely paradise to begin with. They, like, never see eye-to-eye and, just . . . I mean, that's probably why she didn't come this weekend. Didn't want our nosy-ass family to ask questions . . ." She makes eye contact with her uncle, but can't maintain it because it's awkward. *She* feels awkward. She hasn't told anyone about what's been going on at her house. Not even Mel knows the full story.

"Is . . ." Rob stops. Sarah follows his gaze over her shoulder and across the room. Immediately, she spots her auntie Joy standing in the doorway. Even from here, she can see her eyes are puffy and her normally put-together shield has fallen.

Auntie Joy offers a feeble smile before she invites herself in. As she gravitates toward them, the first thing she asks is, "So your dad and your mom are having problems?" while she nods at Sarah. Her voice is a bit gravelly. *Must be all that crying,* Sarah thinks.

Sarah gulps nervously before giving a reluctant nod. "I think so."

Auntie Joy smacks her lips together. A sign of annoyance. Sarah shrinks in her seat.

"Funny," Auntie Joy remarks, and then busies herself with looking around the room.

Rob glances at Sarah before turning to her aunt. "Did you lose something?"

"My phone—my *other* phone," Auntie Joy grunts, as her eyes dart to every open surface. "I've been carrying my personal one around and I think I misplaced my work one. Everywhere I go, I hear ringing, I don't know . . ." She moves about the room in a spacey manner, checking areas she's already looked at and moving things that she moved herself in the first place. It's awkward.

Joy knows she's being awkward.

She just can't seem to get it out of her head. . . .

If Michael and Shelly are having issues, why wouldn't he say anything? Why wouldn't he at least tell *her*?

Joy isn't presumptuous. Obviously, she and her brother don't have the best relationship, and they normally don't communicate about important stuff, but not only is Joy technically a therapist, she also has been through the exact same thing. *He's ashamed of you,* she thinks while she rummages. *He saw what the family did to you and he doesn't want them to do it to him. That's why he's keeping quiet.* She bristles at the thought. It's enough to make her blood run cold. Ooh, he better not think that, especially because one reason the family treated her the way they did after the separation was because of him. All this "family is important" and "family has to be together" bullshit, and his own *wife* didn't come to his mother's seventieth birthday?

Joy shudders. Her temperature rises. She's fucking pissed.

"If any of you find my phone, can you tell me? Thanks," she says. She doesn't wait for a response before leaving.

At first, she's unsure where she's going. Some other room she was in for two seconds at a time, maybe. But by the time she crosses into the main living room, the light cascading through the windows all across the back wall, she realizes she doesn't care about her phone. Nnenna is apparently calling all the party guests, telling them God-knows-what about why it's canceled; her kid is here, her ex-husband is here, everyone in her family is here, oh, except for Michael's son, who's at Oxford, and Michael's wife, who is not at Oxford but is also not here. Hmmm.

Sometimes, God does have perfect timing. Or maybe this is her mom, either in heaven or in the ether of past human consciousness, delivering a message. And that message is: it's time to throw hands.

And then the doorbell rings.

God doesn't want you to be great, she grumbles all the way to the hallway before she calls out, "Who *is* that?"

"Who else, na? It's the reporter!" comes an almost omnipresent response from Auntie Nancy. Her voice all but echoes through the tiles under Joy's feet.

Michael enters the hall, stepping into the entranceway from the staircase. He and Joy lock eyes momentarily before he gestures, feebly, toward the door. "Were you gonna get that?" he asks, though Joy can't help but notice he's technically closer to the doorway.

Typical. She inhales. Exhales.

Michael lets out a sharp breath. "I'll just get it—"

"No, I'll get it. Don't worry yourself," Joy says and makes her way to the door.

Her hand is touching the cool metal of the doorknob when Michael blurts out from behind her, "You left your phone upstairs, by the way." Joy drops her hand and turns slowly to see him waving it in front of her face.

Fight him fight him—

She snatches it immediately. "Thanks."

"I'm trying to get in contact with the hospital, trying to see what the coroner has to say so they can determine cause of death," he goes on. "Uh . . . and then, I guess, a funeral home. We gotta find a funeral home."

"Uh-huh, sure."

"And, um." Michael clears his throat. "I hear David is here."

Every hair on Joy's body stands up, her rage seething through her pores.

The doorbell rings again.

"Oh?" Her voice comes out stronger than she expected it to, and she can tell it surprises Michael by the way he furrows his brow and takes a cautious half-step back. "Yeah, he is. I called him. Jamil was panicking." She was panicking, too, but she refuses to give Michael more ammo than is necessary.

"Well, good of him to show up," Michael replies.

"Why wouldn't he? We're friendly with each other, he's Jamil's dad, they totally speak Italian together when I'm not there, and I'm very cool about it." She was, in fact, not cool about it. "Where's Shelly? Didn't you tell her you were coming for your mom's birthday? Didn't she know it was important?"

Michael's brow furrows deeper, a frown forming on his lips. "Who have you been talking to?"

Joy shrugs. "What? I'm not allowed to ask a question anymore? Why wouldn't she come to your mom's seventieth? Do you think just anyone can reach seventy years old?"

"Okay, it's not a competition, Joy—"

"God, I can't stand you . . . sometimes. Did you know that?"

The doorbell rings again.

Auntie Nancy calls, "Will somebody answer the door? Time is going, o!"

But Michael is frozen at the sound of Joy's voice. His chest rises and falls. He opens and closes his mouth countless times, but doesn't seem to get the words right until, finally, they cascade out like a fountain. "What do you mean you can't stand me? *Me?* Wetin I do you sef?"

She says, "After the separation, you never said *shit* to me except to side with everyone about how stupid you thought I was being," as she narrows her eyes at him. "Mom was wrong about you. You're a fucking coward."

Michael's heart drops. "W-what? Mom . . ." He shakes his head, glowering at her. "What did Mom say about me, except that I'm her son—but *you,* you're her *darling* daughter. Joy amaka, Joy okacha mma—"

"Don't even."

"—and I'm just ejima nna, ejima nna, all the time. She's always treated you better than me! Always. And you're—"

Doorbell, doorbell.

"—really saying this to *me?* Because of what, because my wife isn't here? Which kin' nonsense is that?"

"You can't—"

"And let me be clear, if you'll open your ears to hear it," he presses on, tugging at his own earlobe. "No-bo-dy, Joy, nobody knows why you and David are divorced, o! Nobody!"

Joy frowns. "And why is that a problem? Why is that *your* problem?"

"Because you want to be here, doing yanga, acting like you're better than me. *No.*" He huffs. Joy can see it, the truth he desperately wants to say. It's clawing at his throat. "You don't understand real problems, *real* conflict. You don't." His voice carries such ferocity that it makes Joy tremble with unease. "I'm dealing with things the best way I can, so please, mind your own, okay? For once, mind your own damn business."

Joy stands, shocked. She can hear footsteps approaching, probably coming to see what's going on. Probably coming to see what was inevitable, the not-really-anticipated or well-regarded sibling smackdown.

Or, probably coming to finally get the door.

"You childrens..." Nancy kisses her teeth as she approaches slowly. Her footsteps are less assured. Joy knows she's been listening from the top of the stairs, hearing what she's sure is about to be a catastrophe, and hesitating to interfere. She cautions Michael, "Ekwula ihe ị ga-emesia taba onwegi ụta. You hear me?"

But he shrugs off her words. "Auntie, hapụ m aka, okay? Please."

"Okay, let me just be getting the door first—"

"Because 'Joy amaka' doesn't know what her problem is, so everybody has to suffer, abi?" Michael presses on. From the corner of Joy's eye, she sees James stick his head in from the end of the hallway. Nnenna peeks around the corner from the den, too. Auntie Nancy tries to shimmy around Joy to reach the door, but Michael just keeps going, keeps plowing through his words like a runaway train. "Joy, you know what your problem is? You always have to be in control of everything! Wahala for anybody who doesn't do things your way. You think I'm joking? You picked this house, you picked the DJ, you picked the menu—"

"Because *you* were so available to help?"

"—you picked—oh, so now it's because of *me* that you're like this? Mba, no." He drops his voice and takes a menacing step forward. "Let me tell you very, very clearly, so you never get it twisted again."

She frowns, sticking up her nose as a challenge. "What?"

"The only reason you're behaving like this," he says, "is because you were born a double. Your half is dead and you can't operate on your own. You're overcompensating for Peace being gone."

Oh ... no.

Joy feels the sting of tears immediately. She bites her lip, dead in her resolve not to look like he got to her. But he did, he really did. She would never invoke her sister's name like this. And for what? Some petty argument? He knew this wouldn't be fair for her, and he said it anyway. *He hates you,* she thinks, and it doesn't feel like a lie.

"Ah ... bros," James whispers from the corner. He clicks his tongue against his teeth. "That one too much, o."

"Will you shut up?" Michael snaps at him. When he turns back to Joy, her eyes are watering. Her brother, filled with rage that has finally found its outlet: her.

Auntie Nancy smacks her hands together—

The doorbell rings.

"Ah-ah, this girl." Quickly, Auntie Nancy rushes to the door and pulls it open. She says, "We are bu-sy! Please, give us one minute, na. Ringing door up and down, up and down like money dey inside. Nonsense!" before shutting it firmly again.

Then she smacks her hands together. "Oya, you childrens, that's enough! How can you be saying these things on a day like this?"

Of course, Joy thinks. *On the day my mom just died.*

But then Nancy says, "On the day God has given us a message about my sister's rising," and Joy's mind immediately goes back to the cow.

"I hate it here," she groans, cupping her face in her hands. She narrows her eyes at Michael, chest still rising and falling with anger. "You're not gonna make me feel bad about the fact that I miss my sister. Like, I don't know what you want me to do about that. So I should be punished for it?"

"It's—"

"And you, I mean ... The only time you were responsible was when you married Shelly after you knocked her up, apparently, b-because you said it was the right thing to do." As she speaks, she wipes a tear from her cheek. And another one. And another one.

Michael watches on, stunned. "You weren't even there, so what do you know?"

"*Tch,* I know enough," she scoffs. "And I know because when I got pregnant, everyone told me. Oh my fucking God, it's all anyone said to me. 'You need to get married, you see how things happened with Michael and his wife.' Such *bullshit.* Because *why* was the first thing you told me when I said I was pregnant was to get rid of it?"

Nnenna gasps, bringing her hands to her mouth. She floats into frame, hovering just steps away from Joy's back. "Bros, no . . ." she whispers.

Michael is perfectly still. "That's . . ." He clears his throat, glancing away. "I never said that."

"Are you *dumb* or what?" Joy snaps back. "Because you had more compassion for—for your stupid wife than you did for me, your *sister*, who'd just had to bury her twin, like, a week prior. And that's how it's always been."

Michael kisses his teeth, throwing his arms up in anger. "Joy, please, it's not always about you. God!" He rubs his hands down his face. Restlessness overtakes him. "You know, I never wanted to come to this party in the first place."

Joy rolls her eyes. "Of course, of course—"

"Even Mom left early, somehow," he says. The words shock Joy.

They shock him, too, by the look on his face. Still, he barrels on. "In fact, bless her, she probably decided that today was the last day she could deal with you, Joy. Maybe that's why she died."

"I . . ."

Joy stops. She is completely still.

"W-why would you . . . s-say that?" she whispers. The promise of tears clouds her words.

Michael is stunned into silence. Everyone is. It's only Sarah who has the good sense to rush over and usher her young cousins away. Neither Joy nor Michael realized they were here. The two of them were so locked in their memories, so bound by their harsh words, that they didn't realize the entire family was watching and listening.

Mama, too.

She's probably listening.

The thought haunts Michael immediately. He feels a shiver, a sudden seizing in his chest, and is overcome with the heaviness of his mistake. Of his ugly words. *Why did I say all that?*

He can't think.

Quickly, he turns and leaves. He lets his feet go one in front of the other until they find a place far away from prying eyes.

Why couldn't I have kept quiet?

Walk faster, walk faster.

Mama, o, biko. Ewele iwe . . . I didn't mean it.

He needs to be alone.

I love you. I loved you so much.

— 14 —

It rained outside of Glendale Funeral Home on Albion Road so heavily that they shut the main doors leading into the parking lot, forcing everyone to gather inside whether they liked it or not. Even though all anyone wanted to do was separate and divide and steer clear of one another inside the well-lit viewing room. There were too many people in there, too many aunties and uncles touching its oak tables and reupholstered chairs, talking and visiting as if they'd gotten used to being at a twenty-five-year-old woman's funeral. As if the reason she was dead was no longer strange.

Joy couldn't get over it.

She refused to get over the fact that her sister, her twin, was lying lifeless in a casket at the front of the hall. A *closed* casket. Mom and Dad didn't want anyone to stare at her face for the viewing. "We don't know which kind juju still dey een body," they had said to one another, but to the funeral director, they had sat stone-faced and said it would just be too hard to look at her.

Many people at the hall could've guessed why Peace had died, too. Mom and Dad told everyone it was an accidental overdose of sleeping pills, as was the official cause of death, but deep down inside, the community knew. How could a young girl of twenty-five, healthy and adventurous and beautiful as she was, just up and die like that? It didn't make sense. And besides, as Joy had known herself, Nigerian people were experts at understanding when something was the product of spiritual warfare and when something was just a common cold. And spiritual warfare, the witchcraft, that floated like an omnipresent threat in their lives was more than just an accident. It was the difference between night and day. It was a feeling; a knowing.

Speaking of knowing, Joy *knew* the reason her parents looked so on edge was because Michael still wasn't here yet. She seethed with frustration. Peace was dead so now it was just them two, and he didn't even show up on time for her funeral? She knew her parents wouldn't say anything to him about it. Michael always did things on his own time with little repercussion. It reminded Joy time and time again that he was the favorite.

"Hate him so fucking much," Joy grumbled under her breath. It almost went unnoticed by those around her, the aunties and uncles and cousins who were sitting in quiet contemplation, but it didn't get past David.

"Hate who?" he asked. He was sitting beside her as they watched groups of people saunter by them. Sometimes they stopped and flashed sympathetic looks in Joy's direction. Other times they stared harder, noses scrunched, as they tried to figure out if David was Joy's boyfriend or just a friend from school or work based on how close they were sitting.

Joy noticed and her irritation made her shift closer until she could smell hints of sandalwood in David's cologne. "My stupid brother."

"Michael?" He paused to think. "Isn't he supposed to be here by now?"

Joy nodded so deeply that her dangling earrings rattled. "*Exactly.*" She'd learned not to spill all her vitriol about her family around David, because she was aware it made her sound callous and spiteful, especially today. Instead, she shuddered through a sigh and moved to rest her head on David's shoulder, but didn't because of who she was and where they were.

Normally, she tried to be much more composed. She had many walls and loved to keep them up as high as humanly possible; so high, in fact, that oftentimes *she* didn't even know how to get through them. But she and David had met as friends; she hadn't been on the look-out for intruders, or handsome strangers who pretended to be in her lecture just to say hi to her. By the first laugh, it was too late for her to refortify the breaches. It had been too late for a long time now. He reached for her hand, gave it a squeeze, and she forgot how to resurrect her guard. She forgot why it was necessary.

And then she touched her stomach. The lightest touch still brought the most pressure.

She remembered.

"Do you . . . ?" Joy cleared her throat a few times before she was able to get the words out. She stared at her knees, but she could feel him looking at her. She said she would tell him today, but it was Peace's funeral, for God's sake. Her timing couldn't be worse—like, both Peace's timing of being dead and Joy's timing of being . . .

David gave her hand a squeeze. "Do I what?"

"O-oh, sorry. Did you want a drink?" Joy got to her feet unsteadily. "I can try and find wine, but Nigerian people mostly drink Guinness."

He raised an eyebrow. "At a funeral?"

She cocked her eyebrow as if to say, *What's the problem?* "I'll grab you one. It'll help you blend in," she said with a forced chuckle. "Be right back."

Joy kept her head down as she weaved through the crowd for the refreshment table. She passed aunties who reached out to touch her shoulder, "Ewoh, nwa m, ndo," as well as uncles who exclaimed, pain dripping from their words, "He-ey! Peace is DEAD!" as if they were delivering a sermon on the mountain. Both felt the same in her body: cold, rough, and like she was in the front row at a show she didn't ask to attend.

She reached the refreshment table and grabbed the drinks without asking the attending cousin.

On her way back, she bumped into Michael.

"Joy?"

Her mind went blank, so riddled with grief and confusion that it took her a moment to recognize her own brother.

"You drink Guinness now?" he asked, eyeing the bottles in her hands.

Shut up, shut up, shut up, she thought with unbridled hatred. She wished her brother would just disappear—not die, because how awkward would it be to have to bury two siblings in one day. But at least she had actually liked Peace. *No, that's mean. I'm just sad.*

When she didn't answer, Michael frowned, then scanned the room. "Where's Mom and Dad?"

"I don't know," she grunted.

Again, Michael nodded to the drinks. "Are those both for you—?"

"No, they're not both for me," Joy shot back.

"Okay, okay." He put his hands up in surrender. "Is David around?"

"Why are you always asking about him?" That was a stupid question. Joy knew why. It was because, to be honest, David was always around those days. "Where's Shelly and the kids? Is that why you were late?"

Joy watched as Michael's jaw clenched. He glanced away, squinting momentarily into the crowd as if there were something more interesting there. *I'm right,* Joy thought with a roll of her eyes. *Of course.*

He cleared his throat. "Yeah. Two kids under ten, takes a lot to get everything ready. We would've been on time otherw—"

"Michael, Michael. Ejima nna. He-ey." Auntie Nancy appeared, one hand clutching the funeral program and another holding her black jeweled purse. She reached out for her customary hug. Michael grimaced as he bent slightly to hug Auntie more comfortably. Joy couldn't help but scowl a little. Auntie Nancy was always calling Michael things like "father's face" or "father's twin" just because he looked so much like their dad. It was annoying. Why was it always important enough to comment on?

When Auntie Nancy pulled away and saw Joy, a pained expression came to her face, as if she was out of soothing words to give. "Ndo. Kids."

"Yes, Auntie," Joy muttered.

"Ah-ah. Are you drinking two of those?" She nodded to the bottles in Joy's hands.

"No."

"Auntie," Michael cut in. "Have you seen my parents?"

"Yes, they dey for front," she said, jutting her lips in the direction. Then she sighed loudly before gazing at the both of them. Joy could guess immediately what her auntie was thinking: *Look at them, full-grown adults*, but Joy didn't bother to pursue her doctorate in psychology and now the family will never have a Dr. Okafor like they wanted. Not even Michael had a doctorate. He did engineering work, though, and so he often got out of their auntie's "advice." Or "advise." Auntie Nancy had always used both terms interchangeably.

Suddenly, Auntie Nancy reached out for Michael's shoulder. "Michael, Michael," she chorused with a sadness in her voice. "Take care of your sister, eh? You hear? A sister is a precious thing, and my sister has done well for you. She has, o. She has done well for you and her husband. Now she and this your own sister are grieving, because to lose a child is hard. It is very hard."

"Yes, Auntie."

"And be kind to your mom, as well," Auntie Nancy went on. "She has just one child now. Eh, one *less* child. It's not right."

"Yes, Auntie." Michael bristled. It was so slight that Joy wasn't sure if she was imagining it.

"And you, Joy." She turned to her. "Take heart. Peace is watching from heaven. She is with God now."

Joy forced her face to show any other emotion but irritation. She wanted to roll her eyes so badly. *Peace is not with God*, she thought. *How many nights did I pray for Him to keep her here and He did nothing?* She stopped before she said or thought something horrible. Something sacrilegious. Something that would make her situation worse.

"Okay," Joy said carefully and turned to leave. She knew that she had to be gracious with God now because she wanted to beg Him one favor. A big one. Please, if He could . . . help her. Fix this. Anything.

Dear God . . . or whatever.

Joy gravitated to the front of the room. She could see the casket; she could see her parents.

I need a favor. If You can hear me this time . . .

Mom was bent down, her hands clasped in prayer, by the side of the casket. Dad was standing watch, his arms staunchly at his side. The corners of his mouth were pulled tightly as if he couldn't bear to frown; couldn't bear to show emotion. As Joy approached, she heard the heaviness of his breathing. She placed a hand on his back. He didn't move.

"Dad?" she whispered.

"Joy." He exhaled and glanced at her. "Go be with your mama." It wasn't harsh; it was the only way he knew how to cope. Joy understood that much about her father, anyway. He was always asking them to check up on their mom. See how she was, how she was feeling.

Joy did as she was told, setting the two drinks off to the side, as she kneeled beside her mom. Mom didn't look at her once, but Joy could see a steady stream of tears rolling down her already damp face. The makeup she'd carefully applied that morning had run in streaks down her neck. Joy reached out, placing a hand on her back and rubbing in soft circles, trying to soothe her mom's constant shuddering.

Joy knew there was nothing she could've said or done now, anyway. Some people said being together is good enough, but what was this? Both of her parents could barely look at her because she looked so much like Peace. How could they console one daughter when they'd lost the other? It didn't make sense to Joy.

In fact, none of this did.

She sighed. Her shoulders rose and fell with her breath, and as she gazed at the closed casket, she found herself wondering if she and Peace would have continued to look identical as they aged. As children, they did. Beautiful oval eyes, lush brown skin, high cheekbones, and soft jaws. But as teenagers, Peace had opted to go natural, swapping her relaxer and flat iron for vegan hair butters, while Joy spent every month in the salon getting her hair pressed, weaved, or braided. That was where the differences began. Peace loved rock music. She was fond of screamo for a hot second, even though everyone liked to pretend that phase never happened. Joy was always on that R&B tip, pretending she could sing just to impress the boys.

Peace loved egusi soup. Joy, ogbono.

Peace was obsessed with anime. Joy used to watch soap operas with her mom.

Peace was her father's daughter, stubborn and rebellious. Joy, her mother's. Obedient. Glamorous.

They were so different. *So* different.

It was only a year ago that Peace decided she wanted to go to Mbiri, their father's village in Nigeria. Though Michael was born in Nigeria, Joy and Peace were born when the family emigrated to Canada, and Joy could tell that sometimes their dad felt as if he wasn't doing a good enough job teaching his kids about their culture. So when Peace said she wanted to follow Papa back home, he jumped at the chance to show her all the roadside suya spots he loved.

They had only spent a week there before detouring to Lagos. It was just a week, and . . . Joy was wrapped up in her own life at the time, her own very specific quarter-life struggles, like *should* she stop having sex with her best friend? Wasn't that ruining things? And should she have gotten braids for the summer or go with twists? Stuff like that. So all Joy remembered of that time was Peace texting updates, like, *Just bought suya, almost got run over lol* and *Seen a goat at the side of the road and I thought of you specifically!* Nothing that would've alerted anyone to any trouble.

But when Papa and Peace had arrived back home, Papa was furious and Peace was acting funny. Clutching her stomach, she complained that she'd been feeling sick since the plane ride. She would sleep a lot, or try to, anyway. The tossing and turning was out of control. Joy could even hear the rustling in her room across the hall. She also heard Mama and Papa talking in hushed tones, in rushed and frantic pidgin, when they thought everyone had gone to bed.

They'd said, "Witch."

Joy was confused.

They'd said, "Witch, that witch did something to her."

Joy didn't believe it.

Or, she did a little, but she didn't at the same time.

Growing up in her household, within her culture, of course she believed in things like that. It was hard not to, when supernatural occurrences tended to happen all the time. The elders in her community held a reverence for things like that, witches and unseen powers—juju. They always warned against toying with powers that couldn't be easily understood.

Even though Joy herself couldn't have said she'd ever seen anything herself, the fear was embedded in her. Her *and* Peace. And her sister wasn't an idiot. She wouldn't dare provoke something or someone when she knew what the repercussions might've been, would she? Besides, "The witch did something to her" sounded so vague. What did that even mean?

Back then Peace had spent more and more of her days in bed. Her hair, which she used to keep so soft and proper, hadn't been detangled in months. She was missing work. Her friends, who had tried to keep her up to date on who was dating who, had stopped calling. Even Michael, who had spent many days with Peace bringing her pepper soup and ginger tea, had stopped coming by as often. He probably felt there was nothing more he could do. He probably hated seeing her waste away.

Joy had asked her, "What's going on?" and Peace just shrugged and laughed and said things like, "My stomach hurts? I don't know."

"Your stomach's been hurting for months." Joy frowned. "Are you sick or something?"

Peace shrugged. "I'onno."

"Why don't you go see a doctor?"

"They won't let me" was her reply, as her eyes floated to the top of Joy's head. Past her face. Toward the door.

Their parents' bedroom was across the hall. When Joy realized that must've been what Peace meant, she was heated. How could they be so selfish? Their daughter hadn't eaten properly, been outside to see friends, or attended school regularly since she got back from Nigeria. Didn't they care at all?

That night, while Peace tossed and turned in her sleep, Joy confronted her parents as best she could. Which meant, of course, that she pretended she was only mildly concerned with what was going on.

Her dad was sitting with the remote clutched firmly in his grasp while he flipped channels on the downstairs TV. He looked tense, unapproachable. Mama sat silently, as she often did.

Joy asked, carefully, "Why can't we take Peace to a doctor?"

No one stirred.

She asked again, her voice rising slightly, "Peace should see a doctor. She's . . . I think she's really sick."

Papa snorted, indignantly. "Yes. Why won't she be? Na curse dey do am."

Joy stood still.

"A curse?" she echoed.

Mama slapped her hands together over and over again, as if washing them of something that just wouldn't go away.

"How?" Joy asked, looking at both her parents. "What happened to her?"

Silence.

Mama shifted in her seat, her frown deepening.

Joy gulped, swallowing down her nervousness, and spoke in a stern voice, "She's my *sister*. I wanna know what happened."

Papa glanced at her. His lip turned up in a sneer, at first unwilling to bend. Then he said, "No be, eh, that one witch for village. Papa Onyemaechi's daughter."

"Your papa told her not to go there. Eh? He told her," Mama piped up. She kissed her teeth, cocking her head to the side in frustration. "But your sister, she won't listen. You oyinbo children never listen."

Joy had heard that word too often growing up. She was Nigerian when it was most convenient to her parents, but any time she didn't heed a warning or spoke up for herself or dared to go against the norm, she was oyinbo. And now this otherness had gotten her sister in trouble.

Still, Joy blurted out, "There has to be a—a logical reason, though. Did she get bitten by a bug? Maybe it's malaria."

The more she spoke, the tenser her parents got, until finally Mama snapped, clicking her tongue against her teeth and shaking her head. "Mechi ọnụ! Malaria wetin?" And then she said, "Is it malaria that turned your cousin into a goat?"

Joy's brows furrowed.

Naturally, she had heard stories of family members being turned into farm animals through wicked deeds and witchy dreams before. It wasn't completely uncommon in her community, where generations had grown up understanding these incidents weren't fiction. She'd had an aunt who had turned into a yam after taking money from someone she wasn't supposed to. The first yam in the family, actually.

"Wait, what? Which cousin?" Joy asked, her frown deepening. "Is it—is it a different cousin, a different goat?"

"Cousin—"

"Shh, no." Papa held out his hand, shaking his head firmly. Mama buttoned her lips at once.

Joy groaned. "I'm sorry, *which* cousin is a goat now? It's hard to keep track. You guys are always saying someone picked up money on the road and now they're a cow."

Mama slapped her hands together again. "You see? Life in the village, e no dey easy."

"Mom—"

"If you think say na because of me and your mama? No, o," Papa cut in, indignant. "For this your sister matter, na juju dey hold am. Een spirit no go 'gree see doctor.'"

"W-what? How?" Joy was confused. Peace had insisted that their parents wouldn't let her go to a doctor. Her eyes had floated first to Joy's forehead and then to the space behind her head. She was sure Peace was referring to their parents' room across the hall. She swore it. But now, thinking back, maybe Peace was looking at something that wasn't there.

She went back to Peace that night, whose forehead was dotted with sweat as she tossed and turned in her bed. "Who won't let you see a doctor? Mom and Dad, right?" Joy asked. She was willing to hold out that this was just a simple medical problem; that it was something that could be fixed with proper medication, some pepper soup, or bathing with carbolic soap.

But when Peace rolled over and looked into her eyes, Joy stopped believing. Or maybe she had started believing in something else. The air shifted around them. It grew stale; hollow. Peace's face twisted as if she wanted to cry but couldn't muster the strength. She whispered, "I don't know them," with a break in her voice. Her words lilted across her lips. Joy's heart sank as Peace repeated over and over again, "I don't know them, I don't know them. . . ."

For the first time, Joy panicked. *What if she becomes a goat?*

A week later, they finally took Peace kicking and screaming to the hospital. She was feral with a kind of energy Joy had never seen from her before. Soft, beautiful, rebellious Peace sneered at the doctors who tried to take her temperature and kicked at the legs of tables that held instruments to take blood. Joy couldn't believe it. *Goat-like behavior,* she thought to herself, but not in the fun way siblings normally tortured each other. This time, it seemed a bit too real.

At the doctor's, there was no malaria diagnosis. There was no infectious disease that was eating away at her. "She just needs sleep," the doctor told them, regretfully. Maybe he could tell from then that Peace was a lost cause.

It was silent, and then: "She said she's seeing things," Joy told him without a sideways look at her parents. She could practically feel their disappointment stewing in her peripheral. "She said people she doesn't know visit her."

Mama inhaled sharply, "Eziokwu!" and hung her head. If there was one thing her mom couldn't stand, it was when anyone knew anything about her family. Mama was known to show up in Nigeria without telling her relatives or friends about her travel plans, and by the time they thought to ask when she was leaving again, she'd already touched down in Canada.

"Hallucinations are common with sleep deprivation," the doctor explained. He filled out a prescription, shoved it into their hands. It wasn't his problem anymore.

The pills didn't help, of course. Peace's night terrors only got worse. In the daytime, she would open her eyes and lie perfectly still, as if she was afraid to move. As if she wasn't really there at all.

It went on like that for a year. God, was it a year? Joy struggled to remember. Her sister had been slipping away for a while, and her parents didn't know what to do. Pastors would come and pray over her. They'd slather her in anointing oil until she looked like a slightly burnt puff-puff, but it was no use. The medication increased, and Peace took more and more of it each day. Still, she stopped sleeping, stopped talking.

Eventually, stopped breathing.

No, it didn't make sense to Joy then, and it didn't now as she gazed upon her sister's casket, either.

At the front of the funeral home, Joy had leaned into her mom's shoulder, pressing her cheek against her mom's arm. She wanted to whisper that she was sorry and she was really sad, too, but that she was still here. And she wouldn't go anywhere. In the end, all she could do was whisper: "I'm gonna go sit down now," before rising to her feet and collecting her drinks from where she had hidden them.

Her mom barely moved a muscle as Joy slipped through the growing crowd, past her aunts and uncles—past her brother. They locked eyes momentarily. She wasn't sure what she saw in his gaze, but she was too prickly to care. She remembered how he distanced himself more and more from Peace the sicker she had gotten. She didn't buy his reasons, that Miles had the flu one week or Sarah was starting up dance classes another. *He probably sensed it somehow*, she told herself, *that it was witchcraft.*

When she returned to the far corner of the hall with David, she felt some ease. At least for a second. "Sorry, that took forever," she offered, clearing her throat while she handed him one of the bottles. They cheersed. She let the bitter liquid touch the tip of her tongue before she changed her mind and pulled the bottle away. *Don't be stupid, Joy.*

He watched her hesitate. "You don't like it?" he asked.

"W-what?" Joy's voice wavered. God, why was it so hard for her to appear casual? "N-no, I do. I just—I can't drink it."

"You *can't*?"

"I just don't really, uh . . ." Joy cleared her throat.

Truthfully, she had only found out a few days ago. About the baby. What was she supposed to do, tell him *now*? When she hadn't even told her parents—her parents who were silently grieving their daughter?

No, she thought, *that's selfish*. This wasn't the right time. As she looked out into the crowd of relatives, their shock and sorrow almost palpable from back here, she wondered if the right time would ever come. If God had a plan, the way her parents said He did. If He didn't sleep, the way Mom was convinced He wouldn't.

Then why is Peace dead? Why didn't God save her? What kind of fucked-up plan is that?

Joy took a deep breath. She knew she wouldn't get an answer.

"Cheers again?" she said and reached over to clink bottles with David.

He frowned. "I think that's bad luck."

"Oh?" she said, and then chugged the beer.

— 15 —

Alice Karim had never been treated this way before. Can you imagine! Her, of all people? First, she gets a call from her mother while she was in the middle of her nail appointment. These acrylics don't attach themselves, you know. She had to ask her nail tech to hold up her phone so her face recognition unlock could work. By the time she finally answered the phone, her mom was a split second from hanging up. "Mummy, what's going on? I'm at a nail appointment," she said in an accent so transatlantic that even she wasn't sure where she'd picked it up from.

"Eh, Alice," her mother replied. Alice had to lean in, squinting through her false eyelashes as if the act could make her hear better. "Alice, you must do me a favor."

"Mummy, I'm not going to pick up goat meat."

"Forget that one, na!" Her mother kissed her teeth. "There's *big* news, o! One auntie in our community has died."

Alice bit back a groan. How was this big news? People literally died every day. "Okay, and . . . ?"

"And she's coming back! People are saying she's coming back."

"What?"

"Jesu . . ." Her mother crooned over and over again, murmuring prayers under her breath.

"Mummy, I don't think I understand," Alice said again. "*Who* is coming back?"

"The woman who died, of course. Onyinye Mary. She is being resurrected—praise *God*! You remember her, don't you? She had twins and na juju kill one of them. The other married oyinbo. The boy is an engineer."

Alice frowned, trying to get an image in her head. As usual, none of her mom's descriptions helped place Onyinye Mary amidst the literal hundreds of Nigerian aunties she'd met in her life. "An engineer?" she echoed, thinking. For some reason, that was the one thing her brain latched on to. "W-well, okay. Okay, hold on, Mummy. I'm just finishing my nails. Can I call you back?"

"No," her mother said. "Time is going! I'll text you the address and you must go interview the woman's sister *now*-now."

Alice rolled her eyes. "And how do you know this is real? What if her sister is just lying for the publicity?"

"You see you," her mom grunted. "Her sister received the prophecy from one cow. It wasn't just, you know, it wasn't just normal dreams, o."

"Oh my goodness. A cow?" Alice let out a sharp exhale. If she could rub her temples, she would. "Mummy, AJAfrika is a serious program, o. Not something for your friends to be playing with."

"Taa!" her mother snapped. "Serious wetin? Who is playing? If you don't believe me, just go to the house and hear the prophecy yourself." And she hung up. Hung up! Alice had *never* been treated this way before! Just three weeks ago, she was having dinner in Dubai with her husband and his school friends on a yacht, being entertained in three different languages, and sipping the freshest juice she'd ever tasted. And now she was about to drive down to—where, exactly? She checked her phone and cringed. "Isn't this near *Barrie*?" And interview a woman who apparently got word that her dead sister was going to spring up from the ground like a daisy because a cow gave her a prophecy.

Insanity!

She was used to some degree of sensationalism, being both a media maven with a two-time award-winning news show (the awards came from her husband's companies, but no one had to know that) and being a Nigerian, but this was out of control. Still, she made the long drive all the way to this mini mansion where, allegedly, a woman was supposed to come back from the dead on Easter.

She rolled up with just one cameraman, a trusted freelancer named Tosin who she loved because he never asked for money for new equipment. He was one of those "tech buffs," so he just bought what he liked the moment it came on the market. *Everyone should be like that,* she'd thought. *Self-sufficient.*

She curled one manicured hand and rang the doorbell. And she waited.

Tosin glanced at her. "Are you sure this is the right house?"

"It has to be," she said as she looked around. "There's no other house out here..."

She knocked. Rang the doorbell again. Nothing.

Tosin shifted his weight from his right leg to his left. Impatiently, he took a step forward, as well, and rang the bell. Suddenly, on the other side of the door, they could hear movement. Voices at first, and then footsteps. Then louder voices. Yelling. Harsh words. Tosin gave Alice a weary glance. "Should we come back some other time?" he whispered.

"No. This cow's prophecy might be time-sensitive," she said with a snort. From the look of shock on Tosin's face, she was reminded that she forgot to brief him on what exactly was going on here. "Well—"

Finally, the door flew open.

Alice opened her mouth, ready to dip into her regular greeting, but the woman staring back at her didn't look very welcoming at all. She had a severe look about her, as if she was caught in the middle of the argument Alice and Tosin were just hearing. The woman said, "We are bu-sy! Please, give us one minute, na. Ringing door up and down, up and down like money dey inside. Non-sense!" and shut the door immediately.

Alice's mouth dropped open at once. She was at a loss for words, and she was *never* at a loss for words! She's a two-time award-winning—

"Madam, what do we do?" Tosin asked, his voice small, else the hellish woman on the other side would hear him. "We drove all this way."

"These village people," Alice grunted with a sneer, pushing her hair off her shoulder. "Don't they know who I am? 'Give us one minute,' my ass. I will give them two minutes because this is a holy weekend."

At first, she and Tosin stood on the porch, listening. The voices eventually stopped and they could no longer feel the presence of people on the other side of the door. When they rang the doorbell again, they got nothing. Alice couldn't believe it. One phone call from her husband and these people would probably be *begging* her to come in. They should've had more respect, especially when their story about the cow and the resurrection was so ridiculous that any other journalist, award-winning or not, would've *never* made the trip all the way to almost-Barrie (Barrie, for God's sake!) to validate it.

Now Tosin makes his way to the car to sit inside and wait. Alice stays on the porch, occasionally pressing her ear to the door, wondering if someone will come by and finally let her in. Minutes pass like this. She is two steps away from getting back into her car and making a promise to never drive this far north on Highway 400 again when the door flies open.

There stands a man, bald but with a sense of authority that even her husband would take note of. It makes her stop and pay attention.

"Are you Alice?" he calls to her. Without even waiting for her response, he beckons her forward. Quickly, she and Tosin make their way over, all while the man is saying, "Oya, fast-fast, let's go." It's only when she gets to the front step and he takes a good look at her face, at how her lipstick and eyeshadow make her face pop, that he finally apologizes for the delay. *Men. All the same,* she thinks with a smirk as she steps through the front door.

The luxury of the inside is enough for her to forgive these ... well, how much longer can she refer to them as village people when this house could easily buy seven, eight villages or more? It's beautiful, regal, elegant, outstanding—all things she's used to.

"I'm James Olubisi. Head pastor at New Apostles in Pentecostal

Glory African Church." The bald man reaches out his hand for a shake. He shakes with Tosin first before clasping Alice's hand with vigor. "You are welcome here. It's my in-law that passed away today."

"Alice Karim," she says, then gestures to Tosin. "And this is my cameraman, Tosin. Sorry for your loss."

"It's no problem. She is with the Lord." Then he drops his octave a bit and says, "And she will be back on Sunday anyway."

"Mmmm." Alice isn't sure what to say to that yet. "So where should we set up? I'm thinking a neutral background . . ." She takes off her shoes and tiptoes farther into the house as she speaks. James doesn't stop her. *Perfect,* she thinks, *because I really want to know how many rooms this place has.*

She makes it into the living room before she's stopped by that woman—oh God, it's that same woman who shut the door in her face earlier. "Alice!" the woman exclaims, grabbing her by the forearm and leading her in the opposite direction, around the corner, and to what looks like a den or an office. "No vex, abeg. You know how families are," she tells her. Alice assumes the woman is referring to the eccentric yelling and dramatics she heard earlier.

"It's fine," Alice lies.

"Ah, no, o. Please. Sit." The woman gestures to a lounge chair that doesn't look comfortable at all. Alice scuttles over, leaving Tosin to settle awkwardly on an oak bench that looks like it's more art piece than chair. "My name is Amarachi Nancy. You can call me Nancy. Or Auntie." She chortles at that. "I'm happy you came today, eh. Welcome. Please, anything to drink?"

"Actually, I was hoping we could just get to it," Alice interrupts before Tosin can start asking for water or something. "I'm a very busy woman and, I'm sorry, but I'm not sure I truly understand what's going on here." The way her voice shifts, the way she leans forward and crosses her legs—all of it is to show this Nancy woman that she's not playing around. She might be doing a favor for her mom, but that doesn't mean she's willing to air any old crock on her TV show. "My understanding is your sister passed away this morning."

"Yes."

"And she . . . It was confirmed she had no pulse, correct?"

"Yes."

"And then you received a premonition about her coming back?"

"Are you sure you don't want anything to drink?"

"We're fine—"

"Let's be setting up the camera." Nancy nods to Tosin. Something about her impatience, the strictness in her voice, makes Tosin get up right away, murmur a soft "Yes, madam," and begin to unfurl his equipment.

Alice gives a press-on smile. "Of course."

"And when will this interview be on the TV?" Nancy asks.

"We air nighttime updates, so in a few hours, most likely," Alice explains. "And then everything is reshared to our YouTube page within an hour, pushed across our social media, you know. The usual."

Nancy says, "Good. Because we need to tell more people about the vigil," and Alice's brows furrow with a million and one unexplained things. "Oya, let's begin the interview. Where is James? He's my son-in-law. I would ask my niece and my nephew, but they are fighting like chickens today. Everywhere, just *gpak-gpak-gpak*. Stubborn people. James!"

James and Nancy sit side-by-side on the opposite sofa while Tosin positions them for the camera. He gives them pointers: don't look here, make sure you focus there, don't talk over each other too much, and so on. From the staunch way James nods, jutting out his lips and avoiding eye contact, Alice knows he's probably planning to do the exact opposite of everything Tosin recommends.

Alice does quick touch-ups with her compact as she tells them, "We'll fix a lot of it in editing, so don't worry too much about saying the right thing the first time." She puts her makeup away, says a silent prayer that this isn't a disaster, and cues Tosin.

He gives her a thumbs-up. "Three . . . two . . ."

And she launches into it, full smile and all. "Hello. It's Alice Karim with AJAfrika TV, and I'm joined by two members of the community who have reported a very interesting development in their family." She turns to Nancy and James. "Why don't you two introduce yourselves?"

James manages to get out an "I'm—" before Nancy takes over, calmly but with precision—and, in a new accent to rival Alice's, says, "My name is Amarachi Nancy Akintola. We are from Imo state. Well, my papa was from Imo. Anyway, this is my . . . son-in-law, James Olubisi." She flashes him a regrettable look. "He is married to my daughter, Nnenna. We're all here this weekend."

After a beat, Alice lets out a nervous chuckle. "A-all right." She clears her throat. "Nancy and James. Tell us about the events that have happened here."

James takes a breath. "Well—"

"Well," Nancy cuts in. "My dear elder sister's birthday is today. It's Good Friday. We thank God. But, instead of celebrating her birth, in fact . . . my dear sister has died this very morning."

Alice puts on her best shocked face. "My condolences."

"Thank you, my dear." Nancy nods slowly as she recalls the memory. "My sister was a very vibrant woman, so I thought, *Ah-ah, Amarachi . . . this your sister, for her to just die like that, no be wetin kill Papa George for home?*"

Alice's eyebrow twitches but her smile doesn't falter. *Our people and stories, eh. I swear to God. Who is Papa George?!*

"Anyway," Nancy goes on. "I was crying. Of course. This is my elder sister. You understand? Nwanne m nwanyị na ndụ a. I said, 'Mba, ọ bụghị eziokwu.' Well, you don't speak Igbo anyway. But I couldn't believe it. My husband was driving behind the ambulance and I was praying, 'Chineke, o, God! Gịnị mere? Na me you hate pass?' And my husband was just driving like this, just driving. And then we saw the cow."

Here's the story, Alice thinks. She tries her absolute hardest not to roll her eyes. "Tell us about the cow."

James tries again to get a word in but Nancy places her hand on his shoulder, a strong and firm "don't try it" if Alice has ever seen one. "When I was a girl in the village, I saw one brown cow just like this one. This cow was, eh . . . It would be with the other cows and then, *gbam*, it would disappear. Just like that! Coming and going, and coming and going. But my papa said once that it was a special mmụọ. You don't know what that is. It's a spirit. Like something was holding the cow. You understand? So when my husband was driving and we were going, I saw the cow, I said, 'Ah-ah, na you be this?' And that's when God gave me the message. When me with the cow were looking at each other, Chineke tinye ozi n'obi m. Inside . . ." Nancy recounts the story with candor, using her hands to illustrate where she was in relation to the cow. Alice watches her as if she's told it a million times before. To some degree, Alice figures Nancy must have had to do a lot of convincing with her family for them all to be on board. And they were, weren't they?

Actually, now that Alice thinks about it, it's strange that no one else has come in to join the interview.

Alice nods along as Nancy's story rounds out. "And what does the rest of the family think?"

Nancy frowns. Scowls, more like. "What?"

"Is, um . . ." Alice clears her throat. "Your sister's children must have something to say about this. Can I speak to them?" As she turns, she spots a huddle of kids by the doorway peeking in: a small boy with wide, curious eyes and a girl who looks as if she has questions of her own. When Alice makes eye contact with them, they run.

For a moment, Nancy looks as if she'll refute Alice's claim that Mary has children and that they have opinions, but she softens, eventually allowing herself to show the smallest of smiles. "Yes. Um. James." She turns to him. "Go and tell Joy to come."

James bristles. It's so visible that Alice is sure the camera has picked it up.

Instead of getting to his feet, James calls out, "Yemi!" until the girl from before comes running. "Yemi, go and call your auntie Joy. Tell her to come."

"Yes, Dad," the girl says and speeds off.

Nancy spends the time before Joy shows up recounting small details about the way this premonition entered her body—"It was like the message was already there! She will rise on Easter!"—but Alice is reserving her final thoughts for when she meets this daughter. Surely, not everyone in the family is enamored with this story of divine messages. There has to be something under the surface here.

When Alice sets her eyes on Joy, she sees it immediately.

It's painted across Joy's face; it's etched into her features, the way her eyes take in Alice perched on the chair, and the way she leans against the doorframe, arms crossed, refusing to enter.

It's fatigue. It's grief, actually. *Oh, yes,* Alice reminds herself. *Something tragic* did *happen here. Something really sad.*

"Hello," Joy says in a voice that betrays her right away. It's then that Alice realizes she's the reasonable one in the family; that amidst all this talk of a resurrection, there are still people here who are grieving a real loss.

That's the story I want to tell, Alice thinks.

But before she can open her mouth to invite Joy to the opposite sofa and ask about her late mother, Nancy interrupts. "Joy, tell her about the cow."

Joy takes one step in before finally crossing the room to sit beside her brother-in-law. She rubs her forehead, uttering, "What do you want to know?"

"A-actually," Alice cuts in. "Joy. We've heard the story from your aunt already, about how this tragedy seems to have taken on a new life for you."

Joy purses her lips and nods quickly.

"What would this resurrection mean to you?"

"S-sorry?"

"If your . . . mother were to come back," Alice begins carefully. "What would that mean for you?"

What a question. Even as Alice hears herself ask it, she knows it's crass, opportunistic, and horrid. She'd hate to be asked a question like this, but hey, that's why she's a two-time (husband-sponsored) award-winning host. *My job, o, ee no easy at all,* she tells herself.

Joy takes a shallow breath. Her eyes wander to the ceiling while she thinks. The stilted silence in the room makes everyone antsy. Alice can see how Nancy's jaw grows tighter and how James's eyes bulge and bulge with the worry that maybe Joy will say the wrong thing.

"I think . . ." Joy mutters. She speaks slowly and carefully as if she'll lose the words otherwise. "I think that . . . I do not know what's happening today."

Alice's brows furrow. "S-sorry?"

"I think I'm confused and I'm not really processing anything," Joy goes on. "I think that my mom is . . . my mom *was* . . . someone really s-special." She purses her lips, swallows, to stop from crying. Her voice wavers as she continues, "And I think that, because of that, we . . . want to hope so much. And that's normal, to want to hope. So I'm not—I mean, I don't . . . I don't know. I love my mom a lot. And I know, if she was still here, walking around, she'd probably . . . really appreciate the fact that her family all showed up for her like this—"

"Okay, ah-ah, please." James sits forward. He flashes a scowl at Joy before turning to Alice. "Can we cut that? Abeg. Joy is a therapist, so she's always talking such yama-yama."

"Oh!" Nancy cuts in. "If we drive now, I can show you where the cow appeared to me."

Alice puts on a forced smile. "I, uh . . ." Joy says nothing, but Alice can see in her eyes that she wants to scream.

— 16 —

David is still processing. He feels as if he's been processing a lot of things for a very long time. For example, the separation. About two years ago, when Joy asked him if that's what he wanted, he said, "Wait, let me think," and spent days agonizing over what she meant. Some days, he felt like nothing had changed from the first day he met her. Other days, like that day, he was very sure things had shifted without him realizing. He had come to know there was little room in Joy's world for anything but chaos. And righteousness, always.

Still, no one in his family had been separated, or divorced for that matter, and his parents didn't really look upon things like that too lightly. His dad always said, "You're supposed to know the first time," with regards to picking the right girl to marry, and also choosing fruit at the grocery store. Well, at first, David was very sure. When he and Joy got married, they were twenty-five and expecting a baby, he was newly in law school, and he imagined his life would look incredibly different ten years down the line. Mostly, he thought he would be very rich and own a yacht and private island by thirty through a combination of overcharging wealthy clients and stock trading. Needless to say, that didn't happen.

Raising a kid is hard. And Jamil was easy, considering some of the horror stories he heard from his cousins who had children young, too. He loved his son a lot, loved how bright and vivacious he was, and how he always got very, very interested in things. Not just one "very"; always two.

And he and Joy got each other. They really did. Ever since they were in school together, he was astonished at how easily he could talk to her. How interesting she was, how much she cared about other people, how funny she could be without trying. He had never been so taken with anyone in his life. He hasn't since. She changed so much for him and about him without her even knowing, and soon, it became as if every goal he'd had for his life shifted. Jamil often got seasick, so the yacht pipe dream had to go. Many dreams dissipated this way. For a long time, he figured this was it for him. This was his life, and it was different than anything he'd ever dreamed it could be, but he was happy, somehow.

But no one is the same person they are at twenty-five. Very quickly, he realized Joy was beholden to her family in a way he didn't quite understand and couldn't have known before. "You always pick them over me," he would tell her, first as a joke, and then much more seriously when the reality set in that there was some truth there.

Joy would frown or scoff, saying, "No, I don't. Besides, you're my family, too. Or did you forget?"

"I didn't forget," he'd tell her. "And it's not the same thing. You know it isn't."

Over time, for someone who was always so good at holding space for others, Joy became closed off, boxed in, and quick to say "You're wrong about that" every chance she got.

So it wasn't a surprise for them. The divorce. For everyone else, it made little to no sense. Including Jamil.

Especially Jamil.

Jamil and his dad are camped up in his room with a pack of Briscola cards and a bag of chips. A perfect way to ignore the chaos going on

downstairs. Auntie Nnenna came upstairs earlier to ask if his dad
wanted to talk to the reporter before or after they went to track down
the cow, and his dad told her, "I cannot stress to you enough that I
have no idea what is actually going on here, so no."

To which Auntie Nnenna replied: "Ugh. You sound just like your
wife. Better be careful, o."

Now, *that* made Jamil happy.

In fact, he thinks maybe this is like a Christmas miracle, his parents
being back in the same house for more than half an hour, but except
not on Christmas. So an Easter miracle. Well, a different kind of miracle than the resurrection of Jesus. He sucks in his lips to stop from
smiling. A part of him thinks this might be his grandma's spirit's doing.
Yes, maybe she dropped the ball on stopping his mom and his uncle
Michael from saying horrible things to each other, but with this, everything is evened out.

Quickly, Jamil drops a baton card atop his dad's knight of coins and
says, "Brisc! That's mine."

"What?" his dad gasps as Jamil collects the pile, setting it with his
other winnings. "No, no, aspetta, scusa, com'è briscola already?"

"Papà, sono bastoni, oh my Godddd," Jamil snickers, holding up
the chosen suit for his dad to see. "I probably won. Why are you so
bad at this game?"

"How do you know I'm not letting you win on purpose?"

"I—" Jamil's smile immediately disappears. "Wait, *what*?"

The bedroom door opens.

Joy enters, two phones clutched in her hands. She waves one, says,
"Found my work phone," and quickly tosses it atop her luggage. The
fact that she'll probably forget it's there in a minute is not lost on her,
but she just can't deal with all the buzzing and the ringing.

This time, it's her personal phone going off with tons of messages.
Very odd switch, she tells herself as she swipes it open. Texts upon
texts upon texts from numbers she's saved—Auntie Tessy, Auntie
Meg, Auntie Maureen—and from numbers she's never seen before

in her life. "What the . . . ?" She sighs out as she navigates her way to the bed.

"Mom," Jamil pipes up. "Do you wanna play Brisc?"

"No. I'm no good," she says absently. "When I used to play, I thought I was winning until I realized I had no aces for points, so. You should count before you celebrate."

"Oh my God . . . *what*?" Jamil gasps again, his mouth hanging open in shock. He glances at his dad and then quickly rushes to count how many points he has, muttering, "Like, did I even *win* or has this all been a lie?"

Joy's phone pings again. These messages are getting out of control.

"Who keeps texting you?" she hears David ask from across the room.

"Mmm." She's quickly losing the energy to speak, but what she would've said if she could is: "Aunties from WhatsApp who've heard about the vigil and are starting to see the coverage on Alice's show, I guess."

She scrolls through each message, all asking if what they heard through the grapevine is true; that Mama Mary is dead and that her sister had a premonition about her coming back. When Joy takes a closer look, she sees half these messages aren't even asking—they're *telling* her that they will absolutely be on time for the vigil Saturday night. Joy groans. How . . . *who* is trying to plan a vigil when there's a funeral to plan?

But then, is there still a point to plan a funeral? If she's not dead and all . . .

"Oh no, not me, too," she grumbles, and tosses her phone aside. She is more rational than this; more levelheaded. When Peace died, she was willing to believe that something supernatural took her sister, but that was because she was young. Impressionable. What did she really know? But *now*? Now she's an adult. She can make her own decisions, form her own judgments, and look at things clearly.

And even then, I still . . . I don't know.

Generations of tradition and superstition can't always be wrong, but it hurt her so much to hold out hope this time.

"I have *one* ace!" Jamil declares, pulling it from his pile. He leans forward to search his dad's pile and finds the last three staring back at him. "*How*? Where was I when this went down?"

"I don't know what to tell you."

"You're too powerful. I gotta train with Nonna or I will *never* beat you."

David laughs. "*Train*? Literally what are you talking about?"

Joy's phone pings again. It feels like each buzz puts a spotlight on her; a spotlight she wishes would let her disappear. "Sorry, sorry, sorry, y'all . . ." she mumbles as she rushes to put her phone on silent. Without the constant buzzing, the room feels strangely empty.

Jamil abandons the cards and heads over to his luggage. "So . . ." He clears his throat. He's rifling through his suitcase for something. Joy guesses he's looking for his pajamas. She wants to say, *They're right there*, as her eyes glimpse the dark cotton fabric, but after a moment, she realizes he's taking his time on purpose. "Uh . . . Dad, you're staying, right?"

As quickly as her tired body will allow, Joy pushes herself up on her elbows, looking at David across the room. "Can you? It's pretty late, anyway, to drive back home."

He shrugs. "Yeah, sure, it doesn't matter."

From the corner of her eye, Joy can see Jamil hiding a grin. "Um . . ." He gets to his feet, clutching his pajamas. "So. I've noticed there's only one bed."

Joy shakes her head. "There's, like, a spare room—"

"There's only *one* bed," Jamil says again. Joy laughs. She has to. This isn't even subtle. "So, I can just sleep on the floor or something. Dad said I'm getting really tall these days and I'm all limbs, so . . ." He waves his arms in an exaggerated fashion before jogging to the door. "I'm gonna go change. Talk among yourselves."

He leaves.

Joy breaks into an embarrassed smile despite herself. "I think our son is trying to get us back together."

David smirks, says, "Sure," and wanders to the other side of the bed.

Is it working? she wants to ask, as a joke, of course. It has to be. Because she knows that in between their light banter and casual smiles, the foundation has changed. They're not children anymore. Joy thinks of how Michael said she doesn't know real conflict, and she rolls her eyes. Not all conflict has to be yelling and crying. Sometimes it's just a shift; a knowing.

Like Mama always knew.

In Joy's professional life, she would call this ability to pick up on someone's mood or energy "codependency." What a word. Dozens of studies done on majority white clients tell her that codependency is generally bad. And yes, she agrees that putting your feelings and sense of self in another person isn't the way to go. But she always wondered exactly how they would be viewed from a non-Western standpoint? If someone had interviewed Nigerian clients, or Indian clients, or Korean clients? If someone had seen her family, seen how her mom could tell when something was bothering Joy or when Michael was working himself too hard at school, would they still say that it was wrong? That her mother's way of being was incorrect?

Joy can't help but think of her mom now, imagine her sitting at the edge of the bed with them, silently letting her eyes wash over the two of them. Her daughter and the son-in-law she refused to let go of. *I don't even know what she'd say*, Joy thinks, and it wounds her. How many hours has it been since her mom passed away, and she's so frazzled that she can't even conjure up some timely advice for her situation.

She'd say . . . He's your child. He says this because he can't ask you for what he wants. You have to learn to listen. Which would be bold, since her mom wasn't necessarily always willing to hear her side, or Peace's side. Not even Michael's side. Sometimes she could be stubborn and unforgiving. Sometimes she was callous.

No, I only want to remember the good things for now.

Only the good. But the good without the bad wouldn't be a fair representation of the woman who raised her. Mom always said, "Don't make me a saint," when they were kids. Peace would laugh because what did she mean by that? When you're ten, your parents are gods. When you're fifteen, not so much. "Don't make me a saint, o," Mama would say. And Joy only understood what she meant in the weeks that followed Peace's death.

"Your sister was something," Mama told her. "She was beautiful. She was good. But she was stubborn. Very stubborn. And in death now, you shouldn't forget that."

No, Joy wouldn't.

So she can't go back on her word, no matter what Jamil wants. It wouldn't be fair to her. It wouldn't be fair to Mama, either. Why put her through the separation and divorce just to say that she didn't mean it in the first place? Now that Mom is gone, it'd be like a slap in the face.

But if she comes back . . .

She groans.

Stranger things have happened. Peace died *because she was cursed by a random witch. Why shouldn't Mom be resurrected? Why couldn't that cow be telling the truth?*

Joy presses her hands to her forehead as if to block out the thoughts. There's no way Auntie Nancy got this far into her head. She refuses to believe it.

"Are you good?" David asks her, and she shifts awkwardly to face him on the bed. "I mean, from before, with you and your brother."

Joy attempts a shrug. She's trying not to think about it. She's known her brother to be neglectful and inconsistent, sure, but never mean. Not this hateful. The memory surfaces and she waves it away completely, pushing it as far away as she can. This weekend isn't about her selfish brother; this weekend is about . . . well, it's *supposed* to be about her mom.

"I can't stop thinking about this stupid premonition and I want to scream," Joy mumbles, dropping her hands in her lap.

David chews his lip. "Do you want a distraction?"

"D-depends."

"Okay, so . . ." He clears his throat, pushes a hand through his hair, and waits. Joy sits on edge, preparing for the worst. A message from a pigeon, or something. "You remember when we were talking about what Jamil would be doing in the summer?"

Joy nods fervently. "Yeah, yes."

"And you said, 'Probably tutoring, I don't know'?"

"I, yes, I remember."

"Okay, well, let's now both agree that sounds really boring," he goes on. "And maybe it'd be better for him to travel instead."

Joy frowns. "He's *twelve*. Where is a twelve-year-old going to go?"

"Italy—with me," he adds quickly the moment he probably sees Joy's soul about to leave her body. "I'm thinking I'll go for, like, a month, two months, and it might be cool for Jamil to see his cousins now that he's a little bit older."

"He . . ." She swallows. The thought of her literal baby child going on a plane to another country without her makes her shudder something fierce. Besides, the last thing she's considering now is finding more ways to separate herself from her child. Her child who suddenly speaks better Italian than she realized. Her child who she always felt would take after her, but is becoming more and more like his father with each passing day. Her child who she suddenly feels she is running out of time with.

She inhales sharply. "Could . . ." Could she come with? Does she want to be in Italy for the summer with her ex-husband and his extended family, subjected to the same "So why are you divorced again?" circuit, except with an extra side of Catholic guilt and without the linguistic prowess to defend herself? Wait, should she be learning Italian, too? Shouldn't she try and master Igbo first? Who is supposed to teach her—who is supposed to teach Jamil now that Mama is . . .

Quickly, she drops her head into her hands and takes a deep breath. She feels David's hand on her shoulder and relishes in how comforting it is. "Can I think about it, please?" she asks quietly.

"Yeah, yeah, of course," David is quick to answer.

"It's just that today is a lot, so—"

"Yeah, I know. There really wasn't a good time to ask. Jamil's been asking me about it forever, so I figured"—as he speaks, Joy lifts her head, confusion coloring her understanding of his words—"sooner rather than later . . . would be better," he says eventually.

She frowns. "Jamil knows already?"

The door creaks open. Jamil shuffles in, shutting it behind him with a gentle click. Joy forces a smile, soft and serene, so Jamil won't sense how fast her heart is beating; how overwhelmed and riddled with indecision she is.

But Jamil knows. In a second, Joy can see something switch in his eyes. *It's because you're staring at him like he's going to die.*

He tosses his clothes as close to his suitcase as he can before falling back in the middle of the bed. He tilts his head toward his dad and whispers, "Hai detto a Mamma?"

David pinches his cheeks. "Be?" He shrugs. "Dalle un po' di tempo."

— 17 —

SATURDAY, 9:18 A.M.

Rob is surprised his family managed to wake up as early as they did this morning. He lies in bed for a bit longer, reciting his morning prayers and doing a bit of extra research on Joy's and Michael's behalf, as he hears his dad's footsteps up and down the hall (Ezekiel likes to march back and forth every morning for exercise), his sister's voice in the background, and, unfortunately, his brother-in-law's voice.

He rolls over and waits until they've gone. The last thing he really wants to do is run into any of them without a buffer, whether that's Joy, Michael, or Paul. God, he wishes Paul were here. He wishes he didn't feel so pressured all the time to pretend he wasn't married. What's worse is that it isn't even anything his family has said, it's just how he *thinks* he should be around them. Paul has made it clear to him that whatever is going on is all in Rob's head.

But when Rob finally gets up, makes his way to the door, and nearly bumps into Nnenna on the way out, he knows he's not making anything up. She gasps, stumbling backward. Her bonnet is still fastened around her head while she clutches the strings of her Louis Vuitton robe. "Oh! S-sorry."

"All good," Rob says with an uneasy chuckle.

"You're, uh . . ."

"I just found some stuff for Joy, uh, about the funeral home, so I thought I would—"

"Oh, y-yeah, of course."

The two of them hesitate, not sure if the other will speak first.

Rob is used to this shuffle, this awkward back and forth, with his older sister. It started back when James came into the picture; when James started getting more involved in the family. After that, slowly but surely, Nnenna wouldn't laugh with Rob the same way. It was a slight shift with monumental consequences. It changed everything for him. If Rob couldn't laugh with his family, then who was he supposed to laugh with?

So when Nnenna hesitates, takes a slow step back, then an awkward step forward, he understands. It's James. It's all James. He's in her head.

"Nnenna! Where is my shirt, na?"

Speak of the devil and he shall appear, Rob thinks just as he hears James's voice come booming from their room.

Rob rolls his eyes. He can't stand the way James speaks to his sister and how she, annoyance hidden under flustered features, takes off down the hall at his request. He keeps telling himself it isn't his place to get involved, and that he and Nnenna haven't been close like that for a while, but still, she's his sister. That's for life. He will absolutely punch James in the face if she asks him to.

— 18 —

SATURDAY, 9:37 A.M.

Nnenna dips back into her room and shuts the door firmly. She grumbles, crossing to her vanity and sitting down to get ready. She can hear Zach singing in the bathroom—*He better be putting on cream!* she thinks—and spots Yemi trying to work the remote by the second bed.

James appears from the washroom, fixing his shirt. "This is the wrong one," he tells her.

She grunts in response and takes off her bonnet.

They're quiet for a moment before James says, "I spoke to Michael yesterday."

"Hmm?"

"He was trying to call for a coroner and a funeral home, but because of the holiday, many places didn't answer. He's waiting on callbacks," James explains. "But now that the vigil is happening, I think I should tell him just to forget it."

Nnenna shrugs. "Maybe." Her feelings are all over the place. She believes in her mom, and she'd be the first to admit to having strong faith, but for some reason, in her heart, she just can't . . . commit. She wanted to pray about it but hasn't had time. Everything has just been so crazy, what with this Alice woman showing up.

It takes Nnenna a second to realize James is still staring at her. "What?" she says, confused.

"What do you mean, 'what'?"

"I mean, 'what'?"

"Ah-ah," James tuts, then sneers disapprovingly. "The way you're talking, you're beginning to sound like Joy. Better be careful, o."

Nnenna flinches so hard from his words that she has to cough to cover it up. She shifts, glancing away—glancing at Yemi in the corner and wondering how much of this she can hear. Guilt riddles her. James could be so careless with his words, especially in front of the kids. She never noticed it as much before, but, well, maybe it's the heightened emotions and the lack of proper sleep or extremely stiff bedding, but it really frustrates her now.

She finishes at the vanity and gets to her feet. "Yemi, turn the TV off," she says arbitrarily.

Yemi frowns. "But it's not even on—"

"You people won't let me hear word, ah-ah," Nnenna continues. She rushes back and forth across the room, moving things and wearing things, and yelling things—all to avoid paying James any more attention. She needs to get out of this space.

Quickly, she reaches for the door and steps into the hallway—where she nearly collides with her father.

James steps out afterward, mouth open, complaints heavy, but he swallows it all when he sees Ezekiel. "Pele, o, Papa," James chimes in with his deepest condolences after seeing the disgruntled look on Ezekiel's face. "I hope we have not disturbed Mama."

Ezekiel turns his head slowly, locking eyes with James. "See as your head take style *wide*. And you're asking if you're disturbing my wife."

Nnenna groans, "Dad, please," while James looks on in shock, "Papa, what have I done, na?"

It's no secret that Ezekiel is not a fan of James.

Does he think James Olubisi has been a responsible man for his family? Sure. Does he think James Olubisi has been a shining example of God's love and acceptance? Not always. Does he think James Olubisi has somehow driven a wedge between Ezekiel's only children, and turned his sweet, loving Nnenna into someone he sometimes can't recognize? Absolutely.

Sometimes people marry wrong. Ezekiel knows it; he's seen it all his life. But this family, these people, they love to sing "family is important" up and down, up and down, like they want to come and start beating you with it. He will never win an argument against Nancy, so instead, he keeps quiet, goes where he is needed, and doesn't ever pass up an opportunity to let James know he is lucky he crossed paths with his daughter when he did, as a newly immigrated postgraduate all those years ago, and that otherwise his life would look very different.

"You people should be easy with each other, with your cousins," Ezekiel says. "Especially Michael. That boy has lost the woman he called his mother, the only one he's ever known. Be easy."

Nnenna frowns. "Daddy, what? Joy lost her mother, too—or, 'the woman she calls her mother.' I wouldn't expect you to say something like this."

"So who would you expect it from?"

Nnenna's frown deepens, but she says nothing. He and his daughter both know that this kind of callous phrasing is something of the James Olubisi variety.

— 19 —

Sarah didn't do breakfast, but she woke up feeling ravenous from the night before—and embarrassed. If she was being honest, that fight with her dad and Auntie Joy put her on edge a little. She didn't hear all of it, and she's happy she disappeared when she did, but oh my God, *why* couldn't they just get along? It was so annoying. Grandma literally just died and they choose the same day to say all that horrible shit to each other? It didn't make sense.

So Sarah made a decision: *she* would be the adult, goddamnit. She came downstairs super early (seriously, not even her grandparents were down here yet) and decided to order breakfast for the family. On her dad's credit card, of course. Everyone would be fed, they'd probably be really happy once they realized her dad paid for it all, and she could easily claim that she forgot her dad's credit card was still linked to her food delivery app. Simple.

It's what Grandma Mary would've done, she tells herself, even though she's not completely sure that's true. Grandma had a way of always doing what she wanted, pushing through even when others were still deliberating. Sarah imagines how her grandma would've come downstairs, walking in quick, short steps, and headed straight

for the kitchen without a second look. She'd be halfway through boil-
ing meat for chicken stock before she thought to explain herself. And
if anyone asked her why she didn't ask someone for help, she would
chide them, saying, "So I should be waiting for you, abi?" Yes, Sarah
is sure the best way she can honor her grandma's memory right now
is by ordering a ton of food, force-feeding everyone, and refusing to
explain herself.

The first batch arrives the moment Rob makes his way downstairs.

"Who's there?" he asks, casting a nervous glance at the doorway.
"*This* early?"

He hears Sarah's voice, "It's probably the shit-ton of food I ordered,"
before he sees her emerge from the kitchen. She races down the hall.
Rob sidesteps before he gets completely shuffled out of the way.

Suddenly, his phone beeps. A message from Patricia, the funeral
director he's been emailing, asking to meet with someone from the
family today.

He failed to mention it to his cousins yesterday, but he contacted
a mortician who works with a funeral home that seems to be, if his
GPS is correct, maybe half an hour from where Joy lives. This was only
after he Googled "wtf to do when someone dies? canada ontario" in an
incognito browser. Apparently, after a person dies unexpectedly, the
process chain usually goes 911, coroner report, mortician and funeral
home, burial permit, burial. He hadn't found any information on how
or when a will was supposed to be read, but he figured he'd leave that
to Joy or Michael, and he quickly got to work finding a funeral home
that had good reviews on Yelp.

That's how he came across a place called Glendale Funeral Home
and its proprietor Patricia. Rob thought her name was close enough to
"Morticia," so he felt it was a sign to reach out. When Rob explained
that to her over the phone yesterday, she even laughed. "No one's ever
brought that up," she said, "but I do love *The Addams Family*."

"You're hired," Rob joked. "Jay-kay, I don't have that authority."
Still, he couldn't very well just sit around and do nothing. Joy and Mi-

chael are dealing with so much and no offense to his mom, or his sister, or his brother-in-law, but they weren't really making matters easier.

Oh God, *especially* his mom.

Sarah returns from the door holding bags and bags of breakfast foods and with a grave expression on her face. Her mouth hangs open slightly; her eyes are wide with shock. She lets out a sigh and scuttles past Rob to the kitchen.

"What happened?" he asks her.

"Oh my God . . ." She glances at him while she works quickly to unload all the food. "Like . . . there's hella people outside."

"What?"

"*Mad* people," she says, her voice cracking with nerves.

Rob goes to see for himself. He turns to the door and cracks it open, poking his head out as inconspicuously as he can. He counts at least twenty, thirty people. Maybe more. They're just sitting around and waiting, sleeping in open cars and huddled in groups, as if it's a casual day and they're not on someone else's property. There's a group of people reading a Bible at the edge of the walkway, and the moment one of them notices Rob, he yelps and shuts the door. "Wha-a-a-a-t the fuuuuuck?" An uneasy squeal escapes Rob's lips as he spins on his heel and heads back to the kitchen. "What are all those people doing out there?"

"Probably for the vigil? Probably because of what they've been hearing on Alice's show?" Sarah grimaces. "It's, like, ten a.m. Midnight isn't for another, what, twelve hours? What are they gonna do out there all day?"

"Who are what gonna do where?"

Sarah and Rob startle as Joy enters the kitchen, pulling a robe tightly around her shoulders.

The bags under her eyes are begging for caffeine. She gives a small cough before scanning the infuriatingly pristine countertops for coffee. There is none. She may as well perish.

"Morning, Auntie. I, um, ordered food already," Sarah pipes up with a small smile. Then she says, "And my dad absolutely agreed to pay for everything because he felt bad," for added effect.

The smallest twitch nudges Joy's eyebrow. "Oh, hmm," comes her lofty reply.

"Did you sleep okay?" Rob asks with an apologetic smile.

Did she? This morning, the morning after her aunt received a message from on high about her mother coming back from the dead, Joy crept out of bed, having spent the night sandwiched between her beautifully cunning son and her ex-husband (Jamil *insisted* he slept better on the outside of the bed so there was no way he could possibly sleep in the middle). Joy is almost certain someone from her patrilineal village is using her for ritual.

"Yeah, it was fine," she grunts.

"Good, good," Rob says. "Because, two things—"

"There's bare people outside," Sarah squeaks, then slams her hands against her mouth.

Joy's eyebrow twitch intensifies. "*What?*"

"Well, I wanted to lead with the first thing," Rob says, casting a stern look at Sarah. "But we might as well get into it. People are legitimately starting to gather outside. It looks like whatever my mom or that Alice lady has been saying is working. I think they're waiting to see Auntie Mary actually rise from the dead."

The more Rob talks, the less Joy understands. She utters one more "What?" before his words start to sink in, start to really take root. There are people outside the house waiting for her mom to be resurrected. There are people outside the house waiting for her mom to be resurrected. There are people—

"I don't want to see them." She rubs her hands down her face, massaging and kneading and trying hard to get all the tension out.

Rob gives an exaggerated grimace. "Well, they're kinda everywhere, so you may not be able to avoid them."

"Like, do they actually believe?" Joy peels her hands from her face, casting a scowl over her shoulder toward the door. "Do they? Or are they just here because they, I don't know, because they've all lost their minds just like Auntie Nancy?"

Joy notices Rob cringe. *Harsh. She's still your aunt, and still Rob's mom.*

"I can't take full responsibility for her actions, but I wanna apologize on her behalf anyway," Rob says, biting his lip. He glances away. "I think ... faith is a weird thing sometimes. You know?"

Joy nods right away. "Oh, I know."

"You can believe so hard in something ... like, here." He clears his throat and starts again. "We're Christian—well, we're a Christian family. I still go to church and everything. So when we hear things about resurrection and miracles, it should be normal for us to believe it. But it's not that simple."

"Because logic gets in the way," Joy offers, though the way she says it is more blunt than conversational. She pretends not to notice when Rob twitches a little. "It's true. Your rational mind gets in the way of what your heart wants to believe," she continues. "So even if you've read a million times that ... a person died and was brought back to life, or a blind man started to see again, your mind is still, like, 'absolutely no way that happened because I haven't seen it.' It's natural, honestly."

"Yeah, well . . ." Rob mumbles, and nudges his septum piercing with his finger. She's made him uncomfortable. That's the last thing she wanted. Rob is probably her coolest cousin, and her early morning fatigue coupled with her overall frustration from yesterday plus her grief is making her say things she shouldn't.

Quickly, she rushes to apologize. "S-sorry, ignore me. I don't know why I said all of that."

"W-well, it's true," Sarah chimes in timidly. Both of them give her a look that asks, "We thought this was an adult conversation?" but Joy doesn't have the energy to maintain it. "It is. Two things can be true at the same time. Faith and logic can't always coexist, b-but that doesn't mean one is better or more truthful than the other."

Rob snorts. "Not too loud, or my sister and her husband will come smack you over the head."

Sarah laughs. "Besides, who can really say what's meant to be true or not? Grandma Mary, she passed away on Good Friday—on her birthday, yeah, but it was Good Friday. A holy day. That's ... that's actually insane." A small smile comes to her lips at the thought, and she shrugs. "Maybe it *does* mean something. You never know."

"Y-yeah, I guess." Joy stifles a yawn. She rubs her face again, hiding it, so they can't see the unease in her features. She doesn't really know what to believe. Isn't this a bit too cruel? Talking about her mother rising from the dead, and things like that. She's barely been able to accept the fact that her mom is gone. Last night, she started to remember the sound of her mom's footsteps coming up the hallway in their childhood home. She walked quick, her feet padding softly across the hardwood floor. That's where Joy is mentally: she is nine, hearing her mom come down the hall, ready to rub Mentholatum on her chest, cast spells, and sing prayers about how demons shouldn't possess her small body before she falls asleep.

It's one thing for a bunch of strangers outside to believe it, but for her own family to think she'll come back to life? "It's too much . . ." She sighs out, pressing her hands into her eyes at the slightest sting of tears.

She feels a hand reach across the island to her. Rob squeezes her shoulder. "Yeah, I hear you."

"It's just that there's other stuff to do before then," Joy mumbles as she wipes her eyes.

"Exactly. Which is why I have this." Rob swipes open his phone and turns it around to show Joy. The email response from Patricia stares Joy in the face. Her eyes move quickly across the screen as Rob fumbles through the whole story on how he got in contact with her. "She seems really cool, very open, not at all freaked out about the Good Friday thing—and she wants to meet you today for some initial quotes and to talk about the procedure. I tried to get some info about how long coroner's reports usually take, but it's looking like the consensus is 'a few hours' or something . . ."

Joy zones out the more she reads and the more Rob speaks. One word jumps out at her in the email: Glendale. She shivers, knowing immediately where she's seen that name before. "We held Peace's funeral there," she utters without meaning to.

Rob buttons up. "O-oh?" He and Sarah exchange a nervous look.

"Should we look for another place? I think Michael was still talking to a few other morticians."

She shakes her head right away. Words don't come. She lets the memory of Peace's funeral wash over her, and for a second, she can't help but feel this is all poetic somehow. Mom dying the way she did, Peace being buried with Glendale, a mortician named Patricia, the constant *tap-tap-tap* of anxiety in her heart, the mounds of chin-chin dough still stashed in the fridge. All of it feels poetic.

— 20 —

Nwunye is the first person to call Joy the second she gets out of the shower. "H-hello?" She fumbles the phone. "Nwunye?"

"Joy, ndo, my dear!" Wherever her wayward relative is, it sounds like a party is happening. Loud music begins to dim and she can hear chuckling and toasting in the background, as if it isn't 11 a.m. on a Saturday. "How are you? Long time, o! How is your son? How is your husband?"

"Jamil is fine."

"Eh-heh, and your husband?"

Joy frowns, goes through a string of *How many times do I have to tell people?* in her mind, before finally mumbling, "He's okay."

She chuckles good-naturedly. Nwunye is always in good spirits, even though her reputation among the community isn't one that people look on too favorably. Her name isn't "Nwunye," it's probably Edith or Melissa or something, but people have resorted to calling her "wife" because of her habit of getting involved with married men and breaking up households. Mama would always say, "Some people no get shame at *all*," every time Nwunye came around. When Joy would ask why those couples didn't just get divorced . . . "I mean, if someone so obvious and shallow like Nwunye can break up a marriage," Joy asked, "then maybe the marriage wasn't that strong to begin with. Maybe they're just unhappy being together and they don't want to admit it."

To which Mama would reply, "They're not unhappy, they're Christians. God will help. He doesn't rest."

Well, luckily for everyone, Nwunye didn't rest, either.

"That's good!" Nwunye says. "Ehm, I'm just out and about, you know, and I thought I would confirm the details for the vigil."

Joy grimaces, clutching her towel before it slips. "Um, well, so, about that—"

"To make sure I have the right address. I've been giving people this one, the one your auntie Nancy sent me, and then I saw a different postal code on the one on TV, so I wanted to establish its correctness," she barrels on. Joy can hear tapping in her ear, so she guesses Nwunye is probably scrolling on her phone. She reads out the address for the house. "Is that right?"

"Y-yeah, but, I mean, I can't really guarantee there will actually be a vigil."

"But then what about the poster?"

"Excuse me?"

After a bout of more tapping, Joy notices Nwunye has sent her something. A haphazardly done poster with a picture of Mama and the details for the event listed underneath. This is absurd. It's one thing for people to already be gathered outside, but for a poorly assembled poster of her mom to be circulating? "Oh . . . no, no, no—"

"So we will be seeing each other today, o!" Nwunye chuckles warmly. "Okay, take care, my dear."

"A—"

"Yes." She hangs up and Joy's screen reverts back to the vigil poster. The shining text. The way Mama smiles. Her name, cascading in a corny gradient font. Clip art, most likely. The way her eyes sparkle, even across the flatness of Joy's phone. The way she still looks so warm, so alive, so present.

Joy goes back into the shower and cries.

By the time she gets dressed and comes downstairs, the house feels like a different place. Bustling and lively. It's eerie. She meets a disgruntled Rob grabbing a second breakfast order from the door. He rolls his eyes as he passes her. "He was *late*. I don't wanna decrease the tip, but, like, that is the currency of our capitalist society, so . . ."

As she turns, her eyes catch the slightest glimpse of Michael on the staircase. Her heart thuds in her chest—the panic that she'll have to talk to him and she hasn't really said a word to him since yesterday, and what is she going to do, how is she going to last another day in this awkward, liminal space?

She hears her mom's voice in her head: *He's your brother.*

And her own voice: *He wants me dead, Mom.*

And her again: *Okay, wait, maybe that's a little dramatic.*

Quickly, she turns and makes her way down the hall. She can't be mad at her brother if she never crosses paths with him. *Fuck's sake,* she thinks. *I've turned into one of my clients.*

Joy turns the corner to the kitchen and nearly bumps into David. "O-oh, sorry," she utters as she skirts around him. She feels like she has been skirting around so many things related to David since yesterday that it feels strange he is actually here. She can't stop thinking about the idea that Jamil may be going to Italy for the summer—that he'd been thinking about it for a while and neither of them told her. *Well? Are you mad?* She waits for the anger to come, but it's more like a tired wave coming to shore. It passes before it even touches sand.

"It's cool," David says as he pulls a container from one of the many delivery bags and hands it to Rob across the breakfast bar. "You headed somewhere?"

"Yeah, um, the funeral home. Rob mentioned I should check it out," she answers. Her eyes dance across the counter, eyeing all the food. Sarah and Rob must've ordered a million of everything on the menu. "Should we ration this?" As she asks it, David is already shaking his head. She frowns. "Well, what if it doesn't last until evening?"

"It doesn't need to last anything," Auntie Nancy calls as she steps in from the backyard. Uncle Ezekiel follows, shutting the door gently behind him. Joy remembers how Auntie used to go on morning walks, and how her mom used to join her sometimes. It explains why Auntie looks so tired, her eyes so puffy, after what was supposed to be a refreshing stroll. She must've been thinking of Mama.

Still, it's like she becomes a different person when she steps into the house. She stands taller, her jaw firmer, as she says, "The vigil will be catered, of course. We can't be serving breakfast food to everybody."

Joy touches her chin, keeping exceptionally quiet as Auntie circles the living room for a comfortable spot on the sectional. She desperately wants to ask if Auntie has seen the crowd of people at the front of the house, but she doesn't want to know the answer.

"Ebee k'į na-aga?" Auntie asks her. "To work?"

"No." Joy frowns, feeling a twinge of offense. Does Auntie really think she's that heartless? "I'm going to a funeral home."

"Na ejima nna?"

Joy swallows. "Nope." She's not giving up her plan to avoid Michael so soon. Of course she knows it's in her best interest to try and reach out at some point, but what would she even say? "Hey, you definitely think Mom died to get away from me, so do you wanna come with me to the funeral home where our sister's service was held, or . . . ?" It's fucking ridiculous. God, it makes her skin crawl. She feels prickly and ugly all over again.

Her memories of her childhood with Michael are clouded now, filled with times where their parents would favor him over her and Peace. It made her resentful, and she wonders how much of her interactions with him are tainted by that now. She's sure, in some twisted way, he'd say the same about her. They just don't get along, end of. They don't understand each other at all.

"Okay, go come," Auntie says, waving her away. "Alice will be here soon, so don't be too late with this funeral business. Eh . . . echeghį m na odi necessary to be doing funeral, but you oyinbo children, i kwenyeghi m."

Joy opens her mouth to protest, but a sigh escapes instead. "Okay, Auntie," she says, and turns for the hallway.

Nnenna stops her before she reaches the door. Her glare and confrontational stance are too potent for the morning, especially on a day like today when Joy feels like she is still floating outside of her own body. She swallows down her apprehension and asks, "What is it, Nnenna?"

"Good morning to you, too," Nnenna shoots back. "Where did you sleep?"

"In my room, obviously."

"And where did David sleep?"

Joy glances around Nnenna to the hall. To freedom.

"I'm just curious, Joy. If you truly are *divorced*," Nnenna goes on, indignantly, emphasizing the word, "then you shouldn't be sleeping in the same bed. But, I mean, that's only if you believe in divorce, anyway."

"Look at me." Joy gestures from her head to her toes. "Just look at me."

"Joy—"

"I have to go, Nnenna. My mom is dead, someone has made some ugly Microsoft Paint–style poster with *clip art* for the vigil and is circulating it, and there is an abundance of breakfast food in the house—" Her breathing hitches. *I'm going to cry,* she thinks. *I'm going to cry and she's going to think it's because of the breakfast food.* Quickly, Joy turns and forces her feet into her shoes before she dashes out the door.

And then there is nothing.

Calmness.

Until she opens her eyes to the growing swarm of people gathering outside of the mansion. "Jesus," she sighs out, gaping at how the crowd seems to be growing. Or, that there's even a crowd at all! She takes one step forward before dragging her feet down the walkway and toward where she parked her car. A few people stop and watch her, posing as if they want to ask her a question. *AJAfrika . . .* She groans, remembering that her face might be circulating in interviews across WhatsApp at this very moment.

Quickly, she drops her head and walks as fast as she can to her car. A voice calls out, "Wait, is that Joy?" and she breaks into a run.

She gets in her car and shuts the door. Someone comes over to knock on the window. An uncle she recognizes, or at least she thinks she does. "Joy? Ah-ah, is that you?"

"Oh my Goddddd." A whine breaks from her lips as she revs up the car and drives away, careful not to hit this uncle or any of the other people crowding around the driveway. "This isn't happening, this isn't happening..."

Or *is* it?

She tries to take inventory. Auntie Nancy had a daytime premonition about Mama coming back, and half the family is on her side. The running theory is that juju *might* have taken Mama in the night, but God will bring her back.

And then her and Michael, and their disgustingly offensive fight. Did he really say those things to her? Oh God, did she really say those things to him? Divorce is horrible. Separation is painful. Why would she make light of those things when she knows, for the first time ever, what he might be going through? They could've bonded, finally, and she let it all go to waste because she was so obsessed with being right.

That's what everyone says about her, that her need to be in control is killing her. Her grip tightens on the steering wheel as she realizes she couldn't even get one of her clients to stop calling her yesterday, and today she agreed to visit a funeral home—to visit a place she never wanted to see again. *Why couldn't Michael go? Why didn't you just tell them Michael should do it?*

She already knows the answer. *Because you wanted to be right. About how much you do for others. About how they do nothing for you. You just want a reason to hate him.*

The realization is splitting. Now, without Mama, what's holding her and her brother together? What reason do they have to still tolerate each other? It hurts her to admit. She drives the whole way down the highway and back into the city with her lips pressed firmly together and her jaw clenched.

Does Mom have a will? She would, right? I should check that...

I should ask Michael if he wouldn't mind . . . If he could do that for me.
For us. For our mom.
Maybe, I don't know . . .

Glendale Funeral Home looks the same. It smells of potpourri
and death, she thinks, and she hates it. Joy parks from memory; she
walks into the building without really looking at any one thing for too
long. If she was lucky, if God really was looking out for her, she would
just bump into this Patricia person without having to spend too much
time searching. Because it's in the searching that her body will begin
to realize she's been here before; it'll ease into the space, feel at home,
get comfortable. And she doesn't want to be comfortable in this kind
of place at all.

Peace was here.

She pushes out a sharp exhale from between her teeth and looks
around. A white woman with a tight, low ponytail spots her and immediately walks over. Her smile is warm despite her severe features and
angular physique. "May I help you?" she asks, then gestures loosely
around the foyer. "We're not running at full capacity because it's Easter weekend, but maybe I can be of some assistance."

"Are you Patricia?" Joy asks, and when the woman nods, she
reaches out to shake hands. "I'm Joy Bia—uh. I'm Joy." She forces a
smile, albeit uneasy. "I think you spoke to my cousin on the phone.
Robert Akintola? Rob?"

"Oh! Yes, of course," Patricia says, and leads her to a small office
down the hall. Joy knows this office, its beige walls and harsh, wooden
desk. She remembers sitting in the corner when Mom and Dad were
here to talk about Peace's burial. *And where was Michael? Where was*
he? She groans. Damn, she's exhausting herself.

He might've had a family, but this was his sister, too. Do not let that go,
Joy. Stay right about this one thing, please.

She settles into the chair across from Patricia and folds her hands
atop her lap. Atop her bag on her lap. Clasps them. Unclasps.

"So," Patricia speaks up, startling Joy. She rifles through a set of papers in front of her, including a notepad with some scrawled informa-

tion. Suddenly, she flashes a smile, one of those welcoming ones that's meant to put you at ease and make you forget you're about to put your mother in the ground. "Your cousin is quite a character," she tells Joy.

Joy nods quickly. "Yeah, yep." She can't stop thinking about how she will soon have to put her mother in the ground.

"So, we haven't really spoken to anyone at the hospital yet because we didn't have authorization," Patricia goes on. "But if you do decide to do the service with us, you do have multiple options. We can first look into if the deceased has a will. That's something we can assist you in navigating, if need be."

"Probably. I don't even know if she had one."

"Don't worry about it too much right now. We can work around whatever the family needs."

Joy gulps. *I have no idea what the family needs....* The room feels so big, the air so heavy on her shoulders.

"Can I just ask you a question?" Joy whispers as she leans forward.

"Yes, of course."

"My . . . mom was h-healthy." Joy clears her throat, awkwardly, before she is able to continue. "She . . . I went with her to the doctor, like . . . once a month, once every two months. We did regular checkups. She didn't have any kind of preexisting condition. She didn't live a sedentary life, as much as she could—I mean, she liked gardening, she liked going on walks, she was seventy so there really wasn't much else to do there—a-and, I just . . . I just don't know . . . why this would happen the way it did."

She is fighting tears by the end of it. Patricia reaches into her desk for a packet of tissues, which she hands to Joy.

"S-sorry, that wasn't even a question." Joy dots her eyes. She hates that she's crying in this office, again. Waiting for a funeral director to tell her the way to grieve a dead relative, again. Losing a family member, again.

"It's okay. I understand," Patricia says, her voice softening. "Death is never a welcome visitor, but it's a visitor we all have to let in one day. And sudden passings like these are never ideal. I don't want you to think that just because I work here and I do the job that I do . . . well, it doesn't mean that I'm immune to that kind of grief. I know where you're coming from, and I am truly so sorry for your loss."

Joy nods slowly, her eyes downcast.

"Your mom must've been very special."

"Oh . . . yes." Joy's bottom lip quivers through a teary smile. Her memories come in full force; her mom smiling, her mom laughing, her mom telling her to be quiet when she said something stupid. It's weird, but she misses that the most. Being corrected.

"We can't say anything until we get the coroner's report, really," Patricia explains. "But I have a bit of pull at the morgue, so I can check in on that for you, if you'd like. If you're okay with choosing Glendale, of course. No pressure at all." She gives an uneasy chuckle. "I can't imagine it would take longer than a few hours to get those details for you."

"Y-yes, if you could call, that would be good."

"Of course."

"My sister's funeral happened here."

Patricia smiles, that same welcoming greeting, but she says nothing. Joy isn't surprised. There really isn't much else to say about it. She's not sure why she brought it up.

"I just . . ." Joy dots her eyes quickly before scrunching the tissue in her hands. "It feels so weird. My mom . . . dying on her birthday—it was her birthday yesterday—"

"Oh! Happy birthday to her."

"—and, yeah, but then she's . . . she died. And nothing was wrong with her. She wasn't even that old. And I just don't understand."

"Mmhmm."

"Doesn't that seem strange to you?"

"Life is a mystery," Patricia tells her with a sad smile. "Everything is strange."

Yes, Joy thinks. *A witch's curse killed my sister. Everything is unhinged.* She watches Patricia's smiling face and immediately decides that she will keep that detail to herself.

— 21 —

Michael had been dreading going downstairs all morning. Sarah asked multiple times if he wanted anything for breakfast—"Food magically appeared downstairs! Don't ask who paid for it, though!"— but he always said, "Later," or "I'll be down in a minute." The truth is that he's still anxious about the very public and, if he's being honest, very childish fight he had with Joy yesterday. Not a second has gone by since that he hasn't mentally kicked himself for saying the things he did. He's anxious about staring into his family's eyes, seeing their judgment or their pity, and he's afraid that he will not be strong enough to handle it. He's afraid of this Alice woman coming to ask intrusive questions he can't answer. He's afraid his family is starting to fall for the same shit those people gathering outside are. He's afraid he might be, too.

He's afraid of running into David.

When he really thinks about it, he doesn't understand anything at all. Joy made "being separated" her entire personality for two years. So for her to call David yesterday and him to show up like this is ... it's ...

It's not fair.

Michael is angry without really knowing why. "*Tch*, you know why," he grumbles to himself as he finally pushes off the bed in his room. He gets ready quickly, showering and lotioning and putting on new clothes, all with a knot in his brow and a dull throb in his head.

He tries to call Shelly. It goes straight to voicemail.

It's not *fair*.

His nephew is always quick to say "My parents aren't together, but they don't hate each other or anything," as if it's something they forced him to memorize under fear of flogging. At first, Michael thought it was contrived and he resented Joy for making Jamil recite some stupid adage he probably didn't even believe. But as the separation wore on, and the divorce became final, Michael begrudgingly had to accept that Jamil was not a liar and Joy and David did indeed not hate each other. They didn't hate each other to the point that Joy called him to show up for her mom's birthday-slash-potential-funeral-and-resurrection, and he did—

And then he *stayed*!

What the fuck!

Michael comes downstairs and sees David is currently swerving through game levels on Jamil's device while Zach and Jamil watch from either side of him.

Before he is able to march over, Auntie Nancy speaks up from her place at the kitchen table. Her voice booms. "So you've decided to join us? When day has already broken and your sister has gone, wasting her time talking to the funeral people. Alice will be here any time from now."

Michael swallows a groan and walks over to hug both his aunt and uncle, a painful smile on his face. If they look long enough, they'll see it was just an extended wince. "Joy went where?" he asks.

Auntie Nancy juts out her bottom lip in disapproval. "To desecrate my good intentions."

He sighs. "All right." He can't believe Joy would take it upon herself to spearhead the funeral preparations without even telling him. *Can't you, though? That's how she is. That's how she's always been.* He grunts, glancing away from his aunt. He—

"Ah-ah, but I did not hear 'good morning,'" his aunt says, then gestures to her and Uncle Ezekiel.

"Good morning, Auntie, Uncle."

"How did you sleep, my son?" Uncle Ezekiel asks.

Michael shrugs. "As best as I could."

"Soon, you will know rest," Auntie tells him, which initially sounds like a threat, but as she nods and stares at the ceiling with pride, he realizes she is basking in the premonition.

"Mmm." Michael doesn't know what to say. Instead, he circles the table to greet Rob by the breakfast bar. He spots James sitting with his earphones in, nodding along to a video on his phone. It's probably a sermon. Michael wouldn't put it past him.

Michael breathes out a sigh at the thought of greeting his remaining family members. He's quite tall. He's sure they've seen him enter the room. He's well aware this goes against Nigerian customs—that when you walk into a room, you greet and accommodate your elders first—but he can't be bothered.

Finally, with no other distractions, he sets his sights on David, who has since returned Jamil's device to him. Jamil dashes out of the living room with Zach at his heels, singing, "Can I play? Is it my turn now?"

Michael shuffles over with an awkward gait and sits down in Jamil's vacated spot. "David, hey," he says.

David sits up straighter, pushing his hair from his face. Michael can see a hint of terror on his face. *Eh, fair enough*, he thinks. In all the years David and Joy had been together, Michael never addressed him this directly, or this pointedly. The two of them were never close, but Michael isn't sure if that was because of the age difference or because of Joy.

"Hi," David says finally.

"Can . . ." Michael glances away. He's so aware of Auntie's gaze at the side of his head. He's sure she's probably two seconds away from calling, "Ah, and what do you people have to be talking about?" across the room. Quickly, he gets to his feet while nodding toward the opposite hall. "Can I talk to you for a second? Over, uh, anywhere else but here, literally."

"S-sure," David agrees, but for a split second, Michael swears he can see another flash of terror in his brother-in-law's eyes.

Michael leads the way to a room with dead animals mounted on the wall and shuts the sliding door behind him. Ignoring the obvious confusion mounting in David's eyes, Michael gestures loosely to the empty seating.

"I need to ask you something," Michael says quietly as he sits down, "about . . . divorce."

David furrows his brows as he takes a seat at a nearby sofa. "What about it?"

Michael clasps his hands together. His eyes jump from David to the floor to the wall, where a nativity scene has been re-created with squirrels. He raises an eyebrow. *Why squirrels, though?* His gaze lingers long enough that he forgets what he wants to say. Or, he realizes he had no idea to begin with. God, this was a weird idea. Him and his sister's ex-husband? Bonding? "Actually . . ." He clears his throat and looks toward the door. "Never mind."

"W-well, wait." David holds up a hand before Michael bolts for the exit. "I mean, are you . . ." He chews his lip before saying, "Are you and Shelly okay?"

Michael exhales.

It's just a question, but it feels like a release. He can't help but chuckle a little as the stagnation in his chest loosens. "Not sure how to answer that." He leans back in his seat, slouching on the velvet sofa behind him, while he thinks. "I guess define 'okay.'"

"You're the one who asked me about divorce, so maybe you should define it."

"That's true," he grunts. "I don't know how to describe it. But things have been different at home, and so . . . and so, I guess, I was wondering . . ." He clears his throat; glances at the squirrel who is meant to be portraying Jesus. The words come in heavy, spilling from his mouth and hitting the floor like lead. "At what point do you decide it's just not worth it anymore?"

Michael feels prickly the moment he asks his question, but he tries his best not to show it. There's no reason for him to know this much about his sister's life, right? This is none of his business. He and Joy weren't these kinds of people. And he didn't want to know these things

about her or David; about if the knowledge came for him like a knowing, a quiet "oh" on an evening long after you're meant to be asleep.

David tells him, as calmly as he can, "I'm not sure if I can say that,
definitely. Because it never really stops being worth it . . . you know?"

Michael nods right away. He's sitting up straighter. This is exactly
how he feels.

"Day by day, you just start getting tired. Things feel different. Just
not as cohesive as they used to be."

"Yes, yes, e-exactly," Michael agrees. "I can't really say—I-I don't
really wanna give details, but something is changing, and we're not the
same people. We're not. And I think of Sarah and Miles, and I just . . .
I don't know what to do."

"And therapy is out of the question?"

Michael scoffs. "Shelly won't do therapy. I don't even think *I* believe in it. Don't tell Joy."

David juts out his lips and shrugs.

"But hey, even after everything, you . . ." God, what is he doing?
Here he is not wanting to spill anything about the details of his situation with Shelly, but he can't help himself from asking the most intrusive question that comes to mind. His entire family is nosy. He's only
met a handful of Nigerian people who understand what boundaries
are, and he is not related to any of them.

You still love her, right?

Michael is so curious. He wants to know how different he will feel
once it's all over. *If* it's all over.

David raises an eyebrow, waiting.

Just ask, just ask the question, Michael thinks.

But it's obvious, isn't it?

It is.

David loves Joy in a way that terrifies Michael, because he isn't sure
he feels the same about Shelly. Not after the challenge they are facing.
And he is unsure he can love Shelly the same if they went through with
this. A divorce. A permanent separation.

Suddenly, the door bursts open. Sarah stands, slightly out of
breath, as she beckons her dad and her uncle forward. "Grandma's on

the phone with Auntie Joy, and she's, like, actually crazy," she says, excitement tugging at her words. She even bounces in place while they approach her.

"In what way is this different from yesterday?" David asks in an exaggerated whisper, and Sarah giggles.

"She's telling Auntie to tell the funeral people not to bury Grandma Mary."

Michael stares at his daughter.

At some point, his mouth starts to hang open.

He wants to believe he heard wrong, but he knows—he *knows* that's not the case. He groans with the onset of perpetual irritation. "Ah-ah, Auntie, you won't kill me today, o," he scoffs and starts for the kitchen. Sure enough, his auntie Nancy has commandeered Rob's phone, yelling into it at arm's length and then returning it to her ear to make out whatever Joy is telling her. Michael begins, "Auntie—"

But she holds up a hand to silence him, continuing her tirade over the phone. "You better tell that woman, o! Joy, are you hearing me? If they touch that my sister, if they try to bury her, God will punish them! In fact, eh . . ." She snaps her fingers, a menacing sound that Michael knows is the finishing touch on her outlandish threat. "Tell them that come midnight, they should wait and see that she will rise. Tell them! People are here wait-ing, o! Oya, let me give you my husband's number. When she hears from those hospital people, she must tell us. She should call when my sister is resurrected."

Michael and Rob lock eyes behind Nancy's back. Rob whispers, "It's the way . . . 'when my sister is resurrected' is a real sentence right now." Sarah presses a hand to her mouth to stop from laughing.

Nancy reaches out to smack Rob on the arm. "Will you shut up? Onye nsogbu! Did I ask you to be *ke-ke-ke* while I'm on the phone?"

Rob bites back a smile. "Mom, what is 'ke-ke-ke'?"

"Abeg, shut up, my friend!" She kisses her teeth and turns away, pressing the phone closer to her ear. "Do you have a pen?" she barks. "Please, I don't have time. The reporter is coming soon . . . Ee! Kwụsị ịjụ such questions, na! Okay, it's . . . 410-555-1047. Did you tell her?" The room is silent while Nancy waits to confirm. Only after she's nodded sufficiently does Michael finally exhale. "Okay. Come back. Alice will be here any time from now," Nancy adds.

Michael tilts his head to the side as if he can't believe what he's hearing. "What's 'any time from now'?"

"It's—"

The doorbell rings.

Well, Michael thinks, his mom always said God doesn't sleep and that His timing is best. He watches how Yemi and Zach race each other to get to the door first, and for the first time in a while, he realizes he wishes Joy were here.

— 22 —

Immaculate Edobor won't lie; she loves a good party, no matter who the celebrant is. Now that she's in the best age of her life (why didn't anyone tell her she'd be more attractive in her forties than she was in her twenties?), and her kids are old enough to do what they want without her watching over them, she feels freer than she ever has, and she's planning on taking full advantage. Eh, as if she hasn't been taking advantage in the past. Even when she was carting around two snot-nosed kids and a disagreeable husband, she never missed an event. Immaculate is what the community sometimes refers to as a party crasher, when they aren't referring to her as ashawo. Her gele collection is unrivaled; her beads and tailored clothes unmatched. She has an outfit for every occasion and is always ready to show up and show out.

Based on the amount of people hanging around the Okafor venue house, she guesses she wasn't the only one who had this idea.

Her and her friends Rebecca and Lizzy maneuver their way around a church group, all wearing the same T-shirts branded with their church logo and black pants (or skirts, for the women), who are singing some sort of praise song. Other people are sitting in fold-up chairs, sharing coolers of rice and drinks among one another.

"What's all this, na?" Rebecca whispers from beside Immaculate. "Is this a picnic? Are these people mad or what?"

"There's going to be a vigil," Lizzy responds with a click on her tongue. "Let them pray. Please, what's it your business?"

"But we're still doing the livestream, of course." Immaculate glances at her friends and they give unconvincing nods. How else was she supposed to bolster her follower count—and continue to perpetuate her pseudo-celebrity status in the community—without gaining early access to what's arguably the most salacious event of the season?

She straightens her blouse and checks her makeup in a small compact. *Perfect,* she thinks with a grin.

Lizzy does the same before bringing out a phone to set up the livestream. She gives a thumbs-up. "Yes. Babe, we're ready to go."

Immaculate grins. She rings the doorbell just as a van pulls up in the massive driveway behind them. It drives awkwardly around a group of people who are doing Bible study in the middle of the road. "Who is that?" Immaculate asks, squinting as the van parks. "Is that a news station? Ah!" She yelps when Rebecca jostles her arm. "What?"

"Ah-ah, no be Alice Karim from AJAfrika?" She giggles, bouncing from side to side on the balls of her feet. "Babe, her husband is so *rich.* If she's here covering the resurrection, then it must be true, o! Oh my God, oh my goodness!"

Immaculate scowls without knowing it as they watch Alice exit the van along with a crew of cameramen. They rush to bring out equipment while she stands, fixes her hair, and straightens her pencil skirt. Immaculate seethes. "Who does this bitch think she is?"

"Alice Karim, obviously!" comes Lizzy's brash reply.

"Lizzy, will you shut up—"

Finally, the front door opens.

Immaculate smiles down at a child. She's not sure if she's seen this boy before. He doesn't look like Mama Mary, so maybe he's a relation from the other side of the family. A slightly taller girl appears, too. Immaculate chooses to ignore how the girl's face twists in confusion at the sight of her clothes.

"Hello," the small boy says timidly. "Who . . . are you?"

Immaculate chuckles, then looks over his head into the house. *Ah-ah, see luxury!* Her breath hitches in her throat from what she can see of the main hall and the chandelier. Who does she have to marry to live in a house like this?

Quickly, she looks over her shoulder at Lizzy and nods. "Start the stream." Lizzy logs in and positions her phone.

Soon, the small boy at the door is replaced with Michael Okafor. Immaculate exhales slowly, fixing her clothes, as she gazes into the handsome face of Mama's son. Luckily for him, he looks a lot like his late father. Papa Okafor was such a good-looking man in his old age, and she's sure he was a true knockout when he was younger. Once again, she missed the boat on that one.

"Michael, hello," Immaculate says, putting on her best I've-studied-abroad accent. That hint of "Am I from England? Am I from France?" has really done a lot for her social life.

Michael sighs.

His shoulders sink considerably once he sees who it is. "Nwunye, welcome," he utters. "What are you doing here? Don't say it's for the vigil."

Immaculate giggles, reaching out to touch his forearm. "Wetin, na? Na you I come see, bros."

"Hmm."

Rebecca and Lizzy turn just as Alice approaches. Alice gives them a press-on smile, faltering a little once she sees Lizzy's phone pointed at Michael, but quickly gaining composure. "Can we come and set up inside?" Alice asks him. "We need space for the press room and then enough room for the pastor to give his blessings."

Michael furrows his brow. "A pastor to do what?"

Alice sighs, pinching the bridge of her nose. "Nancy said she would brief everybody."

"Well—"

"We're calling in a . . ." Alice snaps her fingers twice before Tosin whispers a name from behind her. "Yes, that's it. Pastor Lazarus. He's the head pastor and founder of, um . . ." She pauses before the words come to her. "The Righteous Rock of Christ Evangelical Church."

Michael grimaces. His people love a good church name, don't they?

"They're a church in Lagos and we'll have a direct link to them leading up to the resurrection."

"Okay, but please, using the word 'resurrection' feels somehow . . ." Michael says, chewing his lip.

Immediately, Alice holds up a finger, her red acrylics shining in the afternoon light. "Look at me. Look at all these people." She gestures to the pockets of onlookers around them, then fixes her stare on Michael. "Was I skeptical before? Yes. I will admit. But faith lives where skepticism has no place. It's Easter weekend. If there was ever a weekend, if there was ever a time to believe in miracles, it's *this* weekend."

"Amen!" Lizzy cheers from behind her phone.

Alice clears her throat. "Now. Let me in, please. If you think you're getting out of interviews this time, you're mad." Without another word, she sidles past Michael, curling a finger and signaling that her crew should follow her. They do, and much to Michael's dismay, so do Nwunye and her entourage.

One of the people singing around the corner gets to his feet and calls, "Are we being let in?"

"W-what? No," Michael stammers. Wait, did these people eventually want to come in? Is that why they're gathered here? Even he has to admit it would be kind of rude to leave this many people in the driveway when they came here to see his mom come back from the dead. "Just wait first. Sorry."

As Michael shuts the door behind him, he can't help but notice Nwunye's friend Lizzy videoing the entranceway. Every now and then, Nwunye will point to something and whisper toward the phone as if she's dictating what's going on. Michael frowns. "What are you people doing?"

Nwunye steps in right away. "We're keeping people updated about the resurrection."

Alice whips around. "Excuse me? That's my job. I have an interview scheduled and a live segment for the afternoon."

"We're updating local people, na. Yours is international." Nwunye lets out a nervous chuckle. "You and your Lagos pastor."

Alice turns up her nose and makes her way into the house, but not before uttering loud enough for them to hear: "Village people, I swear."

Michael follows behind Alice's crew as they test each area of the living room for proper lighting. He hears her telling Auntie Nancy about the full day of publicity she has planned and he sees Auntie's eyes light up. "Is there another room we can do interviews in? I want it to look dynamic," Alice explains.

"Eh-heh, of course." Nancy nods, then waves Michael over. For whatever reason, James wanders up from where he was perched on the sofa, as well. Michael figures he just can't stand not being included in decisions. "Michael, which other room? There's an office, another office, the house with the plants outside."

Michael shrugs. "There's a taxidermy room with squirrels enacting the birth of Jesus."

James gasps. "Bros, please!"

"No, no, that could work . . ." Alice taps her chin while she thinks. She looks at Tosin, nodding slowly while she evaluates. "So, like a nativity scene? Where Jesus is *also* . . . a squirrel?"

"Yes," says Michael.

"Show me."

He blinks. "What?"

"In the meantime . . ." She snaps her fingers at a few other crew members. "Set up for Pastor Lazarus. They're standing by. Gather the whole family in the living room to watch the prayer, and then we can start the individual interviews."

"Yes, ma'am," they mumble and get to work.

Michael feels stuck in the middle of a storm. The good thing? His fight with Joy is yesterday's news. The bad thing? A pastor from Nigeria named Lazarus will be delivering a sermon in a few minutes and AJAfrika TV will be filming his family's reaction the entire time.

To Michael's surprise, everyone gathers in the living room without much resistance. James has made himself useful by arranging some of the chairs in a way that are facing the huge TV while Alice's people hook up the transmission from Nigeria. Zach snuggles in with his mom, looking like he'd rather be anywhere else but here. Sarah is glued to her phone, as usual. Nwunye and her friends stay on the periphery, and she narrates toward Lizzy's positioned phone about what will be happening. James stands at attention behind everyone and Michael immediately thinks it's because he wants his forehead to be the main thing anyone sees when the livestream starts.

That's mean. Don't be an asshole, he chides himself.

Still, it's probably true.

"Okay." One of the technicians dusts his hands off just as the TV comes on. He gives a thumbs-up. "We're good here. Just give it a few seconds and then we'll get our cameras up and running, too."

James applauds.

Jamil whispers to his dad, "Shouldn't we call Mom?"

Michael overhears and instinctively reaches for his phone to text Joy, but hesitates. She probably wouldn't want to hear from him, anyway. When he sees David give Jamil his phone, he feels equal parts relief that at least someone will tell her what's going on and jealousy that it couldn't be him. Joy's his sister. *Why* can't he just suck it up and text her?

And would it have killed Shelly to call him back after she missed his call? Fuck.

He frowns his way through Pastor Lazarus's initial introduction. Pastor Lazarus has a comforting smile and a chuckle that reminds Michael a little of his dad. He's completely different from what Michael thought he'd be like, too. The second he heard "a pastor from Nigeria is interested," he thought this would be some opportunistic man who was trying to gain clout. But as Pastor Lazarus sings a resounding, "Good afternoon, or is it evening? My Canadian family," Michael thinks he's not that bad. At the very least, Michael can't see a Rolex on his wrist or a Gucci pocket square protruding from his suit jacket.

Mama would like him, he tells himself, and feels comfort in that. *She would say, "Ah, look at this responsible man," and then try to sit in the front row. She would have started praying before he did.* A tinge of sadness colors his face. He swallows quickly to force the emotion away.

"A real resurrection . . . praise God, o!" Lazarus says, holding his hands up to the sky. Behind him, his congregation can be heard applauding and chorusing "Hallelujah."

James calls out a resounding "Hallelujah!" as well and then grins. "Pastor, you are welcome. I'm James Olubisi, head pastor of New Apostles in Pentecostal Glory African Church in Baltimore. In the United States."

Michael feels the pressure swarm his head immediately. Yes, there was definitely an opportunistic pastor here, but it wasn't Lazarus. "James." Michael turns to him, his voice low so Alice's microphone won't pick it up. "James, if you don't shut up that your mouth at *once*—"

James scowls. "Bros—"

"Pastor!" Nancy cuts in. She dons a matronly smile for the sake of the cameras. "Ndewo. Welcome. Thank you so much for joining us today."

"Thank you, my sister," he replies warmly. "Please, before we pray, tell us again of the premonition. Everybody here"—he gestures loosely behind him to what the family assumes is the congregation; Zach cranes his neck to try and see better—"is so interested in how this came to be."

Michael lets out a sigh and rubs his eyes as Auntie Nancy begins to chuckle. "Pastor, it will be my honor to tell the story. It was yesterday morning, on Good Friday, on my sister's birthday, I was feeling something in my spirit. My sister had gone to sleep from"—she snaps her fingers repeatedly, a casual gesture that signifies how long Mary had been asleep—"a long time. The day prior."

What? Michael frowns.

"So I said to myself, 'Okay, let me go and check on her.'"

Auntie can lie! That's not what happened at all . . . Michael watches on in awe at how his aunt completely reframes the story, making both her and the cow the real heroes. She mentions offhandedly that other family members came to cry by his mom's bedside, but she makes no mention of the kids finding her that way. The kids, who will probably be traumatized for years to come. Not only from seeing their grandmother in that state, but from the ridiculousness that is the Mary Okafor Resurrection Tour.

Michael completely zones out during Auntie Nancy's false recollection. He catches a mere hint of her sensationalizing how she came across the cow—"It walked in front of my husband's car! Ah-ah! I said, 'Is this not the same spirit from my uncle's compound?'"—and focuses on his surroundings instead. Nwunye and her friends hang out in the kitchen corner, narrating to her followers as if she's doing the evening news. Alice hanging by the second hallway, talking with her producer about who she'll pull first for interviews.

"Praise God," Pastor Lazarus says eventually. "Death is never an easy thing to digest, but today, we are here to celebrate life. Amen." In the background, the chorus agrees. "There is nothing in the Bible that says… 'Dying on Good Friday is good' or 'Dying on Good Friday is bad.' But that's why we have faith. Eh-heh. We have faith to counteract the doubt."

Behind him, Pastor Lazarus reaches for a Bible with gold-sprayed edges and begins to thumb through the pages. "We must pray for the life of Onyinye Mary Okafor. No matter what. Because now, while she is around us, waiting to make her return, we have to look at her whole life. Let us not only remember the way in which God has called her home, but the way in which God had kept her here. Amen?"

"Amen!" his chorus shouts.

Pastor Lazarus begins reading from his Bible. "If anyone would like to join me . . ." he says as he lifts it to the screen. James shares Bibles with his children and Nnenna loads up her Bible app on her phone. Michael and David glance at each other, and in that moment, Michael knows they're thinking the same thing: *Should* we *have Bible apps?*

Once everyone is settled, Pastor Lazarus launches into his first prayer-sermon hybrid. Michael's eyes begin to glaze over. He can't help it. In his peripheral, he sees Alice signal to him, waving him toward the second hall. He points to himself just to make sure and she nods heavily, *yes.* Michael gets up and tiptoes around the back of the sofa, carefully skirting around James, to reach the hallway.

"So . . ." Alice is all business. She waves him toward the taxidermy room, not bothering to check and make sure that he's following, while she explains, "Viewers will have the opportunity to watch the all-access livestream starting in an hour—"

"Wait, wait." Michael frowns, stopping in his tracks. Alice whips around, clearly put off by his confusion. "What do you mean, 'all-access'?" he says.

"All-access, na." She lets out a disgruntled sigh. "What kind of question is that? When Mama resurrects, your auntie tells me that she can be brought back here to join the festivities. Obviously."

Oh, obviously. Michael's throat dries.

"In the meantime, we'll show parts of the stream with the pastor and your family, then intersperse it with the family interviews, and then I'll go live and talk about the vigil, show some of the attendees—"

"But they're not coming *in* here."

"Yes, they are," she says bluntly. "So you'll invite people to your house for a party and won't let them inside, abi?"

"We didn't invite anybody!" Michael hisses, then looks over his shoulder to make sure his voice didn't carry to the living room. "All those people outside? Most of the people who are tuning into this pastor nonsense and Nwunye's stream? We don't know them, o! They didn't come here to see my mama. They came here to see a miracle."

Alice takes a step toward him and crosses her arms. Her eyes narrow, darting across his face as if there's something there she's trying to read. Suddenly, she says, "Per-fect," and then gestures for him to follow her into the taxidermy room where they've set up camp. Studio-quality lights are positioned around a love seat and wires line the floor everywhere. Two cameramen and a producer are standing by, both talking quickly into headsets as Alice approaches them. "Sit here," she tells Michael.

He does as he's told. "Uh, here?"

"Yes, just here is fine," she says, then clasps her hands together. "Okay. I love the 'rah, we don't know them' angle. It's the perfect opposition to the narrative we're portraying with your aunt and cousin. Can you repeat it again, but this time, maybe let's try more emphasis on the 'all those people' part? As in . . . '*ALL* those *PEOPLE!*' Or"—she drops her voice an octave—"'*all* . . . those people.' You know?"

— 23 —

Pastor Lazarus does another prayer or maybe two. Maybe it's three. Jamil can't tell, but he's so tired of being asked to stand up for ages at a time. At least at church, or at Mass at school, they ask them to sit down or kneel, too. They also have Communion, which is what some of his friends call "breakfast," especially when Mass is before noon.

Jamil feels his soul spring back to life as he sees Pastor Lazarus wrap up his final prayer. Soon, one of the producers with AJAfrika steps in and says they have a break while the next segment is getting set up, so the family can leave. "We want to get everyone in a more candid environment," the producer says. "So don't mind us. We'll be around and we'll be watching you."

"That sounds like a threat," Sarah stage-whispers to Jamil. She's by the kitchen island stuffing her mouth with breakfast potatoes.

Jamil snorts. "What are you doing?"

"Church makes me hungry," and she chortles with a full mouth.

Jamil gets to his feet and shuffles over. He manages to steal one potato before Sarah holds up her hand. "Wait, one second," and she grabs a disposable bowl to fill with the remaining potatoes. A producer watches, eyeing them as if he can't tell if this is worthy of filming.

Quickly, Sarah clutches the bowl to her chest and signals Jamil to follow down the opposite hall. They pass a really bright room where cameras are set up and Uncle James is positioned directly in front of one, holding a Bible to his chest. "Uh, not in here, I guess," Jamil utters as they slip away from the door.

At the end of the hall is the games room. Jamil has only seen it from the outside, but his cousin seems way more comfortable here. It's far enough from the main hall that if someone isn't purposefully looking for them, they won't find them.

He and Sarah settle into the sofa and eat their way through the breakfast potatoes. He sighs as he chews. "Can't believe my mom missed the whole thing."

"Yo, no way," Sarah snickers. "Auntie had the right idea. She's lucky, honestly."

"No, she's not."

Jamil and Sarah startle the moment Yemi appears at the door. Arms crossed and eyes narrowed, she scrutinizes everything about the scene before her. Zach squeezes in under her arm, skipping over to Jamil on the sofa. "Can I play Mario Kart?" he asks.

"Uhh, sure. I think I left it in the living room, though," Jamil adds, nodding toward the hall. Zach disappears before he finishes his sentence.

Yemi slides her way into the room, collapsing on a chair opposite her cousins. She lets her legs swing a little, getting used to the height. "Why's this chair so high?" she mumbles to herself.

Zach returns with game in hand and squeezes in beside Sarah so he can lean against her while he plays. She reaches out, nudging him softly and patting him on the shoulder, as she asks, "You good, son?"

Zach shrugs her off a little, but nods. "Is Grandma Mary gonna be a zombie?"

The urge to laugh hits Jamil instantly, but he shoves another potato in his mouth to stop himself.

But, if he really thinks about it . . . Grandma is dead, and if they keep saying she'll come back, then isn't that technically what a zombie is? "Ah . . . hmmm." He thinks harder. Maybe Zach has the right idea here.

He can tell in an instant that Yemi disagrees. She gasps, "Zach, shut up!" and frowns so hard that her forehead wrinkles make her look at least five years older than him. "Why would you say that? You're so stupid."

"W-well, hey. *Hey.*" Sarah clears her throat. She looks like she's going to laugh.

"Grandma is not going to come back as a zombie," Yemi says, her tone strict. "She will come back as an angel, obviously."

"But then she won't come back at all," Sarah says. "Angels don't live on earth, right? So it's not like she'd come back from the dead and then suddenly be here frying chicken at noon."

Yemi rolls her eyes. "I know that's what *you* believe, but that's not what the Bible says."

Sarah falters. "The Bible mentions frying chicken?"

"No, no—"

"Would Grandma eat our brains if she became a zombie?" Zach murmurs while his fingers jab buttons across the handheld.

Yemi squeaks.

"N-no, she wouldn't." Sarah bites back a laugh again. "Or, I mean, let's put it this way: people don't actually come back from the dead, so the chances of her actually coming back to eat your brains are pretty slim."

"And," Jamil adds, "there's no, like, actual scientific proof that a person can be resurrected . . . right?" He looks at Sarah, who grimaces and shrugs as if she's trying to get out of answering.

Jamil knows why in a second. When he glances at Yemi, she glares back at him, unbridled rage bubbling under her features. "Are you *serious*?" she spits out, her mouth twisting in disbelief. "Why would you even say that on a day like today?"

Jamil frowns. "Like 'today,' meaning . . . ?"

"The vigil is tonight," Yemi goes on. "There's a TV show filming our entire family because of it. People are already outside, waiting, and you're pretending like it's not real. That pastor told us Grandma Mary's spirit is here."

"Okay, but *every* spirit is here," Jamil says with a shrug. "They're called ghosts. The Earth is old."

Yemi's scowl deepens. "I wouldn't expect someone like you to get it. Your mom doesn't go to church, so of course you don't understand why resurrection is important." She rolls her eyes and looks away.

"Okay, wait a second," Sarah chimes in, holding her hands out. She makes chopping movements like she's cutting up the tension. "That's not fair to say. Besides, that's, I mean, this is just an insane convo to be having. You guys are *children*."

In the distance, the doorbell rings.

Yemi smirks, rolling her neck as she says, "That's probably more people for the vigil. So you're all dumb." She pops onto her feet and skips out of the room, humming as she goes.

Sarah lets out an exhale. "Uh, fucking yikes," she mumbles—then slaps her hand to her mouth when she realizes Zach is nestled in beside her.

Jamil, however, doesn't care. He nods in agreement while he stands.

Sarah gets up, too, careful to position Zach on the sofa so he doesn't fall over. "Let's go see who's at the door." After a second, she whispers to Jamil, "How do you say 'fucking yikes' in Italian?"

"I'onno," he lies.

They leave the games room, and as they get to the end of the hall and around the living room—which seems to have been taken over by Auntie Nwunye and her friends—Jamil realizes he can hear his mom's voice in the entranceway. "Mom?" he calls as he rounds the corner.

She is talking to both Grandma Nancy and Grandpa Ezekiel. Jamil weasels himself around them until he can greet her with a hug. She embraces him, petting his back, uttering a small, "Hey, Jamil," before diving back into her conversation. He kinda likes that, this close, she smells a bit like his dad's cologne.

— 24 —

Joy has driven an hour-plus in traffic to a funeral home she never thought she'd ever see the inside of again. She rehashed memories she didn't want to, she cried in front of a stranger, she sang the entirety of Destiny's Child's "Survivor," sobbing up the 400, while she tried not to choke on the weight of her own personal responsibility. She put her work phone on "do not disturb," then felt guilty about it and turned the ringer back on, only to have her colleague send her a *call me ASAP* text, which she then felt obligated to respond to.

"H-hey."

"Joy?"

"Y-yes."

"Are you all right? My goodness, you sound awful."

"Um."

"Did you say something to Coral Lopez, by the way? She's left me a message—and I can't say in particular what it is since, you know, confidential, but she mentions you by name."

"O-oh."

"In any case, when you get a chance, ring her back? I'm going to see if I can get a hold of her in the meantime."

"I—"

"Okay, bye, love."

Joy kept "Survivor" on repeat until she got back to the house.

The driveway is so full that she has to park on the side of the road a good walking distance away. She sees more cars and more vans than she remembered being there the first time, and a group of people have set up a gazebo by the fountain. Underneath, they're playing music and eating rice. *Where did they get the rice from?* No, she won't ask. She wills herself not to care.

It takes her five minutes to walk from her car to the foot of the driveway. She takes several deep breaths on her way up—*This shit does not work, it doesn't work,* she thinks. Suddenly, she feels extra sympathetic to all the clients she's ever told to just pause, breathe, and reflect. She's pausing—*This is the worst experience of my life.* She's breathing—*I want to not be here anymore.* She's reflecting—*I wish I had a different family.*

Don't say that, says the Mama in her head. Joy listens to the lilt of the voice, imagining her mother walking beside her all the way to the house. How fast her footsteps would be. How it would feel like Mama was the one leading. *These are your family,* she is saying. *God gave you this one, and He knows why He did that.*

Joy chews on her lower lip, thinking. Is there really a lesson in everything? Can't it be enough just to . . . *be?*

"Mom, I can't do this," she dares whisper aloud.

Mama replies, *Yes, you can. You're my Joy, na.*

Joy rings the doorbell before entering so she can announce her return without having to say anything. She clutches her phone and slips off her shoes by the doorway. Farther down the hall, she can hear voices, casual chatter, and someone who sounds a lot like . . . *Is Nwunye here?* she asks herself, then strains to listen. Well, if she is, maybe she can keep her brother busy. It's no secret that Michael's marriage is next on Nwunye's list to disrupt.

He's primed for it, and she doesn't even know how easy it would be.

She cringes. *Okay, cheap shot.*

Auntie Nancy appears first, looking as content as Joy has ever seen her. This isn't the face of someone who's grieving, or the face of someone who is ready to rub an impromptu resurrection in everyone's faces. This is the face of a woman with a secret she's ready to share.

"Joy mara mma." Nancy reaches forward for her hug.

Joy hugs back, an awkward smile quivering on her lips. "Auntie . . . is everything okay?"

"Yes. Why won't it be?" Nancy smiles. Over her shoulder, Joy sees Uncle Ezekiel make his way down the hall toward her. "You missed the pastor," Auntie says.

"Oh, damn." Joy kisses her teeth. "Is . . . oh." Her thoughts slow. She stops to really take in her auntie's chipper appearance. It is almost *too* obvious. Joy suppresses a groan. *He said something to them. The pastor said something.*

Auntie Nancy tells her, "The pastor specifically said my sister will rise at midnight."

Joy frowns. "Auntie."

"Joy."

She touches her forehead, softly, then with urgency as she tries to massage a burgeoning stress headache. "A human person told you this to your face?"

"Ah, Joy," Auntie gasps. She glances at Uncle Ezekiel, floundering for the right words, in complete disbelief that her niece would be so heartless. "The way you're asking this question troubles me, o. It's like you don't want to see your mother again."

"I—" Joy's voice cracks. Her hand flies to her throat, then her mouth, to cover up the squeak. The uncertainty. *Of course* she wants to see her mom again. What kind of a question is that? The longer she stares at her auntie, the more her frustration grows. Here she is trying to understand, to make sense of everything that's happened, but they just won't stop pushing and poking and prodding and, why won't they let it go? Why won't they let her rest?

She shuts her eyes.

This is your family, Mama's voice says. *Na only God knows why you dey here.*

Jamil appears seemingly out of nowhere and gives her a hug. Joy glances down, her breath caught in her throat at the sight of her son. If not for him, she would've packed up and gone home long ago. "Hey, Jamil," she mutters, rubbing his back.

"All I am saying is you should be careful with this funeral business," Auntie continues, crossing her arms. "Ị ga-ekwere the, eh, na the pastor. Ọ bụ man of God. He knows better than us—"

"And how do you know he didn't just say that to make you feel better?" Joy shoots back. Her voice is low and sharp.

Auntie's face twists with surprise. "Ị sị gịnị? Joy, you are saying this to *me*?"

Jamil flinches. He detaches from his mom and says, "People are livestreaming in the living room, by the way," while he jogs back down the hall.

"What?" Joy gasps. She looks to her aunt and uncle and then toward the living room, and she just . . . she just . . . "*What?* What even is there to stream?"

"Alice and her people are doing all-access. They are telling everybody of the resurrection, of course," Nancy replies, smug. "Why won't they? It's very important."

"All-access? No, no, no . . ." Joy steps to move past them, but Auntie quickly grabs her arm. "Auntie, please. I just got back from the funeral home, I'm waiting on a coroner's report, I can't have anyone broadcasting to the world that my mother is going to rise from the dead."

"Well, somebody has to, because it's true," Nancy says. Then she holds her hands up, proclaiming, "In Corinthians, the Word says, 'For since death came through a man, the resurrection of the dead comes also through a man.'"

Joy takes a deep breath.

And she screams.

— 25 —

Rob hears the scream from the taxidermy interview room just as he's passing James on his way in. The two of them lock eyes, with Rob exaggerating a grimace because he knows the cause of it must be his mother. It's just a feeling he has. Even he has to admit Nancy Akintola is being way more extra than she normally is this weekend. At first, he thought it was somewhat amusing that she was so wrapped up in this idea of the resurrection. And he believed it, too, a little. It's all so magical. An unassuming death on Good Friday, a prophecy, a sense of togetherness. But even he has to admit his mom is weaponizing her faith in such a way that makes this whole thing really uncomfortable and disrespectful. Auntie Mary's life, the joy of her family, the way she used to make meat pie with the best dough-to-meat ratio every time they came to visit—all of it is being overshadowed by her supposed second coming. *And what about her kids?* he thinks to himself. *What about us?*

"Rob, are you ready for your interview?"

"Yes, abso-fucking-lutely," he says, dancing his way over to the sofa.

Alice directs Rob, telling him to pose more like this or look more like that as he settles in. "Can this come out?" she asks, pointing to her own septum.

Rob frowns, nudging his piercing as he scrunches his mouth. "No. I mean, yes, but no. It's staying."

She purses her lips. "Well . . . I mean, our sponsors may not like it." Rob had it on good authority that the sponsors were all her husband. "But I'll see what I can do." It was probably of no consequence. Will a few more conservative Nigerians tune out if they see a man with a septum piercing on their screens? Well, maybe, but this is about his auntie Mary's resurrection. People are willing to sit through an ounce of discomfort if they know they'll be rewarded at the end.

Rob watches as the cameramen fix their positions and the lighting techs work on making sure the shadows are all falling the right way. Alice takes up her seat across from him and turns to give a thumbs-up to the producer. He counts them in.

"Okay . . ." Alice's smile widens the closer the count gets to zero. By the time they're recording, she's gone full-blown on-screen talent— and her accent seems to have reemerged from wherever it was hiding. "Perfect. We're here with Robert Akintola, a direct relative to Onyinye Mary Okafor. Robert, can you tell us a bit about what you're feeling today?"

Rob gives a nervous smile. His eyes dart from Alice's face to the camera. He can't seem to remember where she said he should look. "Uh . . ." He clears his throat and decides staring into the whites of Alice's eyes is the best way forward. "I feel a bit strange, honestly. Everything is happening kinda fast—"

"Yes, and especially with the crowds that are now gathering," Alice interrupts with a shimmy of her shoulders. "It must be such an exciting time. Tell me, where do you stand on the resurrection?"

Oh no.

"We've heard from some family members who don't completely believe in the strength of the Lord."

Wow, that's a sentence.

"Would you say you believe you'll see your beloved aunt on Easter morning?"

I, uh . . .

Rob clears his throat. He can feel himself starting to sweat under the gaze of the lights and Alice's piercing stare. "W-well, uh." He tries to focus, clasping his hands together in his lap. "I consider myself a v-very religious person, Alice. Um. I go to church every week. And I think that—"

She jumps on his words. "That . . . ?"

"That faith is such an individual thing," he says, then mentally kicks himself because what is he talking about right now? "I miss my aunt a lot. I think we all would love to see her, uh . . . w-when she comes back." At that moment, he knows his mom has officially gotten into his head.

He lets out a sharp breath, shaking his head. "Okay, you know what? No. Mmm, no."

Alice raises an eyebrow, glancing to her camera techs. "N-no?"

"I love my auntie Mary. When I was a kid, she always made extra meat pie when we came to visit. And she never added peas, just for me, because she knew I hated them. I'll miss her—I'll miss the food. But do I believe now that my mother talked to a cow and it told her Auntie is coming back? Do I?" As he speaks, he leans in closer, talks with more conviction. Alice holds her breath, ready to signal her crew to cut if need be. Then Rob says, "I don't *know*!" and Alice lets out the tiniest sigh of relief.

Rob groans, leaning back in his seat. "Like, no one really does. Maybe except for my mom. But y'all don't understand: she's just *like* this."

"Has she ever had a premonition like this before?"

"Well, no, I guess," Rob says. "But one time, she *did* predict a baby's name at a christening. Kwame. But, I mean, the kid was born on a Saturday and the dad was Ghanaian, so. I don't know. Weird coincidence, though."

"What's the coincidence?"

Rob blanks. "What?"

"You said it's a coincidence. What's the coincidence?"

He glances away, shifting awkwardly in his seat. He *did* say he wanted to be more truthful, so here goes nothing. "I, uh . . . w-well. I'm actually going to be moving to Ghana soon for a job. S-so if anyone in

Accra happens to be watching this at any time . . ." He cups his cheeks with his hands and grins. "Remember this face. Hit me up."

"Wow!" Alice gasps. Her TV persona was really working overtime. "That's *amazing.* You're—"

"What's this about Ghana?"

It's hard for Rob to explain just how his blood runs cold or his breathing halts completely when he hears his mom's voice at that very second, especially to someone who hasn't grown up in his household. He's sure Nnenna gets it. Hell, he's sure even Joy or Michael would understand the sheer terror that comes with saying something you shouldn't have in front of your parents. In the vicinity of your parents. In the same city as your parents.

Rob turns slowly, just in time to catch his mom in the doorway, hovering dangerously close. "Uh . . . um." He clears his throat. "Mom?"

"What's this about Ghana?" his mom asks again, this time looking at Alice. "Why would you be talking about Ghana on this Saturday? Everybody knows we are Nigerians."

Alice makes a hand gesture to her crew, telling them to keep film- ing no matter what. "Nancy, why don't you join us?" she asks. Quickly, her staff make room on the sofa beside Rob and widen their shot to get both of them.

Nancy, frowning and filled with discontent, makes her way over to the empty space beside Rob. Rob, who is absolutely losing his mind. His mom, normally omnipresent in a different sort of way, couldn't have picked a worse time to show up. And Alice, she must be eating all this up.

Alice says, "Is—?"

But Nancy interrupts, still frowning. "Why would you be talking about Ghana when my sister has died? Eh, Robert? Ọ gịnị?"

Rob takes a deep breath and lets his eyes finally meet his mom's. In his peripheral vision, Alice is laser focused on him, practicing her best active listening stance. He tries not to think about her, or the maybe hundreds of people who could be watching this interview at any time.

"W-well, um." Rob starts and stops so often that he almost forgets what he wants to say. *Better out than in,* he thinks, and finally blurts out: "Paul and I are moving to Ghana at the end of the month. I got a job offer in Accra and I'm planning on taking it. Uh, we, I already know how to make waakye so I'll be fine." *Why did I say that?*

Nancy is caught by surprise. Her eyebrows shoot up and she turns to stare into the closest camera.

Alice's mouth forms a perfect *O* as she gazes into the camera. "This is such a—a *shocking* revelation on a day that's meant to be about togetherness and family and resurrected siblings!"

Rob rolls his eyes at Alice. "Okay, come on."

Nancy, on the other hand, smacks her hands together with conviction. "Ah! Yes, na! Tufia-kwa!" She looks at Rob, her mouth agape with disbelief. "Why is the job in Ghana?"

Rob gives a stiff shrug and murmurs, "I'onno, Mom, that's just where the company's headquarters are."

"And why is it not in Nigeria?"

"*What?*"

"Robert, nwa m. I didn't leave Nigeria to come to the U-S-A," she begins, using her hands to illustrate her immigration route, "for you to now be coming and going to Ghana."

"I-I know, Mom," Rob answers, his voice sincere. He understands where his mom is coming from, he really does, but she's operating from such a narrow-minded view. Is it because she doesn't think there are opportunities in West Africa? Or just because she doesn't want her family separated?

Maybe, to his mom, it's the same thing; it's the same feeling.

"Your papa and I worked hard for you to be born here, on this side of the world," she continues, her voice betraying her composure. She doesn't meet Rob's eyes as she speaks, and he knows it's because he's right. His mom has been running from something, from hardship, her whole life, all to make sure her kids didn't have to flee from the same beast. She sees anything outside of the life they've built as a struggle, and she won't have it.

"Yeah, b-but it's my life," Rob offers. He sees Alice nodding. "I'm an adult, so what about what I want—"

"Ah! Mba, mba, mba," Nancy cuts in, holding up a hand to silence him. "Don't start talking your diplomatics right now. Okay? I've had enough. You people want to come and kill me, is that it? My sister has died yesterday, and now you see me say I be next, abi?"

"*What*?" Rob's eyes widen. He glances at the camera, a silent plea for help. "Mom, no, that's insane," he tells her. "What kind of a thing is that to say?"

"Robert, I've heard enough. You are choosing to disrespect me on a holy day. And now I know you don't understand. Okay? I know. If you leave for this your Ghana, eh," she says, pointing her finger at him. "Abiakwala ozo. N-nonsense." Her voice trembles with her threat, trembles with her discomfort, as she marches out of the room.

Everyone is silent.

Alice gives the slightest nod to her camera crew. Rob watches them, resolve burning behind their eyes. He knows they're only thinking of the viewers.

— 26 —

SATURDAY, 3:49 P.M.

At one point, Nwunye opens the front door and many visitors start to make their way inside. Luckily for the family, most of the attendees who had found their way into the halls and living room were actual friends of Mary's. "We wanted to see our sister," they'd say as they took note of the chandeliers and the many downstairs washrooms. They see the camera crews and want to get something on film saying how much they loved Mary, and Alice isn't one to turn down free content, so she shuttles them into the taxidermy room one by one.

As time goes on, the house begins to fill with more strangers than the family can count. They walk around saying things like, "It's a miracle! I know. I said it," as they pepper the living room. Women dressed in their finest george lace; men donning suits or agbadas. All these people who held Mary dear in their hearts.

One of the guests sitting in a giant armchair calls out. "Eh, madam." Once he gets Nancy's attention, he greets, "Ndewo."

"Yes, welcome, sir." Nancy smiles.

"Please, is there malt?"

Nancy looks over her shoulder at the kitchen where Nnenna, under James's instruction, is clearing space on the kitchen counters.

"Nnenna, where is the malt?" Nancy calls over the commotion. Another man chimes in, "Yes, please, I need malt."

Nnenna lets out a groan as she stands straight.

God, will no one let her have peace today? James tells her to rearrange the pillows on the chairs for the guests. Then he says she should clear the breakfast food and pack everything into boxes. Oh, but the only problem is that there's no room in the fridge because of all this dough the caterer left, so she has to somehow move this and put that—and now the campers from outside are moving inside; that woman Nwunye won't stop livestreaming; Alice's people are considering setting up a second set outside, talking about, "This looks like where we might hold the vigil"; and ugh!

"Mom, do it yourself!" is what Nnenna wants to scream.

"Mom, we don't have malt" is what she mumbles instead.

"Ah-ah," the man gasps, craning his neck to look into the kitchen. "You don't have malt? You get Guinness?"

"How can you be drinking Guinness today when a woman is about to be resurrected?" the man's wife chides.

Nnenna feels like she will scream, just like Joy did.

Joy, who they had to sequester upstairs because she seemed to be overwhelmed by the sudden escalation of events. As Nnenna turns back to the fridge to fish out the dough and replace it with some of the leftover breakfast food, she doesn't blame Joy for hiding upstairs. Nnenna is excited about the resurrection, too, but a small, niggling voice in the back of her head keeps telling her that this is all a little bit much. Where is the humility? Somehow, this doesn't feel very Christ-like at all.

Her mom approaches, her voice low as she says, "We have to order more food. These people will be here until midnight."

Nnenna scoffs. "Order food from where, Mom? We're not from around here."

"I have the caterer's number," James jumps in. "Mama, don't worry, I will call. We'll ask them to deliver the food we ordered for the birthday party. It's paid for, anyway."

Convenient, Nnenna thinks.

"Excellent," her mom says.

Nnenna steps away. She knows where she's not needed. While her dad seems to think James is a stain upon their family, her mom is always impressed when he does the bare minimum.

God, what's wrong with me today? She's never had thoughts like these before. She watches as Joy enters the room, holding a small notepad and her phone, and Nnenna can't help but think that too much time in a vulnerable state around her wayward cousin has weakened her temperament. No, she has to stay strong. It's Easter weekend, after all. Isn't this the biggest test of faith? She won't waver and she won't quit. She won't become like Joy.

— 27 —

Auntie?" Joy's voice barely carries through the room. She can't believe the sheer amount of people in this house who really showed up early—early!—for a supposed resurrection. She wishes Nwunye would stop telling people to come. She wishes this Alice woman and her ever-growing crew would disappear. Who knows how many people will drop by just because they're watching the coverage on AJAfrika? Joy wasn't even aware people actually watched that program!

She scans the room again. "Auntie?"

"Why are you shouting? I'm right here." Auntie Nancy waves from the kitchen.

Joy marches over, skimming through the notes she took from her call with the coroner. "It's a holiday weekend and everything," he had said. "So I thought it would take much longer to get you a pre-liminary report, but when Patricia called, I thought I'd take a closer look . . ." Joy took careful notes of everything he said, even asking him to repeat certain things several times. She drew lines and put her thoughts in brackets and created this intricate recollection of their conversation, but . . .

"I spoke to the coroner," she says. "And he says from first look, e-even though he hasn't done a deep dive or anything—it seems she died of a heart attack."

A heart attack.

"Are you sure?" Joy had asked him for the millionth time. "She was healthy. How could that happen?"

"Sometimes, these things can be sudden," he told her. "To add to that, I didn't see anything that would indicate an external or brain-related cause. No, for now, until maybe toxicology comes back with something in a few weeks, or we perform a full autopsy at your request, it's looking like a heart attack. In an official report, you'll likely see it referred to as 'natural causes.'"

Natural causes.

Even saying it aloud now does little to put Joy at ease. It sounded so vague but so direct at the same time. It could mean anything and nothing at all. *So she was just taken, then . . . for no reason.*

But Auntie Nancy smiles that same wide, wry grin from before. Her voice dissolves into a breath while she croons, "Hallelujah." Joy purses her lips. Of course to her fanatical aunt, Mama dying of natural causes makes perfect sense. Of course if the good Lord was to take someone on Good Friday, it wouldn't be because of a terminal illness or an accident. It would be because it was God's will, just like it is His will to return her to them.

This indeed, Joy thinks, will be a celebration.

Nancy turns to Nnenna, smiling while reaching out for her wrist, and says, "Oya. Order food. Let's start frying the chin-chin."

— 28 —

By the time evening sets in, the house smells like sweet oil and spicy rice, and there are more guests sitting in the living room, pulling dining chairs, and lining the halls than Michael is personally comfortable with. When Mama Okezie showed up with her grandchildren, two rambunctious boys who kept trying to dig the meat filling out of each meat pie, she took up what Michael deemed as "the last chair." Now there was nowhere really to sit, unless you were okay with crouching on the floor, hopping on the countertop, or sneaking off to one of the rooms upstairs. So this is what Michael decides to do. He hides for the better part of the afternoon and waits until nightfall.

He had absolutely no will to greet the growing crowd, a crowd of people who would weep at his feet or tell him how much he looked like his dad. Nor did he want to cross paths with anyone from Alice's team, or they'd stop him for another interview, this time finding a way to ask even more intrusive questions. No, he'd rather sit in his room, scan every streaming app on the Smart TV, and find something mind-numbing to watch.

"What about a *Real Housewives*?" Sarah had suggested.

Michael scoffed. "I'll leave that for you and your mom."

In actuality, he couldn't bring himself to entertain that idea because *Real Housewives* tended to be a thing Joy watched. He associated it more with his sister than he did his wife.

His wife, who still hasn't tried to call him back.

He's stopped hearing footsteps up and down the hall outside. Once he's absolutely sure Sarah has gone to keep an eye on her young cousins or steal chin-chin from the kitchen, Michael brings out his phone. A heavy sigh shakes from his chest while he swipes into his wife's contact and redials her number.

It rings once.

Twice.

And again. *"Hello, you've reached Shelly Okafor, please—"*

Michael hangs up and tosses his phone on the bed. He's never known Shelly to be *this* avoidant or careless. All he wants to do is talk. And at the very least, he'd like to tell her his mom is dead. He's sure she'd like to know that. Mama was nice to Shelly, giving her a lot of leeway when they first got married. At first, Michael felt his parents didn't understand why he'd want to marry a girl who wasn't Nigerian. They were convinced it would be hard for him.

Mama, in particular, worried that a girl who couldn't cook Nigerian food wouldn't make a very good wife. It was archaic, but these were the kinds of concerns his parents had. "So what will she be feeding your children? Common burger and fry?" she had said, which made Michael laugh more than he should've. *We were arguing,* he remembers. *She was really angry, honestly. She was genuinely concerned about her grandchildren.*

Over time, Mama softened. First when Miles was born, and then with Sarah. She did omugwo both times, coming to bathe the babies and bring fish pepper soup for Shelly. She even taught Shelly how to cook ogbono soup—though she remained eternally put off that Shelly added chicken to it. For a while, she'd call Shelly "Madam Chicken." It was a joke, but Michael could see how uncomfortable it made Shelly, so he asked Mama to stop referring to her that way. And she did, at least to her face.

His phone starts buzzing in the center of the bed. It catches him off guard, and as he twists backward to reach for it again, it doesn't cross his mind once that it might be a returned call.

It's Shelly.

Seeing her name flash on his screen so suddenly makes him freeze. Even though he's been trying to get a hold of her all weekend, well, that doesn't necessarily mean he's emotionally ready to talk to her. Yesterday, sure, but *now*?

"Bad idea," he grunts to himself—then accidentally accepts the call. *Shit*, he kisses his teeth, and slowly brings the phone to his ear. "Hel . . . lo? Hello?"

"Mike." Shelly's voice sounds curt over the line. Tired, too. "Did Miles text you?"

Michael frowns. "No. Is he all right?"

"He's all right. He's just asking about spending the summer over in London." She sighs, as if the thought is exhausting for her. "I told him we're not sending any more money and he's got to get a job or something."

"Which kind of job do you think he'll find in Oxford?"

"*Tch*, I don't know, but he's got to find something," she says. He can almost see the way she's probably rolling her eyes, too. It wasn't as if they were struggling for money or anything, but sometimes Shelly could be thrifty to a fault. At what point was it okay to spend money? he wondered. She rarely even lent money to her relatives when they asked. He didn't really understand that way of living. For years, his parents would send money back to Nigeria for their relatives who had trouble finding work or getting their head start in business. Sure, not all families did that, but he became so accustomed to it that he never questioned it, either. *Maybe that's just not what her family life was like*, he'd tell himself. *It's not a reason to castrate somebody.*

What was wrong with him? Wanting to pick fights about everything.

"I called you yesterday," he says slowly. "You didn't call back. Is everything okay?"

Right away, she sighs. "Mike, I was just tired. Couldn't talk."

He purses his lips, nodding. .

"What happened?"

"What?"

"What happened?" she asks again, this time softer. "You sound like it's something bad that's been going on. Is it about Sarah?"

"N-no, not Sarah."

"You better watch that girl, eh?" She kisses her teeth. "Make sure she's actually spending time with the family. I swear, every time I bring her anywhere, she's always on that damn phone like she's talking to someone more important. And who can be more important than her family?"

He's not sure what to say. The version of Sarah that Shelly sees can sometimes be so different from the Sarah that he sees. She's been so good with her young cousins, and she's always been fond of her uncle David, and her uncle Rob. It's . . . he's . . . In the end, he sighs. "Shelly."

"I'm serious now, Mike. Take that phone away from her," she instructs, her voice wavering for a moment. It sounds so unlike her, as if there's something sinister or unwelcome about an eighteen-year-old having a cellular device.

Michael tries again. "Shelly."

"What, Mike?"

"My . . . mom is dead."

Shelly gasps over the phone, a string of, "Oh, no, no, no . . ." spilling out before she's able to collect her thoughts. She starts rambling, "Oh my goodness, Jesus Christ, oh my goodness," and a part of Michael, a small, slightly sadistic part, finds her panic to be like music to his ears. *She cares,* he tells himself. *She cares about* something *at least.* This is the Shelly he remembers, the one he originally fell in love with. The one who has feelings; has compassion. It's weird to say that her momentary outburst, her outpouring of emotion, sounded more like her than their recent interactions. He feels guilty for thinking it, but it's true.

She hums, moans, and feels into her sadness. "I'm so sorry, baby. I'm so sorry. That's just horrible."

"It is, yeah."

"I . . ." She takes another deep breath, utters a "Damn," then stays quiet.

The line is so quiet, in fact, that Michael is afraid she has hung up. He strains to hear her breathing, for that hint of reassurance.

And he battles with himself. *Ask her to come.* The words don't formulate the way he wants. Michael imagines it was so easy for Joy to ask David, and equally as easy for David to say yes. He resents that so much, even in this moment where his thoughts should be consumed by the devastating loss of his mother.

He's afraid she'll say no.

Give her the chance, he chides himself, *to disappoint you.*

He shuts his eyes for a moment, hanging his head while he lets his thoughts get carried away. "Yeah," he sighs out. Pressure builds in his chest, making it harder to concentrate. It's anger, or it's frustration, or something mixed between the two. He hates that it's there and that it keeps growing unchecked to the point that he can't really pinpoint its source.

In the end, he says nothing. Just lets the feeling fester.

It's fear.

You're afraid because you know. *Already, you know.*

He hears his uncle Ezekiel calling his name from down the hall.

"Uh, um." Michael clears his throat and rubs a tired hand down his face. "I have to go. Call Miles and tell him for me. There's just so much going on here. . . . Did you call Sarah?"

"Hmm. Tell her I said hello," Shelly responds quickly. "And, Mike, I *am* sorry."

"Mmm." He hums as Uncle Ezekiel's "Son, where are you?" rings out again. "Don't worry, okay, no problem. I'll try and call again."

"A-all right."

He hangs up and gets to his feet, pocketing his phone, when he hears his uncle's final call: "The spiritualist is here! Come downstairs."

"The what?" Michael frowns as he steps out of his room. He is thinking of Shelly and how right he was about her. *I didn't want to be,* he thinks, and it bothers him how quickly the Shelly in the present has replaced the Shelly he once knew. The one he loved.

He makes his way to the staircase. Uncle Ezekiel stands at the foot, staring up with a stern expression on his face. Quickly, he waves Michael down, ushering him to come faster so as not to miss anything. Michael, dumbfounded, tries to remember exactly when or how this "spiritualist" was contacted. When he reaches the ground floor, he asks the first question he can think of. "Is he a friend of yours?"

Uncle Ezekiel scrunches his nose. "No. Why would he be? Because I am *old*?"

Michael laughs. "No, Uncle, ah-ah."

"Oya, just be quiet and come," Ezekiel chides and marches on to the living room.

His uncle must be unfazed by the sheer amount of people who have begun to fill the hallways, all snacking on food that Michael swears wasn't here an hour ago. He even spots Nwunye and her crew taking up residence in the den, lounged over furniture, sipping on malt and beer. He notices Alice's people sticking microphones and cameras in guests' faces as everyone recounts their best memories of his mom.

"How many people are here, Uncle?" Michael whispers to him as they walk.

"I don't know."

"Shouldn't we stop people from coming? Tell this Alice to stop broadcasting?"

"Eh, I don't know."

Uncle Ezekiel bypasses the kitchen and living room with ease, moving between groups of people and stepping over cords. Michael can't help but notice he hasn't seen one family member since coming downstairs. He opens his mouth to ask yet another question, but Uncle Ezekiel pauses by the sliding door to the backyard and pushes it open. He gestures for Michael to step outside, where he sees his immediate family sitting on chairs facing a makeshift pulpit at the edge of the yard.

Before he can shut the door, Alice appears from inside the house. Michael thought he was imagining it, but no, she really is pouting. "Mr. Akintola," she says to Uncle Ezekiel. "Please, I dey take God beg you, o. Let us film outside a little bit. It'll be so good for the show."

"Alice, I've already given you my answer," Uncle Ezekiel says, then gestures to his family outside. "This isn't for other people to listen to."

"But everyone already knows everything," she goes on. "Mary's daughter is divorced, your wife wants to get custody of the cow, and your son is going to Ghana."

Uncle Ezekiel frowns. "*Who* is going to Ghana?"

"*That's* the only thing you heard?" Michael chuckles. "Okay, let's go. Alice, we're sorry, but later you can get reactions or something. Interview people as they come in."

"I—" Alice opens her mouth to argue, but Michael can tell she's really mulling over the idea. Probably trying to figure out how she can work this to her advantage, he assumes. "All right," she concedes, and then steps out of the way. Uncle Ezekiel grabs Michael's wrist and ushers him outside, shutting the sliding glass door behind them.

Sarah waves, pointing to a seat beside her in the first row. Michael shuffles over, feeling self-conscious as his family watches him get settled. Joy sits two seats down and only glances over once while he gets seated. That's more of an acknowledgment than he was expecting from her.

"Is that everybody?"

The man's voice rings out with a raspy coolness that reminds Michael of an elder in a village. He wears a patterned red-and-white hat, which Michael thinks is called an okpu agu, but he's not sure. Many of his male relatives in the village wear something similar while donning a singlet and wrapper.

Auntie Nancy speaks up. Her voice is timid for the first time all day. "Yes, sir," she tells him.

He grins, showcasing the straightest, whitest teeth Michael has ever seen. "Ngwanu," he speaks in a low voice. Something about it is so eerie, the way it gets under your skin. From one quick glance around the yard, Michael can tell he's not the only person who is affected. Yemi clutches her hands together tightly. James wipes sweat from his head. David and Jamil exchange curious looks.

"Ndewo nụ," the doctor says, then spreads his arms out before placing them on his chest. "I am Maazi Jaja. Are we ready?"

— 29 —

Maazi Jaja washes his hands in a basin that looks like it was a decorative bowl from the kitchen. He rinses them, then flicks out specks of water behind him, all while muttering. Michael's Igbo isn't that good, so he can't really make out what Jaja is saying. He is used to hearing Igbo traditional prayers and sometimes he misses the staunch but poetic way they were recited when his family used to gather for celebrations. Those were all Christian prayers, though. All "Ọ bụ n'aha Jesus" this and "N'aha Jesus" that. Christianity had seeped its way into Igbo traditions, making a home where there wasn't one, but so much of their traditional cadence had survived. This was no different, Michael thinks. As he watches Maazi Jaja prepare the rites, he realizes who they are as people isn't something that can be altered on the surface.

"I have been asked to, ehm . . ." Jaja clears his throat while he turns back to face the family. "I have been asked to call upon the spirit of one Onyinye Mary Okafor today. I can say that . . . normally, I can't always talk to the person I want to talk to," he explains. At one point, his gaze falls on David and he makes a direct effort to be as transparent as possible. "Ehm, sometimes, some spirits don't want to be found."

"Yes, but, Nna, our sister has just left us yesterday," Nancy pipes up, drawing Jaja's attention. "And ... Ọ hapụrụ anyị ngwa ngwa, ọ bụ ya mere anyị ji chee na o nwere ihe ọ ga-ekwu. That is all."

Michael nods along. He only caught some of that. *She left so fast? Leaving so fast? So ... we think she ... has something ... something.* A part of him regrets not taking Igbo more seriously as a kid. When they immigrated to Canada, all he wanted to do was fit in and get rid of his accent. *Well, joke's on you. Now you sound like every other man who grew up in Scarborough.*

Jaja nods as well. "Ee, aghọtara m. Ngwa, let me begin the ritual."

Michael watches with bated breath as Jaja retrieves a set of kola nuts from a small pouch. Instinctively, he shudders, remembering the extreme bitter taste of the seed that they eat after any sort of ceremony. Whenever a relative moved into a new house, or when a new baby was born, or sometimes even when a kid got into any notable university, everyone would gather and, after a prayer, they'd break the nut and share minuscule pieces among everyone present. It was customary for everyone to eat it, no matter how bitter it tasted.

"It's medicine," his father would say to him.

Michael definitely agreed. He though kola tasted like chewed-up Tylenol and Advil and tree bark.

He missed his dad sometimes.

Especially now, watching Jaja raise a nut in the air, his eyes closed, while he chanted Mama's name. Michael's dad couldn't talk to spirits like Jaja apparently can, but he always led these sorts of prayers or ceremonies for their family before he passed.

"Onyinye Mary Okafor, bịa nwere ọjị," Jaja says boldly. His voice echoes in the open air. His boldness, his candor, makes Michael shiver. He glances at Joy a few seats down and sees her bottom lip tremble. She's thinking of Mama; she must be thinking of Papa, too.

"Onyinye Mary Okafor, bịa nwere ọjị," Jaja repeats. He repeats it again and again, like an anthem or a chant, and it swarms the backyard. Even James, in all his righteousness, mutters under his breath, echoing the chant.

Suddenly, Jaja gasps, "Aha!" and breaks into a wide, slow smile. He says, in a low voice, "Ama m na ị ga-abịa. *Mary.*"

Nancy grins, reaching out to clutch Ezekiel's hand beside her. "He found her. Praise God," she sighs out.

"Mmm." Jaja shuts his eyes and tilts his head back. Honestly, Michael isn't sure how much of this is him just making a show of it. Something about Jaja feels real, though. Like the way you step onto the ground and feel its pull. Like the way you touch water and understand life. *It's magic,* Michael thinks, a certain type of magic that he hasn't experienced before. But by the looks of Auntie and Uncle, it's something they are intimately familiar with.

This magic killed Peace, remember?

No. Michael quickly shakes the thought from his mind. This is not the magic that took his sister at a young age; this is the magic of stars and planets and Earth and life. This is something different entirely.

Jaja says, "Ezinaụlọ gị kpọrọ gị ebe a. Ma-ry. Eh-heh. Ị nwere ihe ị ga-ekwu?" and waits. The waiting feels like agony. They watch as Jaja tilts his head like he's listening. It makes Michael feel a bit creeped out, if he's honest. He wonders what Jaja could be hearing; if it sounds like Mama's real voice.

Soon, Jaja looks out to the crowd and says, "It was her time. She says . . . where she is, with her family, she says she is with her Mama. Ehm. Which one again is Amarachi?"

Auntie Nancy brings a hand to her chest, her lips wobbling so much she can barely speak. "It's me."

"Amarachi, ndo," Jaja begins. "This your sister, she is telling me you are . . . ehm." He clears his throat and tries again, certain the words will come this time. "She is saying you are like twins, but you're not. That in this life, you two waka-waka like this," and he holds both his index fingers together. "You see?"

Nancy nods regrettably. "Ee."

"But . . . you see how this finger comes from this hand, and this one, na this one get am." He separates the fingers, separates the hands. "Una get ee own life . . . for this life. You understand? She says, 'Amarachi, abatala ebe a.' Don't come here, don't follow me here."

Almost immediately, Nancy folds. She holds her face in her hands and breaks into a wail so loud that several guests inside the living room turn to the window for the source of the sound. Ezekiel puts an arm around her, and from the row behind, Zach reaches out to place a hand on her back, but nothing can heal the fact that Jaja is right. Michael knows, from hearing stories about his family. Auntie Nancy has always followed Mama up and down, up and down, until she herself grew tired. And this is one place she can't go.

"And twins." Jaja looks around the group, trying to suss out who is intrigued by this mention. His eyes home in on the woman in the front row who startles at the word. "Is it you?" he asks.

Joy nods. "Y-yes. Maybe."

"Are you Joy?"

"Y-yes," she breathes out just as Jamil gasps "Whoa. . . !" at the accuracy.

"Your Mama says she is with her daughter. She says, 'Mụ na nwa m nwanyị nọ ebe a.' Is that your sister?" As he speaks, Joy's eyes well up with tears. She sucks in her lips, nodding. Michael wishes he could reach out, reach down the row and squeeze his sister's hand, but he doesn't dare move an inch. Jaja continues, "The girl is resting. She is fine. Your mama says she is okay."

Joy opens her mouth to say "Thank you," but she can't get the words out.

"Ehm, Maazi Jaja," Nancy pipes up. Her voice comes out raspy and groggy after she's been crying. She dots her eyes, asking, "Is she saying anything else? About the family, about seeing us again?"

A chill runs down Michael's spine. He's not sure he wants to hear an answer to that.

"Yes, of course!" comes Jaja's eruption of a reply. "She says she will see you all again. She is here and she is ready."

Nancy breathes a sigh of relief, then looks over her shoulder to the rest of the family, smiling weakly at this revelation. In her eyes, she is saying, *Tonight, we will celebrate.*

Nancy's relief is contagious, it seems, because Michael sees many of his family members' shoulders drop, their eyes shut in prayer. Including Joy. He watches her clasp her hands together. She sits impossibly still.

"Maazi." Auntie Nancy speaks up again. "Please, is there anything else she can tell us?"

Jaja tilts his head again as if to listen. Then he frowns. "She is still asking about twins."

Joy furrows her brows.

Nancy looks on, confused, as well. "Twins?" Then it hits her. "Oh! Ejima nna."

But Michael isn't listening. He shuts his eyes momentarily and clasps his hands together. He can feel the presence of his mom, the warmth of her touch and the earthy scent in her skin, and he decides he has his own words to speak. His own prayer. "Mom, I'm sorry," he whispers so quietly that no one hears him. "Mom, I'm sorry. I am."

He waits for the response. Trying to drown out the sounds around him, how Jaja continues on in Igbo and how Auntie Nancy keeps muttering, "Yes, of course, yes," over and over again.

Nothing comes.

He thinks again, *Mom, biko, please answer me. I'm sorry. I said something horrible to Joy. I told her she was the reason you died. Mom. Mama, o.*

Nothing.

His chest feels heavy; his head, all over the place.

Mama. I shouldn't have said it.

And then, out of nowhere, a voice. But not from inside his head.

Jaja says loudly, in English, "She has forgiven you, o!" to the group.

It's only Michael who exhales a shaky breath, feeling both tears and a smile cut through his strong exterior.

"She has forgiven you," Jaja says again.

It could mean so many things.

But it's Michael who Jaja turns to.

He says, "She is saying she wishes she could talk to her husband's son one last time," while raising a finger in the air. His face morphs with sorrow, as if he is channeling the sadness in Mama's words. As if he is feeling them so acutely that they're turning an invisible dial in his chest from hot to cold. As if he is so hung up on the sorrow in . . . Mama's husband's son.

It dawns on Michael immediately that that's a strange thing to say. The phrasing is off, as if he went out of his way to describe, for example, Joy as "Nancy's sister's daughter."

Yes, exactly. As if he went out of his way.

"Husband's son?" the words spill from Michael's mouth unknowingly.

Down the row, Joy turns her head, only glancing momentarily at him. When he looks up, they miss each other.

Still, something in Michael feels unsettled. Call it intuition; call it his mother's spirit, ever-present. He looks Jaja in the face and asks, "Oga, what does that mean?"

Jaja startles. "Wetin?"

"Why does my mom want to talk to her 'husband's son'?" Michael asks. "Who? Who is that?"

Suddenly, Auntie Nancy smacks her hands together so loud that they create a thunderous sound. "Chineke, God!" she cries, then turns her head to look at Uncle Ezekiel. The two share a look so grave—and so suspicious.

A creeping uneasiness makes its way up Michael's spine.

He asks again, "Does she have another son?"

Jaja takes an uneasy step to his side, glancing nervously at the ground. "Ah-ah. I don't understand. Is she not your mama? Shouldn't you know who she is talking about?"

"No—"

"Yes." Ezekiel's voice rings out crystal clear. The family's attention is on him. Michael's attention, too, and this is all that matters to Ezekiel. He glances at his wife, but she turns away from him, her lips twisted into a scowl. Ezekiel frowns. "Nancy, it should be time to talk, na. Time has been going."

"So if you want to talk, then talk," she erupts suddenly. Her nervousness is on full display in the way her leg taps in place, and how she can't sit still. It makes Michael sit at the edge of his seat, and then eventually rise out of his chair.

"Someone better start talking," he says. He doesn't feel half as confident as he sounds. Inside, something in him is quaking. *Mom, is that you?* he wonders, but no answer, no certainty, comes.

Ezekiel, disgruntled at his wife's bullishness, rises to his feet, as well. "Michael. How old are you now? Do you know what happened the night you were born?" He points to him loosely, as if both instructing and warning him about the events to come. "You came out screaming, like any other baby boy. Very proud. Like the world should be coming out to greet him."

Michael's breathing deepens. His eyes stay fixed on his uncle.

"But . . ." Ezekiel sighs, shaking his head in defeat. "It was not your mama who born you."

Michael holds his breath.

"It was another woman."

A hush falls over the family.

"*W-what?*" Michael stumbles backward into his chair. Sarah reaches for him, trying to steady him, but he throws her hand off in a hurry. He keeps moving backward, backward, backward, until he's out of the row. Away from the family. All the while, he utters, "No . . . what? How? What?" each word becoming more pointless than the last.

He says, "It's not true."

Ezekiel sighs again. "A woman named . . . what was it?" He nudges Nancy, but she refuses to look at him. Michael knows right away: they both were keeping this from him. They both knew. "Ah! Caroline. Caro. She was someone who lived in the same village as your papa—"

"N-no, stop!" Michael rubs his hands down his face, slowly at first, then with fervor. "Uncle, that's enough, na, that's enough—"

"You're asking why your mama's spirit said what she said," Auntie Nancy interrupts, getting to her feet as well. She doesn't sound like her usual self. This time, a desperate plea is hidden in her words. *Don't be mad,* it says to him, though it feels too late for that. "Michael," she says, and he freezes at once because this is the first time he can remember she's referred to him by name. "Michael . . . my sister was a better woman than most. Even though your papa betrayed her, she still kept you—"

"Why?" Michael snorts. "Because it was disgraceful?"

"Ah-ah." Nancy frowns. "No, o. Because she *loved* you."

He scoffs.

"Ejima nna. You look so much like her husband and she raised you as her own. You *were* her son. Nwa ya nwoke."

"Nwa di ya!" he shoots back. "Her husband's son. You heard her. Abi? Is it not so?" He uses his lips to gesture toward Jaja, who cowers at the accusation.

"I don't understand . . ."

Joy's voice pierces through the confusion. Soon, it's her who's locking eyes with Michael. His heart does a mile a minute, his nerves threatening to undo him. He hasn't said a proper word to Joy since their fight, and now she stares back at him, frustration knotted in her brow. It puts him on edge immediately, like nothing has changed between them. The remorse he felt just moments ago dissipates.

He sneers. "*What* don't you understand?"

"I just don't get it, like . . ." Joy glances away. "Mom always treated you better than us. They both did—"

"Joy, this really isn't the time," Michael snaps back. "For once, can you not make this about you?"

"I'm not, I swear!" she says, holding out her hands in defense. "I just—it's just—they liked you so much that they treated you better than us. *Always.* You were their actual favorite."

Michael's cheeks burn with embarrassment. His temperature rises in the blink of an eye and he—God, he can't even look at her anymore. "You're . . . obtuse," he growls. "Don't you see now? It wasn't favoritism. It was fear. Fear that someone would find out about their secret."

Nancy begins to shake her head. "Ah, no, na. Eji—"

"Don't call me that!" His voice breaks free from his lips, and with it a sob. A choke. He loses his composure under the watchful gaze of his family. Of his daughter. The shock in Sarah's eyes is almost too much for Michael to deal with.

Quickly, he stumbles backward until he gets to the path leading to the house. "Wait!" He hears Joy call after him, but he doesn't turn.

The moment he reaches the sliding door, he startles once he realizes that a group of people had been gathering on the inside, staring out into the yard, watching and listening. Alice, too, has a camera pointed directly at them. Their eyes betray them before he can even say anything. They know; they heard. They are waiting.

Of course, he thinks. *These people came here for a show.*

— 30 —

Joy reaches the sliding door a second too late, her fingertips grazing the hem of Michael's shirt before he begins muscling his way inside and past the crowd of people. "Damn," she curses and attempts to do the same, but the wall of onlookers is ironclad. They reach out to touch her shoulder, nudging her and asking, "What's going on? Is it true?" while she tries to smile politely and move through. She hears Alice behind her, "And maybe we can get more information from Joy, Mary's daughter . . ." but she doesn't turn around. She has no answers for them. In fact, she's sure the only people who do have answers are either not willing to elaborate (her aunt and uncle) or aren't here any longer (her mom and dad).

My God . . . what a secret, though. As Joy sidesteps a gaggle of children crowding around an auntie's leg, she swallows down the bitterness that arises when she thinks of Michael and their childhood.

I don't get it . . . they loved *him*, she thinks. Her dad would always treat Michael like a king, as if he could do nothing wrong. Peace assumed it was because he was the eldest and also a boy (she always called it a deadly combination), and for a patriarchal culture like theirs, it meant that sometimes Joy and Peace fell to the wayside, if they were acknowledged at all.

Doubly so, because they were twins. What Michael could do, they could not, and it was made very clear time and time again that though it was good to be ambitious, their greatest ambition should always be marriage and children—namely, marriage and a son.

Her parents had forgiven Michael *so* many things, too. Joy bites her tongue, pushing this bitterness as far down as she can, while she thinks about how they allowed him to remove himself from the family whenever he wanted. He didn't have to go to church if he didn't want to. He didn't have to apply to the schools they thought he should if he felt he knew better. And her dad would always say, "Wetin, na? He's becoming a man. Let him go," as if that was reason enough for the favoritism. The neglect.

"Michael, wait!" Joy calls at his retreating figure.

He doesn't slow down. Instead, he flies toward the front door with alarming speed. *This is so like him,* she thinks. The need to escape and the privilege to do so.

She jogs faster and grabs on to his arm with both hands, trying to root him in place. He throws her off without a second look, keeping his gaze focused on the doorway, on his way out. "Michael, wait, please—"

As fast as he threw her arm off, he whips around, face crunched into a frown. Tears streaming down his face. He doesn't bother wiping them away. "H-how long did you know?" he splutters out.

Joy can't move. She's paralyzed by the sight of him; how she's never seen this kind of anger, this kind of sadness, etched into his features before. It shakes her. She reaches forward for his hand, but he moves back, never closing the distance between them.

She swallows. "I . . ."

Behind her, the crowd starts to hover. She can feel them. Michael glances at them, and frustration takes root. Joy wishes she could tell them to leave them alone, to let them have this *please*, but she can't move. Can't form the words.

Finally, Michael swipes at his eyes, forcefully wiping the tears from them, before he erupts. "Tell me, how long did y-you—did you know? Did you? Did *everyone*?" His voice rises, shaky and panicked, with each word.

"I-I didn't know, I didn't," Joy stammers. She slides a foot forward, carefully—

"Don't come near me!" Michael shoots back. "No one come near me! God, this—this fucking family—"

"Michael, I swear to God, I had no idea." Joy puts up her hands in surrender. "Peace didn't know, either. Mom never told us anything a-and Dad never said anything—"

"Can you imagine?" He scoffs. "My own father let himself *die* before he told me the truth? Je-*sus*. Jesus, o . . ."

"B-but it doesn't matter," Joy says, taking another careful step forward. "R-right? None of it matters. You're—you're still my brother. My full brother. Y-you always have been—"

"No, I haven't," Michael interrupts with another scoff, loud and disbelieving. He presses his palms into his eyes, groaning, saying, "I haven't, I haven't, and you *know* that, Joy—"

"I don't—"

"Yes, you do!" He pulls his hands from his eyes so he can look at her. She stares back, trembling and unsure. They've barely gotten to the point of forgiveness and they're already on shaky ground. It seems like it'll always be this way for them. Here, with this growing rift that she can't quite cross, she has never felt more alone.

Uncle Ezekiel steps forward easily through the crowd, a grave look on his weathered face. "Michael," he calls softly. "Pele, o. Come. Come, let's talk."

"Uncle, biko, I can't, I'm s-sorry," Michael chokes out with a firm shake of his head. "I can't be here anymore."

"Don't say that. Please." Uncle Ezekiel approaches slowly, holding out his hands as if to embrace Michael, but he doesn't get that far. He pauses beside Joy. "Okay, that's enough, na. Come back. Come back to us."

Michael swallows down a sob, but it twists his face, contorting it with pain and regret. He says, "It doesn't feel like there is an 'us.' You people let me believe I'm part of this family, that I deserve to be grieving today, when I don't."

"Ah-ah, but you are, and you must," Ezekiel explains with a frown.

He glances at Joy, how she cries silently beside him, and in a moment, she can see that he knows this has gone on for too long. This rift caused by deceit. Quickly, he beckons Michael forward. "Mary did well for you, or did you forget? She is the only mama you know. When Caro died in childbirth, other people in the village were saying it was you who killed her. They would have left you to die, but Mary was there for you."

"Then she was a fool," Michael growls.

"He-ey . . ." Ezekiel's frown deepens. "Don't say that. Don't talk about your mama like that. She was doing what the best of us could not. What the best of us should not have had to do. And she loved you like her own son."

Michael caves. His shoulders hunch and he sobs, deep and pained, at the invocation of Mama's memory.

Joy watches, her bottom lip trembling. She stares at him. Her brother. She thinks of her mom. How she looks more like Mama. How Michael never did, not even a little. How no one said a thing about why.

How no one said a thing.

And now she is at a loss for words.

Joy takes a step forward and reaches out for Michael's arm. "Can you . . . come back outside?" she asks quietly. The onlookers behind her hover ever closer, and Alice is narrating everything that's going on to her audience, but Joy doesn't care. This entire weekend so far, her family—hell, her life—has felt like a spectacle. She felt as if her sorrow had to be curated, that her words needed to be watched—but this is different, this is her brother. This is her only brother. Jesus Christ, this is the only sibling she has left. She wants to tell him this, that it's just him and her forever now. That all they have is each other. But her throat is dry and her thoughts feel jilted—and this is Michael she's talking about. She *knows* him, and looking at him now she knows he doesn't care.

He'd rather be alone.

Joy wishes she could tell Michael that loneliness is overrated. That, yes, he was right before: she is a twin who doesn't know how to be a single, and it will haunt her for the rest of her life. She wants love and she wants attention but can't create the space for any such thing to grow in her life because she's afraid. She's afraid of this loneliness that follows her around like a bad dream, a nightmare come to life. And she hates it, and she hates it, and she *hates* it.

She doesn't fault him for not seeing things her way, but this time, she wishes she could see things his way. For once, she wishes she could understand him.

"I can't stay here," Michael grunts, then turns to the door.

A knot in Joy's throat forms while they watch him leave.

Whispers begin, taking hold in Joy's ears. "So he's not Mama's son?" and "Jacob was a wicked, wicked man" make Joy prickle with unease. She turns on her heel, quick to pounce and tell off whichever rumor-mill auntie thinks it's not too soon to gossip about this, but is stumped to see Sarah standing directly behind her.

Sarah stands in silence, her face perfectly still. The whispers continue around them, but Joy shivers, clasping her hands together, while she watches her niece. She doesn't move an inch. "Are . . ." Joy clears her throat and tries again. "Sarah, I'm so . . . sorry."

The corner of Sarah's mouth twitches, upturning in a regretful smile.

Joy reaches out for her, but before her hand touches her arm, Sarah stumbles back. "I-I'm sorry, I, um. I'm gonna go." She clears her throat and, quickly, scans the front hall for her escape. Just like her dad.

The staircase is unobstructed, so Sarah races for it, maneuvering around her aunt and grandfather with ease. She keeps her head down while jogging up the stairs, but from where Joy and Ezekiel are standing, they can see the frustration, the powerlessness, the tears.

— 31 —

Nothing is louder than the stares of a hundred people waiting to see a miracle—or, the stares of a hundred of your fellow Nigerians trying to understand the ins and outs of your family business. When Michael disappears and Sarah runs upstairs, Joy feels the spotlight shift to her. Guests who had heard the altercation don't even pretend they weren't listening. Joy spots an uncle, William or Benjamin or something, making his way through the crowd to her and she slips away, trying to lose him between other visitors. All she knows of this uncle is when he sat her down at the ripe age of fifteen and told her that if she doesn't learn to cook correctly, she'll never get married. It's no secret that this uncle had a tryst with Nwunye years ago, so if Joy was looking to take anyone's advice or consolation at a time like this, it wouldn't be his.

She ducks into the den, where a group of teenagers she doesn't know are watching videos on their phones. *Perfect, yes, teenagers,* she thinks, *they won't give a shit about me at all.* Finally, she can take a breath. Finally, she can think.

What is going on?

She leans against the wall, waiting for the chatter to die down in the hallway. For all her emotions, her mind is blank. She wishes her mom were here, now more than any other time. Her mom would know what to do. She'd tell everyone off. The thought makes Joy laugh. Mary Okafor would tell everyone to stop staring. "You foolish people," she would tell them, making sure to look everyone in the eye. "Is this how you people want to start behaving?" It wouldn't matter if she were right or wrong. Mama never cared about anyone's opinion but her own, and if she was slighted, she'd make sure everyone knew it.

Joy used to hate when her mom would get like that, argumentative and unforgiving. But at a time like this, Joy wishes she could be the same.

She cries. Joy cries quietly, pressing her hands into her eyes as each sob shudders through her. She—

"Yo . . . Auntie, are you okay?"

Joy pulls her hands from her face abruptly to see the gaggle of teenagers staring back at her. One tries to hold up his phone and film her, but she points a finger at him. "Don't you—don't you dare!" she hisses. He drops it immediately.

One girl pouts. "Do you need a hug? Or, like, some water?"

"N-no thanks." The last thing Joy needs is a hug from a random teenager—who are these kids, anyway?

Quickly, Joy wipes her face and leaves the room. Eyes trail her as she makes her way down the hall, but the DJ has restarted the music in the living room, so many guests have gravitated there, swaying back and forth to the playlist. Joy is thankful for the distraction.

The kitchen is relatively empty, save for Nnenna. She and her cousin lock eyes the moment Joy comes into view, but neither of them speak as Joy settles into the space beside her. They lean against the kitchen counter, watching the guests meander through the room.

And Joy feels lost.

Her heart thumps; her nerves spike.

I have no idea . . . what to do.

It should be sobering, but the thought is scary.

Joy *always* knows what to do. Even when she and Nnenna were in the room with Mama, Joy remembers how Nnenna jostled her shoulders, asking what the next steps were. Because someone like Joy always knows the answer. Her eyes sting again with tears when she realizes she doesn't this time. Not one thing that happened this weekend has so far been in her control. Nothing went as planned. Nothing in her life ever goes as planned.

"What's the point, then?" she mutters. Nnenna tilts her head in her direction, but says nothing. Joy wishes she'd get an answer. Even an "I don't know" would be better than nothing. Why does *she* always have to be the one to know? Why not anyone else?

Her family who lean on religion in times like this would say it's because she doesn't believe; that all she needs is faith to get her through. But you can't touch faith, and that's what bothers Joy. She has always believed in the tangible—herself, her kid, her family. That's what matters to her. That is what she could always control.

Or maybe she never could.

Maybe control is an illusion and the façade has finally lifted.

She wrinkles her nose. She watches a small child run by with a water bottle.

"We might run out of water," Nnenna says.

Joy nods.

Nnenna lets out a heavy exhale and crosses her arms.

She asks, "Should we call Michael?"

Joy scratches her eye.

"No," she says.

Nnenna glares, turning to Joy. "Ah-ah. Are you being serious?"

"I am."

"So?"

"So he won't answer if we call," Joy grunts. "I know my brother well enough to know that."

Nnenna's glare deepens. She kisses her teeth, scoffing as she turns away. "You're not even trying."

Joy takes a deep breath. Her eyes well up with tears. All she has been doing is trying, but this is all the proof she needs: it doesn't matter, it didn't matter, and it will never matter to people who aren't willing to see that. To her family, this is what it always is. She will never be able to try hard enough.

"You're right." Joy clears her throat. "I'm not."

— 32 —

Nnenna leaves the kitchen just as Rob makes an appearance. She can deal with one or the other, but definitely not both. They like to make light of things instead of being serious about what's important. This kind of family secret is no joke, and yet Joy doesn't think it's worth trying to call Michael. To try to track him down?

My wayward cousin, once again, doesn't know right from wrong, Nnenna thinks as she moves to the outskirts of the living room. The thought doesn't carry the same amount of frustration as it normally would for her. Somewhere in her heart, she feels for Joy and what her side of the family is going through—what they're *all* going through. Michael is still her cousin, too, and she cares about him.

"*Tch,* I'll just call," Nnenna grumbles as she reaches for her phone. She dials his number and waits.

And waits.

The line cuts. "He hung up on me?" she gasps, staring down at her phone screen.

Well, maybe Joy was right about one thing. But only *one*!

Nnenna kisses her teeth, crosses her arms, tosses her hair over her shoulder. She checks the watch on her wrist, fixing it slightly so the diamond-encrusted face stares back at her. "Time is going," she mutters to herself while she fidgets with the watch. With each passing second, a heavier weight crushes down on her shoulders. She hates being in this weird limbo, not knowing what will happen next . . .

She bites her tongue hard enough to feel the sharpness of her teeth in them. *Don't be like that,* she berates herself like a child. *Auntie Mary is coming back.*

She waits.

All around her, she sees nameless guests crowd the living room, fill the kitchen, and take up the hallways. They've even taken up residence outside in the backyard, where Alice and her team are setting up a projector for the all-access stream from the morgue and inviting some of the campers from the front yard to join her. But even in all that confusion, Nnenna does a close scan and realizes she doesn't see her husband anywhere. Finally, she breathes a sigh of relief. She lets doubt roll around in her mind unfettered.

It's not just doubt, though. Of course I believe in the resurrection. But to say Auntie Mary will come back . . .

Okay, but then, why shouldn't she? Yesterday was her birthday. It was also Good Friday. It was also the day she died. Think about it, Nnenna! Who else has been born and has died on the same date?

Shakespeare . . . I think Shakespeare.

No, I think, actually, it wasn't the exact day . . . I think he died before he was born, right?

Or—as in, he was born first and then died several years later on a different—in a different year. He wasn't born and dead in the same year.

I wish I could drink.

Nnenna's gaze falls softly on a bottle of Guinness held firmly in an uncle's hand. The man talks quietly with his wife in the corner, the two of them barely moving their mouths, while their eyes bounce from surface to surface.

Nnenna is almost sure they're criticizing everything in their peripheral, but she doesn't pay that any mind. She just wishes she could have a cold beer. Or any beer! God, it's been so long since she's drank anything that wasn't Communion wine. And, to be honest, that was only if she was lucky. Their church didn't often do Communion, so she's gone years and years without anything that has more than 0.5 percent alcohol. There was one time she thought she'd start drinking kombucha, because she heard it was good for your gut health but also contained questionable amounts of alcohol for a soft drink. She couldn't stand the thought of things fermenting and growing in the bottle.

That, and James had convinced her that kombucha was the devil's juice.

She touches her wrist again, finally pulling her eyes from the beer bottle. James has convinced her of a lot of things over the years. He wasn't a bad person for it, and she wasn't worse off because of it, either, but just . . . Why is it, at a time like this when he's nowhere to be found, all she can hear is his voice?

"Nnenna, why do you stand like that? Try to stand straighter. Eh-heh. Like that. Good."

"Nne, what are you feeding this boy, na? As you see him sef, you don't see he's getting too big?"

"Nnenna, where is the other lipstick? This one makes you look like ashawo."

"Nnenna—"

"Nne, this food has too much salt. It's like you don't know how to cook again."

"Nn—"

"Nnenna, why—"

"Nne—"

She pushes out a strong sigh and tosses her hair over her shoulder again. She chews her lip. Suddenly, she wants to cry.

"Mom . . ." Yemi approaches without Zach. Nnenna is willing to bet the kids have taken up residence in the basement. She hopes they have, honestly. It's better they play there than be out here, with Alice and her vultures looking for an inside, unfiltered scoop.

Nnenna reaches out to smooth her hand down Yemi's braids. "What is it, dear?" she asks.

"There's just three hours left," Yemi says with a toothy grin.

Nnenna doesn't smile back. Something about her face . . . it's just not working. The mechanics. All she can do is stare at Yemi until the poor girl shrinks in her presence, and it makes Nnenna feel like a shitty mother. Here her daughter is excited about seeing her dead grandma again and Nnenna can't keep her apathy to herself. If she can even call this apathy.

"Let's try and clear up the living room, then," Nnenna says with a sigh. "We should find more chairs for people to sit in here."

Yemi nods right away.

"Where's Zach?"

"Playing," Yemi answers dutifully. "He's playing a video game."

"Okay—"

"Should I tell him to stop?"

"Tell him to come help you arrange this place," Nnenna says instead. "We can put the chairs better so that everyone will have room."

Yemi races back down the hall and returns moments later with her brother.

Nnenna gestures to the furniture. "Okay, come, let's start to move some of these tables." It might only be three hours to time, but it'll be a long three hours. As Nnenna shifts an end table to make room for an uncle who's sitting on a fold-up chair by the wall, she wonders what it would feel like to be drunk. Completely lose control.

"Good. We need somewhere to dance."

Nnenna whips her head around at the sound of a man's voice behind her. A sturdy-looking guy dressed in agbada has gotten to his feet, staring around the wide living room. When he finally stops and looks at Nnenna, he reiterates, "We need a dance floor."

"O-oh." Nnenna clears her throat. "Okay."

"So it's good you're moving these things," he goes on, gesturing to some of the tables and decor lying around. "And it would be nice if someone were going to give a speech. Either here or outside."

"Eh-heh, now you're talking," says another uncle a few steps away. "Please, what is the program?"

Nnenna frowns. "We don't have one."

"Which kind vigil no get program?"

"I-I don't know. We just don't have one."

"And who are you?"

Nnenna bristles. She finds herself standing up taller while Yemi gives the man a dirty look. "I'm Mary's niece. First lady of New Apostles in Pentecostal Glory, in Baltimore. In the United States."

The man doesn't seem amused. My God, these Canadian people were really something else. "Okay, and so?" He turns up his nose at her. "We are asking for a dance floor and you're here making mouth."

Nnenna gasps. "Sir, we're clearing the floor now. Please sit and stay where you are, or we'll move you with the furniture. Non-sense." She kisses her teeth and turns away. She wishes she could swear in Igbo like her mom. No way Nancy Akintola would let this man draw another breath before she raked him across the coals by his forehead first.

— 33 —

She won't stop moving furniture. Why does she keep moving furniture?" Joy stage-whispers to Rob. He snorts loudly, not even pretending he's hiding it. As Joy watches Nnenna direct her mini-me around the living room while a group dances in the center, she can tell Nnenna's running on fumes and anxiety right now. Generic Afropop fills the downstairs, but it doesn't do much to quell the friction in the room. Everyone is spooked. Everyone is anticipating what's to come.

Michael still hasn't returned.

Joy tries to push the thought out of her mind. The image of his face, contorted with agony, staring back at her. That's why she focuses so hard on Nnenna, not letting her mind slip for a second, else she'll start trembling with thoughts of her brother. Of her mom.

Two more hours until . . . something *happens.*

She takes a deep breath.

Rob notices and reaches out to put his hand on her shoulder. "You good?" He winces the moment he says it. "Never mind, d-don't answer that. I'm being dumb. Obviously you feel like shit."

Joy winces this time, though she really shouldn't have.

Because he's right. And she's absolutely fucking freaking out.

She is.

It starts slowly, but her palms gradually grow sweatier; her heart-beat is pounding ridiculously fast in her chest. Her head is cloudy. Every now and then, she tries to take a deep breath, but she can't seem to breathe. It's weird. She blinks once, twice, sees Nnenna, watches Nnenna go, and all at once, she's not sure if she's even breathing at all. If she's even here.

She shuts her eyes for a second.

Trying to think of what it'll be like . . . after the fact.

After Mama sits up in the morgue and walks all the way to the rental property.

Or, drives.

How would she even drive? I mean, it's an impossibly long walk, but where would she get a car?

Without warning, a loud whine from the center of the living room breaks her concentration. She blinks her way back to the present while she watches Yemi throw arguably the biggest tantrum that she's ever gotten away with: groaning and stomping her foot a total of one time.

"But it's not fair!" Yemi grumbles, her face scrunching with disappointment.

"Did I ask you about 'fair'?" Nnenna barks back. "Abeg, just do what I say."

Yemi can't stop frowning. "Yeah, but—"

"But nothing!" Nnenna says. "Do you ever stay up past this time on any other night?"

"No, but . . . this isn't just any other night," Yemi says. Suddenly, she gasps, a last twinkle of hope in her eyes. "If I promise to wake up really early, can I stay? Mom, please?"

"Yemi, don't try me, o," Nnenna says, pointing a finger at her. "You and your brother should go to bed right now. Don't let me catch you awake."

Yemi's bottom lip begins to tremble. She looks around the living room, for anyone to come to her defense, and her eyes fall on Joy and

Rob standing in the kitchen. She tries to lock eyes with Joy, but Joy can't meet her gaze.

Rob looks at Yemi and is quick to say, "Listen to your mom."

Yemi grumbles. "This isn't *fair!*" She stomps her foot one final time before marching down the hall to the staircase.

Nnenna sighs. She turns to Joy, ready to pounce, her face twisted with malice. "Don't give me that look," Nnenna warns, taking in Joy's listless expression. "I've had enough today. Please, it's not only you who is suffering. We're all grieving in our own way, okay? So don't just look at me."

Joy can't bring herself to nod her head. She's still stuck in this weird paralysis.

Wait, paralysis?

Oh, Joy thinks. *I'm . . . having a panic attack.*

She knows this because she's studied it, read articles and books on how it presents differently for everyone. She knows about the shakes, the dizziness, the nausea, the hyperventilating. She knows about the sudden weakness. But she wasn't prepared for anything like that to ever happen to her. In a way, it feels inevitable. This moment feels like it was orchestrated from the second she stepped foot into this house.

Okay, be clear, Joy. What do I have to be anxious about, aside from literally everything? Her therapist brain is trying to reason with her normal person brain, and it's a catastrophe. It feels like one part of her wants to lie down while the other is stretching for a 6:00 a.m. jog. She hates both versions equally.

Joy blinks rapidly. She has no idea what Nnenna just said.

"I need air," she croaks, and turns to leave the room. She heads straight for the staircase, letting the tail end of Rob's voice linger in her ears: "Well, what did we expect, right? Her mom *may* be resurrected soon . . ."

Oh yes. A new worry. A new challenger has appeared.

Joy blindly heads to the staircase, stalks her way upstairs, feeling the weight of each step. She passes someone on the staircase she thinks is Michael, but it isn't—he's just some other guy who may or may not be related to someone in Nwunye's entourage. Nwunye, who is downstairs, chatting up guests and filming things as if this is a party. A celebration.

This is a nightmare.

Wake up, Joy, please.

Mom . . .

Joy's phone buzzes in the distance.

Yes, this is a nightmare.

She stops dead in her tracks at the top of the stairs, feeling light-headed from the jog. That buzzing . . . God, she swears if she gets through this day alive, she's going to either break her phone or eat it.

Why would you eat it?

"Uhmmmmmrrr . . ."

Go lie down, sis.

Her feet trod one after the other toward her room, toward the sound of that horrid buzzing. She nearly bumps into David on the way in. "Hey, are you okay?" he asks, concerned. "I've been looking for you everywhere. Jamil says Sarah can't get in touch with Michael . . ."

He's talking. He's talking a lot.

Then he brings up a phone, *her* phone. "Oh, is that mine?" is what she wants to say, but her mouth isn't moving. She can't make out the words. He tries to hand it to her and it takes her two tries to grab it.

"I think it's your work phone, right?" he asks. "It's been buzzing nonstop. I ignored it for a while, but it kept going. Every twenty minutes, then every ten, then every five."

"Mmmmhmmrr."

"Like contractions," he says.

Joy remembers when she went into labor with Jamil and how he tried to calm her down by counting how often her contractions were. The memory is almost like a balm—happy thoughts, Jamil being born, excruciating pain, lots of drugs, ooh, a baby—and helps relieve some of the tension in her chest. She is able to say one word: "He . . . lp."

David raises an eyebrow. "With what?"

Joy's breath hitches in her throat. She shuffles by him, squeezing herself between him and the frame until she is safely in the room and face down on the bed. She breathes in its cotton tresses. She forgets to breathe out.

Soon, she feels David's hand on her back. "You're okay, you're okay," he says over and over again.

Joy begins crying. This, just like the panic attack, feels inevitable.

"It's . . . almost eleven," David says.

"Mmhmmmrrr."

"Uh . . . it sounds like a wedding downstairs."

Joy would roll her eyes if she had full control over them. He's been to too many family events not to realize that Nigerians treat every event like a celebration. Does he not remember how their wedding and Uncle Festus's funeral had the same DJ?

She pushes herself off the bed, trying her hardest to sit up. Wiping her eyes frantically, she tries to take another breath. She looks at her phone. It *is* her work phone, of course, so she doesn't even need to check to see who's trying to contact her. Coral. Who else would be ringing her around 11:00 p.m. on a Saturday?

Joy flings her phone into the corner and tries to fold her hands into her lap.

David sits beside her, quietly staring at the wall opposite.

They sit this way for a while. Joy scrunches her toes into the carpet. She feels her heartbeat slow.

Eventually, she swallows, feels around for her voice, before mumbling, "It's . . . soon."

He glances at her. "Midnight."

"Y-yeah."

"Are you scared?"

"I . . . I am."

"Uh-huh."

"We're divorced. Aren't we?" She doesn't mean for the question to come out so ominously, or for it to come out at all, if she's being honest.

David glances at her again, a curious look on his face. "Yes?" He answers with a question. "Uh. You signed the papers first."

"Mmm."

"You were always very . . . efficient."

That didn't sound like a compliment. Joy frowns, turning to him. "I've been trying to take . . . deep breaths all weekend, and th-that shit does . . . *not* work." She coughs, bringing a hand to her mouth, before she continues. "I wasn't efficient. I-I am *not* efficient. I'm just . . ."

He waits, then says, "Terrified of losing control of any situation ever in the history of everything."

Joy grimaces. "Okay, damn. Didn't realize this was honesty hour."

"We lived together for years and you're not very good at hiding anything, so." He shrugs, as if that explanation makes up for exposing her in this way. "Plus, we went to therapy for, what? A year? Two years?"

"Fine. But—and I didn't wanna say it before—that shit did not work, David, and you wanna know why?" She points her thumbs shakily toward her chest. "Because of me."

He frowns. "What? No."

"Yes. I *am* terrified of losing control a-and I'm unstable. My brother is really my half-brother, my mom is dead, and my cousins and a reporter and a fucking *cow* have convinced me she might come back to life. And the worst part is that I th-think I *believe* it . . . you know? Or I *want* to believe it. I want . . . I miss my mom." She rubs her hands down her face. A crass chuckle escapes her lips. It bursts out painfully, as if all the deep breaths she's been taking have chosen to expel themselves at the same time.

She feels David sigh beside her. She is so embarrassed that she can't even look at him.

"I . . ." Joy clears her throat. "I, um. When you said you told Jamil about Italy already, I felt a type of way. I can't lie to you."

He is quiet. Then, after a moment, he asks, "Such as?"

"Jealous . . . ? Jealousy." She swallows.

"But why?" *He sounds disbelieving,* Joy thinks, as if he's hearing things about a different Joy, one who would never be so petty. "Did you wanna come or you're just mad I didn't tell you?"

Joy frowns, testing out both answers. "I don't know."

"Jesus, Joy," David groans. "Are you jealous of Jamil?"

"I'm—no—I'm jealous because you're—the two of you—h-he speaks Italian!" She throws up her hands in defeat, suddenly feeling more her son's age than her own. "I feel so stupid. I had no idea he was that good a-and now you're taking him for the summer, and when he comes back, I'm afraid he won't be anything like me."

Anything like me, anything like . . . my mom.

She feels stupid. Petty. Vulnerable.

She can't look at David. He must hate her, she thinks. Jamil isn't any more hers than he is David's, and she knows it. But now she's let fear get in the way—the kind of fear that penetrates and makes the irrational feel like a safe space. Makes control feel normal because the alternative is scary. The alternative is not knowing what tomorrow looks like. It's misunderstanding a gesture. It's coping with a tragedy. It's putting hope in something you can't really comprehend.

Joy glances at him. Quickly, she mumbles, "I don't mean anything by it. I'm sorry. I just thought . . . it's stupid." She exhales in a rush. "I just thought he'd have more t-time with her. With my mom."

"Yeah, no, I know." He nods slowly. "Don't worry too much about it."

"I just . . . I wish . . ." She sighs. "I wanted him to learn so much more than the language. My mom was so . . . I-I mean, I'm not like her. I grew up here. I feel disconnected sometimes," she mumbles, feeling her cheeks burn with embarrassment. At her big age, she's still going through the same identity insecurities she experienced in high school and university and ugh. Seriously, when will it end? When will she be safe and secure and feel Nigerian enough to occupy her own body? When will she feel it's finally enough?

"I know what you mean," David utters.

Joy chews her lower lip, nodding slowly. David doesn't talk a whole lot about it, but she knows he feels strange sometimes being so different from his Italian cousins who grew up in and around Rome. He would always say he had an accent when he spoke Italian, though Joy couldn't tell the difference. She knew it made him insecure sometimes, though, being a part of the diaspora. Not that there's anything wrong with that, since that's what he is—what they *both* are. But it's hard when the image you have of yourself in your head isn't the same as what people see. She couldn't explain how. It just is.

The sounds of singing continue downstairs, filtering through the floorboards up to their ears. This uncomfortable silence does little to quell the anxiety in Joy's heart, because the more breaths she takes, the closer and closer the clock inches to midnight. She wants to check the time, but she's afraid.

Jamil isn't, though.

He sits just outside the room, out of sight so neither of his parents will know he's there, and so he won't be seen from the staircase, either. He watches the clock tick by on his game device. Each minute comes with a new prayer.

Uh . . . God? Are you there?

Is Grandma really coming back? Everyone thinks she is.

I wanna believe she is.

We read the Bible yesterday. It's boring so, not gonna lie, I wasn't really paying attention. I feel bad now.

I remember the verse. Numbers 6:24–26. I lied and said I forgot because I didn't wanna seem like a loser.

I'm sorry for that, too.

God? Is Grandma really coming back?

Jamil takes shaky breaths with each minute that passes. He has never wished for anything harder in his life than he has for this. He has never prayed for anything like he has now. If God could answer one prayer . . . no, wait, if God could answer two prayers, then for the first, he wants his Grandma to come back.

For the second, he wants his parents to only have one house again.

— 34 —

SUNDAY, 12:00 A.M.

It's midnight.

— 35 —

SUNDAY, 12:01 A.M.

There's nothing.

The music downstairs has dimmed a little. Alice's crew hovers by Auntie Nancy, who is homed in on Uncle Ezekiel's phone, waiting for a call from the morgue.

In a bedroom upstairs, Yemi recites clumsy prayers with her comforter over her head. She wants to wake up to a miracle.

— 36 —

There is no call.

This *ba-boom, ba-boom, ba-boom* sound from Auntie Nancy's chest is deafening. It gets louder with each second.

No one is standing in the living room. Seats are filled with nervous bodies and restless minds. Onlookers in the backyard gaze into the house, looking for confirmation. A reason to celebrate.

No one is praying.

— 37 —

Uncle Ezekiel takes a deep breath. His eyes have been focused on his phone for who knows how long, waiting for some sort of buzz or twitch. Something that will put everyone's mind at ease, but mostly his wife's mind.

He takes a moment to stare into the crowd of people. Most of these people are Mary's friends, people she held dear and people who cared for her so much in life.

Alice is narrating quietly toward the camera. "It looks as if there hasn't been a call yet. No word on the resurrection . . ." *When will this woman stop filming?* he thinks. She's been doing this for hours and is no doubt the reason so many people showed up on such short notice. In his day, they just sent paper invitations or requests when they wanted to hold an event. Oh, so-and-so is doing their fiftieth birthday, or my daughter-in-law just had a baby. Elaborate papers, beautiful fonts.

Now it seems as though Mary's worth is defined by this livestream. There will be nothing concrete to mark her passing today.

Not even her resurrection.

He lets his head fall back so he can see the ceiling, and he sighs.

Now that it is quiet, now that every voice isn't trying to talk over the other, he realizes he feels calm. He realizes what he knew all along: that Mary is not coming back. That it is impossible, and not even his faith could make him see things differently. Jesus is the Son of God. There was meaning in His resurrection. Mary's passing, though auspicious, isn't the same. It just isn't.

But oh, his poor wife. Ezekiel turns to Nancy, whose deep frown and buttoned lips do little to hide her frustration. He can almost hear her voice in his head: *This phone better ring or wahala for all who dey here.*

He reaches out a hand to place on her shoulder. "Ndo," he says softly. She doesn't move an inch.

A man in shades stands up at the far end of the living room. "Oya, eh . . . will someone give a speech?" he asks loudly while he looks around. Several guests stir, but no one dares look at him. "For Mama Michael, na. Let's try and cheer up."

Ezekiel feels Nancy shudder at the suggestion. Honestly, he's not sure how to feel about it, either.

"Yes, he is right," says a woman as she adjusts her blouse. "I think everybody would like to hear what we have to say about our sister."

Alice nods. "Yes, I agree. Quick, can we get more lighting here—"

Nancy pushes back from the countertop, pushes away from the phone. It's not a rough gesture or one that makes a lot of noise, but somehow everyone seems to notice. From the corners of their eyes, they watch Nancy, how she straightens her clothes, and how she keeps her head held high while she turns from the kitchen.

Ezekiel steps forward, trying to place his hand back on her shoulder. "Nan—"

"Leave me, jor," she hisses, shifting away from him. The room is silent as she walks out, heading toward the staircase and up.

Nancy's mind is a blur. She feels something in her chest rattle while she goes. It knocks her, twists her, makes her feel small. *Why?* is the only word in her mind she can make out. Why would . . . ? How could . . . ? She was so sure. She was *so* sure.

Now she doesn't know what to feel anymore.

"Ah!" She gasps, taken aback by Jamil crouched on the floor outside his room. "What are you doing out here?"

Jamil quickly scrambles to his feet. He is wearing the same somber look that everyone downstairs has. Nancy scrunches her nose at once, eyes flicking from his head to his toes. Jamil averts his eyes as he says, "Uh-uh, nothing."

"Go to bed. It's late," Nancy grunts while she walks past. "There is church in the morning."

"I-I know." By the time he says it, she's already disappeared into her room. She shuts the door with a loud click that can probably be heard downstairs.

"Jamil?"

He turns at the sound of his dad's voice. Quickly, Jamil pokes his head through the door of his parents' bedroom. "H-hey," he utters.

His mom waves him forward and he follows, nudging the door closed behind him. Both his parents look tired. At one point, he could hear their conversation through the door, but it turned into hushed voices and words so quiet that he couldn't make anything out.

Jamil sits cross-legged in the middle of the bed. He feels awkward and he's not sure why.

"Grandma Nancy went to bed," he whispers. "She looked kinda sad."

Joy sighs, wiping her eyes. Had she been crying? Jamil didn't notice. "Well..." his mom says quietly. "She must be. I'm guessing no one from the morgue called."

Jamil nods slowly, but then shrugs, trying to play it off casually. "I mean, I knew it wouldn't happen." He glances at his dad, as if gauging whether that was the right thing to say. "You didn't believe it either, right?" he asks him.

David gives a half-smile. "It's not for me to say. Everyone believes things differently."

"But did *you* believe it?"

"I..." His parents glance at each other, before his dad sighs. "People don't just come back from the dead, Jamil," he says in a quiet voice. "It just doesn't make sense."

Jamil frowns, his brows furrowed. He knows that, of course, so he doesn't get why he's so frustrated right now. Maybe it's because everyone had hyped this up all weekend and it amounted to nothing. Maybe it's because he allowed himself to imagine what it would be like when she came back, and how he would still get to spend time with her.

Maybe it's because Grandma is actually dead now.

She didn't really die until this moment. For him, for anyone.

"Can . . . ?" Jamil clears his throat, though his voice still comes out tired and small. "Is . . . ? Can we say a prayer? For Grandma?"

His mom freezes, her expression unreadable. "Um." She looks at his dad immediately. Jamil might be imagining it, but he swears he can see a hint of panic.

"O-oh." David looks at Jamil and puts on his best fatherly voice. "Do you wanna lead? I feel like this is something you're really passionate about."

His mom bites back a smile. *Parents are weird*, he thinks. "I agree," she adds, turning her attention to him. "I bet Grandma would love to hear from you."

Jamil is nervous. Usually at every family gathering, it's the adults who do the prayers. He has no idea what to say and this is way too much pressure. But then he thinks of his grandma and what she was like, how she always smelled a bit like menthol and the sweetness of melon seeds, and he gets a warm feeling inside. She always knew what to say. She always knew how to be.

He swallows down his nerves. "O-okay, um . . ." *I can do this*, he thinks. He has to, for Grandma. "So. Close your eyes."

His parents do as they're told. He shuts his eyes, too.

"In . . . the name of the Father, the Son, and the Holy Spirit . . ." He does the sign of the cross, and exhales. "Dear Grandma. We miss you a lot . . ."

— 38 —

SUNDAY, 9:34 A.M.

On Sunday morning, the house feels quiet; eerie. The driveway, once littered with vehicles parked haphazardly up and down the road, and gazebos and tables where onlookers were gathered, only has a handful of cars now. Still, the tire tracks tell a different story. Something happened here last night. The people and the sounds have disappeared in the calm sunrise, but their mark is permanent.

Michael drives in, aligning his car beside James and Nnenna's rental, before killing the engine. He waits. His breathing sounds so loud in his car, and he finds himself trying to breathe quieter so only the rumble of his stomach matches the engine. Unfortunately, he didn't pick up any food on the way here and he can barely remember the last thing he ate. As he gazes out the window toward the house, he says a silent prayer that there's food in the fridge he can munch on.

Last night, after Michael took off, he drove for hours.

He doesn't know this city well—if he could even call it a city. He's such a Toronto man, honestly. Anything outside of the Greater Toronto Area is a "town" or a "village," he thinks. He finds it hard to look at the rolling grass in the distance and the one-lane roads and see beauty, but last night, as he drove, he felt peaceful. He felt like he was flying. He let his GPS take him as far down the road as it could before he ended up on the 400 going south back into the city.

He thought about driving home. He didn't.

He thought about calling Shelly and asking her why she couldn't be more of this or less of that. He didn't.

He thought about leaving a voicemail for Sarah, telling her that he just needed some air and he'd be back soon. He didn't. That one hurt. He remembers how Sarah looked at him last night with pain and confusion in her eyes, and he regrets not saying something to her before leaving. What kind of father is he? He didn't even say goodbye.

And now here he is, back at the house, hoping for any reception that doesn't include his own family flogging him in the yard.

Why would they? They're the ones who were wrong. He frowns, stepping out of his car and shutting the door behind him. For years, they could've told him about Mama and what happened when he was born. For *years*. He shudders when he thinks about it. He'll be, what, forty-seven next year? His two children are practically adults. Miles is at Oxford, for fuck's sake. Did his parents think they could just get away with it? That he'd die the way his dad or his mom did, and it would be okay if they never said anything?

Did they think he didn't deserve to know?

He clenches and unclenches his fists as he walks quietly toward the house. He doesn't want to be angry with his mom, but he is. She was so kind and loving and this and that, but she kept this one secret from him. *The* one secret, the one thing she should've made time to explain. He can't help but feel a twinge of bitterness when he thinks of her now. His memories of his mother will always be tainted this way.

And his father. He was no better. Who knows, maybe he even asked Mama to keep quiet about the whole thing. Michael would believe it. That was such a prominent thing in their community, unfortunately; wives lying for their husbands. To keep peace, whatever that meant. It was a cop-out. All of it was a cop-out. You can't find peace through lies.

"Why did I even come back here?" he grumbles to himself as he approaches the front door.

He reaches for the knob and tries to twist it, but it won't budge. For a moment, he contemplates ringing the doorbell, but that would lead to the exact opposite of what he wants. What if Auntie Nancy came to answer the door? Uncle Ezekiel? Or, worse: What if Joy answered? He knows he'll have to speak to her at some point—he'll have to speak to *everyone* at some point—but not now.

Michael dips around the corner of the house, following the stone path to the backyard. He jogs toward the sliding glass door. He presses his face to the glass, scanning the inside quickly to make sure he won't find a family member staring back at him. *Good,* he thinks once he realizes it's empty. *Even better.* He exhales in relief after he tugs on the handle and watches it slide open. Everything must have been so hectic last night that they forgot to lock up properly. He wonders what time everyone left, including Alice and her crew. *What if she's still here?* He shudders.

Michael carefully slides the door shut behind him. The downstairs area is a bit of a wreck. Chairs where they shouldn't be, food left out in foil pans covered haphazardly with aluminum, half-full drinks, and bottle caps on every surface. He tsks, takes off his shoes, and carries them to the front. Someone will have to clean all this up and he doesn't want it to be him. Yemi and Zach will probably do it, since they're the youngest and James is very old-fashioned that way. Joy would probably suggest they hire cleaners. Auntie Nancy would freak out at the idea of paying for labor when there are children around.

He feels strange thinking about them all now. His family.

Before Michael heads upstairs, he ducks into the kitchen for a handful of chin-chin. It's not ideal, but it will quell his grumbling stomach for a little while.

His footsteps are soft on the staircase (thank God for this disgustingly plush carpet), but he tiptoes anyway because he can hear voices and stirring in the rooms. It's Sunday morning, after all.

Not just any Sunday, he thinks while he chews on the last few pieces of chin-chin. *It's Easter Sunday. Jesus is risen. Hallelujah, I guess.*

He twists the knob and pushes against his bedroom door slowly. He doesn't notice Sarah staring at him from her bed until he closes the door behind him.

"Dad?" she asks, as if it could be anyone other than him. He sees her eyes are puffy and dry, probably from crying. From lack of sleep, too. He knows she's been trying to call him all night, and he feels horrible beyond words now. "Dad?" she repeats.

Michael steps forward. "Sarah. I'm sorry. I saw your missed calls and I . . ."

She frowns. "Where d-did you go?" Her voice shakes mercilessly, and when Michael hears it, he's afraid she'll cry. He doesn't think he can deal with that right now. Sarah snatches her phone from beside her and holds it up. "How come you never picked up?"

"I know. I know. I'm sorry." Michael repeats as he approaches her bed. She won't stop frowning, and in her eyes, he can see the deepest form of hurt: rejection. He has every right to be mad at his family, but Sarah doesn't deserve all this. When he thinks about how he left her alone here, he feels embarrassed. It's not that the family would've made her life a living hell; it's that, in the midst of his feelings of betrayal, he didn't realize he was doing the same to his own daughter. "I shouldn't have left," he concedes, a lilt in his voice. "I didn't think I would stay out so long. I went for a drive a-and then—"

"Mom said she'd call you. Did she?"

"No, she didn't." As he says it, Sarah deflates more than Michael thought possible. Right away, his mind jumps through hoops to try and blame Shelly for something, anything, but as quick as the fire comes, it dissipates. He sits on the edge of Sarah's bed, though he can't make eye contact with her. The shame is too much. "I don't have an excuse," he utters. "I don't know what to say."

Sarah doesn't, either.

Quiet fills the room and holds them hostage.

Down the hall, they hear voices becoming louder. "Hurry up, wear this" and "Don't make us late, o!" pepper the hallway in voices that sound like Nnenna and Nancy. Michael looks toward the doorway before asking, "Is something going on?"

Sarah chews her lip. "Uncle James found a church nearby, so they want everyone to go for the Easter service," she says.

Michael sighs. He figured as much. James and Nnenna are the kind of people who spend as much free time as humanly possible at their church back home, so there's no way they would survive a weekend without some form of communion. Besides, it's Easter. Michael was always taught this was the holiest day in the Christian calendar. He can see why James would try and finesse everyone into a service, today of all days.

Michael looks around the room for a clock, unsure if there even is one. "What time is the service? What time is it now?"

"I think ten thirty," Sarah answers, though Michael can't tell which question she's responding to. She shifts so her vision is directed at the wall behind him.

Michael asks, "Do you want to go?"

Sarah says nothing.

"To the church," he continues. "You don't have to if you don't want to."

She raises an eyebrow defiantly. Michael can't help but feel she looks a bit like Shelly when she gets angry.

A stampede of footsteps pass the hall outside their door. James's voice calls out loud and clear: "We're going, o! I have sent everybody the address. You people, don't be late!"

Michael is willing to bet he and Sarah will be the only ones left in the house. He gets to his feet and heads for the door, poking his head into the hall briefly.

"You're not gonna tell people you're back?" Sarah asks.

"Ah . . ." Michael sighs, turning to her. "I will. I just . . . I need to call your mom." The admission throws Sarah off a little. He can tell by the way her eyebrows shoot up and her mouth twists. "If you know you want to go to the church, you should go get ready," Michael tells her as he fishes in his pocket for his phone.

Sarah stays where she is.

Michael turns to face the window the moment the call connects. "Shelly?"

"Mike," Shelly begins. "Sarah says you left somewhere yesterday. Where'd you go?"

He sighs, rubbing his hand across his forehead. "I needed to clear my head. A lot of things happened yesterday."

"I bet," she says. He might be imagining it, but did she just scoff? "So, where's Sarah? You talk to her this morning?"

Michael stays quiet. *This feels weird,* he thinks, replaying her words and her tone in his mind. Is he being unreasonable wondering why she wouldn't ask what happened? Is it presumptuous of him to think she'd be more thoughtful? Or is he just heated because he's hungry?

He glances over his shoulder at Sarah, who watches him as if she knows she is the topic of discussion. That makes him uneasy—it makes him realize just how often she's been the topic of discussion between him and his wife. Perhaps a bit too often. Michael frowns while he responds, "Sarah's fine. She's here."

"You take that phone away yet?"

Michael bristles. "Ah-ah. Why would I? She pays for it."

"I don't want her talking to nobody."

"Like *who*?" he challenges.

She doesn't say. Instead, she exhales sharply. Michael can sense her frustration, but God, for once he wishes she'd just say what she wants to say with her chest. Just fucking be honest. Say that she thinks Sarah spends too much time talking to one of her female friends. Say that it worries her or scares her or makes her uncomfortable. Say that her love for her child is contingent upon one thing.

Shelly clears her throat. "When are you coming home? Tonight?"

"Maybe," he answers. "It depends. Maybe tomorrow."

"Okay. Well, just call when you're on your way. Bye." She hangs up.

Michael drops his phone on the bed, feeling the rumblings of anger in his chest. He doesn't know what to do, so he sits still. He tries that breathing thing that Joy is always on about. Deep breath in, deep breath out.

In. Out.

In.

Out.

Damn. This shit is working.

He makes a mental note to tell Joy later. Maybe.

Sarah crawls off her bed and comes to join him. "My . . ." Sarah clears her throat and begins again when Michael turns to her. "My, um . . . my friend, she always takes deep breaths in through her nose and out through her mouth. She counts for five both ways. It helps her a lot."

The corner of his lips twitch. "Your friend?" he asks.

Sarah nods quickly, feeling her cheeks warm. "Uh, yep. She has anxiety, like, officially. She was diagnosed. Not saying you have anxiety," she rushes to add, "but I mean, it works for her, so, yeah."

Michael tries it the way Sarah suggests. Every time he sighs out through his mouth, he feels a bit lighter. It's magical.

"Do you hate Mom?"

He's shaken from his peace by Sarah's question. His eyebrows raise, thrown off by her directness. "I don't hate anybody," he says simply.

Sarah chews her lower lip, glancing away. "Do . . . you hate *your* mom?"

He frowns. "Sarah."

"She never told you about . . . you know." She shrugs, sheepishly. "I'm just wondering."

"No." Michael surprises himself with how fast his answer comes, and how true it feels for him still. In fact, when he thinks of his mother now, his heart aches with the memories he has of her. The good ones. Where she would praise him, or teach him, or laugh with him, or cry with him. Where she mothered him, even when she didn't want to. When she didn't need to, either.

"No?" Sarah asks.

"No," he says. "I miss her."

— 39 —

Joy hears the loud gaggle of people pass by her door—"We're going, o!" calls James in his most authoritative voice—and she feels her stomach lurch. She is almost ready, wearing a shimmering dress that is maybe too flashy for an Easter Sunday service, but her bare face stares back at her from the bathroom mirror. *Just wear the lipstick, Joy,* she tries to reason with herself, but it's no use. She's not feeling very religious, very spiritual, or very much of anything.

Aside from pain, that is.

Late at night, when everyone went to bed, Joy lay awake feeling her life crash down around her. Even when she tried to sleep, the pressure continued to build. Concealer won't hide this particular brand of scarring. She sighs, turning away from her face in the mirror, and pops her head from the en suite bathroom into the bedroom, where David is helping Jamil with his tie. *Shit, he's already dressed.*

Jamil spots her the moment she appears. "Mamma," he says quickly. "Mom, I don't wanna go, I don't wanna go, I don't wanna go—"

David tsks, and pinches Jamil's cheeks. "Quiet."

"Dad's not going, either," Jamil shoots back. "He said he doesn't have to go."

Joy swallows down the urge to be angry—*He's right, I mean he's technically right. I mean, no, he's not right, how dare he*—as she treads softly into the room, approaching them. Realistically, David doesn't need to be here. He doesn't really owe her anything, and it was kind of him to come in the first place and keep her company. Oh, and Jamil, it was nice of him to keep Jamil company, too. Of course.

"I . . ." Joy inhales, and she continues, ". . . don't want to go, either."

Jamil gasps.

David's eyebrows shoot up. "Oh?"

Joy groans but the sound is swallowed by Jamil's snickering. He grins, looking at his parents. "Yes! I knew it. So can we stay home? Please?"

"I just . . ." Joy folds her arms across her chest as if she's cold. "It's just . . . I need a break." The words settle in her ears. It takes her a moment or two to feel into them, to understand what she means, but when she does, she begins to nod. "Yes. That's exactly it. I need a break."

After a moment, David snickers, "From your family."

Joy's eyes widen. "N-no, who said that? *I* didn't say that." She shakes her head right away, though her eyes flit cautiously toward Jamil. "I didn't, uh, don't repeat that outside of this room, please."

Jamil smiles.

"Well, I mean, if you're not going, uh . . ." David clears his throat. Joy already knows what he wants to say: "I should probably head out." She sees the hesitance on his face—and she's sure Jamil does, too. Where she is trying her hardest to mask her feelings, her son can't be bothered. Jamil stares at his dad, brows furrowing curiously, as if he knows what he's about to say.

David tries to get in front of it. "I gotta go into the office tomorrow," he says, more so to Jamil than Joy. "And it's still a bit of a drive back, so, you know."

Jamil makes a face like, *Okay and . . . ?* "Mom also has to go to work tomorrow and she also drives," he says bluntly.

"Jamil—"

"No, wait, wait," Joy cuts in. "It's fine. Honestly." She reaches forward, pulling Jamil into her embrace, as she gives him a squeeze around his shoulders and a kiss against the side of his head. He rolls his eyes the entire time. "It was really nice of your dad to come all the way out here, even though he didn't have to. Right?" She smiles briefly, glancing at David. He stares back at her with softness in his eyes. *Do not milk this,* she tells herself. *You are divorced. This is disrespectful to your mother who told you divorce was stupid.*

Your mother who can't be here to see that maybe she was right, just this once.

Joy drops her head a little to quell the surge of emotions. *She was not right, no. You're confused. This is grief, it's just the grief talking. Also, you're hungry.*

She digs her face into Jamil's hair, and only reemerges when she feels more composed. David watches her carefully, concern etched on his features. "It's fine, really," Joy reassures him with a fragile smile. Then she says, "My mom, she really liked you. You know that, right?"

He nods slowly, a hint of regret on his face. "Yeah, I know."

"She would've been so happy you drove all this way," Joy continues. Her eyes sting with the arrival of tears, but she tosses her head back and blinks rapidly to stop them from falling.

Jamil shifts slightly until he is facing his father. Joy hears him say, in a low, taunting voice, "Papà. Mia nonna è morta e vuoi tornare a *casa tua*? Really?"

And David chokes on a laugh.

"W-what?" Joy releases Jamil in time to catch falling tears from her eyes. She watches as David grabs Jamil's face between his hands and smushes it, with Jamil chuckling, "Right? I'm right, right?" over and over again. "What?" Joy sniffles, touching her nose. "What did he say?"

"Nothing, it doesn't matter," David cuts in with an easy shrug. "I can stay."

"O-oh?"

"We're not going to church. Jamil, you should change."

Jamil grins and bounces back and forth on his heels. "Yes! Yo, learning another language is really working for me. I think I found my calling." And he darts off to the washroom.

Joy purses her lips, pushing back a chortle. She's thankful she has such a vivacious son; someone who can distract her from the depth of her own feelings. Who tends to say and ask the things she wishes she could. *I could've just asked David myself,* she chides. *Why couldn't I just say it?*

I'm not brave, like she was.

Like my mom.

Mama always said she was named after her grandmother, Onyinye. In Igbo, it means "gift." Growing up, Joy always thought that name sounded prettier in Igbo, because she couldn't imagine someone going around simply named Gift. The word had no poetry on its own, in English. She found a lot of things didn't, and again, as she rifles through her clothes for something more homey to change back into, she wishes she spoke more of her mom's language. Of her family's language.

It's too late for that now. Joy sighs. *There is . . . no family left.*

She grimaces.

No, that's—why would I think that?

It's just her and Michael, really. And who knows if he'll ever want to talk to her again. Who knows where he even is, honestly?

Even though it was Jamil who was most excited to ditch church, it's Joy who's the first to change back into comfortable clothes. She feels so much lighter now, just like when she was a teenager and successfully lied her way out of going. Peace was always a bit more direct. "I'm not going, I don't feel like it," she'd say. When Dad would ask her again, she'd reply in pidgin, "Papa, I said I no dey go," which would always lift their parents' spirits, even if they were still annoyed. Dad would scoff and say, "Okay, o. I have been laboring since I came to this country, so me, I must go and give thanks. Na wa for you." He legit said it all the time. Why was it always the same phrase? He never said anything different.

Well, he did sometimes, to Michael.

Joy doesn't have very many memories of Michael skipping out on church. He always said yes whenever their dad asked something of him. Joy wonders if maybe something in him had known all along.

She pokes her head out of the doorway. Michael and Sarah's door is firmly shut across the hall.

Maybe he's back now. What if he came back in the middle of the night and didn't wanna say anything?

"I'm just gonna check something," Joy utters offhandedly while she tiptoes into the hall. There really is no need to tiptoe since the carpet is so thick that the floor doesn't even creak with her weight. She approaches Michael's room carefully, slowing her breath and straining to hear sounds of life from the other side. Still, she is hesitant to get too close. *What if you see him?* she thinks. *What the hell will you even say?*

"I'm sorry?" she whispers aloud, trying out the words. No, that sounds pretty empty and, well, who's she kidding? One feeble "sorry" from her won't be enough. "I'm sorry, we didn't know?" No way. "I'm sorry . . . you're my brother and I love you."

The slightest creak comes from the other side of the door and Joy stumbles back. Her breathing quickens. She's too nervous for this. She does the fastest about-face and shuffles in the direction of her room.

"O-oh."

Joy comes to a halt when she notices an open crack in the door to Mama's room. That's so strange. Why is it that . . . ? It's just . . . She would've closed it after the paramedics came and left. Seeing it ajar is so disarming. She can't stop her eyes from drifting to the open space.

Honestly, she hasn't even thought about going back into Mama's room since the incident. Since they found her. Joy knows now how unrealistic that is. Someone's gotta pack up her stuff. Someone's gotta make the bed, or the curtains have been jostled open. *It doesn't always have to be you,* she scolds herself, but standing in the middle of the hall, she realizes that maybe this is the one time it does. Who else would do it? Auntie Nancy and her entire family are at church. Michael is missing. No, really, this time, it's her responsibility.

Joy inches forward and nudges the door to Mama's room open. A wave of sadness washes over her immediately as she takes in the details. It is largely untouched. In her mind's eye, she can see the scene exactly the way it was. How she walked in, saw the light cascading on her mom's sleeping figure.

She wasn't sleeping, Joy. Get that through your head.

How her mom stirred slightly in the—

She was dead already.
Stirred in the afternoon sun—
Dead. She was gone by the time you saw her.
The memory fades.

Joy takes a deep breath and sinks into the reality of an empty room. Mama left her suitcases half-open, clothes spilling out here and there. Her purse is on the night table. As is her Bible. A plastic bag containing sandals is tucked away in the corner just outside the en suite bathroom. The curtains are half open. There is too much sun.

Joy takes quick steps, crossing to the window. The sun creeps in, filling every corner and every crevice as if it knows how desperately it's needed here. Joy stands in its warmth for a second longer. She shuts her eyes and scrunches her nose and does all those things you're supposed to do to feel centered and grounded, but she really just feels like shit.

"What am I doing in here?" She lets out a disgruntled sigh. This isn't some Hollywood movie. Coming in here and being close to the place her mom died won't make her feel whole, and it won't give her life purpose, or whatever else those narratives sell you. It just makes her feel lonely. It makes her regret everything she's ever said to anyone at any time. It makes her feel like a shell of a person whose soul will forever be fragmented by this change.

She begins to sniffle, signaling the onset of some nameless emotion come to claim her, and spins around to make her way out of the room.

But from the corner of her eye, near the night table under the Bible, she sees one of her reusable bags. She frowns, unsure how or why this is even in here, but as she approaches, she realizes it makes perfect sense. Inside the bag are old music tapes that Mama specifically requested for the party. Onyeka Onwenu, Chief Stephen Osita Osadebe, Prince Nico Mbarga, and Oliver De Coque. Several CDs of Sister Agatha Moses, Mama's latest obsession. Joy bites back a bittersweet smile. If she has to hear "Glory be . . . ! Adoration be . . . !" one more damn time. But then, she thinks, she won't have to hear it again if she doesn't want to. There will be no one here to force her to listen.

She sits with that, sinking into the side of the bed while she clutches the CDs and tapes to her chest, and she cries. She didn't know it was possible, but she feels worse. *Mom won't be able to listen to these anymore.* And she wails to herself because somehow that is the saddest thing. The music that her mother loved so much can't reach her where she is now and that realization digs into Joy's chest, plows into it, without remorse. Grief overtakes her without remorse.

"Joy?"

She startles. She must be dreaming.

The last person's voice she expected to hear was her brother's.

— 40 —

Michael didn't realize she was crying. He could guess as much, seeing her hunched over and clutching something as if she couldn't bear to let it go, but he wasn't certain until she turned around. Tears streaking down her face, she frowns at him, blinking rapidly as if trying to place his face somewhere.

He knows. It's not that he looks different; it's that he's here at all.

After such a public, shameful display, he's surprised he even had the gall to approach Joy like this. From his room, he could hear rustling down the hallway. Voices. "I guess not everyone went to church," he'd said offhandedly, casting a glance at Sarah on the opposite bed. She barely moved. Her eyes were glued to her phone.

It was then that he got up, peeked outside. He saw Joy's room door slightly open, but most of the rustling was coming from his mom's room. *Odd.* He headed down the hall, fast footsteps growing slower as he heard more, saw more. Joy crossing the room to the night table. Retrieving a stack of CDs and tapes. Flipping through them. And that sigh. He knew he had to come in after that.

Now that he has, he isn't sure it was a good idea.

Joy gets to her feet immediately, while she uses one hand to wipe frantically at her face. "W-what are you doing here?"

Michael winces at the sharpness of her voice. He holds up his hands, taking a pensive step back. "I didn't mean to walk in on you—"

"No, I meant, like what are you . . . ?" She gulps, wiping the last of her tears. After another breath, she says, "I didn't know when you got back, so. Yeah."

"Yeah."

She watches him. He could always tell when she was watching him because her gaze was so intense. How could people stand it? There was little else you could do in her presence but cower or fight, so he chose the latter, always. Get her before she gets you, he'd think. *Oh God . . .* He suppresses a groan. Is that really how he's always viewed his younger sister? She was literally a baby when he was heading to middle school. She and Peace would've looked to him for guidance, but he couldn't be bothered to be the person they wanted him to be. Or needed. It was too much pressure and he just wanted to be a kid. He vaguely remembers how hard it was to emigrate to Canada; how he had to adjust. People drew attention to his accent and his foreignness in a way that he'd never had to think about before. *Why* then would he come home and want to spend time with his baby sisters, both of whom wouldn't be othered in the way he was? Not in the exact way. They were born here. That came with a privilege many don't often speak of.

But it wasn't their fault. Why would it be? They were babies.

It's no one's fault, really.

Isn't it?

He cringes. "Damn . . ." He takes a hesitant step into the room before deciding he no longer cares about Joy's scrutiny. He goes to sit down on the bed.

To his surprise, Joy joins him. She is still clutching the CDs as if dropping them would be blasphemy.

Michael says, "What are those?" as if he doesn't already know.

"CDs," Joy replies.

"Oh."

Silence.

Joy clears her throat. "I, uh . . ." She throws her head back, shutting her eyes briefly. With each passing second, Michael knows she's trying to come up with something "good" to say—something that Mom would've said. Something Joy's clients expect from her.

I don't want anything from you, he thinks. But he can't say it. He doesn't trust himself to get the words out right.

So he waits, lets Joy wrack her brain for the Right Thing to Say.

"Okay." She tries again. "I'm . . . we—"

"Honestly, don't worry," Michael cuts in, his voice soft. He juts out his lips, a sign of disagreement. "You don't have to say anything profound. I'm not one of your, you know, one of your coaching people."

She glances at him. "I wanna say something profound, though."

He scoffs. "Well, you're not good at it, so."

Joy bristles, and Michael can see a small nudge in her eyebrows, a hint of anger. *She should know that every time she's tried to say the right thing to me, it's backfired,* he thinks. They always argue.

"Okay, well, then . . . fuck that," Joy says with a shrug. "I'm not gonna try to be profound."

"Good."

"I just wanna say that I-I'm sorry." She looks at him for a reaction, but he gives her nothing. Just stares ahead toward the window, squinting in the morning brightness. "I didn't know about Dad. I know that you might think it doesn't matter either way, but, like . . . bro."

He waits for what is sure to be a stunning end to her point, but it never comes. The shortness of it makes him want to chuckle. A vague, nonthreatening smirk is all he can muster. "'Bro'?" He snorts. "That's all you have?"

"That's all I have," she mutters with a nod. "I thought you'd never come back, so . . . I figured I had infinity time to prepare."

His smirk widens despite himself; despite how shitty he feels. He can see on Joy's face, the cautious way she looks at him and the delicate candor of her words, that she is afraid. She's a girl clutching old CDs and tapes her mom refused to throw away, even though online streaming is now a thing. And she's scared. *Of course,* he grumbles. *You're older. She can't fix this for you. It's not her job.*

He thinks of how so many things ended up being Joy's job simply because of him, and he finds the words "I'm sorry, too" bursting through before he can evaluate them. In the end, the things he wants to say find him before he's able to pin them down. "I was so mean a-and for no reason. I said things to you I shouldn't have. I wasn't there when I should've been. I've b-been a disgrace—" His voice breaks and he pauses, clenching his jaw in case tears follow.

Michael takes a moment to compose himself before continuing, "When Peace died, I felt it, you know? I felt that things would be different."

A frown stretches across Joy's lips.

"I knew you guys only had each other, and I didn't even—Joy, when I tell you I *did not* even care." His face contorts with anguish. It's so palpable, and soon he is crying, fully sobbing, into his hands. Each sob rattles his shoulders and muffles his voice. "I didn't think about any of you. I just went on with my life. So th-this, *now* . . . Joy, it's karma. Learning about m-my . . . about Dad and h-having a different mom is like . . . it's what I deserve, y-you know?"

"No." Joy scooches closer and places a hand on his shuddering shoulders. "No one deserves that."

"You don't have to be all diplomatic," he groans. "You said it for years. I was never there for you guys."

"Mi—"

"I never took Mom to the doctor, I never visited when I should. After Dad died, I just—I checked out." His voice rises with each word, brimming with more and more anger. "It's like a part of me *knew*. Mom probably didn't wanna hold it against me because she *knew* all along I wasn't hers—"

Joy smacks him on the back, hard.

He straightens up, scowling at her. "Ah-ah! What the hell?"

"You're spiraling," she says quietly.

"Don't use your therapy language on me, o."

"You're talking smack. None of it is true."

"Na you know? You said half those things yourself—"

"Yeah, and I was angry," she says, letting her hand settle back in her lap. "Michael, I have been"—she swallows—"I have been *pissed off* at you for most of my life."

He stays quiet. All he can do is bite his tongue, purse his lips, try not to cry again.

"I always wanted a d-different brother." She turns away. Immediately, Michael feels himself tensing up. He knows; none of this is new for him. Still, he doesn't want to be sitting here listening to these heavy things in a room where their mom took her last breath.

Joy chews her lip anxiously. "I wanted a brother who I felt I knew. But you didn't wanna have anything to do with me, and after Peace died, a-and when Dad died, it just got worse . . ." Her voice begins to waver. Her lip quivers. "Someone dies—someone *dies* and you run away. But we're all we have left . . . it's just you and me now. S-so what are you gonna do?" She turns to him. He can't take one look at her before breaking down.

"I know, I know, I know . . ." Michael dissolves into a puddle of tears, each sob pulsing its way through his body. Years and years of guilt and shame and anger and frustration come pouring out of him all at once. He has never cried so much; he has never been so wide open.

God, please . . . He chokes on a scoff. Calling God now feels like a joke. It makes him feel hollow, though he can't really explain how. He is angry with God, but he can't really say why.

Because He left you.

You left Him, and He left you.

Loneliness envelopes him like a cold blanket. It's only when he feels Joy's arm around him and her chin on his shoulder that he feels a bit like he can get through it. It hurts, this sudden opening. His chest feels like a fresh wound is forming and being tickled by the wind. It's sour and bitter and makes him want to cover up. It makes him feel visible, the kind of visible he wasn't sure he could ever feel.

Michael doesn't know how long he cries.

He's not sure when Joy's chin lifts from his shoulder or when her hand leaves his side.

There are voices down the hall, but he can't make them out.

And his tears taper off, drying out naturally, once the well of emotions is done running over. He feels silly. A man of his age, crying like this. When he glances at Joy, she doesn't budge; doesn't show any sign of disgust. *She's used to this,* he tells himself. *She probably sees adults cry all the time.*

The two of them sit in silence. There's a weird lull, Michael can tell. For the first time, it feels as though Joy has no reason to attack and Michael has no reason to defend. The sun inches higher in the sky. The shadows shift around the room. Michael glances at Joy. She's still clutching those CDs.

He nods to them. "Does doing that help?" he asks, his voice gravelly from the crying.

Joy snorts. "No."

"Huh."

"I can't let go of them, though," she says with a sad smile. "I keep thinking that, like . . . I don't know. I don't know."

"Same." Michael sighs. "I wonder if going to church would've helped. Auntie and them went, and sometimes I think they're dealing with things better than I am, because they have the church and all that."

Joy raises an eyebrow. "You think they're dealing with things better than us? Need I remind you of the cow?"

Michael snickers. "Okay, well—okay, fine. But something *is* different. I've seen it with Shelly's family, too." He pauses a minute, thinking about holidays and birthdays he's had to spend with them. "Yeah, they really lean into their beliefs. They have that community. It's like a foundation."

"*We* have that foundation, too," Joy pipes up. "But we chose not to use it."

"Well, would you?"

"I don't believe in it anymore," she says, her words clipped. It sounds so final that Michael can see how it shocks her. He gets it. He knows it's not that Joy doesn't believe in God or the angels or the divinity of being; it's just that she thinks the Bible is a crutch. And a bad one, at that. After seeing how their family behaved this past weekend, how could they think otherwise? It didn't bring the comfort they were promised.

Michael doesn't push it. He sees the lines in her face, how rigid they've become, and realizes she's still processing things in her own way. He understands that Joy is angry with God, too, just like he is. He wants to ask her about it—he *should* ask her—but he doesn't have the words yet. Maybe one day when the wound isn't so fresh, they can talk about how a promise and a premonition came undone before their eyes.

And the eyes of approximately thousands both here and in Nigeria via a broadcast that was sanctioned by a pastor named Lazarus.

"Alice will say that it was a hoax, eh?" Michael says with a shudder.

Joy groans. "Yeah, I know. Not excited for that backlash."

"Y-yeah . . ." *At least we have each other, though,* he wants to tell her, but he doesn't.

They're silent for a moment before Joy speaks up. "How are things with Shelly?"

"What?" Michael startles, at first confused as to why she's asking, but then he realizes he opened the door himself by bringing her up. "Um . . ." *No point in lying now.* He says, "Honestly? Not great," while Joy rushes to add, "You don't have to answer." He lets out a humorless chuckle. "Oh, *now* I don't have to answer?" It's supposed to be a bit of a joke, a touch of lightness in such a heavy place, but he can tell from how Joy shrinks that she misread him. Again. *We just don't understand each other. I don't know if we ever truly will.*

He tries again. "We've been . . . not seeing eye to eye on a lot of things."

Joy frowns. "I'm sorry. That sucks."

"Eh." Michael shrugs. The shrug is almost too casual for how he feels about the whole thing. Truthfully, his world is being ripped apart. Truthfully, the person he was supposed to love the most is turning out to be someone he can't recognize anymore, and that hurts him more than he can say. He folds his hands together, leaning forward, and lets out a strong exhale. He wants to push this feeling out of his chest.

"Are you . . ." Joy begins. "Are you guys gonna be okay, do you think?"

He scoffs, tasting bitterness in his words. "I really don't know."

She says nothing.

"How do you know when it's time to . . ." His voice trails off, uneasily. Then he shuts his eyes momentarily and forces out the question: "How do you know when things aren't worth fixing anymore?" When she doesn't respond right away, he tilts his head back to look at her face. He doesn't say that he asked David the exact same thing, though even now he can see the same sequence of emotions play out on her face.

She says something similar: "There isn't a real time w-when that decision becomes obvious," and Michael has to scoff. He simply must. *Just like I thought: my situation is completely different.*

Because for him, there has been.

He thinks—no, he is certain he knows when it was.

"There's something wrong with that girl," Shelly had said. It was a Wednesday afternoon, years ago now. Maybe longer. The days are starting to blur together and Michael can't place the exact date because, at the time, it felt harmless to him. This conversation wasn't noteworthy, until it was. Until it became the spark behind the fire.

Michael had only stopped at home to grab a file before heading back to the office. Shelly handed it to him from across the kitchen island. She didn't look at him as she spoke, so Michael was uncertain if he heard wrong.

He waited a moment before asking, "What girl?"

"Sarah," Shelly said quickly, as if she'd been waiting to spit out the name from the moment Michael walked in.

Michael didn't get it. Sarah was a teenager. She was a bit moody and Michael suspected that she was hiding alcohol somewhere in her room, but to be fair, he did the same thing when he was her age. He had actually been trying to find ways to bring it up with her, just to make sure she was being responsible and not hanging around anyone who would influence her to, you know, drive drunk or drink until she blacks out or something else stupid. He just didn't know how. He'd never had that talk with his parents, them opting to go the more traditional "don't drink or you'll go to hell" route of parenting, so he had no blueprint. But surely, that couldn't be enough reason to say there was something wrong with her.

"Why? Where is she now?" Michael asked. "Is she upstairs?"

"Yes," Shelly responded. "I told her to stay there until you got back. And I took her phone. These people she's talking to, I don't trust them, y'know."

Michael's brows furrowed in confusion. "Who's she talking to?"

Shelly's answer was immediate; sharp and unforgiving. "Girls," she spat out.

"Girls?"

"Different girls. Different *kinds* of girls."

Michael will never forget how Shelly looked at him that day. Or, rather, how she didn't. How she danced around the kitchen, busying herself with things that didn't need her attention, and didn't stop once to look her husband in the eye. Tell him to his face that she was worried her daughter wasn't straight.

It only worsened from that day forward, and even when Michael tries to think about it, his memories become one unpleasant swirl. The day when Shelly yelled at Sarah and tore up the jeans Sarah bought with her own money, saying they were boys' clothes and why would she want them? The day when Sarah was set to get a nose piercing, but when Shelly found out, she all but locked Sarah in the house. The day when Sarah joked about wanting to shave her head and Shelly slapped her. The day when, the day when, the day . . . So many instances where Michael could feel Shelly's dislike building. So many instances when Michael had to step in and smooth things out. He comforted Sarah; bought her new clothes. He reasoned with Sarah; promised he would pay for her next piercing. He hugged Sarah; tried again and again to explain that her mom didn't hate her, no. How could she? This was her mother. The woman who birthed her; the woman who loved her unconditionally. Who was supposed to love her unconditionally. Hatred was such a foreign thing.

Well, it *was*. Recently, it had begun to build its home in their house and he wasn't sure how much longer he could stand by and say nothing.

Sarah is his daughter and he loves her. He has lost a father and he has lost a mother, and he knows that this—love, the way he feels about his children—is the most important thing. He can't call himself a father if he sacrifices that.

Joy stares back at him curiously, watching his thoughts play out through emotions on his face. "Michael?" she nudges.

He doesn't miss a beat when he says, "I think Sarah has a girlfriend."

Joy's eyes widen. "Oh!" she exclaims, perhaps a bit too shocked. Michael can see the emotional journey on her face—feeling awkward for being shocked, feeling shocked for being shocked. She asks, "How . . . do you know?"

Michael moves his thumbs as if he's texting, surprising himself when a humorless chuckle escapes his lips. "She's always on that phone. I hear her talking to someone named Mel. Or Mal. They don't sound like just friends."

"*Oh.*"

"Y-yeah." He sighs. "And . . . Shelly, she . . ."

Suddenly, Michael can see a wave of understanding wash over Joy's face. It's like a lightbulb goes off in her head and it's cascading a soft light over him, over his situation. As if she hadn't seen him clearly until just now.

She extends a hand and places it on his back.

He gets it right away. How strange that words were never good enough, but these simple gestures seem to speak volumes.

"Yeah," he sighs. His bittersweet smile begins to waver. "She's my kid, Joy. She's my child. And I love her."

"I know," she answers softly.

"But I'm so scared, eh?" He lets out a crass laugh, pressing his hands into his eyes and letting out a low groan. When he finally pulls his hands away, he sits up straight. "My God, I'm terrified. Because if anyone says anything to her—*anyone* says anything to my kid about how she is—I'll straight up slap them."

Joy's face breaks into an easy smile and she laughs. "Anyone?"

"Anyone."

"James?"

Michael doesn't hesitate to do a swift slapping motion, imagining a figurative James standing before them. "*Pop*. In fact, because it's James, eh? The way his head is so wide, it'd have to be a *pop-pop*." He does a fronthand and a backhand.

Joy laughs harder. This is the first time Michael can remember laughing with his sister in . . . in ages. He can't even think of one memory the two of them shared where they were this open. And now, here they are, laughing about slapping their cousin-in-law while sitting on the bed where their mother died.

Joy's next chuckle forces the CDs to slip out of her grasp onto the floor. They hit the carpet with a soft thud. "Oh, shit," she says, her words almost swallowed by her laughter. She drops to her knees and begins to scoop them up.

Michael comes down to help her. "You'd think Mom would've at least gotten an MP3 player or something."

"MP3 player? How old *are* you?"

Michael hides a smile. Joy never jokes with him like this, and he can't deny it's a bit strange, but it feels good to be on this side of things. It feels strangely . . . normal. "Well, maybe she could've put music on her phone or something," he says. "You know, really get into the You-Tube to WhatsApp Nigerian auntie pipeline."

"You realize *we're* the aunties and uncles now, right?"

Michael blanks.

"Besides, she was all over WhatsApp," Joy says with a casual roll of her eyes. "But what she needed was a YouTube playlist. Something way more portable than this shit." She holds up an old CD before flipping it around to look at it.

Michael nods slowly, staring back at the face of Oliver De Coque in Joy's hand. "Hey . . ." A smile creeps onto his face. "Do . . . you wanna do something dumb?" Joy looks back at him with raised brows at the suggestion. She doesn't look combative; she doesn't seem to have misread him. That brings a wave of relief that he never thought possible. Him and Joy, not quite understanding each other, but not at each other's throats, either. It's an Easter miracle.

"It's the best way I can describe it," he continues, getting to his feet. "It's also the best way I can think to honor Mom."

Joy grins. He extends a hand to her and she hoists herself up. "Sure," she tells him. "I love doing dumb shit."

"*You?*" He scoffs.

Her cheeks burn with embarrassment. "F-fine, fine! I can learn to be okay with doing things that aren't very productive every once in a while, sure."

— 41 —

Joy wants to laugh as she follows Michael out of the room. He looks left and right down the hallway, as if he's a kid trying to sneak out of the house at midnight without anyone hearing. He knows what he's doing; he's been that kid. Crawling out of bed, tiptoeing past her room, and hissing threats at her—"You better go back to bed, o. You didn't see me here"—before eventually making it out the door. She knows that when he was a teenager, he'd meet up with friends at the corner to smoke cigarettes or get high in someone's car. And she bets he thinks he got away with it, but when he'd waddle back in at 5:00 a.m., Dad would be there, early riser that he was. Joy wonders if he got in trouble, but judging by the amount of times Michael had snuck out, she guesses not. Dad always forgave him. Always kept room for him.

"Where are we going?" Joy asks from behind him.

"Downstairs. Come on." He speeds down the carpeted stairs and jogs into the living room, all the while being shady, checking each room to make sure no one is there.

Joy is chortling. She's never seen her brother act this strange—or this childlike. He gets to the living room and begins to look behind the

TV, on the shelves, in the drawers. "What are you looking for?" she asks as she joins him.

"Bluetooth speaker."

"How do you know there's one here?"

He makes a face, sour and disbelieving. "Just look at this place. Each room has complimentary wine," he says, gesturing around them. "A Bluetooth speaker is jara."

"*Tch,* sure."

He finds one, nestled under the TV. After some tinkering and five minutes waiting for the devices to pair, he's able to connect his phone. Joy watches as he opens up his streaming app and keys in the first of many names: Sis Agatha Moses. Joy gasps. "*Please* no!"

"Thought you could escape, eh?" Michael snickers, searching up more old-school artists and adding them to a queue. "Today, we can celebrate Mama with all her favorites."

"Please let's leave off this song—" Joy startles when the music blares mercilessly from the speaker. For such a small device, it really is loud. Igbo gospel fills the downstairs, bouncing off the walls and windows, at an alarming volume. She winces, signaling for him to turn it down. "You're gonna disturb everyone upstairs!"

"Everyone?" He raises an eyebrow. "Everyone's at church, right?"

"Not everyone—"

"What about this?" Michael changes the song. There's a bit of a lull before "Sweet Mother" starts blaring. "He-ey!" he choruses, pressing a hand to his chest. He shuffles his way to the center of the living room, his feet moving in time to the music, before he breaks out in full-on dancing. He holds his hands above his head, swaying, while he sings: "'Sweet mother, I no go forget you, for the suffer wey you suffer for me, yeah...'"

Joy laughs, smacking her hands together. "Are you dumb?"

"Come and dance, na!" He beckons her forward. "Do you remember when Uncle Festus would say, 'Come, come and dance!' every time this song started playing?"

"Yes!" Joy's shock surprises her. For one, she can't believe she and Michael had an almost identical experience growing up, even though she swears she can't place him in her memories. She remembers her and Peace trying to get away from Uncle Festus, but she can't believe Michael and some of their older cousins had to dodge him, too.

Joy does her best impression of Uncle Festus, squeezing her face the way he always did. "'Oya, come and dance for your mama!'"

Michael snickers, snapping his fingers. "Yes! No matter where we were, if 'Sweet Mother' came on, he would find us, one by one, and be like, 'Oya, come!' like it concerned him."

"He was so annoying . . ." Joy rubs her eyes, rubs the idea of her annoying uncle from her mind. When she pulls her hands away, she sees Michael gesturing for her to join him while he mouths over the words. She laughs and steps forward to dance with him. She's never seen this side of her brother before, the one that's so carefree and open. He almost seems like a different person.

She says loudly, as best she can over the music, "I can't believe you never inherited any rhythm!"

He gawks like he misheard her, but then scrunches his lips, shaking his head, and doing exaggerated leg movements that are barely on beat. "When people ask you to come and dance, they don't care how bad you are. You're dancing for someone's memory. That's the point!"

He does a dance move that looks like it was popular with Nigerian kids five years ago and Joy pauses to show him how it's supposed to be done. "Like this?" he asks.

"N-no, wait, stop—stop moving your leg—"

"Like *this*?"

"You can't do legwork. Please stop."

He flashes a grin while he continues trying anyway. And Joy keeps laughing.

When the song gets to the "stop, stop . . ." part, an awkward pause where people never actually stop dancing, Michael freezes, but Joy doesn't. "He-ey, see you," he chides. "And we used to make fun of those people who never stop dancing when the man *clearly* says we should."

"In memory of Mom," Joy tells him. "I thought I would ignore the instructions, you know, one last time."

"You no well, o."

"What's . . . going on here?"

Michael and Joy turn to see Rob slowly shuffling into the room. They exchange confused looks: Rob was *here*? This whole time?

Yes, in fact, Rob was here!

James had specifically written down the directions and the address of the church he found, and handed the sticky note to Rob earlier. "Come on time," he said, even though they were all about half an hour from being late.

Rob stared down at the sticky note, plastered a prickly smile on his face, and said, "Sure thing," before closing the door in James's face. He turned, rolling his eyes, as he approached his bed. There was no way Rob would be caught dead in a pew next to James.

Quickly, he reached for his phone. Paul had sent him a good morning text, like he always did, and Rob was in the middle of recounting everything that went down the night before.

That sounds horrible, wrote Paul.

It was, replied Rob.

How's your family taking it? Paul texted back.

Decent, I think!

How's . . . the cow taking it?

Rob sent several skull emojis and a barrage of butto mashing to his husband in response.

He had no idea how the cow was taking it, but he knew how everyone else—the hordes of people at the house yesterday, that is—were taking it: horribly. He's been seeing a lot of news articles this morning based on the AJAfrika coverage. Headlines like "Local Family Dives into Religious Hoax" peppered his feed. It was embarrassing and infuriating at the same time, though even he had to admit, his personal favorite headline—"The Latest Religious Hoax Is *Beefier* than You Can Imagine"—was quite clever.

After his scrolling, he pulled out his Bible and said a small prayer like he always did. The words "the Lord is risen" wafted off his tongue and he felt warmth in his heart and comfort in his soul. His version of worship didn't look like his mom's or his sister's, but that didn't make it any less valid. He had to remind himself of that often.

For a moment, he wondered if everyone else in the family had succumbed to James's requests. He guessed Sarah wouldn't be going to the church on account of her dad being missing, and he wasn't sure about Joy and her situation. Honestly, sometimes, he wasn't sure Joy was even sure of her own situation.

In the end, he shrugged and fell back against the bed. He stayed like that, scrolling back and forth on his phone for what felt like ages. While he was two minutes into a video of Alice explaining how she was duped by the premonition, his eyes rolling so often they might as well have been generating wind power, a surge of sound came from downstairs. He sat up right away, and uttered, "What . . . ?"

He crawled off the bed and poked his head out of the door where he heard what sounded like an old Nigerian song coming from the living room. "Sweet Mother." "Who in the hell is playing this relic?" Well, maybe "relic" was a bit harsh. He adored "Sweet Mother." It may as well have been the Nigerian national anthem, not only because it was so popular, but because it was definitely as old as the national anthem as far as he was concerned. He'd heard it every year, at every party, since he was a fetus, most likely.

Rob took a step into the hallway and turned just as the door to Joy's room popped open. He waved at David, who looked even more perturbed than he did. "What's going on?" David asked.

Rob shrugged. "I couldn't tell you." He watched Jamil wiggle his way into the hall, shuffling past his dad, and quickly called to him: "Jamil, where's your mom?"

"I couldn't tell you," Jamil repeated.

"Ha." *Does Joy know her kid is cooler than her?* he thought. She had to have known. Parents always knew that sort of thing.

Rob inched his way toward the staircase, looking over it as best he could. "I'll go see what's up," he told them offhandedly, taking the stairs one at a time. The music grew louder and louder still, drawing him in the closer he got. But, my God, he wasn't prepared to see Joy and Michael—Joy *and* Michael, in the same room, alive and breathing—dancing in the middle of the floor.

Rob and Joy are close in age, and Michael was always an elusive brother figure for him, too. He'd rarely seen Michael look jovial; he could count the times he saw Joy and Michael have a civil conversation on one hand—no, actually, on one finger. And it was this. They laughed with each other. Joy was trying to teach Michael a dance move and the poor man was just not getting it. *Rhythm is truly a gift,* Rob thought as he had the unfortunate pleasure of watching Michael's attempt at legwork. Then, when the "stop, stop . . . stop, stop" part in "Sweet Mother" came on, Joy danced through it and Rob found himself groaning. *The man isn't just saying stop for fun,* Rob thinks. *When will my people free themselves from this?*

"What's . . . going on here?"

Joy, a hand to her chest while she tries to suppress a giggle, walks over. "What the hell? Didn't you go to church?"

"Didn't *you* go?" Rob teases. He mimics her hand-on-chest stance. For that, she smacks him in the arm. "He-ey!" He leaps. "Well, no one asked you to be playing 'Sweet Mother' at the ass crack of dawn."

"Day has broken," Michael says while he dances.

"Yes!" Rob raises his hands, dramatically swaying with the music. "It's Easter Sunday. White Jesus has risen. He's in the sky. Hallelujah!"

"Abeg, shut *up*, man," Michael snickers. "Come join us."

"Can we play something a bit cooler?"

"What?" Joy snorts. "'Sweet Mother' is beyond your normal conception of what's cool and what isn't. It transcends. It just *is.*"

Rob gives an exaggerated roll of his eyes. "Yeah, whatever."

He dances with them. Michael threatens to start the song from the beginning, but Rob specifically dances beside his phone and the speaker, doing exaggerated arm movements to stop him. *He's a way better dancer than Michael,* Joy thinks. Not like it was hard to be.

Damn, did I know Michael was this bad? She ponders the question, combing over details in her mind, until she realizes it doesn't matter at all. This version of her brother is the one she wants to keep in her head. She says a silent prayer that tomorrow morning, when she wakes up and the magic of Easter is gone, replaced by the dull tug of grief, that she will remember *this* Michael.

Another chorus of "Sweet Mother" starts up (seriously, how long *is* this song?) and as Joy dances around to the kitchen, she notices Jamil peeking out from the hall. "Kid!" Joy calls, which is uncharacteristic for her. Jamil stares for a moment like he's not sure who she's talking to, but when she beckons him over, he does so, dragging his feet. "When did you come down? Where's your dad? Come dance with me," she babbles on while he floats into her embrace. God, he's getting tall. She threads her hands through his hair, absently. It reminds her of how her mom used to be with her, always poking and touching and smoothing her hands over Joy's face and hair.

Jamil mumbles, "I don't really want to."

"Oya," Joy begins, channeling her best Uncle Festus. Jamil doesn't often get to experience being strong-armed into dancing with the adults, so she feels she's doing him a favor. It's a cultural experience. "Ah-ah, don't give me that look. Come and dance."

"Mom—"

"You can't be worse than your uncle. I mean, honestly."

"Mama, I no say I no sabi dance, o," he mumbles again, this time in pidgin.

Joy freezes, her mouth falling slack in equal parts disbelief and intrigue. "*What*?" She feels weird; she feels blindsided. Since when could Jamil speak pidgin? And why is his accent better than hers? Wait, wait, should she have known this? Have there been signs that she completely overlooked?

Jamil tenses in her embrace. "Uh . . ." He clears his throat. "Did I . . . say it wrong?"

"N-no!" She rushes to correct him, her hands smoothing their way to his shoulders. "No, I just—it's, uh . . ." She feels her cheeks warm, a surge of emotion rushing through her. *How embarrassing for me, honestly.*

She bites back a chuckle; she blinks away the sting of tears. This entire time, some weird gremlin in her mind had been telling her she wasn't enough of this or enough of that for her son to be much of anything. The thought haunted her, made her resistant to the idea that her son could be and very much is two wholes, not two halves. And he is just like her.

She hides her face immediately, turning from him. Jamil is freaked out. "Okay, I'll dance if you want me to," he says hurriedly.

He reaches for her arm to guide her back to the living room, but she halts, tugging him back. A teary smile graces her face as she tries her hardest to keep it together. "I think you'll have a really good time in Italy this summer," she tells him.

A spark flickers behind Jamil's eyes. His excitement is almost palpable, buzzing through him as he rocks back and forth on his heels. "Ooooh my God, Moommm, legit?" He bites his lip, already anticipating the answer.

"Legit. Yeah." Her smile widens. The smallest hint of anxiety nudges her, somewhere in the back of her throat, but she lets it stay there. She hasn't seen Jamil this excited in a while. And he's her kid; she should want him to be happy above all else. Mama would want that, too. "Where, um . . . do you know where you'll be going when you get there?"

Jamil nods right away—then freezes, as if he's going over a plan in his head. Glancing away, he says, "I don't know, mostly around Rome? Staying with Nonna Bruna, washing tomatoes or whatever."

Joy snorts. No way a twelve-year-old wants to sit and wash tomatoes. He hated going to the farm with Mama here, buying bushels of tomatoes to wash, grind, and store for the winter, so she's sure that not even the early morning Italian sun will suddenly inspire her child to want to do labor. "Whatever," she mimics, and pulls him into a close hug. "Just don't start any bad habits while you're there."

"I won't, I won't—"

"Stay close to your dad. Do not take things from strangers. Don't start smoking."

"I'm *twelve*, Mom, jeez."

He's right. Kids, on average, start smoking around fifteen. *Don't be-*

come a teenager, please, she thinks as she shuts her eyes, inhaling the scent of his hair. *And stop growing.*

When she opens her eyes, she spots David walking toward her from the hall. Immediately, she notices what he's carrying in his hands: her work phone. "Oh no," she grumbles, letting Jamil slip out of her grasp.

"Uh, yeah," David answers, handing it to her. "I swear I can't be in the same room as your work phone. It literally never stops going off."

"I'm so sorry."

"It's fine. Just . . . keep it away from me forever," he says. His easy smile is marred with an undercurrent of frustration.

Joy looks at the phone, quickly swiping through the last few calls. She groans. "Good God . . ." Almost all of them are from Coral. There are voicemails, too, six of them. Some from Coral, some from the head office, others from unknown numbers. Colleagues. Her supervisor. With each new message or missed call notification, her impatience grows. Are these people serious? She asked for one weekend off—it's *Easter*, and even if it wasn't, it's a Sunday, for goodness sake! And . . . and . . .

"My mom is *dead*," she says. Her brows knit together and a scowl takes root on her face. These . . . these heartless bastards. She asked for two days off and they couldn't give her that? Just two fucking days?

She looks up at David.

He stares back at her. "What?"

"I . . ." Her grip around her phone tightens. "I am leaving my job."

"Oh?"

"Yes." Her hand twitches. Without a second thought, she turns and throws her phone down the hall and toward the front door. Jamil jumps at the sound of it crashing against the wall. Michael and Rob glance over, trying to find the source of the noise.

Joy shakes her shoulders. Pushes off the weight of responsibility, of other people's expectations. Her mom is gone. Things won't be the same for her going forward. Her mom is *gone*. She has to change.

The adrenaline is fading with each passing second. With whatever courage she has left, she reaches her hands out to David and says, "Come. Dance with me."

— 42 —

Over time, the volume of the music lowers until it becomes a comfortable background hum. The dancing stops. The cleanup begins. Rob begs them to put on something other than old highlife music, and Joy finds an updated Afropop playlist to fill the space. She sways back and forth, picking up overturned cups and separating garbage from recycling.

Across the room, Michael bends, touches his knees, and lets out a crass laugh, one that feels like it's years in the making. He's not as young as he used to be, and so many of his poor decisions in his twenties and thirties continue to haunt him. Every time his knees ache, he curses the times he never warmed up or stretched properly at the gym, thinking he could just avoid it or that it wasn't a big deal. Well, he's learned his lesson. He does quick leg stretches, which makes Sarah chuckle. Sarah, who has since vacated the room and arrived downstairs, just as Jamil rushes by her with a filled garbage bag.

Michael beckons Sarah over, then points to a row of half-filled pop cans and beer bottles. "These need to be emptied," he says simply. "And then recycled."

"Uh, save the empties," Rob calls from the opposite side of the room as he walks past with an ottoman from the taxidermy room.

Sarah nods, glancing away. "Yes, sir."

Michael slides a table across the floor, but Joy waves her hand to get his attention. "Wait, I think that went over there." She points to a spot by the wall.

"Really?"

"I-I think so."

Michael sighs and gives his back another crack before bending to push the table over. Now he understands why his dad and all their parents used to ask the kids to do things. As he watches Sarah cross the living room back and forth, seemingly gliding as she goes, he realizes he just doesn't have the energy he used to. "Sarah, bịa," he says with a huff. He points haphazardly to the scene in front of him. "Clear this up for me."

"Sure." She gives an exaggerated salute before getting to work.

— 43 —

Two things happen that make Joy reconsider her stance on belief.

She is putting away a stack of dishes that David washed and left by the side of the sink. For what it's worth, she was prepared to wash everything. "I don't mind doing it, honestly," she told him before he flashed her a most condescending look.

"I know," he said. "You don't mind doing anything, Joy, that's kinda a problem you have. No offense."

She pursed her lips, feeling her jaw clench—*Is he serious? I say no to a lot of things!*—before she realized he was right. Funny, that. The moment she was able to breathe through it was the moment she realized, actually, yeah, she did mind. She hated doing the dishes.

"Fair," she said pointedly, ignoring the smug smile he flashed her as she waited to dry and put away the stack of plates.

Jamil shuffles by every now and then to watch. When Joy turns and sees him lurking, she waves a dish at him. "Okay, come help me, then—"

"No, no, no, you guys are fine on your own. Together, but on your own together," he says quickly, and races away.

He nearly bumps into Rob, who's just stepped in from the backyard. "Hey!" Rob yelps at the same time Jamil calls, "Sorry, Uncle!" over his shoulder.

The living room has emptied out some, aside from Joy and David, and Sarah dusting one of the tables. "Guys, everyone, hey." Rob holds up his hands, waiting until he has their attention. Then he does his best impression of Auntie Nancy. "I've had a premonition."

Joy gasps. "Too soon!"

"I've just seen a pigeon—"

"Uncle!" Sarah chortles, rubbing a hand down her face.

Rob grins. "So my parents and sister will be back from church soon, and I had an idea." He looks around. "Where's Michael? Someone call him. And find Jamil."

"I'll go," Sarah says.

While Sarah disappears upstairs, Joy watches Rob position himself in the center of the living room. He's in the optimal place for everyone to see and hear him, including Michael and Jamil, who come waltzing in just moments later. He grins. "Are we all ready?" Confused glances are exchanged across the room. Rob continues, "Let's have a wake for Auntie Mary, like, right here."

Joy is immediately hit with the need to protest.

Michael cuts in, "How? With what?"

"With, I don't know, the backyard." Rob gestures over his shoulder. "I was just out there, and the weather is pretty nice. Plus, I think we owe it to Auntie to give her a proper send-off while we're still all together."

"Ah-ah." Michael frowns. "You're talking like you won't come for the funeral when we hold it."

"We will," Rob says. "But we're all here *now*. So why not? We're one phone call away from the outdoor decor and catering coming back. We have the original guest list of people we can call. We have an army of stuffed squirrels. And, besides, I don't think there's any religious reason as to why we can't do it." He taps his chin, thinking. "Christians usually have a week to do the funeral, right? Or two weeks. Either way . . ." He looks around, letting his eyes inevitably fall on Joy. The way he's looking at her makes her feel as if he's ready for her to attack.

But, actually, Joy isn't fixing to bite anyone's head off. That look Rob sees? It's relief, and then relief about feeling relieved. This is the first thing that makes her feel that faith isn't all that bad. Because Rob's idea isn't only a damn good one, it's an idea that she feels she should've had herself. Or she could've. *You can't do everything by yourself, Joy*, she thinks, and it makes her smile because now she feels she might not have to. It's trite, but she remembers all the times she'd given this kind of advice in sessions with clients, telling them to let go and let the best come to them. Well, now she figures she should take her own advice.

It's Mom's doing, probably. She's watching.

She doesn't sleep, either.

Her heartstrings tug. All she can do is nod, smile, signal Rob to keep going. If she opens her mouth, she's afraid she will cry again.

Hearing Rob's suggestion rekindles her belief in a higher power. But seeing Michael agree with her, nodding while he gazes at her with a knowing she's never seen from him before; well, that's the second thing. *That's* an Easter miracle if she's ever seen one. Hallelujah, the Lord is risen, indeed.

— 44 —

After church, Nnenna gets a head start on leaving the building. She has a press-on smile ready for every parishioner who who greets her with the customary "Christ is risen!" and for every other parishioner who wants to ask her where she got baptized. She hustles to the car, knowing acutely that she has about four seconds of peace from the moment she shuts herself in the rental car.

One: *These people can stare, ah-ah! As if they've never seen Louboutins!*

Two: *Zach has never been this antsy before. Maybe he shouldn't have been playing with that game thing his cousin has.*

Three: *I can't believe Mom made me come out here. I can't believe James thought this would be an acceptable church.*

Four: *Where in God's good name is the rest of the family?*

Done.

The doors fly open and the car is filled with voices: James rapping off how unhappy he is about the way the pastor conducted the service; Yemi and Zach arguing about who can sit in the middle; her dad complaining the service was too long; her mom chiming in about the service being too short. Nnenna massages her temples through it all, biting her tongue so as not to say anything over the top. The voices cascade louder around her—"Mom! Mom, Zach is being stupid!" and "Nne, set the GPS, na!"—and it takes every ounce of strength she has not to scream.

Suddenly, she turns and hisses, "Sit down, sit down!" to Yemi and Zach. She wrestles her kids into their proper place as best she can from the passenger's side. Zach looks like he might cry. "What is it?" Nnenna asks, trying to temper her tone.

"Yemi hit me!" he whines.

Yemi immediately gasps. "Nooo, what? I didn't even touch him!"

"Yemi, did I ask you to be beating your brother?" she warns, pointing a stern finger at her. "He's a baby. It's Easter. Would Jesus be beating his brother?"

Yemi grumbles, crossing her arms with such ferocity that it almost looks like it hurts her to do so. She scowls out the window, her chest rising and falling quickly. Papa Ezekiel reaches out to give her shoulder a squeeze from the backseat. He says, "Pele, my dear, it's all right," and Yemi sighs.

Nnenna glances back to see her mom sitting quietly. She stares out the opposite window as James backs out of the parking lot and pulls onto the road. Nnenna can't help but observe her mother's solemnity, but she doesn't know what to say.

Luckily for her, James seems to have been watching, too. "Mama, o," he calls, trying to lock eyes with her in the rearview mirror. "How did you like the service? Eh . . . I thought that pastor was too *pompous*," he says, overpronouncing the word. It ends up sounding incredibly vulgar. "Instead of him to just deliver the Word, he was acting like God came down to personally make him deliver the news. Nonsense."

Nnenna blinks into the distance. Somehow, that sounds a lot like someone she knows.

Her mom's reply doesn't come. Awkward silence blooms as James's last comments circle the air.

Her dad speaks up. "It is Easter. The man is a pastor. Which one concern you?"

"Papa, I be pastor, too," James says.

"And yet, nobody here is asking you to start preaching," Ezekiel says.

Nnenna groans, her head falling back on the seat. "Dad, honestly . . ."

"He is preaching how God has asked him to preach," Ezekiel continues. "You, too, will preach how God asks you. So what's the problem?"

"I—"

"Okay, enough," Nancy cuts in. She kisses her teeth and shifts so she's facing the window. "Just enough, please."

Silence envelops the car again.

Nnenna watches her parents in the rearview mirror. She sees her dad reach for her mom's hand, and when she doesn't give it, he pats her on the forearm. It's obvious her mom hasn't been her normal self since yesterday and understandably so, but it still hurts to see her like this. They all traveled here from Baltimore for a birthday party, they expected there to be dancing and to have a good time, and, and—and she didn't even get to say goodbye. *That must be the worst part,* she thinks. Her mom never got to say goodbye to her sister.

She feels for her, but she's not sure what to do. The two of them have never been close the way that Joy and Auntie Mary were. Or, the way Joy and Auntie Mary became as Joy got older. Nnenna's mom had held her to the same standard from the day she was born and, even now, it hasn't let up. *So many standards,* Nnenna thinks, swallowing down the bitterness in her throat.

It takes half an hour for their car to pull into the rental home's driveway. As Nnenna steps out, she realizes she will miss the luxuriousness of this house, its modern architecture and all-glass everything, but she can't wait to leave this country and get back home. Get back to some level of normalcy.

Because she for sure won't find it here.

She's the first to the door and, when she pushes it open, she's surprised to find the house in way better shape than when they left it. In the background, she can hear— "Is that Wizkid?" she murmurs, noticing the soft twittering of a song in the distance. Behind her, she hears gasps from her children, and aggravated whispers from her husband and parents. She is too tired to scowl or throw a fit or posture in front of her family. Instead, as she floats in through the main hall, she just looks around for someone who can answer her questions.

"Joy?" she calls out as she passes the den. Jamil appears carrying a set of throw pillows, which she remembers being part of a set in the living room. "What are you doing?" she asks him. "Where's your mom?"

"She's, uh, I don't know. Ask Uncle Rob. He has the schedule," he says before rushing into the den to drop the pillows.

Nnenna's eyebrow twitches. "Excuse me?"

"Ị sị gịnị?" Nancy comes up from behind Nnenna, leaning in for a clarification. When Nnenna doesn't respond, Nancy asks, "Schedule ke?" with a sharpness in her tongue that Nnenna thought she'd never hear again.

Something about seeing the house clean, hearing that Rob has a schedule, and lo-fi Wizkid playing in the background sets Nancy off. She sidles past Nnenna, marching into the living room, ready to find the object of her frustration.

Immediately, she spots Rob cross-checking something on his phone. "Robert!" she says, her voice shrill.

Rob looks over, his eyes falling on his immediate family, as his mother approaches. She stares back at him, her mouth twisted in the most disgruntled frown. Rob blanks. Quickly, his eyes flit from corner to corner, seemingly trying to find the source of Nancy's anger.

He gulps; tries for a neutral smile. In the end, his nervousness pulses through. "Mom? Y—"

"*Why* did you people not go to church?" she spits out, jutting a finger menacingly at him. "It is Easter, for goodness sake! If anything, you people should have been right behind us, driving to the church your-your-your brother-in-law has found."

"Mo—"

"And what is all this?" She throws up her hands, staring around the house. "So you didn't go to church because you wanted to stay home and clean, abi? Which kin' excuse is that?"

"No, actually," Rob cuts in. "Uh, so, we decided, in your absence and amid a series of very mean, but very punny, headlines written by Alice's team, that, uh, what would be better than holding a wake for Auntie Mary while we're all still here, right? So that's what we're doing . . ." The more Rob talks, the more severe Nancy's face becomes. Rob rushes to add, "Don't worry. I have a full schedule; it's doable. Everyone agreed to help, a-and we're calling back some of the vendors and the guest list . . ." Nancy has now started to emanate heat. She's reaching a fever pitch. "Right now we're planning for five p.m. today, and we're using the backyard area, just like we originally planned for the party. I'm thinking about getting a cake, but, like, all the bakeries have Easter cakes that say, 'Jesus Is Lord,' so we're just gonna have to ignore the writing." He fans out his arms, as if to say, *Take your best shot.*

Nancy fumes in silence. Her chest feels like it will combust; her throat constricts so much she can barely speak. Unfiltered anger rushes through her. As she stares back at her son and takes in what he's said, she struggles to find which insult to hurl at him first.

But she cracks.

And she says, "Easter is my sister's favorite holiday!"

Rob furrows his brows. "Oh, well, then—"

"And you are—you are taking this time, instead of giving thanks to the Lord, you are doing what? Throwing a *party*? N'oge dị ka nke a? Robert? Ro-bert? You no well, o."

Nnenna steps forward, carefully. "Mom, i-it's not a party. It's a wake—"

"Abeg, will you shut up, as well?" Nancy kisses her teeth, casting a stern glance over her shoulder. "Is it not the same thing? Will they still not be dancing on my sister's grave?"

"*What?* Mom . . ." Nnenna groans, touching her fingers to her temples. "I just—I can't—I can't do this anymore," she says, and then snaps her fingers at Rob. "Show me the schedule. I want to help."

Rob's eyes light up as Nnenna approaches. James says, "Nnenna, what are you doing?" but she doesn't turn around. Rob brings up the list he has on his phone and tilts it so his sister can see better. "So, here we go. The kids are folding programs in the den—Sarah was putting it together with Jamil, so maybe if, uh, if Yemi and Zach are interested—"

"Yes." Nnenna turns and signals to her kids, both of whom don't look prepared to do any sort of labor. "Go and find your cousins and help them. Yemi, stop squeezing your face like that."

Yemi turns on her heel and speeds down the hall. Zach follows, decidedly less dramatic.

Rob continues, "Right. We have Michael and David in the backyard going over furniture placements." James suddenly perks up. "I'm calling up guests from the original list, seeing who can be down here in a few hours. Between that, I'm fixing up some playlists. Then we have Joy calling the caterer and seeing what they already made that they can just run back. She's somewhere, maybe upstairs—"

"Got it," Nnenna says. "I'll go help her."

"Joy doesn't need help calling people on the phone," Nancy hisses, stomping her foot on the ground. "In fact, who is she calling? She shouldn't be calling anybody! All these people are harlots!"

Nnenna ignores her and maneuvers her way around the sofa toward the hall. James reaches out for her arm—"Where are you going?"— but Nnenna shakes free of him and keeps walking.

Rob holds up his phone. "Anyone else need an assignment or are we good?"

James steps forward, ready to argue as usual, but Nancy watches his attention drift to the glass back doors. "Ah-ah. They should have consulted me first. I arranged the place before," he utters, watching Michael and David move chairs around in the backyard. His brow furrows the more he watches and soon, he finds himself gravitating toward the sliding doors. "No, no, that setup is wrong." He kisses his teeth. "Where will we put the pulpit? Didn't you people arrange for a pulpit?" He turns on Rob.

Rob holds up his hands in surrender. "We can get a pulpit."

"We *must*," he presses into the word before seeing himself out.

Nancy stomps her foot again. "Ah-ah! I can't believe this! My own fa-mi-ly chọrọ igbu m. Ha chọrọ ka m suffer, o!" She cries. Her frown deepens; her breathing quickens. Rob takes a hesitant step forward— "Ah, no, don't come near me!" she shouts. The sound rings out in the emptiness of the room. Its sadness lingers long after Nancy has finished speaking. She, herself, can't bear it.

When the first tear falls from her eyes, she shakes a fist at Rob. "Easter i-is my sister's favorite holiday," Nancy says. Her voice wavers, but her words hold Rob captive. Her sorrow makes him still. "Every year, she . . ." Nancy pauses, letting the next wave of sadness wash over her. She feels it all; the times she spent the holiday with Mary and the times she didn't. Her memories color her words and soon she is crying, rambling, without inhibitions. "She looked forward to it. She was—she loved being with her family, because her birthday was close, but also th-th-this was a time she, we, could celebrate and give thanks for all we had. Everything. Ụmụaka, ọrụ anyị, ezinụlọ anyị. Ev-ry-thing."

The more she speaks, the more her shoulders shake, her voice breaks, and she cowers. Ezekiel is at her back, carefully holding on to her.

"And you . . . she . . ." Nancy chokes on the words. She wipes her eyes forcefully as if to stop the tears. "He-ey . . . Chineke, God, o. She should be *here*, na ezinụlọ ya ebe a. *Here.*"

She crumbles. Rob flies forward, but Ezekiel is already there, guiding her safely to the nearest sofa. Nancy wails, tortured and loud. She whispers, "Ewoh, God, o, please . . ." over and over again, while Ezekiel rubs her back and shoulders. "Ewoh, God, o . . ."

Rob kneels at her feet, holding on to her hand. He closes his eyes and says a quiet prayer for her.

— 45 —

Rob helped his mom to bed an hour ago. He wanted to make a joke, say something lighthearted like "You're exempt from duties" while he walked her to her room, but he couldn't do it. He'd never seen her so shaken up, so broken down. She had lost a sibling. *Imagine how that feels,* he thought. It made him shudder. He and Nnenna aren't the closest, but as he watches her with Joy in the hallway upstairs, he still feels as though there's hope. He's only thirty-seven. He and Nnenna don't have an insane age gap so there's less space to traverse. *One day,* he promises to himself. *I'll cross it one day.*

In the meantime, he has a wake to plan.

Before he decides to do another checkup, he heads back to his guest list, calling the next name on it. If he's being honest, he hasn't had much luck with those he's reached out to. He tried the professional approach: "Hi, this is Robert Akintola, Mary Okafor's nephew. We're holding a wake for her later this afternoon, and we were wondering if you could make it." That yielded little to no results, with many even saying that they couldn't grasp what he was telling them.

Then he tried a more casual approach: "Hi, this is Mary Okafor's nephew, Rob. Can you come to her wake this afternoon? It's at the same address as the party. And the vigil. You saw the livestream on AJAfrika, right?" Still, no one was keen to come. Someone he called, someone named Mr. Uzezi, pointedly said that he had to work. "What?" Rob asked. "Work? Today? On Easter?"

"Eh, y-yes," the man responded.

He isn't sure what provoked him to say such a thing, but Rob spat back, "If Auntie Mary had come back from the dead and was being interviewed by Alice Karim, would you still need to work? Wouldn't you have been here drinking malt until sunrise?"

Uzezi hung up immediately.

It was too late by then. The damage was done. Rob didn't want to think this way, but with each rejected invitation he received, he wondered just how many of these people would say yes if there was more of a spectacle to see. They were all keen to watch a miracle, but a wake? That was the definition of ordinary. People died and stayed dead every day. It wasn't worth their time.

Rob seethes with frustration, but he knows there's more to be done. He decides right then and there that this wake isn't about all of Mary's flaky friends; it's about her family. He owes this to Joy and Michael.

Rob leaves the guest list and makes his way around the house, doing his quarterly round of checkups. First: himself. He makes sure he's got the music playlists ready. He plans to start with a selection of highlife instrumentals. Sarah said there'd be a speech section, so the instrumentals would be perfect for that.

As he's switching songs in the queue on his phone, Yemi appears, flying down the staircase and looking in way better spirits than she did an hour ago. Rob holds his hand out for a high five as she approaches. "Hey, kid."

"Uncle," she begins, high-fiving him. "Change of plans, maybe. Sarah says all the kids should give speeches at the same time, but I think we should have separate timing. She told me to ask you." Here, she crosses her arms and stares plainly, waiting for him to try and disagree.

Rob swallows a laugh. *She really is Nnenna's child, damn.* "Okay, what about this? We can do, like, all the kids giving speeches, but we can stagger them and we can go in order of age."

She narrows her eyes. "Youngest to oldest?"

"Oldest to youngest," Rob tells her. "So you go after Jamil."

Yemi growls. "Uncle, I'm older than him!"

Yikes. "So you are."

"Did you forget? I'm thirteen and he's twelve. My birthday is in December."

"I will remember that forever," Rob says, reaching out to give her a pat on the shoulder. "Sarah, you, Jamil, Zach. Got it."

Yemi skips back to the staircase. The moment Yemi is out of earshot, Rob lets out a sigh of relief. "Yo, I'm so afraid of that girl," he whispers to himself. Thankfully, no one hears—

"Robert."

Rob turns to find his dad walking toward him. He's carrying a glass of water that Rob is sure he's bringing for Mom upstairs. Rob can't help but notice how frail his dad looks now after the events of the weekend. It's such a different look for him. Ezekiel Akintola is much sturdier than this, even at his age, but seeing his family crumble this way must have really affected him.

So much so that the first words out of his mouth are: "Robert, you should go to Ghana."

"Sorry?"

Rob stands perfectly still, an abundance of questions rushing through his mind. *How did he even know? Did Mom tell him? Did he watch it back on the livestream?*

Ezekiel says again, "Robert, you should go to Ghana. You and that man you live with."

Rob flinches.

"My husband, you mean," he says.

"Yes." Ezekiel clears his throat. After an excruciatingly long moment, he asks, "Why didn't you bring him this weekend? He doesn't like Nigerian food?"

Rob wants to laugh. Of course his dad—scratch that, his family in general—would boil someone's absence down to their opinion on food. "No, Dad," he says with a sigh. "He just . . . h-he had other stuff going on."

Ezekiel frowns, tilting his head to the side. "You didn't ask him?"

"I did!"

"Robert, you have to let us be in your life," he explains calmly, softly. Beneath it, there is a warning. Rob knows there is frailty and fear that his dad will have to relive this weekend's grief in a different way: being emotionally separate from his child. Somehow, that feels like a bigger chasm to cross. "That's all I'm going to say. Go to Ghana. Both of you. You have my blessing," he adds with a nervous glance to the floor.

"I do . . ." Rob swallows. He's ready to protest, ready to say he's been as open with his family as possible, but he knows that's not true. It's just like Paul has been telling him: he's operating off his projection of what his family will accept. The problem with that is that it's not true.

"Well," Rob continues, "what about Mom? I mean, did you talk to her? Is she okay with me leaving?"

"Your Mama? Heh, no," his dad says. "I saw the interview."

"Oh God."

"Your mama can *vex* like nobody else," he continues. "But a lot has happened this weekend. We are not ourselves. No one can be, in the face of grief. Nothing hurts like death."

Rob gulps, nodding slowly. He only saw a glimpse of how this has affected his mother, but he can't possibly know how she will be in the coming days, weeks, or months. Grief takes time, and only time can heal this sort of pain.

"She loves you," Ezekiel continues. "She wants you here because that is how my wife is. She wants everyone to be . . . like this." He squeezes his shoulders in, trying his hardest to appear smaller and more put together. "But that can't always be possible. Only God knows a man's destiny. So if you . . . if you are supposed to be in Accra, making . . . shito and your favorite waakye—"

"Dad, please."

"I don't know what people do in Ghana. Okay? But you have to go. You have to."

"Well, we can wait to decide when Mom wakes up, or when she's calmed down a little—"

"When your Mama wakes up and when she calms down will be two different days," Ezekiel tells him. "You can't wait for her."

Rob breathes a sigh of relief. His dad is a fair man who understands things at a higher level, even when others can't. It's not enough to quell Rob's anxiety about going, or about disappointing his mom, but . . . isn't one change enough? His dad said that the day his mom will wake up and the day she will calm down are separate. What's wrong with at least waiting for one of those days to pass?

— 46 —

The house falls into a quiet hum as time goes on. It's like the day is moving on, pushing life forward, whether they like it or not. Joy finds herself gravitating to her room, circling it when she's upstairs, or thinking of it when she's downstairs. Once 3:00 p.m. hits, she finds Jamil narrating a story with the taxidermy squirrels in the games room with his cousins. "What are you doing? Don't answer that. You guys should go get dressed," she tells them.

"Isn't it early?" Sarah asks, clutching squirrel Joseph with both hands.

"Nope," Joy says simply, and finally takes the stairs to her room.

She rifles through her suitcase for her navy dress. It's not quite black, but Mama really liked this one. Mama had a dress in this color that she wore to church all the time. Joy wonders if that's the dress she would've liked to be buried in. *No.* Joy snorts immediately. *It's not colorful enough. It's too simple. Mom would've liked purple and gold lace or something.*

By the time Jamil comes upstairs, Joy is dressed, sitting at the edge of the bed while she applies a layer of foundation. She dusts her cheeks lightly before she notices Jamil studying her hard. "How do I look?" she asks with a cheesy grin on her face.

Jamil snorts. "Pretty."

"Good. Go find your dad."

"I think he's outside already."

"Tell him to find and put on a suit. For me," she adds.

Jamil's eyes light up. He speeds out of the room, saying, "I'm gonna tell him you said that!"

One day, Joy will have to examine her feelings from this past weekend. She will need to separate the grief and longing and anxiousness and fear from what she believes to be true. In a way, she acted more like herself than she ever has. In other ways, she is terrified when she remembers her thoughts and actions since . . . since the incident.

She owes David an apology.

She owes her cousins, her brother, apologies, as well.

She owes herself one.

She knows no one is coming to the wake.

This is the real reason she decorates her face and lotions her legs a second time. She knew this in her heart from the moment Rob suggested they plan something, that it would just be them. The family. *I guess that's fine. That's how it should be, right? It's okay.*

No fancy pastors or village men who can talk to spirits. No live-streamed vigil or crowd of people begging for Guinness at different temperatures. No animals. Just her, her family, and her mother. The spirit of her mom.

The backyard is set up so beautifully. The chairs and decorations are reminiscent of what the party could have looked like, or would have looked like, had it been downscaled. In the background, soft music plays, filling the open air with a sweetness her mom would be proud of. It feels vivacious and tranquil at the same time. It is familiar.

Joy doesn't wait for anyone before she sits down in the front row. James got his way and managed to have a pulpit moved in from God-knows-where. Unfortunately, Joy loves it. At its front, there's a table with flowers, Mama's collection of CDs, and a framed picture of Mama in her best clothes. It takes some time before Joy is able to look at it, but when she does, she sees serenity in her mother's face. It's slightly unnerving. Her being gone is such a disastrous, difficult thing, but the peace Joy sees on her face in that picture puts her at ease. She realizes this is the third time she's looking at a serene picture, a framed image of a family member who's gone. She feels she should cry, but the tears refuse to come.

Eventually, the seats fill up around her. To her left, Michael and Sarah. To her right, Jamil and David. Jamil is holding a Bible. Joy has absolutely no idea where he got it from. Across the aisle, Nnenna, James, and their children sit patiently. Rob, too. Uncle Ezekiel holds Auntie Nancy's hand. And she looks as stoic as ever, as if nothing can touch her. Except now they know that's not true.

For a moment, there's nothing but the sound of the wind.

Then Nancy speaks up, her voice hoarse and small. "Somebody should say something."

"The kids should," Nnenna says.

Yemi jumps up, but immediately shrinks when Joy's eyes fall on her.

"C-can I read something?" Heads turn when Jamil speaks. Joy takes a closer look at the Bible he's grasping and realizes it belongs to her mom. *Oh, thank God,* she thinks. It wouldn't be a bad thing for him to have commandeered a Bible on his own. Just odd.

Joy gives his shoulder a comforting squeeze. "Yeah, go ahead. Anything you want."

"Okay." He gets to his feet and makes his way to the pulpit. Joy clasps her hands together, trying her hardest not to dissolve into a puddle of tears.

"Um." Jamil clears his throat and flips open the book. "S-so . . . early on Friday, Grandma asked me to help her pick out a verse to read. And, um, it's this one." He scans a bit until he gets to the right page. "Numbers . . . 6:24–26."

Yemi gasps.

Jamil reads: "'The Lord bless and keep you; the Lord make his face shine on you and be gracious to you; the Lord turn his face toward you and give you peace.'"

Peace.

Joy feels her heart swell; feels the sudden onset of tears. Mama picked this for her, for *them*. Joy shuts her eyes and she swears she can feel the presence of her sister, too. She blinks back tears when she opens them. Jamil comes to sit beside her, placing a hand on her back in comfort. It is bizarre to her that she can feel so alone and so full of love at the same time, but she does. She really does.

Down the aisle, Auntie Nancy slowly gets to her feet, but something stops her in her tracks. "Chineke . . . God," she breathes out. Her eyes are fixed on the podium and then on the table in front of it.

Joy watches as a single butterfly makes its way to the corner of Mama's picture. She holds her breath. It isn't that she knows what butterflies symbolize or anything like that. In fact, it isn't about the symbolism at all. It is about a living thing that's come to touch the face of a person who is no longer here. It is about arriving in the presence of family. It's her mom.

Nancy settles back in her seat, eyeing the butterfly with reverence. "Nwanne m, ndewo," she says. "You are welcome here."

Acknowledgments

Hello hello and thank you for reading.

It always pays to take a leap of faith and I'm happy I landed on my feet with this one and not, as I feared for the better part of a year, flat on my face with a broken nose and my childhood gap tooth come to haunt me.

I've always had a strange relationship to faith, I think mostly because I naturally believe in everything but was taught from religious tradition to only believe in one thing. It was conflicting for me for a long time, but I'm at peace with it now. The beauty of my cultural heritage is that there's so much richness in it already, and to diminish and limit what belief and faith means, specifically by using a Western or colonialist lens, would be diminishing and limiting the culture itself. Part of that was what I wanted to explore with this book. The other part was that I thought the premise would be funny.

Anyway, thank you to my family, both at home and at home. Happy to be here, honestly!

Thank you to my agent Claire, who has been a tireless advocate for me at all levels. When I pitched this idea to her, it was the best "Yes, and . . . !" moment of my life. Who knew a story about a potential resurrection and Nigerian comfort sensationalism would've been the kind of story that would become my adult demographic debut. I'm happy it is, though. I'm forever grateful we connected.

Thank you as well to the editorial, design, and marketing teams at

Atria Books and HarperCollins Canada, especially my editors Melanie Iglesias Perez and Jennifer Lambert. It was a bit nerve-wracking writing for a different readership, so I'm really thankful to have had your expertise on this one!

A special thank-you to Mama Uyoyo, my sweet mother who helped me proof all the Igbo. If anyone reading feels it's wrong, or that it's not a dialect you're familiar with, that's none of my business. Feel free to argue with my mom. She's very good at it.

About the Author

Louisa Onomé is a Nigerian Canadian writer of books for teens and adults, including *Like Home*, *Twice as Perfect*, and *The Melancholy of Summer*. She holds a BA in professional writing and a MA in counselling psychology. Her debut young adult novel, *Like Home*, was critically acclaimed, receiving several starred reviews, including from *Kirkus Reviews* and School Library Journal.

When she is not writing, she works as a narrative designer in games. Her hobbies include language study, obsessing a healthy amount over her favorite video games, and perfecting her skincare routine. She currently resides in the Toronto area. Find out more at LouisaOnome .com.